HISTORICAL

Your romantic escape to the past.

The Trouble With
The Daring Governess
Annie Burrows

The Earl's Marriage Dilemma
Sarah Mallory

MILLS & BOON

THE TROUBLE WITH THE DARING GOVERNESS
© 2024 by Annie Burrows
Philippine Copyright 2024
Australian Copyright 2024
New Zealand Copyright 2024

First Published 2024
First Australian Paperback Edition 2024
ISBN 978 1 038 93561 8

THE EARL'S MARRIAGE DILEMMA
© 2024 by Sarah Mallory
Philippine Copyright 2024
Australian Copyright 2024
New Zealand Copyright 2024

First Published 2024
First Australian Paperback Edition 2024
ISBN 978 1 038 93561 8

® and ™ (apart from those relating to FSC®) are trademarks of Harlequin Enterprises
(Australia) Pty Limited or its corporate affiliates. Trademarks indicated with ® are
registered in Australia, New Zealand and in other countries.
Contact admin_legal@Harlequin.ca for details.

MIX
Paper | Supporting
responsible forestry
FSC® C001695
www.fsc.org

Published by
Harlequin Mills & Boon
An imprint of Harlequin Enterprises (Australia) Pty Limited
(ABN 47 001 180 918), a subsidiary of HarperCollins
Publishers Australia Pty Limited
(ABN 36 009 913 517)
Level 19, 201 Elizabeth Street
SYDNEY NSW 2000 AUSTRALIA

Cover art used by arrangement with Harlequin Books S.A.. All rights reserved.

Printed and bound in Australia by McPherson's Printing Group

The Trouble With The Daring Governess

Annie Burrows

MILLS & BOON

Books by Annie Burrows

Harlequin Historical

"Cinderella's Perfect Christmas"
in *Once Upon a Regency Christmas*
A Duke in Need of a Wife
A Marquess, a Miss and a Mystery
The Scandal of the Season
From Cinderella to Countess
His Accidental Countess
"Invitation to a Wedding"
in *Regency Christmas Parties*
The Countess's Forgotten Marriage

The Patterdale Siblings

A Scandal at Midnight
How to Catch a Viscount
Wooing His Convenient Wife

Brides for Bachelors

The Major Meets His Match
The Marquess Tames His Bride
The Captain Claims His Lady

Visit the Author Profile page
at millsandboon.com.au
for more titles.

Annie Burrows has been writing Regency romances for Harlequin since 2007. Her books have charmed readers worldwide, having been translated into nineteen different languages, and some have gone on to win the coveted Reviewers' Choice Award from CataRomance. For more information, or to contact her, please visit annie-burrows.co.uk, or find her on Facebook at Facebook.com/annieburrowsuk.

With many thanks to Harlequin
for making my dream of becoming
a published author come true.

Chapter One

'**B**ut I *lo-uh-lo-uh-love* him!'

Oh, dear, thought Rosalind, pausing with her hand raised to knock on the study door, from behind which came Lady Susannah's anguished protest. A protest which had now turned into a wild mixture of sobs and screams.

No wonder Lady Birchwood, Susannah's widowed aunt, had looked so distressed when she'd come, in person, to order Rosalind to get down to His Lordship's study and *'deal with the gel'*.

Since that was Rosalind's primary function in this household, she'd risen from her chair and come downstairs straight away. It was only now that she could hear how badly Lady Susannah was behaving that she hesitated, pondering how best to deal with her over-indulged and therefore rather pettish charge.

It sounded, from the few intelligible words she'd been able to make out before Susannah had become incoherent, as though Lord Caldicot was trying to put his foot down over the attentions of one of Susannah's suitors. Probably Mr Cecil Baxter, if Rosalind had to guess. It had been *Cecil says this* and *Cecil did that* for weeks now.

Actually, there was probably no point in knocking on the door, she reflected, lowering her hand. Neither of the people in that room was likely to hear it over the high-pitched wailing that Susannah was making now.

So she just squared her shoulders and went in.

The scene inside Lord Caldicot's study was pretty much what Rosalind had expected. Susannah was lying on the floor, thrashing about as she gave vent to her outrage, putting Rosalind in mind of a toddler who'd dropped her cream cake in the pond and seen the ducks devour it before anyone could get it back for her.

Yet she'd had the presence of mind, Rosalind noted wryly, to give vent to those feelings on the hearthrug, which was a soft, thick sheepskin, rather than on any other portion of the study floor, which had no carpet at all.

Lord Caldicot himself was standing behind his desk, ramrod straight as befitted a man who'd spent so much of his life in the military. He'd also selected the one sure defensive bulwark in the room, behind which he could duck, should Susannah take it into her head to start throwing things. He was no fool.

He did, however, look like a man who had almost reached the limit of his patience. Though his exasperated expression changed the moment he noticed her come in, to one of heartfelt relief.

'Take this silly chit back to her room,' he said irritably, 'and keep her out of my sight until you've talked some sense into her.'

Rosalind had been so pleased by the way he'd welcomed her arrival with such evident pleasure. But this tactless remark effectively doused her brief moment of joy.

Didn't he know his ward at all? Talking *sense* was never going to get through to Susannah when she was in one of these moods.

But then, of course, he didn't know her, did he? He'd been abroad, fighting for his country, when his cousin, the Fifth Marquess of Caldicot, had died and he'd become not only the Sixth Marquess, but also legal guardian of his predecessor's only surviving child, Susannah. From what Rosalind had gathered, since she'd taken on the role of something more than a governess, but not quite a companion to Susannah, everyone had thought that a bachelor, and a soldier to boot, would have no idea how to rear a girl child. So a succession of female relatives had taken turns to move into Caldicot Dane with her, to supervise her care. And all of them, without exception, had petted and cosseted the wealthy little orphan until she'd become almost unmanageable.

It was at moments like this, Rosalind reflected, regarding Susannah's flushed cheeks and thrashing limbs, that she was sometimes sorely tempted to take a glass of water and fling it into the girl's face. The trouble was that, if she were ever to succumb to such a temptation, she'd lose her job. Nobody, but *nobody*, had ever raised a hand to the girl. And for her to do so would result in instant dismissal.

Anyway, although Susannah was what some people described as *'a bit of a handful'*, this was by no means the worst position Rosalind had ever held. She wanted to keep this job. So she contented herself with merely imagining for a moment or two how Susannah would look, with cold water dripping down her face, before applying the only method that she'd ever found worked on her charge.

She went over and knelt down on the rug beside Susannah.

'I know, I know,' she crooned in apparent sympathy. 'He is a nasty brute. He won't pay any heed to your tears, you know. Come upstairs with me,' she said, holding out her hand.

'He has no right to say I may not marry Cecil,' said Susannah, abruptly, sitting up. 'No right!'

Ah. So that *was* what had brought on this latest storm.

'I have every right,' said Lord Caldicot, rather unwisely in Rosalind's opinion. Susannah had just stopped crying, sat up and begun talking. How she wished she had the right to advise him that the thing to do now would be to distract her, not reopen the argument that had started her off. But of course she didn't have that right. And it would never occur to him to *ask* her for advice. 'I am,' he persisted, 'your legal guardian.'

'You aren't!'

'I am.'

'No, you're not! I have trustees who…who…well, my aunts have always consulted with them, whenever I need something, and—' she gulped '—they let me have whatever I want!'

'The trustees,' said Lord Caldicot, firmly, 'acted on *my* behalf, while I was away fighting, and was not able to make those decisions in a timely manner. And let me tell you, young lady...'

Oh, no. Please don't, thought Rosalind.

'That had I been consulted,' he continued, impervious to Rosalind's silent plea, 'you would not have been indulged to the extent that nobody can now do anything with you!'

Well, on that score, she thought Lord Caldicot might have made a good point. Had somebody made any attempt to discipline Susannah, rather than passing her off to the next set of relatives when they'd started to find her temper tantrums tiresome, then she might not have turned out like this.

Had anyone stood by her, instead of walking away whenever she'd gone through one of her 'difficult' phases, Rosalind was certain she would have abandoned this sort of childish behaviour long ago. But nobody had. Instead, people blamed the girl for being unable to control her temper rather than wondering whether it might not be the end product of being alternately spoiled, then abandoned, by people who claimed to have her best interests at heart.

However, saying what he had did nothing to help matters. On the contrary, it provoked Susannah into sucking in a huge, indignant breath, then holding it for a split second, as though deliberating whether to use it to scream, or tell him exactly what she thought of his opinion and what he could do with it.

Rosalind took advantage of that pause to lean in and murmur into Susannah's ear, 'I shouldn't bother if I were you. Whatever you say now will only make him dig his heels in harder. We need to regroup and plan our next move. In private.'

Susannah's head swivelled in Rosalind's direction. She appeared to be considering Rosalind's advice.

It was touch and go. Rosalind could never tell which way Susannah's mood would swing, during one of these tantrums. But this time, to her relief, Susannah gave a decisive nod, got up, stuck her nose in the air and swept out of the room, without deigning to give her poor beleaguered guardian as much as a glance.

Rosalind didn't give her employer a glance, either, as she left the room and headed up the stairs in Susannah's wake, but not, she was sure, for the same reason as Susannah. Rosalind simply didn't dare. Oh, not that she was afraid of him, for all his martial demeanour—no, it wasn't that. It was worse. Far worse, to her mind. She was just scared that if she ever looked him in the eye, at a moment when he happened to be looking in her direction, then he might somehow perceive that she had a…well, that she thought he was…

No. No, she mustn't even *think* about the way she'd started to feel whenever she was in the same room with him of late. That would be to…to feed it. And she mustn't. No, she must starve that feeling. Or…or strangle it, or something. Because if he were to guess, or if anyone was to guess, that he made her heart flutter, and her pulses race, and her silly imagination run riot… well, they'd all think she was a complete ninny. Which was the exact opposite of the image which had landed her this position.

Lord Caldicot had hired her, on one of his infrequent trips to England, because, he'd told her, he thought she looked *sensible*. And *stern*. Attributes which, he'd said, Susannah's governess would need if ever she was going to make the girl fit to make her debut by the time she reached seventeen. He'd hired her because he believed she'd be able to make Susannah behave herself.

'*You look as if you have backbone,*' he'd said. '*Which is precisely what is needed, in my opinion.*'

If he knew that the *sensible* governess he'd hired was prone to silly, romantic, impossible daydreams…

Although she'd never had any before they'd all moved here, at the start of the Season, had she? On the contrary, she'd actually been a bit nervous about what it might be like to have a man permanently in residence, after having enjoyed living in a mostly female household for the previous five years. So nobody could justifiably accuse her of being *prone* to silly daydreams…

'I hate him!'

Susannah's bitter exclamation snapped Rosalind out of her reverie.

'And I hate Aunt Birchwood, too! She…she actually stuck up for Lord Caldicot,' said Susannah, shaking her head in disbelief. 'Said that even though Cecil was from a very old family, he is only a younger son, with no prospects, and that I ought to be aiming for a much more brilliant match.'

Having uttered her opinion of Lord Caldicot and her aunt's treachery in agreeing with him about Mr Baxter's unsuitability, Susannah flung herself face down on the bed and burst into another bout of noisy sobbing.

Rosalind, who had grown used to scenes of this sort since she'd come to work for the family, bit back the urge to sigh and went to sit on the most comfortable chair in the room while she waited for Susannah to calm down. It was right by the window and gave a really good view over the square, and the people wandering around down there.

She did not make the mistake of glancing outside, however. She'd done that once and Susannah had caught her doing it when she ought, to the girl's indignation, have been paying her attention.

It was safer to sit and look down into her lap, so that when Susannah eventually grew tired of weeping and sat up to find out why Rosalind wasn't fluttering about her, the way her aunts did, the way she thought everyone should when she was causing a scene, she wouldn't find her looking out of the window. There were several breakable objects stationed within Susannah's reach, and she had a remarkably good aim, even when she appeared to have lost control of all her other senses.

Then, all of a sudden, as was Susannah's habit, she sat up and turned to look at Rosalind.

'Stop scowling at me!'

'Was I scowling? I beg your pardon,' said Rosalind, mildly. 'I didn't mean to. I was just thinking, very hard and my thinking face must look so serious that you mistook it for a scowl.' It was probably why Lord Caldicot had hired her, she mused. She'd been determined, at that interview, not to take another job where there was any risk of some male member of the household thinking he had the right to take advantage of her.

She'd decided that since she was eighteen years of age, it was about time she started to make decisions about her future for herself, instead of relying on others to make provisions for her, so she'd signed on with an agency. And when they'd sent her for the interview for the post as Susannah's governess, she had asked Lord Caldicot at least as many questions about what she might expect if she went to live at Caldicot Dane, as he'd asked her.

He'd leaned back in his chair, at one point, and chuckled, remarking that he was beginning to wonder exactly which of them was conducting the interview. When she'd retorted that a girl had to be careful, he'd nodded and said he liked the fact that she hadn't backed down when he'd challenged her. That his ward needed someone who wouldn't stand any nonsense. That she seemed like just the kind of person who could bring some much-needed discipline into Susannah's life.

She supposed she did appear stern, when really that was not her nature at all. She'd noted it on looking in the mirror recently. It was because of her thick eyebrows. Perched as they were above a beak of a nose, they couldn't help making her look decidedly formidable.

But then nobody would describe Lord Caldicot as classically handsome either, would they? His nose was not a beak, like hers, but neither did it look as though it had been chiselled out of marble. His hair was not wavy, flopping across his brow in a romantic fashion, or at least, he kept it cut so short that no waviness or floppiness dared to make an appearance. No, it was his eyes that had first made her think him...compelling, to her as a female. The clear intelligence in them. The way they narrowed, ever so slightly, when anyone said anything particularly fatuous. And then there was the way he behaved. With such *integrity*.

She didn't care what anyone else said. Rosalind could not fault him for only selling out, apparently with great reluctance, so many years after he'd inherited his title from his cousin. England was at *war*. He'd stayed at his post until it was time for him to supervise Susannah's come-out, in person, displaying, to her mind, the perfect balance between duty to his country and his family.

Then there was the upright way he carried himself and the air of...well, she couldn't describe it as anything but cleanliness. He didn't give off that sort of greasy, repellent atmosphere that had hung about the wealthy, titled men she'd encountered in her previous post. The men who'd regarded females, especially females in menial roles, as fair game.

'Thinking?' Susannah's face turned hopeful. 'About a way to bring Lord Caldicot round? So that he will let me marry Cecil?'

'Er...' Far from it! But the prospect that she might be was enough to make Susannah look in a better frame of mind. And she had persuaded her charge to come upstairs on the pretext of *planning their next move*, hadn't she? So it was only natural that Susannah would expect her to come up with a plan, wasn't it?

'I suppose,' ventured Susannah, 'that with all those books you read, you must have read about all sorts of ways of rescuing persecuted heiresses from the clutches of evil guardians.'

There were so many things wrong with that statement that Rosalind wasn't sure which misconception to deal with first. Susannah didn't need rescuing, for one thing—she needed to learn to listen to advice, even when she didn't like it. And her guardian wasn't evil, nor was he persecuting her. He just wasn't treating her with the sugary, flattering, doting manner that she'd grown to expect was her due, that was all. Trying to lay down a few rules, which was something none of her other relatives, so far as Rosalind, had observed, had made much attempt to do.

'In all the fairy stories I can remember,' Susannah continued, while Rosalind was still debating the wisdom of saying what she really wanted to say, 'when the king forbids a suitor from marrying the princess because of some stupid thing such as he is merely a swineherd or something, the princess persuades the king to let him prove his worth by going on a quest.'

'A quest,' Rosalind repeated, trying not to laugh. If Susannah thought that anyone could persuade Lord Caldicot to send her Cecil on a quest to prove his worth...or to persuade him to do anything he didn't want, come to that! Didn't Susannah realise what kind of man he was? He was a military man, used to giving orders and having them obeyed instantly.

'Well, not a quest, exactly,' Susannah said, pensively. 'There aren't any dragons for him to slay, or, or magic lamps for him to find, not in London, these days...'

'Er...no,' agreed Rosalind, faintly, wondering what on earth must go on in Susannah's head for her to come out with such comments.

'But he could show... I don't know...loyalty, or bravery somehow, couldn't he? And persuade Lord Caldicot that he is not merely dangling after me because of my fortune.'

Ah...so that was what had caused Susannah to throw such a dramatic tantrum just now. Not so much Lord Caldicot's refusal to grant permission for Cecil to marry Susannah as the implication that he only wanted her for her fortune.

'He *loves* me,' Susannah protested. 'And I love him!'

Susannah reached for a handkerchief to dry her eyes and blow her nose, and began to look much more cheerful.

Rosalind didn't take much comfort from that, because Susannah now had that look on her face that she always wore when she was plotting something.

'You will just,' Susannah decreed, 'have to help us elope!'

She might have known it.

'But I thought,' Rosalind pointed out, 'you wanted to persuade Lord Caldicot that Cecil could be loyal and true...'

'Oh, yes, well of course Cecil could do all that,' said Susannah dismissively. 'But I don't see why I should have to wait while Cecil is changing Lord Caldicot's mind. And don't you think it would be romantic? Eloping?'

'What, climbing out of a window,' Rosalind pointed out, rather ruthlessly reminding Susannah of her fear of heights, 'at the dead of night?'

Susannah turned white. So badly did she fear heights that, the moment they'd arrived in London and she'd seen that her bedroom had a balcony overlooking the rear garden, she'd ordered Rosalind to swap with her. Even though it meant taking a much smaller room.

'It wouldn't have to be out of a window!' said Susannah. 'Or not one that was very high up...'

'Well, I suppose you could just meet somewhere as though by chance, during the day,' Rosalind mused, as though turning over the scheme with a view to making it happen. 'Oh, but then,' she said, regretfully, 'you wouldn't be able to take any luggage. Someone would be bound to ask why you were carrying trunks and hatboxes about in broad daylight…'

'I wouldn't need luggage,' Susannah scoffed.

'No? Oh, well, I suppose it wouldn't matter that you didn't have a clean change of clothes on the journey. I suppose the romance of it all would carry you through the unpleasantness of wearing the same clothes for a week…'

'A week! Why should I be expected to wear the same clothes for a week?'

'Well, I am not entirely sure how long it would take you to reach the border, but I do know that Gretna Green is in Scotland, which is a very long way away. And you would have to go there, you know, to get married, because you are still not of an age to marry without your guardian's consent in England.'

'How do you know that? Oh, from all those books you read, I suppose. But that is infamous!'

'What is infamous?'

'Having to travel to Scotland to marry without your guardian's consent,' she said petulantly.

'And only think,' Rosalind continued, warming to her theme, 'of how ill you get travelling in coaches. We had to stop three times for you to get out and walk up and down, just on the journey from Hertford when we first come up to London. And that,' she reminded Susannah ruthlessly, 'was in a very well-sprung coach. I don't suppose your…um… Mr Baxter would be able to afford such a luxurious one.

'And even if he could,' Rosalind put in hastily when she caught a militant look spring to Susannah's eye at the reminder that Cecil was not well-to-do, 'what with all that getting out and stopping, Lord Caldicot would be bound to catch you up before even one day was out.' She would guarantee it. There was no way he would permit Mr Baxter to spend a night with Susannah, thereby ruining her.

At that point, there came a firm rap on the door and Lady Birchwood's maid, Throgmorton, stepped in.

'Begging your pardon, Miss Hinchcliffe,' she said, sounding not the least bit apologetic, 'but Her Ladyship sent me to remind you that it was time to be getting ready.'

'Getting ready?' Susannah drew herself up indignantly. 'Aunt Birchwood cannot possibly expect me to go out tonight as though nothing has happened. How can she, or anyone, expect me to…to carry on as normal, to dance the night away, when my heart,' she cried, flinging herself backwards on to the bed, 'is broken?'

Throgmorton took a deep breath. 'Her Ladyship said to remind you that this is not just any ball. It is Almack's.'

'I don't care!' Susannah cried.

No. But Lady Birchwood did. And so would Lord Caldicot. A girl who cared about her reputation didn't shun Almack's without good reason, not after all the effort Lady Birchwood and several of Susannah's other female relatives had taken to obtain vouchers.

Throgmorton turned to leave the room, her lips pursed in disapproval.

Rosalind hurried over to the door, opened it and stepped outside.

'Tell Her Ladyship,' she said quietly so that Susannah wouldn't be able to hear, 'that I will do my best to make sure Susannah is dressed and ready within the hour. But don't, I beg of you, send her maid to attend her until I ring for her.' It would end in certain disaster if Pauline bustled in before Susannah herself had decided she was ready to change into her ball gown.

Throgmorton inclined her head very slightly before going away to relay the message to her mistress, in a manner calculated to remind Rosalind of her superior position in the household hierarchy. Throgmorton was, after all, the personal maid to a lady who was the daughter of the Fourth Marquess of Caldicot, the sister of the Fifth Marquess and cousin to the current holder of the title, even if her late husband had been merely the Earl of Birchwood.

When she'd gone, Rosalind mentally rolled up her sleeves. At the end of her interview with Lord Caldicot, he'd suggested that she take the job for a trial period and offered her a generous rise in wages if she managed to last a full quarter without Susannah driving her away with her tantrums. And, perhaps more significantly, without Susannah demanding her dismissal, the way she'd done with so many other hapless governesses over the years. Then, when he'd returned to England in readiness for the Season, he'd also promised her a staggering amount of money if she could steer Susannah successfully through her Season without her creating a scandal in one form or another.

He'd drawn her aside, not one week after he'd moved into Kilburn House with them. And, in the very same study in which Susannah had just been displaying the worst of her temperament, had said, 'Lady Birchwood may indeed have better connections than her sisters and no doubt she does have the entrée to the kind of places that matter to a girl of Susannah's rank, but...' He'd paused, lowering his head and toying with the paperknife on his desk. 'Well, she doesn't seem to be able to exert much influence over the girl. Or at least, so far I have never seen her do so. Or attempt to do it. So...'

So Rosalind was going to get Susannah dressed and ready to go to Almack's, no matter what it took. And it wasn't just because of the bonuses, or at least, not entirely. It was because Rosalind could understand exactly why Susannah behaved so badly.

Almost from the moment she'd met Susannah, Rosalind had felt a sense of kinship with her. For Rosalind, too, had been treated poorly by her own family. They had made her feel unwanted and inconvenient, too. And she had often lashed out in frustration, as well. But, most importantly, it was because Susannah had asked her to stay with her through her Season. And Susannah needed someone who *would* stand by her, not flounce off muttering that she was impossible, just when she most needed someone to...to...*steady* her.

She closed the door and leaned on it, regarding Susannah thoughtfully.

'I was just wondering...' she said.

'Wondering what?' came Susannah's muffled response, since she'd rolled over to bury her face in her pillow.

'Well, if you intend to stay at home, how on earth you are going to contact Mr Baxter?'

Susannah went very still.

'I mean,' Rosalind continued, gazing up at the ceiling, 'you are going to have to tell him that although your guardian has forbidden the match, you are not so spineless that you are going to take it lying down, aren't you?'

Susannah sat up. 'Absolutely not! We will find a way!'

'Precisely so. Only...' she shook her head and sighed '... I cannot see how you are going to come up with a successful plan if you stay at home. I mean, I shouldn't think Lord Caldicot will permit Mr Baxter to call on you...'

'No. He wouldn't. He has forbidden me to even *speak* to him again! As though I could cut him, if I should meet him on a public street!'

'Ah. Well, don't you think that, should you stay here, weeping all evening, he might think that he has won? That he has defeated you?'

'Oh! Yes, that is *precisely* what he would think! But he shan't,' cried Susannah, leaping off the bed. 'Ring for hot water, Miss Hinchcliffe! I *shall* go to Almack's.'

Where, with any luck, Susannah's coterie of admirers would provide some distraction from her distress.

'You...you will,' said Rosalind, 'be careful, won't you?'

'What do you mean?'

'Well, if you make it too obvious that you are only going to Almack's to meet Mr Baxter and plan your next move, Lady Birchwood might report back to Lord Caldicot, and...well, then they might both do something...drastic, to prevent you contacting Mr Baxter at all.'

'Like sending me back to the country, I suppose. Yes, I wouldn't put it past them. But I am not going to give them *any* excuse for cutting my Season short.' She gave a peal of rather manic laughter. 'I will be the model of good behaviour, I assure you.'

Which was all that Rosalind could hope for. For tonight. And as for tomorrow...

Well, never mind tomorrow. She'd think of some way to survive whatever tomorrow threw at her, when tomorrow came.

And in the meantime, with Susannah out at Almack's, Rosalind would have the evening to herself. Peace and quiet, in which to read the latest novel she'd borrowed from the library.

Bliss.

Chapter Two

'The thing about women, Lord Caldicot,' Lord Darlington slurred, leaning forward as though uttering a confidence, 'is that they ain't like chaps.'

Michael didn't bother to reply to that inanity. Of course women weren't like men! It didn't take a genius to work that one out.

'Chaps, you see,' Lord Darlington continued, 'are like dogs.'

'Like dogs?'

'Yes. We stick together. Like a pack of hounds. Don't see hounds going off on their own when they're after a fox, do you? Eh? Loyal, that's what they are. Faithful. Women, though...' He shuddered, and took another gulp of wine. 'Like cats,' he said and belched. 'Can never tell what they're thinking.'

Michael suddenly remembered the waitress in that little tavern in Lisbon. The way she'd had to weave her way in and out of the tables, dodging the customers trying to either pinch or slap her bottom as she served their drinks. He'd always been able to tell *exactly* what she'd been thinking. Her disdain for the whole pack of them had been written all over her pretty face.

'Walk alone, do cats,' Lord Darlington continued. 'Look at you with their calculating eyes, weighing you up. Can't trust a cat. Like you can't trust a woman.'

It had been a mistake, Michael reflected as he swirled the wine round in his glass, admitting to Lord Darlington that he wasn't finding it easy to follow in his cousin's footsteps. His esteemed cousin, the Fifth Marquess of Caldicot, had always known he'd inherit the title from his own father. The Fifth Marquess was the sort of chap who loved all the pomp and the adulation that went with his rank, not to mention all the endless paperwork that piled up on his desk every day.

Michael would warrant he had never had a moment's trouble from any of his sisters, either. Not to judge by the way they kept on singing his praises. That last part, about the Fifth Marquess's troop of sisters, was all he'd admitted to Lord Darlington, but that one admission had been all that it had taken to prompt the elderly peer to launch into that ridiculous theory about cats and dogs.

Give him a piece of open ground and a battalion of men, Michael mused, with an enemy approaching over the crest of the next hill, and he'd know exactly what to do. Dispatch men to the flanks. Look for cover to conceal sharpshooters. Position the guns on the high ground. Form the infantry into a square…

Yes, out on a battlefield he could make plans, shout orders and be confident of gaining the desired result.

In Kilburn House, however…

He shook his head and sighed.

In a way, he *supposed* he could see what Lord Darlington was getting at with the dogs and cats analogy. He could admit that there were times when he did feel a bit like, well, a large bull mastiff, outnumbered and baffled by kittens. Though he was both physically, and legally, far more powerful than any of his female relatives, they…they somehow constantly managed to undermine his authority by being…well…either fluffy or striking out with their little claws.

All except that Miss Hinchcliffe, the young woman he'd hired to bring some discipline into Susannah's life. She was like a… like a swan, he supposed, if he was going to stick to comparing people to creatures. She glided along, looking down her long slender nose at the rest of them, totally unmoved by their antics.

No, not a swan…if anything she put him in mind of those

magnificent eagles he'd sometimes seen, soaring above the Pyrenees, apparently effortlessly, making use of some mysterious power that enabled them to rise above the sordid realities that kept mere humans earthbound. Just as she rose above Susannah's tantrums and Lady Birchwood's fits of the vapours, or his own raised voice, with scarcely a flicker.

'Chaps,' Lord Darlington said, cutting through his own train of thought regarding the likeness of various members of the animal kingdom to his own female dependants, 'stick together.' He banged his glass down on the table. 'Like a pack of foxhounds.' As though to demonstrate the validity of that opinion, he threw back his head and gave a good impersonation of a hound baying when catching scent of a fox.

And all round the room, for no reason that Michael could determine, other men began baying, too. Or barking, or braying, or neighing like horses. The only man who showed no interest in joining in was a glassy-eyed youth who was sprawled on a chair with his legs splayed out in front of him, looking as though the only reason he hadn't slid down to the ground altogether was because someone had hooked the collar of his jacket over the chair back.

'See?' Lord Darlington waved his hand expansively round the room. 'That's why you join a club like this. Always have chaps to back you up! Even when they don't know why they're doing it.'

Yes, well…that wasn't exactly a great recommendation for joining, not in Michael's opinion. He neither wanted to behave like one of a pack of slavering hounds, nor had he any ambition to become a leader of such a brainless bunch of buffoons. He'd accepted the invitation to dine here tonight because his predecessor had been a member, because he'd been told it was an honour granted only to a very select few and because it had therefore felt as though it was something he ought to do, now he held the title.

The only thing he'd achieved, by coming here tonight, was to confirm his belief that he didn't belong with this set.

No, make that two things. It confirmed that he didn't *want* to belong.

Was he ever going to feel like a marquess, rather than just plain Major Kilburn? Was he always going to feel this uncomfortable in civilian clothing? So...*other* from the company he was now expected to rub shoulders with? In the army, he might have had to undergo hardships, but at least he'd had the comradeship of men he could trust and respect.

Cats and dogs, for heaven's sake! You couldn't divide people into two groups like that. People were...people. Some were stupid, admittedly and some were aloof.

And the ones in this room were just plain drunk.

All of a sudden he couldn't remember ever having felt so alone.

'Another bottle,' shouted Lord Darlington, breaking into his musings, 'over here, waiter!'

'Sorry,' said Michael insincerely, getting to his feet. 'I have, er, something else I need to do...'

Lord Darlington grinned and winked. 'Of course you have. Of course! Women have their uses, eh? Can't do without 'em, in that respect!'

He made no comment, but left the room, mentally shaking his head. If that was the cream of English society, it was a wonder the country hadn't been overrun by the French years ago.

For the first time, he thought he could understand why his commanding officer had been so amenable to him selling his commission and returning to England, citing his need to find a wife and secure the continuation of his family line. The Colonel might even have meant what he'd said about England needing men of his stamp at home, as much as out on the battle front.

He paused on the front steps of the club to look up at the sky. The night was fine and clear. The air outside far more wholesome than the stuffy, overheated rooms of that so-called gentlemen's club.

Where to go now? He could go for a walk, he supposed, though the streets held no great interest for him. He supposed it was not a very patriotic thing to think about the capital city, but London, to his mind, couldn't compare with the bleak splendour of the Pyrenees, or the sun-baked plains of Portugal.

But he'd yielded to his family's increasingly impatient demands that he return to England. They'd pointed out that his ward was now of an age to make a come-out and would be wanting him around to steer her through the shoals of her first Season, and that while he was at it, he could do worse than look about for a bride for himself, too, and secure the succession.

They were right. He had put off that particular duty far too long already. But how could his cousin's girl have grown to the ripe age of seventeen already? It seemed only five minutes since he'd received the news that she'd been born. Less since he'd heard that his cousin himself had succumbed to a stupid fever and that Michael was now, legally, the Marquess of Caldicot.

And that was another thing, he mused as he set off down the steps. That girl, Susannah. He should have... He shook his head. It was no use now wishing he'd been more involved in her upbringing. Besides, any bachelor would have believed, as he'd done, that her female relatives would have a far better notion of how to bring her up. And she'd known them all, since his predecessor's sisters had been frequent visitors to the family seat, even after they'd married, whereas he was a virtual stranger. A sprig of a younger son, who'd only rarely seen the vast property that the Marquess of Caldicot could call home.

How was he to have guessed that they'd spoil her so badly that she could, at the age of seventeen, still think it acceptable behaviour to roll around on the floor screaming because he'd pointed out that Cecil Baxter was not a suitable person for her to know, let alone marry?

He'd stood there, watching her in disbelief, reflecting that at the same age he'd already become a subaltern. He'd fought in battles. As for Miss Hinchcliffe, she'd hardly been much older when she'd turned up for that interview and impressed him with the strength of her character.

Thank God for Miss Hinchcliffe, the only one among them who never turned a hair when Susannah enacted one of her scenes.

Not only had she been spectacularly unimpressed by Susannah's antics today, but, in spite of Lady Birchwood's dire predictions, she'd coaxed the girl out of her temper and into an outfit suitable to make her debut at Almack's.

Where he ought to be, too, he reflected. Had he gone there, as Lady Birchwood and the rest of them had expected, he would not have had to witness the drunken idiocy of the men who he was supposed to now regard as his peers. But after that scene with Susannah he hadn't been willing to face the prospect of spending an entire evening enduring Susannah's pouts, while fending off droves of matchmaking mothers who wanted their spindly spotty sons to attract Susannah's notice, or worse, their giggly, vapid daughters to attract his.

And that was another thing. It was all very well deciding he ought to do his duty to his family and find a suitable wife. But his idea of suitable did not stretch to girls just out of the school-room, no matter how impeccable their lineage. If he was going to live with a woman for the rest of his life, he had to be able to imagine holding a conversation with her, occasionally. That wasn't too much to hope for, was it?

At that point, he suddenly discovered that while he'd been in a brown study, his feet seemed to have carried him to the family residence in Grosvenor Square: Kilburn House. The house Lady Birchwood had insisted he host Susannah's come-out ball at the start of the Season, because it was the place from which *she'd* been launched into society as a girl. The place he was suddenly supposed to think of as home, but which still felt like his cousin's property. He'd only ventured inside a couple of times before he'd inherited it along with all the rest. And both times, after making his bow to his cousin, he'd been sent off to amuse himself in the garden.

His spirits lifted, just a fraction, as he remembered the time he'd spent playing there. The garden was a good size for a property in London, with paths leading to banks of shrubs where an enterprising young boy could make a den.

But as for the house... His spirits sank right back to where they'd been. It held no fond memories, as it did for the likes of Lady Birchwood, who'd run tame there as a girl. She still seemed to think that, even though she was a widow, she had a right to consider it as her house, not his.

Although, since Miss Hinchcliffe had somehow worked her magic on his troublesome ward, Lady Birchwood wouldn't be there, would she? In fact, the whole lot of them would all be at Almack's.

So the house would be empty. Or at least, empty of his female relatives.

Which meant that he'd be able to sit in his study, one of the only two rooms he'd so far been able to stamp his own personality on, with a book and a brandy. A pastime far better than carousing with a bunch of men who aspired to nothing more than being part of a pack, like so many sheep. Or searching in vain for a female who would meet both his family's, and his own, standards.

With a lift to his spirits, he began to mount the front steps.

Only to stagger back when the front door opened and Miss Hinchcliffe came flying out, so intent on fleeing that she didn't appear to have noticed he was there until she'd cannoned right into him.

He caught her by the arms just above the elbows to steady her. Or himself. And sighed.

'I thought,' he said, on a wave of disappointment, 'that you were made of sterner stuff. I never thought that Susannah would be able to drive you away, like she has done with so many of your predecessors.'

'Susannah?' Miss Hinchcliffe gave him a wild-eyed stare. 'I'm not running away because of Susannah. It is far worse! Oh, do let me go!'

He released her arms, but did not move out of her way, which was clearly what she wanted him to do.

'If not because of her, then...' He looked her up and down. She had a small case in one hand, from which something white and fluttery was trailing, as though she'd packed in a hurry. Her coat was buttoned up the wrong way and her hair was straggling out of a bonnet which was even now slipping down over one ear.

She gulped, dropped the case and pressed her hands over her face for a moment, then lowered them, to about the height of her throat, and gazed at him. Her shoulders drooped.

'I knew,' she said despairingly, 'I wouldn't get away with it this time.'

He felt the hairs on the back of his neck prickle. The way they did, sometimes, when the enemy had laid an ambush.

'Get away,' he said, 'with what?'

He might have known she was too good to be true. No woman who clung to a post managing a girl like Susannah could possibly do so unless she had some very good reason. Who was, in short, so desperate for work that she'd put up with anything. Why hadn't he realised this sooner?

'Let me see what you have in your case,' he said sternly.

'My case? Why should you be interested in that?'

'I want to see what you have tried to steal,' he said grimly, 'before deciding what to do about you.' He could hardly blame her for snatching whatever she could and making a run for it. He'd been tempted to get on his horse and make for the hills on many occasions, recently.

'I am not,' she said indignantly, 'a thief!'

'No? Then why were you leaving in such a hurry? And what exactly was it that you feared you wouldn't get away with? *This time?*'

Her eyes filled with tears. 'Well, I didn't mean to. Honestly I didn't. But all the same, it appears that…that I've killed him. I've killed Mr Baxter!'

Chapter Three

'Killed? Mr Baxter?'

His predecessor, the Fifth Marquess, would no doubt at this moment be expressing horror on hearing such news.

It just went to show how unfit he was to hold the title of Sixth Marquess that his prime response was that of envy. Yes, envy that she'd had the privilege of putting a period to the existence of that slimy worm who'd thought him gullible enough to grant him Susannah's hand in marriage.

He should have been the one who'd wrung that young man's neck, not the governess! He'd only managed to restrain himself from doing just that, earlier on, by reminding himself that one simply couldn't do such things in London. Particularly not in one's own house, with the female members of his family hovering outside the door.

'Did you wring his neck?' he couldn't resist asking her.

'What? No!' She looked horrified. 'I told you. I didn't mean to do it at all!'

'You just couldn't help yourself,' he said, nodding sympathetically.

'No! Well, yes, I mean...'

'Perhaps it would be better,' he said, extending one arm to

the front door, 'to go back inside and tell me exactly what happened.'

She looked appalled at the prospect.

'In battle,' he mused out loud, 'chaps do sometimes kill people they didn't mean to. A rocket goes astray, or a shot ricochets, for example. I am sure you will have some equally plausible explanation as to how you came to *accidentally* kill someone in London.'

'I suppose,' she said morosely, all the fight appearing to go out of her, 'I would have had to explain to Grandfather why I had to leave this post as well, in the end. So there was never any hope of keeping it secret.'

'Secret?' The word dropped into his brain with the force of a bell ringing. 'Is there,' he asked, the moment he'd shut the front door behind them and they were standing in the hall, 'anyone else in the house? Could anyone else have heard anything?'

She looked at him with wide eyes. 'No. Well, that is, the male staff have all taken the opportunity to go to the tavern and the housemaids have all gone to bed. Oh!' She looked at him with a sort of wild hope in her eyes. 'Are you saying that it might be possible to hush this up? Hide the body, somehow? Perhaps…' Her face fell, abruptly. 'No, that would be *wrong*.' She wrung her hands. 'And yet,' she added, looking straight at him, 'if anyone could dispose of a body, that person must be you.'

'What? What sort of man do you think I am?'

'An intelligent one,' she replied without hesitation. 'A resourceful one! And…and possibly a *grateful* one.'

'Eh?'

'I mean,' she said, that wild light of hope gleaming in her eyes again, 'you must be jolly glad that Mr Baxter is no longer able to pursue Susannah, mustn't you?'

'Let us not,' he said drily, 'get carried away. There is a vast difference between wishing to put a bullet between a man's eyes and actually doing it.'

Her shoulders slumped again. She rubbed one hand over her forehead. 'Yes, of course, you are right. I don't know what I was thinking.'

He was thinking, all of a sudden, about the school of anatomy. They were always, so he'd heard, glad to have fresh bodies to dissect and weren't always fussy about knowing where, exactly, they came from...

But first things first. 'You still haven't told me how it happened. I mean, to look at you, one would never guess that you went round accidentally killing men on your evenings off...'

'I don't! I didn't!'

'And yet you said *this time*. As though you have tried to dispose of hapless males who strayed across your path on several occasions. And, also, you mentioned explaining your dilemma to your grandfather. *Again.*'

'Oh, but the other times were nothing like this! Oh, dear, how bad that sounds. What must you think of me?'

As she shook her head in a fashion that he could only describe as woebegone, he wondered—what *did* he think of her?

Well, for one thing, he'd always wondered what it would take to ruffle her feathers. 'The same as my family, I suppose,' she continued, despondently. 'That I am not fit to live in a house with...civilised people.'

'Not fit to...?' How could they? 'Your family? I didn't think you had any. When I hired you, you said you were an orphan...'

'Well, yes, of course I am an orphan. But everyone had parents at one time, didn't they? And mine were both from good families, to their own way of thinking, before they married each other against their respective fathers' wishes and got cast off, or cut off, or both, actually—'

'So, this grandfather you mentioned,' he cut in when it looked as though she was about to veer off at a tangent, 'to whom you were about to flee...'

'He is my mother's father. He always steps in to rescue me when I get into trouble.'

'And he's had to do that frequently, has he?'

'More than he would wish,' she confessed, gloomily. 'But this is all beside the point, isn't it? Why are we standing about in the hall, talking about my grandfather, when there is a dead body...' she stopped, suddenly, and lowered her voice, 'in the back garden.'

Sensible as ever, he reflected with admiration. Even though

she'd clearly had a nasty shock, she'd only succumbed to talk-ing nonsense for the briefest of interludes before pulling herself together and getting right back to the matter in hand.

'Oh, you killed him in the garden, did you? What did he do?' he asked, realising that he was enjoying this encounter more than he ought. 'Surprise you while you were walking about with a lovely sharp spade in your hand?'

She glared at him. 'I wasn't in the garden at all. I was sit-ting in my room, reading, when he tried to climb in through my window.'

'The devil you say! I mean,' he corrected himself when her jaw dropped at the sound of his cursing, 'what cheek! Naturally you pushed him off your balcony.'

'I did no such thing,' she said with great indignation. 'I hit him with *Sense and Sensibility*!'

It was with great difficulty that he bit back a sudden urge to laugh. Instead, he asked her, in as serious tone as he could muster, 'Which volume?'

'Does it matter which volume?'

'I was just wondering which part of the story he interrupted. If it was a particularly exciting part, no wonder you got up and bashed him over the head with it.'

She gave him a look of exasperation. He supposed she was going to chide him for veering off the topic again and remind him that he ought to be worrying about the fact he had a body lying in his back garden. Which would be a pity. Because the dead man, clearly, wasn't going to go anywhere. But Miss Hinchcliffe might, if he didn't find more ways to keep her here talking.

He never could just talk to her, as a rule. She was always in the background, keeping decorously in her place. Which was all right and proper of course. He couldn't fault her for that. But he'd been feeling increasingly frustrated that he couldn't just strike up a conversation with her, when she appeared to be the only sensible person in the household. The only one he could imagine having anything worth saying.

'There are no exciting parts in *Sense and Sensibility*,' she said, gratifyingly engaging with his nonsense, rather than obliging him to be…well, sensible. 'It isn't that kind of story. And I didn't bash him with it,' she said indignantly. 'I threw it at him!'

'Hard enough to knock him clean out of the window? I confess to being impressed. You must be stronger than you look.'

'Well, he was off balance,' she replied modestly. 'With one leg half over the balustrade.'

'That's a very sporting thing of you to admit. Most men would have bragged about scoring a direct hit on the fellow's nose, or something of the sort. But you aren't a man, are you? You are a woman.'

'Have you only,' she said scathingly, 'just noticed?'

'No, of course not!' Far from it. But she worked for him. And he detested the kind of men who looked at female members of their staff in an impure way. So he did not do it. He *refused* to do it. 'It is just,' he continued, 'that you don't generally behave the way most other women do. Or at least, not the ones I've been unfortunate enough to have come across since I've sold out.'

Less than half an hour since, he'd been comparing her to an eagle, soaring effortlessly far above the turmoil created by his ward. But right his minute, he reflected, narrowing his eyes to examine her more keenly, she put him more in mind of a hen. Just after a fox had tried to get into the hen house, with her bonnet askew and her coat buttoned up incorrectly. Though even if she did put him in mind of a chicken with her feathers ruffled, she was still a very impressive chicken to have fended off the marauding fox.

'I suppose,' he said, feeling rather more sympathetic all of a sudden, 'you must have been scared out of your wits when a man attempted to climb into your room, at night, when nobody else was in the house. No wonder you panicked.'

'Panicked? I did no such thing,' she said indignantly. 'I told you. He took me by surprise, and I just acted without thinking! I do tend to…er…go on the offensive when I feel threatened.' She started twisting her hands together, in what looked like an expression of remorse. Or possibly vexation.

'But then, if a woman ever shows the slightest sign of weakness when approached by a man determined on making mischief, like calling for help and hoping someone may hear, or worse, fainting, which would only serve to put her entirely in his power...' She paused, biting down on her lower lip, as though annoyed that she'd let it say too much.

'It sounds as though you have had plenty of experience with mischief-making men,' he said, examining her more closely than he'd ever allowed himself to do before.

She was tall, for a woman, and angular, with ferocious eyebrows and a nose which had put him in mind of the beak of some bird of prey. So not conventionally pretty. And she'd only been eighteen when she'd applied for the job as Susannah's governess. Which meant any experience she'd had of that nature must have happened before that. No wonder she'd scowled at him all through that interview. No wonder she'd asked so many questions about the conditions of her service.

How he wished he could find out what man had tried to take liberties with her, when she'd been scarcely more than a girl. He'd teach them to prey on defenceless females!

She shifted from one foot to the other. 'Well, not as bad as *this.*'

'What do you mean,' he asked, 'not as bad as this? Or,' he added, 'do you just mean that you do not make a habit of pushing men out of windows?'

'Of course I don't,' she said, looking agonised. 'And I didn't push this one, either. I told you—'

'Yes, yes,' he interrupted, in what he hoped was a soothing tone, 'you simply threw the book at him. Although I cannot help wondering,' he continued, finding himself inexplicably fascinated by Miss Hinchcliffe's hitherto unsuspected history, 'what you did to your previous victims?'

'Does it matter? Really? Should we not be concentrating on what we are to do about...*him*?' She gesticulated wildly in the direction of the servants' quarters, though he supposed she meant to point to the garden, where the body was lying.

'You are right,' he admitted, with regret. 'We should leave all that for another time. Though I cannot help wondering,' he mused out loud, 'why he was trying to climb into your window at all?' He'd heard some unsavoury rumours about Baxter.

But he couldn't for the life of him see what the man thought he would achieve by climbing into the governess's room.

'I suspect,' said Miss Hinchcliffe, 'that he thought it must be Susannah's room. After all, it is the only room at the back with a balcony. He must have assumed it would be hers. And I also assume that it was with the intent to either seduce her or persuade her to elope with him.'

'Yes. That sounds about the sort of sneaky thing a fellow like that would do,' he agreed, feeling his lip curl. 'Also, it probably looked easier to get in that way, than by a window which was shut. You were sitting there with the window to the balcony standing open, I take it? If you were able to throw your book and hit him without breaking the window as well?' It occurred to him that his brain was beginning to clear. Had he had more to drink than he'd meant to, earlier on, that he'd been so muddled, up to now? It would certainly explain why he was comparing people to chickens and eagles.

Oh, and kittens, at one point.

And also why he was finding this encounter rather enjoyable, when a more staid sort of fellow would have found it shocking. But then, he reminded himself, he was not the sort of chap who ought, ever, to have become a marquess.

'Yes. Well, it is a very warm evening,' she reminded him. 'I was enjoying the breeze. And I think there is a nightingale...'

'He really did ruin your evening off, didn't he?' he remarked, leaning back against the wainscot and folding his arms across his chest. 'He absolutely deserved that you threw your book at him.'

'Well, thank you for trying to make me feel better. But actually *killing* him...' She shook her head, and tucked her hands under her armpits, as though unsure what to do with hands that had so recently behaved so badly.

'And you are sure that he is dead, are you?'

She paled and gave a stiff nod. 'First I leaned over the balcony railings and saw him lying in the bushes...'

'The bushes? But doesn't your balcony overlook the terrace?'

'Well, yes, but he'd climbed up at the side of the balcony.

There is, as I noted, a drainpipe there, which must have offered decent handholds.'

'Of course, that explains it,' he agreed. 'Only, if he fell into those bushes, they might have softened his fall,' he suggested.

'Well, yes they might, but I cannot believe that anyone lying at that precise angle could possibly be...be...' She petered out, turning pale.

He straightened up. 'So you didn't check him closely?'

'Well, I did go down to retrieve the book,' she said.

'To retrieve the book? Not to see if you could do anything for the man you'd just assaulted?'

'Well, it came from the library!'

'Of course. That makes all the difference,' he said drily.

'Well, it does! I couldn't just leave it lying on the grass. It would have been ruined! And it will have to go back, you know. So I just ran down and grabbed it, and fortunately it was lying some distance away from...him, so I didn't have to...see very much...' She swallowed, as though she'd just been obliged to eat something very unpleasant. 'And I put it on my dressing table,' she continued, 'with a note explaining that I'd had to leave in a hurry and asking someone to return it...'

'Never mind the blasted book,' he said, as a horrible thought suddenly struck him.

Her eyes widened at his second use of a curse word and she gave him the kind of look she'd so often used to quell his ward. Though, since he was not an impressionable girl, but a battle-hardened, seasoned veteran of many bloody campaigns, he felt only the mildest touch of shame that she'd made him forget his manners.

'Keep to the point, madam,' he said as sternly as he could, considering she was not one of his subalterns hauled up on a charge. 'Which is—how certain are you that Baxter is really dead and not just stunned, since you didn't look at him closely?'

'As I was saying, I went outside to retrieve the library book, once I'd packed my overnight bag, and piled all my other possessions into a heap on the bed, hoping someone would be kind enough to send them on later...only I don't suppose that would have been sensible, would it, once they'd discovered the body.

Oh, how disordered my wits are tonight!' She raised a hand to her forehead. A hand which, he noted, was trembling.

'Take a deep breath,' he suggested, 'then tell me how you became so certain he is dead.'

'Well, for one thing, he had neither moved nor made a sound by the time I'd run round the bedroom pulling everything out of the cupboards and writing a note about the library book. And for another...' She gulped.

'Yes?'

'Well, there was blood. All down his front.'

He frowned. 'Blood? How the deuce...' He'd assumed the fellow must have fallen on to the paving stones of the rear terrace and that, therefore, there was nothing anyone could do for him. But this changed everything. If the fellow was just injured, he ought to be seeing if there *was* anything to be done. Without further ado, he stalked down the hall to the breakfast room in which there was a set of double doors that led out to the terrace, providing the quickest route to get to where Baxter lay. He heard her footsteps pattering along behind him. When he reached the double doors and paused to open them, she ran full tilt into his back.

He turned, steadying her by taking hold of her shoulders.

She blushed. Gasped. Trembled. But not, he didn't think, with horror. On the contrary, something sparked between them. Something that usually led to kisses, in his experience.

'You don't need to come out and view your handiwork again,' he said gruffly, setting her aside. He had no business to be thinking about kissing her, after the dreadful night she'd already been having. Hadn't she already suffered enough shocks? First to have had a lecher like Baxter climb in through her window, probably with evil intent, and then the horror of accidentally killing him.

But when he stepped outside, she followed closely behind him. All the way along the terrace to the stone parapet that separated it from the shrubbery. In which lay, as she'd warned him, what looked at first glance to be a shapeless bundle of clothes.

'You see?' she said, though when he turned to look at her, she'd closed her eyes. 'He cannot possibly still be alive, can he?'

But just as he was about to agree with her that nobody who was lying in that position could possibly still be alive, the shapeless bundle of clothing let out a groan.

Chapter Four

Rosalind gasped and opened her eyes. Looked up at her window and then down at the bushes. It wasn't all that far, now she came to think of it. Could he really have survived the fall? If he'd been the sort of boy who'd climbed trees, he would surely have learned how to fall from much higher than that, without breaking *very* many bones.

'It might not mean anything,' she heard Lord Caldicot mutter darkly, as he swung one leg over the parapet. 'Wind has to escape, whether a fellow is dead or alive.'

What? Did he mean Mr Baxter might be still be dead, even though he was making…those sorts of noises?

'And sometimes, it can sound very convincing…' He stopped talking as he bent over the body.

Then he straightened up, rather abruptly, and let out a curse. The third one she'd heard him utter. Though she ought not to be keeping count. Her behaviour this evening was bad enough to make *any* man curse, although, she couldn't really understand why he was so angry right now. Though, to be honest, he had not reacted to anything the way she might have expected since he'd caught her trying to flee from the house. He hadn't sounded the least bit shocked, for instance, when she'd admitted to accidentally killing a man. If anything, he'd seemed…

amused. So what could he have learned, from that one swift inspection of Mr Baxter's body to make him look so cross? And
say such an ugly word?

'What,' she therefore asked, 'is the matter?'

He turned to her, his expression grim. 'I am sorry to have
to inform you,' he said, making her heart sink, 'that Baxter is
not dead.'

'Well, but that is a good thing, isn't it?' He couldn't possibly
really wish she'd killed the man. 'I mean, you couldn't possibly
have wanted to have to preside over a murder trial, not during
Susannah's debut, could you? You specifically said,' she reminded him, 'you didn't want her Season ruined by scandal.
Surely nothing could be more scandalous than a girl's governess murdering a suitor, could it?'

Was she talking gibberish? He was certainly looking at her
as though she'd taken leave of her senses.

'And also,' she added, 'how can you possibly be so certain
he isn't dead? You scarcely looked at him.'

'I didn't need to look at him. He spoke.'

'He spoke? I didn't hear him.'

'No, well,' he said drily, 'I dare say your teeth are chattering
so loudly with nerves that you couldn't hear him.'

'My teeth,' she objected, 'are not chattering.' Though she
was trembling, she had to admit. Just a little.

'Then I fail to see why you did not hear him say turpentine!'

'Turpentine? Why on earth would anyone say the word turpentine, at such a moment?'

'Well, there is no accounting for the absurd things some
men say, is there,' he said bitterly. Then he bent down over the
body—well, Mr Baxter, that was. She couldn't refer to him as
the body if he wasn't dead, could she?

When Lord Caldicot straightened up, he had something in
his hand. Something that looked dark and sticky.

'This,' he said, giving her a strange look, 'is what you thought
was blood, isn't it?'

Just as she was about to nod, he tossed it up in the air.

It showered down, like confetti.

'Rose petals,' he said with derision. 'The silly chump climbed up to your window with about a dozen of them stuffed down the front of his waistcoat.'

And the fall from the window had crushed them.

Not blood.

Not dead.

All of a sudden she began to do more than tremble just a little. Before she could do something foolish, like fall to the ground because her legs had given way, she groped her way to the parapet, sat down, and bent over, resting her head on her knees.

She heard a scuffling sound, then Lord Caldicot was beside her. 'You aren't going to faint, are you?' He sounded anxious. Far more anxious, she noted, than he had when she'd told him she'd killed Cecil Baxter. 'Aren't you glad you won't have to stand trial?'

She glared up at him. 'If that is your attempt at trying to defuse an awkward situation with humour,' she said, suddenly deciding that this had been his modus operandi from the moment she'd run into him on the front steps, 'then I have to tell you that it falls short of the mark. Besides, I distinctly recall telling you that I *never* faint! Only a…a pudding heart would faint in a situation like this!'

'And you are certainly not that,' he agreed, wiping his hands of the last remnants of crushed rose petals.

'Perhaps I am,' she said despondently. 'After all, I could not make myself look at him all that closely. If I had, I wouldn't have had to go through all this…this…'

'Drama?'

'Anxiety,' she corrected him, sitting up. 'Instead of running around like a chicken with no head, throwing clothes into my bag and writing a note that was so hysterical I shouldn't think anyone would have been able to make head or tail of it, I would have just gone straight out and fetched a doctor. And, oh,' she cried, turning to him and clutching at his sleeve, 'that is what we ought to do now, isn't it? After all, he's been insensible for ages.'

'Probably from the moment of his birth,' he said, enigmatically.

'Oh. You mean he has never had any sense, I suppose. Very

droll. However, that doesn't alter the fact that now we know he isn't dead, but badly injured, we ought to fetch a doctor to him.'

He sighed. 'Now that you have suggested it, I suppose that is what we should do, yes.'

'Of course we should!'

'I just said so, didn't I?'

'Yes, but you sighed first.' All of a sudden she realised her fingers were still clutching into the cloth of his coat sleeve. And that he hadn't made any attempt to remove them. What did that mean?

'Well, a man cannot help how he feels,' he said a touch defensively, 'can he? About men like Baxter, particularly. And how could you guess what I was thinking from the fact that I sighed?'

She had no idea. After all, she couldn't begin to guess why he hadn't immediately brushed her hand from his sleeve. It was such a very forward thing for her to do.

She'd better let go of him.

And she would, in a minute. It was just that, for the moment, she didn't think she could make herself. He was so solid. So unflappable. She would have thought that most men would have been furious to come home and find an employee fleeing the scene of what they'd thought was a murder. Instead, he'd been calm. And hardly shown any signs of being cross with her at all. Not even now that she was clinging to his sleeve like a drowning man clinging to a lifeline.

'It was the *way* you sighed.' She suddenly realised that had made her think he was reluctant to send for a doctor. 'All... regretful.'

'Perhaps I was thinking of the bill I shall have to pay on that cur's account,' he said, nodding his head in the direction of the shrubbery.

'As if you aren't rich enough to care nothing for such things!'

He turned his head sharply and gave her a look that she guessed he had employed in the past to make his subalterns quake in their boots. It didn't have the effect upon her that he was probably hoping for. Instead of making her nervous, it made her wish she hadn't said something so personal. Now he must think she was not only an idiot, but a rude, tactless one as well.

It was just as well she'd never been able to cherish any hope he might think well of her, because he certainly wouldn't after this night's work.

She removed her hand from his sleeve under the cover of getting to her feet. 'We have delayed for too long already. I should have seen if there was anything I could do for him straight away instead of just trying to avoid looking...' She shivered.

'No,' he said, getting to his feet as well, so that he could glower down at her. Not many men could do that. They usually had to glower *up* at her, which tended to make them far crosser than they might have been with a shorter woman, she'd always suspected. 'You shouldn't have tried to do anything, not if you have no medical experience. You might have made things worse.'

'Oh! Do you really think so?'

'Absolutely. And since I have few medical skills either, *I* shall go and fetch the doctor. Which,' he said, giving her a look of resentment, 'was exactly what you hoped I'd do once you suggested going yourself, wasn't it?'

'I am flattered,' she retorted, 'that you think me capable of planning anything at all at a moment like this, when I still feel decidedly headless chicken-like.'

His expression softened. 'Then forgive me for thinking such an uncharitable thing. I have just grown so used to females trying to manipulate me since I've inherited the title that it has become hard to take anything any of you say at face value.' He rubbed his hand over his face in a way that revealed how weary he was.

'I promise you,' she said on a wave of compassion, because she understood exactly what he meant about manipulative females, after working for his family for the last five years, 'that I shall never say anything to you that is not the complete and utter truth.'

He looked at her for a moment. 'After the whiskers I have heard you telling Susannah, in order to get her to toe the line, you expect me to believe you?'

She flinched. Surely he could see that she'd had to make use of strategic ruses in order to improve Susannah's behaviour?

And as for her telling whiskers—no! She'd *never* done that. She might have drawn the girl's attention to factors that would help her to understand why certain types of behaviour were preferable to others in terms that would mean something to her. Such as pointing out all the things about eloping she wouldn't like, when Susannah had been turning over plans for doing so.

Why couldn't he see that? For a while there, it had felt as if he'd understood her. Sympathised with her. That they'd come to a sort of understanding.

It had clearly all been a bag of moonshine, brought on by wishful thinking. Of course a man like Lord Caldicot would not consider her in that light.

Dropping him a perfunctory curtsy, she turned and strode along the terrace.

'Just where,' she heard him say, 'do you think you are going?'

'To my room, sir,' she said over her shoulder. 'As you bid me.'

She thought she heard him mutter yet more curse words. She wouldn't blame him. He must be heartily sick of her by now. And the mess she'd made for him to clear up.

But at least she hadn't killed Cecil Baxter.

It wasn't until she reached her room and shut the door behind her, then caught sight of the open balcony window, that her legs finally went out from under her, making her drop to the floor halfway to her bed.

She might have killed a man!

It was only by the merest chance that he'd fallen into the bushes, rather than on to the terrace. And only the greatest of good luck that she'd run out of the front door just as Lord Caldicot was returning from wherever he'd been. If she'd gone, leaving that incriminating note…

She broke out into a cold sweat. She'd almost thrown away this job along with any hope of ever gaining another one. When would she learn to…just stop and *think*, before lashing out? Hastily, she went over to the dressing table, picked up her running-away note and tore it into little shreds, then put the shreds in her washbasin, lit a taper from her bedside candle and put the taper to the shredded remains of her evening's folly.

Only when the flames had reduced the letter to a little pile of ashes did she go to her bed and begin to return the belongings she'd piled there into their proper places in the room.

When that was done, she sat down for a moment or two, her hands raised to the sides of her head. What was she to do now? She didn't think she could possibly get herself ready for bed, not until the doctor had been to tend to Mr Baxter. She wouldn't be able to get to sleep until she'd learned how badly she'd injured him.

She could only learn that by going downstairs and asking Lord Caldicot, but she couldn't do so once she'd donned her nightgown and cap. Imagine, walking into his study, in her patched and darned flannel nightgown with her knitted shawl over her shoulders and her hair all bundled up under her ancient nightcap! And the look of revulsion she'd surely see come over his face at her frightful appearance.

The very thought made her blush all over.

She leaped to her feet again, and tried to relieve her feelings by striding back and forth. There was plenty of room to do it. Thanks to Susannah's fear of heights and her consequent reluctance to have the room with a balcony overlooking a drop of some twenty feet, Rosalind had by far the best room on this floor. She had not only a bed, wardrobe and washstand at one end, but also several chairs and tables at the other, with the balcony window between the two halves.

Though no amount of pacing could help to calm her nerves.

Eventually, after she felt as if she'd been pacing back and forth for about an hour, she heard the sound of men's voices floating in through her open balcony window.

He was back with the doctor!

She edged over to the open doors, hoping that she might be able to hear exactly what they were saying, without either of them being able to catch a glimpse of her.

But, frustratingly, the voices seemed to be getting further away. As though the men had gone inside.

They had done so, she discovered a few moments later, when she heard two heavy sets of feet coming up the stairs and heading along the corridor to her room.

After knocking on her door, Lord Caldicot came straight in, his face set in grave lines.

'Miss Hinchcliffe,' he said, giving her a piercing look. 'I have brought Dr Murgatroyd to see you.'

To see *her*? Why on earth had he done that?

Chapter Five

He shot her a warning glance, hoping to goodness that she was as intelligent as she usually appeared to be when dealing with Susannah's tantrums or Lady Birchwood's vapours. Hoping she'd understand that he was trying to conceal what had gone on in this house this evening.

Then he turned to the doctor, whom he'd prevented from barging in on her by remaining standing in the doorway, his hand on the latch.

'Miss Hinchliffe insisted she did not need a doctor, but as her employer, I have a duty to care for her. I hope, Miss Hinchliffe,' he said, turning to address her again, hoping that she'd understood that what he'd just said was as much for her benefit as the doctor's, 'that you will not be too angry with the good doctor. After all, he is only following my orders. And when I told him how agitated you became when you claimed to have seen an intruder in the grounds, he agreed to come and check that you have recovered from the...er...shock.'

'*Claimed* to see an intruder in the grounds?'

She looked so indignant he feared she was about to give the game away by reminding him that Baxter had intruded right into her room and that he'd seen the fellow lying in the shrubbery. But then her eyes darted to the doctor, who was trying to sidle past him, and she swallowed back her objections.

Thank heavens she *was* as clever as he'd hoped! She might not fully understand, yet, why he'd come up here with the doctor in tow, but she was prepared to play along until she found out.

So he stepped aside, allowing the pompous little man who was Lady Birchwood's favourite physician to oil his way into the room.

'Miss Hinchcliffe,' he said, in a voice so full of syrup that it invariably set his teeth on edge whenever he reported back to him before depositing his hefty bill on the study desk, 'Lord Caldicot and I have made a thorough check of the garden and we can assure you that there is nobody there.'

He saw understanding spread over her face. In the interval during which he'd been fetching the doctor, Baxter must have recovered and taken to his heels.

He'd tell her later that when he'd reached the spot where he'd left him lying, with the doctor in tow, but no patient to tend to, he'd swiftly gone over in his mind what he'd told Dr Murgatroyd. Realising that he hadn't specified exactly why he wanted him to come out at that time of night, he'd decided to provide him with an alternative patient, since the one he'd had in mind had done a runner.

The doctor looked over at the open windows and frowned.

'My dear girl,' he said to Miss Hinchcliffe, 'have you no idea how injurious the night air is to delicate constitutions?' He strode over to the window as fast as his little legs would allow and pulled the window shut. 'No wonder you have become prone to hysterical fancies, if you will breathe in the noxious miasma of the night air. It would not surprise me to learn that you are in the early stages of a feverish condition. Only look at those spots of colour in her cheeks, my lord,' he said to Michael. 'And the feverish glitter of her eyes!'

The spots of colour in her cheeks probably stemmed from temper at the patronising way the oily little man was speaking to her. And the glitter in her eyes warned him that she was within a hair's breadth of giving them both a piece of her mind.

'It is as I thought, then,' Michael said, shooting her a glance which he hoped denoted the sympathy he wished to convey. 'She is ill. Or,' he said, glancing at the doctor, who always made him feel a bit queasy, 'about to be.'

'Sit down, my dear,' said the doctor, indicating a chair next to a small table on which rested two volumes of *Sense and Sensibility*. The first and third, he noted absently. Did that mean she'd thrown the second volume at Baxter?

She went to the chair, with her lips pulled into a mutinous line, and sat down with clear resentment.

'I shall take your pulse,' said the doctor, reaching for and grabbing her hand. Because he was pulling out his pocket watch as he spoke, he didn't notice her clenching her other fist, then gradually uncurling her fingers, while her jaw worked, as though she was counting slowly to ten.

'Tumultuous,' said the doctor, snapping his watch shut, then patting her hand before releasing it. 'I think,' he said, looking at the books on the table at her side, 'that you may have been addling your wits through reading too much, rather than going to bed at a sensible hour and getting your rest. Women,' the doctor continued, turning to him, 'should not sit about, inactive, while their minds get all worked up over these sorts of silly romances,' he said. 'It can often lead to episodes of hysteria.'

If anything was likely to induce a fit of hysteria in this particular woman, he would warrant it was having an ignorant quack like this one coming up with such a demeaning prognosis. And far from being silly, the particular novel she'd been reading had come in jolly handy. Why, it had almost become a lethal weapon!

She was breathing heavily now and barely managing to keep herself sitting still.

'I shall,' said the doctor, turning away to the bed where he'd dropped his bag a moment before, 'mix up a soothing draught for her. It will help her to sleep. And from now on, I prescribe less reading and more exercise, to restore the balance of the humours.'

She was so livid now, that steam was practically coming out of her ears.

'Perhaps,' Michael couldn't resist saying, 'I should remove

the offending items from her vicinity, in case she is tempted to make use of them again.' As he went to pick up the two volumes of *Sense and Sensibility*, he met her eye. Oh, how she would love to have got to them first and hit someone with one of them. Probably the doctor, who was busy mixing up some powder from a packet he'd taken out of his bag with some water that he'd poured from a jug he'd found on her nightstand. Or possibly him, now that he was teasing her by appearing to go along with what the doctor was saying.

'Now, drink this up like a good girl,' said the doctor, holding out the glass of cloudy liquid.

'Must I?' She gazed up at him with entreaty in her eyes.

'I am afraid,' Michael said, 'that you must. It will help you sleep, you know,' he added.

'Yes,' she said and sighed. 'I suppose I was finding it hard to…to be at ease…while you were out fetching the doctor.'

She took the glass, downed the contents in one go, shuddered and made a face.

What a trump she was!

After seeing the doctor off the premises, he ran back up the stairs and knocked on her bedroom door again.

She opened it so quickly she must have been standing just inside it, waiting for his return.

'I know, I know,' he said, holding up his hands in a gesture of surrender. 'But when I got to the spot where we'd left Baxter burbling on about turpentine and found he'd vanished, I had to think of some reason why I might have summoned the doctor with such urgency, in the middle of the night.'

'And a hysterical woman,' she said tartly, 'was the best you could come up with?'

'Well, I didn't know who else was in the house. And I couldn't very well say I was in desperate need of a quack at this hour of the night, since I'd gone to him myself and could have consulted him in his own rooms. Besides, I knew you'd catch on to what was afoot and play along.'

'You did, did you?'

'Well, I hoped, at any rate. You have always struck me as being of above average intelligence.'

'Huh,' she said. 'Pardon me for pointing it out, but a short while ago *you* were accusing *me* of telling whiskers!'

'So you will completely understand why I had to resort to doing the same. Sometimes, employing a ruse of that sort is the only way to scrape through a tight spot, isn't it?'

'Huh,' she said again, although she did look slightly less annoyed. 'Well, at least,' she said pragmatically, 'I looked the part, didn't I? After you took that vile little man away, I took a look at myself in the mirror. And I *do* look positively demented.'

'Well, who wouldn't after the things you went through? Most women would have indulged in a fit of the vapours long before that doctor shoved his oar in. And how you kept a straight face when he pointed out the dangers of *Sense and Sensibility*,' he said with admiration, 'I cannot imagine!'

'I was within an ames-ace of showing him exactly how dangerous books can be, I admit,' she said with feeling. 'Only I had just been scolding myself for acting before thinking and thought it would be better to count to ten. Or relieve my feelings by hitting something, *after* he'd gone away.'

'You did the right thing. If you had hit him—not that I would have blamed you, after all the provoking things he said—he would only have thought that it proved he was right. But anyway,' he added, glancing over his shoulder, 'we cannot stand about discussing the doctor's stupidity, or we will be here all night. And my ward and Lady Birchwood are likely to be returning fairly soon. The last thing I want is for them to discover me in your room.'

She blushed. 'Yes. And now you have mentioned it, might I remind you that you ought not to be in here?'

'I don't need a reminder. I know it is rather unorthodox. But I just needed to make sure that you were aware of the facts. Baxter has vanished. Which, in one way, I suppose, is a good thing. That is to say, it must mean that he cannot be that badly injured or he couldn't have got up and run off.'

'We don't know that he ran…'

'Whatever speed he went, the point is he made himself scarce the moment the coast was clear. Which means he's out there, on the loose, planning his next move. Which means we will need to start planning *our* next move.'

'Our...next move? What do you mean?'

'Just that now we know how unscrupulous Baxter can be—for what decent man would attempt to climb into an innocent girl's room, with flowers? We will need to be on the alert for further attempts to...win Susannah away from her home. And since it would not be proper for me to remain here, at this hour of the night, and anyway we are likely to get interrupted by the last persons we want to know anything about this night's work, then I suggest you attend me in my study in the morning after breakfast. And help me thrash out a plan.'

'Pardon me for being stupid, but why don't we want Susannah to know about Baxter trying to get in by the window to see her? Surely, forewarned is forearmed?'

'Isn't it obvious? If she knows the lengths to which he will go to thwart my wishes, I wouldn't put it past her to think of that as the epitome of romance. Or some such nonsense. Besides, we don't want her to know that you threw him out of the window, do we?'

'*Knocked* him out of the window,' she corrected him. 'By accident.'

'However he went out of the window, the point is that at the moment Susannah trusts you completely. Otherwise, why would she have insisted that you came to London? In spite of Lady Birchwood being equally insistent that she was the proper person to preside over her presentation.'

'Yes, well, Lady Susannah's aunts have been passing her from one to the other to suit their convenience ever since I have been working for the family,' she said. 'So, for the last few years, I have been the one person who has stuck with her through thick and thin.'

'There, you see? If she should find out that you dislike the man so much you caused him actual bodily harm, that trust is bound to get dented, if not destroyed completely. And I need her to trust you. At the moment you are the only person on my staff that has any success at keeping her in line. Unorthodox though your methods may be. Look,' he said, seeing her eyes take on a glassy sheen, 'I can see that whatever the doctor gave you is beginning to take effect. You are not thinking as clearly as you usually do.'

She frowned. 'You could be right. I do feel rather...lethargic.'

His conscience smote him. 'I apologise for foisting that nasty little man on you. And for allowing him to give you a dose of what I suspect is laudanum. But he regularly doses Lady Birchwood with it and she has never come to any harm from it.'

'No,' she said, making a dismissive gesture with her hand. 'I am already getting sleepy, but it won't do me any harm. Though I do wonder if she may have come to rely on it too much. I recall, when she was first widowed, that it really did help her. From what I could observe. Only...' She blinked, rather owlishly. 'That is to say...to be honest, without it, I wouldn't have been able to sleep at all, I shouldn't think. Before you came in I was...pacing,' she said with a rueful shake of her head. 'Back and forth. Getting nowhere.'

'Then let us bid each other goodnight and meet again in the morning to discuss tactics.'

'Tactics, yes,' she said, giving him a rather wan smile. 'In the morning.'

'I shall look forward to it,' he said. As he closed the door on his way out, he realised that he had spoken nothing but the truth. He *was* looking forward to meeting Miss Hinchcliffe in the morning and having what was bound to be a completely unorthodox conversation with her.

To think that when he'd left the army, he'd feared his life would become one long tedious round of duties. Well, so far, it had been. At least, a great deal of it. Having to spend so much time in London, dancing attendance on his ward, who was the most spoiled little madam it had ever been his misfortune to encounter. And having inane exchanges with fluttery debutantes.

But this evening, or at least, from the moment Miss Hinchcliffe had run into him on the front step, babbling tales of murder, mischief and library books, he hadn't felt the slightest bit bored. For the first time since he'd returned to England, he'd felt like...himself.

It was probably reprehensible of him. But then he'd never

been a staid sort of chap, had he? Not like his pompous cousin, who'd never put a foot out of line. No, life in the army had suited Michael's character perfectly. He'd enjoyed being on the move, with no knowing what adventure each new day would bring.

A smile pulled at his lips as he laid his hand to the door latch of his own bedroom. For it sounded as though Miss Hinchcliffe, under that stern, unflappable front which was all she'd permitted him to see before tonight, was the kind of person around whom things *happened*.

And he, for one, couldn't wait to find out what might happen next.

Chapter Six

Rosalind woke with a start and sat bolt upright, her heart pounding.

The room was stuffy, probably because the sun was shining in through the window. The closed window.

She looked at the little clock which she kept on her bedside table, groaning when she saw that it was past eleven. No wonder the room was so uncomfortably hot. The sun must have been shining in for some time.

She flung back the covers, got out of bed and strode over to open the window. As she stepped over to the balcony, to breathe in some fresh air, the events of the previous night came flooding back to her.

Her stomach roiled. She might have killed a man! For a few dreadful hours, she'd believed she had. Only for Mr Baxter to make a remarkable recovery, before vanishing into the night, leaving Lord Caldicot to clear up the mess he'd made. Or she'd made.

But never mind that. Why hadn't someone come and woken her up? It was well past the time she normally rose and broke her fast. Even on nights after balls, when Susannah slept past noon, she made sure she had the first part of the day to herself, before her charge began making demands on her.

It was only after she'd taken a wash in rather dusty water that had been standing there all night, since she didn't want to waste time ringing for hot water, and waiting for someone to fetch it, that she noticed a slip of paper lying by her bedroom door. Just as though someone had pushed it under the door while she slept.

She hurried over and picked it up.

When you awake, come to my study straight away.
M.

M.? Who was M.?

Him. He was *Michael*, Lord Caldicot.

But why had he signed it M? They were not on such terms that she might expect to address him by his first name.

Or perhaps, after last night, he thought they were.

But they weren't. Still… She took the note to her dressing table, took out her writing case and slipped the note inside, then slammed the drawer on her sentimental piece of foolishness, before scrambling into her clothes. He was her employer and the note reminded her that he'd clearly been waiting for her to keep the appointment they'd made the night before. Nothing more, no matter what significance she might wish it had, from the way he'd signed it by his given name rather than his title.

He must already think badly enough of her for all the trouble she'd caused. It was what had made her swallow that vile medicine with such meekness—the feeling that she deserved to be punished for her crimes. Or, if not quite a crime, since it appeared Mr Baxter hadn't died after all, then…her reprehensible behaviour. For it was only by the greatest stroke of luck he'd landed in the bushes, rather than on the terrace.

Oh, when would she ever become the person she'd tried to pretend to be since coming to work for Susannah's family? A calm, dependable, rational person who didn't go about throwing things at stray men and knocking them out of windows?

Once she'd taken a swift glance at her reflection in the mirror, to make sure she looked as much like the stern, dependable governess companion she was trying so hard to be, she ran down the stairs, and tapped at the door of Lord Caldicot's study.

'Come in,' she heard him call out.

She squared her shoulders and went in.

He looked up at her from behind a mountain of paperwork and grinned.

Yes, *grinned*.

'I was wondering when you were going to emerge,' he said, without the slightest sign of irritation. 'That stuff the doctor gave you must have been stronger than usual. Lady Birchwood quaffs gallons of it and it never makes her sleep so soundly that she doesn't even hear a person knocking on her bedroom door.'

'You knocked on my door?'

'No, of course not,' he said, looking surprised. 'I sent a maid up, to see if you were awake yet, after I'd had my breakfast. I don't make a habit of going into a female's bedroom, not during the hours of daylight. Um, I mean...'

She felt her cheeks heat as she thought of why he might enter a female's bedroom during the hours of darkness.

His own cheeks had darkened, too, she rather thought.

'That is, last night was different,' he said, in a rather defensive tone. 'I acted in an unorthodox manner, yes, but there was nobody else about. At least...' he shifted in his chair '...that would normally not be a sufficient excuse, but the maids must have been up in their attics. If Baxter falling out of the window and the arrival of the doctor and all that didn't alert them, then me running softly up the stairs and tapping on your door wasn't going to, was it?' His cheeks went darker still. 'Besides,' he said, rallying, 'surely you must know that the last thing I want is to sully your reputation.'

At that moment, fortunately, before the encounter could become any more embarrassing for either of them, her stomach emitted a most unladylike rumble. His eyes shot to that portion of her anatomy, meaning he had heard it. Right across the other side of the room. Oh, how much lower could she possibly sink in his estimation?

His brows drew down.

'Haven't you had your breakfast?'

'No. Your note said I was to come here the moment I woke, so...' She spread her hands, to demonstrate that here she was.

'Yes, because we have some serious matters to discuss and time is of the essence. But I didn't,' he said, giving her a look of exasperation, 'mean for you to appear so famished that you might faint away at any moment.'

'I never faint,' she retorted before she'd thought about how insubordinate she must sound. Oh, dear. It appeared that all that...arguing and bantering they'd done the night before had robbed her of the ability to speak to him with the deference due to his station. Or...no, it couldn't be that. It was more probable that, having thought she'd killed a man, and been in such a state, only to find him being so...solid, so calm, so...dependable that she'd come to look upon him in a different way to anyone else. And he hadn't helped by signing that letter with an M., as though they were on terms of intimacy, had he? But it wouldn't do. She bit her lip.

But he was grinning again. 'Yes, so you told me last night,' he said. 'How stupid of me to forget.'

'I don't think you did forget,' she was goaded into retorting by that grin. 'I think you said it to be provoking.'

'Hah!' He barked out a laugh. 'Nothing gets past you, does it, Miss Hinchcliffe?' He got to his feet, went to the bell pull by the chimney breast, and tugged on it. 'I will order some food, so that you may eat while we are talking. It will save time,' he said, going back to his desk and sitting down. 'And you'd better sit down. We might be here for some time.'

As she took a chair across the desk from him, Timms, the butler, came in answer to Lord Caldicot's summons.

'Miss Hinchcliffe is in need of some breakfast,' said Lord Caldicot, waving his hand at her.

Timms turned to her and raised one brow.

'Well, go on,' said Lord Caldicot in an impatient tone of voice. 'Tell him what you'd like.'

Rosalind hesitated, then decided that since she had the chance to order whatever she wanted, for once, then she was going to make the most of it. 'I would like two slices of toast, well done, with butter and marmalade on the side, two rashers of bacon, crispy, one poached egg, a spoonful of mushrooms, some fried potatoes, a pot of tea and an orange.' She might not have room for the orange, after the eggs and bacon, but she could certainly slip it into her pocket as a treat for later.

Timms's other eyebrow rose, but after giving Lord Caldicot a deferential bow, he made his stately way out of the room.

'Are you sure,' said Lord Caldicot, with all appearance of being serious, 'that will be enough?'

'It is a bit late to be asking that, isn't it? Timms has gone.'

'Well, I didn't want to embarrass you in front of the man. But you look to me as though you need to eat a great deal more than most women.'

'What do you mean by that?'

'Only that you are twice as tall as most of them,' he replied smoothly. 'Since I've been in London I've begun to feel like Gulliver among the Lilliputians. You cannot think how much I appreciate being able to speak to someone without getting a crick in my neck.'

'Oh.' That was the first time anyone had said that being tall was a good thing. She was far more used to being called a maypole, or a long Meg.

'What,' he enquired, 'did you think I meant?'

'Oh. Um…only that perhaps I eat too much.'

He looked her up and down. 'It looks to me as though you don't eat anywhere near enough. You are very thin.'

'You are very rude,' she snapped back before she could help it. She couldn't help lacking feminine curves. And normally she was glad she didn't have any. So why was it that it stung her to the quick when *he* remarked upon it?

'You are in a bad skin this morning,' he replied, with a chuckle. 'I wonder—are you always like this before you have breakfast, or is it an unfortunate by-product of that medicine the quack forced on you last night?'

'I should like to blame the doctor,' she said. 'I mean, what kind of idiot thinks that reading books could make someone hysterical?'

'On the other hand, one could argue that you demonstrated just how dangerous books can be,' he said, with a twinkle in his eye.

She couldn't help letting out a huff of laughter as he reminded her just how dangerous *Sense and Sensibility* had proved, last night, to Mr Baxter. Which made her drop her guard with him, yet again. 'I fear,' she admitted, 'that my mood this morning has more to do with the fact that you somehow have a knack of making me blurt out what I'm really thinking. I usually manage to behave in a perfectly proper manner with everyone else.'

A strange sort of expression came over his face. A sort of... arrested look.

And then, as quickly as it had appeared, it vanished. He bent his head and moved a sheet of paper from one of the piles on the desk to another. He cleared his throat.

'Perhaps it is time we got down to the matter in hand.'

'Yes, indeed,' she said with some relief. So far, this interview had been most peculiar and most unsettling.

'Firstly,' he said, leaning back in his chair and looking at her more keenly, 'I want you to explain some of the things you told me last night, when you were also not guarding your tongue.'

'Which things?' She could barely remember any of the things she'd said last night, she'd been in such a pucker.

'You told me that your parents were both from good families *"to their own way of thinking"*. What does that mean?'

'Oh.' Well, that was easy to answer. 'My mother's people were rather proud of being connected to the aristocracy, although it was some way back, while my father's people were self-made. My mother's people therefore regarded my father's family as vulgar mushrooms, while my hardworking, dissenting father's family thought my mother's lot were idle parasites.'

'So...you father's family were wealthy, while your mother's family were merely well connected?'

'Exactly! Or so I've been told. I was too young when they died to be aware of the discord. It was later that I picked up bits and pieces, from what people let drop.'

'Might I enquire who this distant, aristocratic connection might be?'

'Oh, well, the Earl of Framlingham.'

'Is that so?' He studied her for a moment or two. 'If that is not so very far back in your lineage, you would have the right to be attending all the events to which Susannah is now being invited.'

She snorted her derision at that. 'Not Almack's! Don't forget, on my father's side I am tainted by the stench of trade.'

'Not Almack's, admittedly,' he agreed. 'But then the patronesses are notoriously picky about whom they admit.'

'Why are you even mentioning it?'

'Wouldn't you like to go to balls and picnics, and things?'

'I have been to several picnics and things with Susannah,' she said bitterly. 'Any event to which Lady Birchwood suddenly finds herself too fatigued to attend, during the day.'

'Yes, she claims she needs to recoup her strength for attending the events to which Susannah is invited in the evening. The events,' he added, with a twinkle in his eye, 'that she actually wishes to go to herself.'

'Precisely!'

'Well, you know,' he said slowly, looking as though he was about to say something outrageous, 'the doctor did recommend that you get more exercise.'

'Oh, no,' she said, with deep misgiving. 'What are you plotting?'

'Before I tell you, I wish to ascertain a few more facts.'

'So you *are* plotting something!'

'Well, it depends.'

'On what?'

'On what you meant, precisely, about those other victims you mentioned.'

'I never did!'

'Ah, but what was I to think when you said that *the other times* were nothing like last night, but that they made your family think you were not fit to live in a house with civilised people?'

'Do you,' she said with resentment, 'remember everything everyone tells you?'

'Not usually. But what you said last night must have been particularly fascinating. I found myself, later on, lying in bed imagining you leaving a trail of broken, bleeding men strewn across the countryside...'

'You didn't!'

'Coupled with the rather ominous-sounding way you described the behaviour of predatory men, pouncing on defenceless females…'

'Oh. Yes.' She lowered her head. 'I suppose I did gabble on in a rather indiscreet fashion.'

'Come now,' he said, 'you had better make a full confession. You will feel better for it.'

'You don't really believe that, do you?'

He looked up at the ceiling, as though he was considering how to reply. 'Well,' he eventually said, 'that is what I've heard. But you are right. I am just eaten up with curiosity. You cannot dangle such fascinating titbits of information about your past and then refuse to elucidate me. It would be most unkind. After I was about to dispose of your latest victim, too!'

'Oh, were you?'

He nodded. 'Had it been necessary, you can be sure I would have hushed it up to the best of my ability.'

'Because you don't want any whiff of scandal marring Susannah's come-out.'

He gave her an enigmatic look. 'If you like. But never mind Susannah for now. Stop trying to distract me and give me a straight answer to my question. What, exactly, had made you flee to your grandfather, on several previous occasions? And, while we are at it, who precisely *is* your grandfather?'

She sighed. 'The grandfather who keeps on coming into my life to straighten it out,' she said, preferring to answering that question, than delving into the murky depths of her past disgraces, 'is General Smallwood.'

He sat up straight. 'General Smallwood? Not *the* General Smallwood? Scourge of the Spanish Sierra?'

'I haven't heard him referred to by that name,' she said. 'But he did spend a lot of time with Wellington in Spain, so he might well have scourged something Spanish. He certainly struck terror into his family, whenever he came back to England,' she added, with feeling. 'So much so that, against their judgement, one of his sisters took me into her home.'

'Wait a minute, I thought you said you were an orphan. And

that both sides of the family cut off your parents for marrying against their wishes.'

'Yes. So that when my parents died, I ended up on the parish, as they say. In a shabby little orphanage in Leeds. Picking oakum and the like. Only, when Grandfather came home on furlough and learned that his daughter had died and that I was in that…place,' she said, unable to prevent herself from shuddering at the memory, 'he was furious.'

'With whom? I mean, surely he was the one who'd cast his own daughter out?'

'Yes, but you cannot expect a man of his temper to behave with any consistency. There is no knowing what will cause him to fly into the boughs and bark orders left, right and centre. Many of them contradictory to ones he's uttered before.'

'Yes, that sounds like the Scourge of the Sierras right enough,' he said with evident amusement. 'On campaign it made him rather an effective leader, strangely enough. He was so terrifying in one of his tempers that subordinates took great care not to provoke him. And, since they were far more scared of him than the notional enemy, his unit became renowned for bravery in action.'

'That doesn't surprise me,' she said, thinking of the few times she'd met him and the way his whole family quaked at the prospect of *seeing* him, never mind offending him. 'Anyway, I think what happened was that he took it into his head to decide that my father's family had no right to complain about the connection. He told me that they should have taken me in and brought me up. After all, they had so much money they'd bought up half of Derbyshire. He was so angry with *them* he forgot about not wishing to acknowledge me.'

'And how old were you when he snatched you from the orphanage and told you what he thought of your father's family?'

'About twelve, by then.'

'He must have scared you, shouting like that.'

'Well, that's the funny thing. He never did, because—'

'You,' he cried as though experiencing an epiphany, 'have a temper just like it!'

'No. At least, I *do* have a temper, but I don't think anyone can match Grandfather for irrationality. It is just that I was so glad to have been rescued from that orphanage that I didn't care how much he shouted. And he wasn't actually shouting at me, you see. Only about how annoying everyone else was.'

'The orphanage was very bad, was it?'

'It was...' She bit down on her lower lip. It was always hard to think about that place, let alone speak about it. Not that anyone else had ever asked her much about it. Because nobody else had been interested. Not in her, specifically, only what she represented.

'It was a shock, going to a place like that after living with loving parents,' she told him, unsure why she had started with that, when really it had very little bearing on what she'd meant to say.

She pulled herself together. 'But the worst thing was the hunger. I was always so hungry and there was never enough food to go round. And I soon learned that having manners was a positive hindrance to survival. Polite little girls always ended up at the back of the queue for what little food there was. Polite little girls tended to have whatever they did manage to get stolen from them.'

'So you abandoned what manners you had.'

'By the time Grandfather descended on the place, all guns blazing, I had, let us say, learned to survive.'

He leaned forward, as though he was about to ask her something of great importance, when someone knocked on the door.

Timms, with her breakfast.

Naturally, he couldn't ask whatever it was while the butler was there, fussing over dishes and covers, and the teapot.

She could only hope that by the time Timms left, he would have forgotten whatever it was he'd wanted to ask her. Because he'd already dredged up too many memories which she'd thought safely buried.

And she didn't like the way she kept on confiding in him.

Why did she keep forgetting he was her employer? That he could turn her out of her position, and therefore her home, without a reference in the blink of an eye?

She had to stop treating him as though he was her friend,

just because he'd been so surprisingly understanding about last night's incident with Mr Baxter.

And remember just how much she had to lose.

Chapter Seven

He saw her face shutter.

That was a pity. Because she'd been confiding in him in a manner that had moved him in a way he wasn't able to put into words. But it had felt...good. And he'd been hoping for more of the same.

But then, as she picked up her knife and fork, her face changed again. Expressing relish.

'You *were* hungry, weren't you?' he said, as she tucked in with gusto.

'Mmm,' she agreed, with a nod.

Was she really that hungry, though, or was she using the excuse of table manners to avoid speaking to him with her mouth full?

He wouldn't put it past her. She was a fascinating mixture of behaviour, was Miss Hinchcliffe, as he'd somehow always suspected she would be. Alternately frank, in a way that few people ever were, then retreating behind a façade of prim and proper manners. Although good manners didn't seem to apply to the rate at which she was consuming her meal. Just as if she feared that if she didn't clean her plate swiftly, someone else might come and snatch it away. A habit she'd fallen into at that orphanage?

Still, it meant that she wouldn't have the excuse of having her mouth too full to answer his questions, for all that long.

'So,' he said, leaning back in his chair with a smile. 'You learned how to survive in that orphanage. And the habits you'd learned, I presume,' he said, eyeing the way she was demolishing her bacon, 'went with you into your new life.'

She nodded again.

'But, for all his blustering about your condition, I presume General Smallwood didn't take you into his household?' He rarely returned to England, so far as Michael knew. He much preferred being in the thick of the action.

'No, he forced one of his sisters to admit me to her household, since she had children of a similar age to me and governesses, and what have you.'

'From the expression on your face, I gather it was not a happy experience. Unless there is something wrong with the mushrooms?'

'No, the mushrooms are delicious,' she said. And carried on eating.

'And your aunt's household?'

She paused. Then sighed. '*Not* delicious. But I didn't last there very long, anyway. And I suppose you want to know why they threw me out?'

'Did you, perchance, threaten to eat them out of house and home?'

She glared at him with a forkful of mushrooms halfway to her mouth.

'You are—' She snapped her mouth shut and blushed.

'You were saying?'

'Well, I very nearly did,' she admitted, 'but then I thought better of it.'

'You remembered, perchance, that I am not the most obnoxious man,' he said silkily, 'you've ever met?'

'Oh, no. Far from it,' she said with feeling.

'Yes, you said something to that effect last night,' he reminded her.

She lowered the fork to her plate. 'Yes, I did, didn't I?' She looked at the mushrooms, then, with a shrug, lifted them to her mouth and chewed for a moment or two.

He waited, sensing that she was thinking about how to respond. Which he found he didn't like. He much preferred it when she spoke without thinking. When she just said what she really meant.

'I will just tell you of the incident which pushed my great-aunt to expel me from her home, I think.'

'Very well.' If that was all she was willing to tell him, for now, he'd have to accept it.

'I was, as you have reminded me, always hungry. And there was an orchard on the property. So, naturally, when the apples ripened, I went off to pick some. Only...my cousin, an odious boy who had decided, from my first day under his parents' roof that it was his prime duty to remind me that I didn't belong with decent folk, followed me out there. I tried to avoid him by climbing a tree, but he was persistent. He had got halfway up the tree I'd chosen and I was certain that he would have pushed me out of it once he caught up to me, so I...well, I just kicked out at him. I only meant to dislodge his hand from the branch he was holding, but unfortunately, from his point of view, I caught him square in the mouth.'

'Ouch.'

'Indeed,' she said, spearing her egg with deliberation, so that the yolk flowed out across the plate. 'I found it hard to be sorry that he lost some teeth, or that he claimed I'd broken his nose. Because he'd so frequently held that very nose whenever I walked into a room, saying that he could smell the foul whiff of my origins. A phrase he must have picked up from his parents,' she said, slashing the unfortunate egg completely in half.

No wonder she hadn't been able to credit the fact that he might have attempted to hush up her part in what might have been an accidental death, just to spare her feelings. For it sounded as though nobody had taken her feelings into account for so long that she expected nothing but mistreatment.

'So where did they send you?'

'To school,' she said, in a voice that was rather more cheerful than when she'd been dwelling on the failings of her family. 'They paid for me to go to a place where girls of a similar station to mine learned how to earn a living when they grew old enough. Well, even my grandfather hadn't expected them to launch me into society, not with my father's family owning mills. That would have meant finding a dowry big enough to tempt some man into demeaning himself by taking me on,' she said with a slight shrug, which he supposed was meant to look nonchalant, but which, to his eyes, portrayed a good deal of hurt.

'There, I learned how to teach little children to read and write, and, when they found my intelligence was more than that of some of the other girls, and how much I loved books, how I might be able to teach older girls how to go on in society. How to play the piano and how deeply to curtsy to people of varying ranks and all that sort of nonsense,' she added, wrinkling her nose.

Well, that did it! He thought it was about time she had some fun to make up for the years of hardship she'd endured so bravely. 'Did they teach you how to dance?'

'Yes,' she said, looking bewildered, 'although I don't see what that has to do with anything.'

'That is because I haven't yet told you what I have in mind.'

He could see her working it out. He'd asked her if she knew how to dance and he'd asked her about her background, saying that she had almost as much right as Susannah to go about in society, and so...

'No,' she breathed, shaking her head. 'You cannot mean that you want me to attend balls?'

'That is exactly what I mean.'

'But...but...'

'Come now, you know that we are going to have to watch Susannah closely, now that we know to what lengths Baxter will go.'

'*We* are going to have to watch her?'

'Yes. Clearly Lady Birchwood is just not up to the task. Baxter must have got to know Susannah while she was supposed to be watching her. And he must have had unfettered access to her, or he would not have managed to worm his way so deeply into the girl's affections that she declares she loves him and throws herself on to the hearth rug when I refuse to give my permission for them to marry.'

'No,' she said, laying down her knife and fork, in a manner that signified the subject was closed.

'May I remind you,' he said, 'that it is entirely your fault that Mr Baxter is at large?'

'It is not!'

'If you had not insisted I go and fetch the doctor, he would not have had the chance to sneak off when I wasn't looking.'

'Fustian!'

'Or,' some imp of mischief prompted him to add, 'if you had done the job properly in the first place...'

'If I had done the job properly, as you put it,' she retorted, 'then Susannah would be so angry with me you would have had to dismiss me.'

'But not for committing murder?'

'I'm beginning to suspect you wouldn't have considered *that* cause for dismissal,' she retorted.

He let out a bark of laughter. 'You malign me. I cannot have a woman with a propensity to go about murdering people left in charge of an impressionable girl.'

'I haven't murdered anyone!'

'The way you spoke last night gave me the distinct impression you had left the countryside strewn with your hapless victims.'

'Well, last night my wits were disordered.'

'Or you would not have revealed what you did,' he agreed affably.

'Though I definitely remember telling you that I have never harmed anyone *deliberately*.'

He sighed, in mock regret. 'That is a pity, because what I really need from you is to act as a sort of...guard over Susannah. And I am sure that after last night, Mr Baxter, for one, will definitely think twice before attempting anything similar, if he sees you hovering about the ballroom.' He leaned forward to emphasise his point. 'I doubt he will dare go anywhere near her.'

She took in a sharp, offended breath. Opened her mouth. Closed it. Took another breath as she tried to marshal her arguments. And, true to form, it was not long before she came up with a corker.

'If I am going to have to attend balls and things, when, exactly, am I going to get any time off? I trail around after her all day. I regard the evenings as my own.'

'If you recall, I said *we* are going to have to keep a close eye on her.'

'Ye...es...'

'Which obviously implies that I, too, will take my share of guard duties. With about as much enthusiasm as you show for it, I must admit. Though I would have thought you would have enjoyed getting dressed up and going to balls.'

She snorted her disgust of such an assumption. 'What, so that I can watch feather-brained females making fools of themselves over vile men?'

'Not all men are vile...' He had been about to say that he was sure Susannah could meet someone perfectly acceptable, if only they could keep the worst sort of fortune hunters out of her orbit.

But she forestalled him by exclaiming, 'Well, I should like to meet one!'

'Are you not looking at one, right now? Or do you consider me vile, as well?'

She blushed. 'Oh, well, I mean, I thought it was clear that I didn't mean you. Although,' she added, her brows lowering, 'you are capable of pretty reprehensible behaviour, aren't you?'

'Me?' He tried to look the picture of innocence.

'Yes. Saying that you wished I had succeeded in doing away with Mr Baxter...'

'I never said that!'

She thought for a bit, as though swiftly reviewing all their conversations. 'Well, you definitely implied it.'

'It comes from spending so much time in the military, I dare say. I have grown so used to just putting a bullet into any enemy I come across that it chafes, yes, positively chafes me to have to rely on governesses to toss such fellows off balconies.'

'I did *not* toss *anyone* out of...oh,' she spluttered, 'you...you are outrageous!'

She regarded him for a moment or two, and then, just when

he'd begun to give up on her, she burst out laughing. 'Oh, you have been roasting me!'

It amazed him how different she looked when she laughed. Not only less guarded, but also far younger. He would wager that the things she'd endured thus far in her life were what had drawn her features into such disapproving, disappointed lines. Without them, she was, he saw with satisfaction, an attractive woman. Not pretty, precisely, but...handsome. No, not that, either. What showed in her face, he decided, was character. Intelligence, too, with those heavy frowns and the sarcastic twist to her lips she indulged in so often.

'So,' he said, shaking off the speculation about what it was about her that made him find her attractive, 'I have your agreement, then?'

'You have nothing of the sort!'

'Come, come, Miss Hinchcliffe, you know that we are the only two sensible people in this household. We are the only two capable of protecting her from herself.'

'But...' She looked positively pained.

'We can draw up a roster, if you like.'

'A roster?'

'Yes, a chart, detailing who will be on duty at any given time...'

'I know what a roster is! I am not, as you have already pointed out, an idiot.'

'Oh? It was just you did not seem to understand.'

'I don't. I mean, I don't understand why you would propose such a thing.'

'Well, because you are, as you pointed out with such belligerence, entitled to time off. So we will have to divide up the days into watches, so that between us, we can keep Mr Baxter at bay.'

'Oh.' She looked nonplussed.

'Did you expect *me* to treat you shabbily, just because circumstances have obliged you to work for your living?'

She blushed. Again.

'I beg your pardon,' she said stiffly, 'for misjudging you, but it has been my experience so far that men of your class, or rather *people* of your class,' she corrected herself, when he frowned, 'do not consider the feelings of their servants to any extent.'

'Perhaps I am not doing so either,' he said. 'Perhaps I am just thinking that if I drive you too hard, you will either run off, screaming into the night, like so many other of Susannah's governesses, or collapse with exhaustion.'

She gave him a reproving look. If she'd worn spectacles, he reflected with amusement, it would have been over the top of them.

'Once again,' she said, 'I suspect you are roasting me. You know I am not so faint hearted that I would do either.'

'Well, I do hope not. Because you are going to have to start right away. Today.'

'You think Mr Baxter might attempt to contact Susannah, in a...clandestine manner, today? But...he must be pretty badly injured. I mean, he did not stir for such a long time that I believed him to be dead!'

'Yes, but then the minute we both left him unattended he got up and ran away.'

'Oh. You mean...he might have been shamming it?'

'He is the kind of man who is shamming it all the time, I dare say. It would have been second nature to him to lie still until he was sure the coast was clear.'

She frowned, thoughtfully. 'So...how are we to explain to Susannah that I will be suddenly going to balls and such from now on?'

'Oh, because the doctor recommended it, of course!'

'What?'

'Yes, don't you remember him saying that you ought to get more exercise and read less?'

'I remember him saying all sorts of stupid things,' she said darkly.

'Yes, but Susannah won't know they're stupid, will she?'

'I...but—'

'So,' he cut in ruthlessly, while she was still sputtering instead of coming up with a coherent objection, 'as soon as she emerges from her room, I will inform her that she is to take you shopping.'

'Shopping?'

'Yes. You do know what that is?'

'Of course I know what it is! I just don't see why I have to do any!'

'Oh? Your cupboards are stuffed full of ball gowns and the fripperies to go with them, are they?'

'No,' she said, looking dejected.

'There you are then. You need to kit yourself out and Susannah, I would warrant, will love having an excuse to go out spending my money, which will kill two birds with one stone.'

'You mean…while she is overseeing my shopping, I will be doing my part as a guard dog?'

'See? You're catching on. Then, when you come home, you will need to inform me how Susannah plans to spend the rest of the day, so that we can divide the guarding duties between us.'

'You want me to spy on her,' she said glumly.

'Protect her,' he corrected her firmly.

'For how long? The rest of the Season?'

'And beyond, if necessary. Like you, I have no intention of running off screaming into the night. Susannah may be a bit of a handful, but it is my duty to protect her. And I shall carry on doing so until I have seen her married to a man of honour.'

She smiled at him with approval, which gave him a warm glow inside.

He cleared his throat. 'In the meantime I shall think of a way to put a spoke in Baxter's wheel, permanently. I have already thought of several ways that I might be able to achieve that, without going to the lengths of doing him irreversible, physical damage. Men like Baxter are usually motivated by greed. If I can find him and come to some sort of arrangement…a sort of stick-and-carrot approach…'

She nodded approvingly again. Then frowned.

'But it isn't just Mr Baxter, is it? London is probably heaving with men of his stamp, attempting to dupe rich young heiresses out of their fortunes.'

'Exactly. Which is why we will both be doing our utmost to protect her.'

She sighed. 'Very well. You have convinced me.'

'Capital!' He leaned back in his chair, smiling. Not only because he'd won her round regarding his plan to watch over Susannah, but also because it would mean he'd now have all sorts of reasons, valid reasons, for spending time with her.

Chapter Eight

When Rosalind told her, Susannah clapped her hands with glee.

'Shopping for you? Oh, famous!'

'You don't mind?' Rosalind had been unsure how her charge would react to the news that she was going to have to abandon whatever plans she might have made for the day and go shopping with her governess–companion instead. She'd braced herself for a bout of the sulks, so this display of pleasure was a very welcome surprise.

'Oh, no! I love shopping. And I have always thought that you could look much better if only you didn't dress in such dowdy clothes.'

Rosalind bit back the response that sprang to her lips. That she had never had the means to buy anything that was either in fashion, or of good quality. Or had even wanted to look... *better*. For better, in Susannah's estimation, probably meant attractive to men. And that was the last thing Rosalind wanted. She'd learned during her previous post as a governess that if a woman in her position dressed as though she wanted to attract male attention, then she would get it. And would then heartily wish she hadn't.

'And now that Lord Caldicot has said we can send the bills

to him, you can have whatever you want! Oh, this is going to be such fun!'

It was at times like this that Rosalind so often experienced strong surges of affection for her young charge. For Lady Susannah was perfectly capable of thinking of others and not solely of herself. If only someone had nurtured that side of her when she'd been younger, rather than encouraging her to be so self-indulgent...

Although, not half an hour after they'd entered the first modiste's shop, which Susannah had insisted they should visit, Rosalind began to wonder whether Susannah was treating her more like a doll to dress up for her own amusement, than as a person with feelings.

'That blue crepe,' Susanah said, pointing to a bolt of pale material draped across the counter. 'That would look wonderful with an overdress of silver gauze.'

It probably would look charming on a girl of Susannah's age. But on Rosalind, who was not only older, but also taller and far thinner, she had a suspicion it would make her look like a streak of blue pump water.

But there was no point in complaining. What did she care what she looked like? This whole exercise was about keeping Susannah safe and occupied in a way that put her beyond the reach of men like Mr Baxter. And the one thing of which she was certain was that men like Mr Baxter did *not* spend their days in establishments like this one.

'Does Madame,' said the modiste, probably noticing the look of resignation on Rosalind's face, 'approve?'

'Oh, Miss Hinchcliffe has never had the chance to buy clothes like this before,' said Susannah blithely, 'so she can't possibly have much of an opinion.'

'It is very pretty material,' said Rosalind with complete honesty. For it was. She just wasn't convinced that it would do anything for her. Not that she wanted it to do anything for her. Apart from having a fleeting, and extremely silly, wish to find an outfit that would make Lord Caldicot see her...differently. As an attractive woman. 'Lady Susannah,' she said, pulling herself back from the brink of wistful longing with an effort, 'is being most kind in giving me her advice.'

Susannah beamed at her and carried on discussing such mysteries as spangles and shell scallops and Circassian sleeves with the modiste while Rosalind submitted to being measured and draped in a variety of materials.

'Now,' said Susannah, after declaring that she'd done as much as she could in that particular establishment, 'we should go on to a milliner. And then we must think about shoes. And gloves.'

'Must we?'

'Of course we must! Oh…' she peered at Rosalind's less than enthusiastic demeanour '…are you tired? Of course, at your age this must be terribly tiring, especially since you are not used to it.'

'Um…' Susannah probably thought she was being most considerate. For her, that was a huge step in the right direction. So Rosalind decided not to tell her that mentioning a lady's age was not at all polite. Or remind her that Susannah was only six years her junior.

'So let us go to Gunter's for tea and cake, before continuing with your wardrobe.'

Gunter's. The kind of place where anyone might *accidentally* meet with someone they were forbidden from meeting anywhere else.

Was that why Susannah had seemed so keen to come out, with only Rosalind for company? Did she think she was a fool?

'I think,' said Rosalind, 'I would prefer to carry on shopping until it is all done, then return to Kilburn House.'

'You don't want to drink tea at Gunter's? Honestly, they do far better cakes and things than that cook Lady Birchwood engaged for the Season. And ices! Oh, you cannot imagine how delicious they can be on a hot day.'

'Well, perhaps, later on…' And anyway, when she came to think of it, what harm could Mr Baxter do in a tea shop? There would be plenty of other people about.

'Hurrah!' Susannah clapped her hands again.

She was, Rosalind reflected with deep suspicion, in a very

good mood today, considering the fact that only yesterday she'd declared herself to be heartbroken.

'You haven't,' Rosalind therefore said, as they climbed into the carriage, so that they wouldn't have to have the tedium of walking all the way from Bruton Street to Conduit Street, 'told me anything about Almack's last night. Did you enjoy it?'

She had been a little surprised when Susannah had the ba-rouche brought round for their shopping trip, since they could easily have walked such a short distance. But perhaps Susannah had done enough walking for one day, she reflected as she'd climbed in and sat beside her. Perhaps she preferred to conserve her strength for all the dancing she was bound to do that evening. And she was not about to complain about the fact that having a carriage also meant they had the protection of a driver and a footman. Plus, somewhere to deposit their parcels, rather than having to either carry them all home, or have them delivered later on.

Susannah pouted as she arranged her skirts more tidily once she'd sat down. 'It was terribly stuffy. So many rules, you cannot imagine. But I was a perfect paragon of good behaviour, you know. Throwing dust in everyone's eyes. Everyone will think that I've forgotten all about Cecil, I was so…gay and charming to all my partners!'

'You had plenty of dance partners, then?'

'Of course I did,' she replied with a look of astonishment that Rosalind could ask such a silly question. 'I am so wealthy, and well connected, that even the highest sticklers can find no fault with me.'

As long, Rosalind reflected darkly, as they didn't examine her too closely and learn how temperamental she could be.

'I suspect,' Susannah confided, with a mischievous grin, 'that my Aunt Birchwood believes that I was so flattered to be singled out by such a notoriously good catch as Lord Wapping that it put all thoughts of the lowly Cecil completely out of my head.'

'Lord Wapping?'

'Yes. Only a baron at the moment, but he's the nephew of the Duke of Yardley, who is about to expire at any moment, apparently, and the only male in that branch of the family. So that although he is not a duke now, it won't be long. And his wife will of course therefore be a duchess. And Lady Birchwood,' she said scornfully, as the carriage pulled up outside a shop whose windows were full of the most terrifyingly flamboyant hats Rosalind had ever seen, 'thinks that it must be every girl's ambition to become a duchess.'

'But not yours?'

'Absolutely not! When I marry, it will be for love,' she declared, as she climbed down out of the carriage. 'Not rank or wealth!'

As Rosalind followed her charge into the shop, she felt a surge of admiration for Susannah. Many girls of her class *did* only marry for position, or wealth, and nobody thought any the worse of them for that. Furthermore, nobody seemed to think it wrong that, once such girls had done their duty by their husbands, in presenting them with a legitimate heir, they would then go on to take lovers.

At least, she mused, as Susannah launched into an animated conversation with the milliner, the girl meant to love and honour her husband, whoever he might be, rather than use him as a stepping stone on the way to some nebulous goal.

But then Susannah had the freedom to choose. Almost in the same way she could choose one of the many hats the milliner started bringing out for her inspection. Within certain limits, of course. Lord Caldicot was not going to grant his permission for her to throw herself away on a man of Mr Baxter's character.

If his character genuinely was bad. Now she came to think of it, she had no real evidence upon which to base her distrust of the man. Apart from the mounting irritation that had grown over the weeks while Susannah kept on saying how wonderful he was.

Oh, and the way he'd crept into her room via the balcony—there was *that* to consider.

But then Lord Caldicot surely wouldn't have refused, point blank, to permit the man to pay his addresses to Susannah, simply because he wasn't wealthy, would he? He *must* have more reasons to refuse the match than the fact that he was a younger son with only a tiny income.

Then again, Mr Baxter *had* climbed in through the balcony window. No decent man would do that. Unless, perhaps, he was deeply in love and acting out of desperation...

Was there a clue, in that word he'd moaned? Turpentine? Might he be an artist? Struggling to make a living...

'If you don't like that turban,' said Susannah with a giggle, 'you don't have to scowl at it like that. Just tell me and we'll find something you do like.'

Turban? Oh. The milliner was holding out a bundle of blue wrappings, heavily interspersed with cordage and tassels. Which she was meant, she presumed, to balance on the top of her head.

'The colour,' said Rosalind, after due consideration, 'will definitely match the material that you are having made up into a ball gown for me.' And at least it wasn't covered in flowers like so many of the confections she'd glimpsed, with horror, in the window.

'Precisely!'

Susannah waved her hand and the milliner set the blue monstrosity on top of Rosalind's head.

Then brought her a mirror.

The sight that met her gaze put Rosalind in mind of a story she'd once read about a mythical creature called a gorgon, who had hair made out of snakes. Whose stare turned mortals into stone.

She was still trying to work out how to explain her dislike of the headgear, in terms that wouldn't sound ungrateful, when Susannah declared it was just the thing, the milliner was removing it, and placing it reverently into a box lined with tissue paper.

Perhaps, Rosalind reflected, watching the milliner putting the lid on the box, thus hiding the gorgon headdress from sight, she didn't have much taste. At least not in terms of what was fashionable, or what suited her. For Susannah always looked attractive, in whatever she wore, and she'd had free rein to choose her own clothing for some time now. Or at least, she corrected herself, the females who had been in charge of her before had stopped trying to talk her out of buying whatever took her fancy.

'And now,' said Susannah, having told the milliner to deliver the headdress to their house and to send the bill to Lord Caldicot, 'Gunter's!'

Rosalind, like most of the females who'd been nominally in charge of Susannah before, surrendered. Not only because she chose her battles with the strong-willed girl carefully, but also because she'd never been to Gunter's before and couldn't resist the chance to sample its famous delights.

When the barouche drew to a halt in Berkeley Square, Susannah surprised Rosalind by making no move to alight. Instead, she sent the footman, who'd been sitting up beside the driver, over to the shop to summon a waiter.

'Won't we be going inside?' she asked Susannah.

'Oh, no. Nobody goes *inside* on a lovely day like this,' said Susannah, with a giggle.

Rosalind supposed she meant nobody of the *ton*, since she could definitely see people going in and not coming out again.

'We just sit in our carriage, then, do we?'

'Yes, and in a minute, the waiter will bring us whatever we want. Do you want to try an ice? They do all sorts of flavours. Like parmesan and lavender.'

That sounded disgusting. 'I think I would prefer a cup of tea. And some cake.'

For what Susannah had said about the cook at Kilburn House had been no less than the truth. She didn't seem to have much skill at baking. There was nothing wrong with the savoury dishes she cooked. But it was sometimes hard to decide whether she'd produced small cakes that had failed to rise, or biscuits that were strangely spongey.

Once the waiter had dashed out, taken their order and dashed back to the shop again, Rosalind noticed that Susannah was looking round at the occupants of other open carriages, dotted about the square. As though she was searching for someone.

She very much doubted that Mr Baxter would have access to a carriage that he could park up in the square, even if he wasn't in bed nursing half a dozen broken bones, which was where he most likely was today.

So she decided not to remark on the fact that Susannah was clearly hoping she might see, if not him, then someone.

'I must admit,' Rosalind therefore said, 'that it is very pleasant, sitting here in the shade of the trees while a waiter fetches refreshments. Much better than going into a crowded room where we might have to rub shoulders with heaven alone knows who.'

'I know! I knew you'd enjoy it. Oh...' Susannah sighed '...if only Mr Baxter might decide to take a walk in the square just now and happen to see me sitting here, then he could come over and we could chat, with perfect propriety. It is so silly,' she said petulantly, 'for Lord Caldicot to have taken against him. Without knowing the first thing about him.'

She sighed, pouted and leaned one elbow on the edge of the carriage, then her chin upon that hand, as she gazed wistfully about her.

Lord Caldicot *must* know something to Mr Baxter's detriment. He must! Or he would not have put his foot down so firmly. Or spoken so scathingly about him, when he'd been lying in a broken heap among the bushes.

Mustn't he?

Of course he must! He wouldn't act so unjustly, without any reason at all, not when Susannah was so clearly in love.

Would he?

Unless he had some sort of prejudice against men who had to work for a living, the way one side of her family had against her own father's people. If Mr Baxter was an artist...

At that moment, the waiter returned, with a tray held aloft, and began doling out dishes, plates and cups.

After one taste of her lavender ice, Susannah pulled a face. 'This tastes like soap,' she cried. 'Oh, I have never been so... bamboozled!'

For some reason, that use of the word struck Rosalind with the force of a stone dropping into a lake. Had *she* been bamboozled? By Lord Caldicot?

Until this afternoon, she'd assumed Susannah was the one who'd been deceived, by Mr Baxter. But now she was starting to wonder if *she* was the one who'd been deceived, by Lord Caldicot.

After all, hadn't she accepted every word he'd said and approved of everything he'd done *without question*? Not just because he was her employer, either. She'd never had any trouble taking anything her former employers, or any of the aunts who'd drifted in and out of Susannah's life, had said with a hefty pinch of salt. No, it was, she suspected, because she had a tendre for him.

There. She'd admitted it. She'd behaved in just as silly a fashion as Susannah, allowing herself to be taken in by a man about whom she knew hardly anything at all. Apart from the fact that he was tall and manly. And rather curt in his ways with his female relatives. Oh, yes, and very nonchalant about discovering apparently dead bodies in the shrubbery.

Put like that, it wasn't much of a recommendation, was it?

'Oh, no,' breathed Susannah, as she set aside the ice she'd been longing to try and now denounced as completely unpalatable. 'The very last person I wanted to see.'

Rosalind followed the direction of her gaze, to see Lord Caldicot striding along the pavement. Her heart did a little bounce. Probably, she suddenly perceived, the kind of bounce that happened in Susannah's chest whenever she saw Mr Baxter.

He altered course when he saw them sitting in the carriage and came over.

'Out enjoying the lovely weather?'

'We have been shopping,' replied Susannah scornfully. 'As you might have gathered,' she added, indicating the boxes littering the floor of the barouche, 'if you had the slightest bit of intelligence.'

'Yes, but you are not shopping now,' he countered. Then his eye fell on the melting puddle in Susannah's dish. 'Never say you fell for the lure of the lavender ice?'

Susannah sucked in an indignant breath.

'Well, at least now you have learned it is completely inedible,' he finished cheerfully, before Susannah had a chance to tell him how unkind it was of him to taunt her. 'Waiter!' He snapped his fingers in the direction of the shop and, somehow, a waiter appeared as if by magic. 'Take this away and bring the ladies something more to their taste. What do you really like, Susannah?' he asked her.

She pouted and shifted in her seat, but finally admitted, 'Chocolate cake.'

'Then you shall have some.'

Susannah frowned at him with suspicion. 'Why are you being so affable today?'

'Well, perhaps I felt you deserved a reward. For being so kind to Miss Hinchcliffe. Taking her shopping is one thing, but treating her to tea and cake from Gunter's is going the second mile.'

I am here, Rosalind wanted to say, as they talked about her, rather than to her. But, of course, since she was merely an employee, she had to keep her mouth firmly closed.

'Oh.' Susannah was flushing. 'It is nothing, really. I... I wanted to come myself, you know,' she admitted.

'And did you,' he said, finally turning to Rosalind and speaking to her, 'wish to come to Gunter's and sample the ices?' He glanced down at her lap. 'I see you had too much sense to fall for the lavender ice, at least.'

An incoherent noise burbled from her lips. Typical! After she'd been resenting the fact that neither of them had been speaking to her, the moment he *did* address her, she lost the ability to reply. It was just...he was leaning on the railings, looking all...well...much more tempting than a dish of ice cream, anyway. And she'd just been thinking about how he made her heart flutter and how she oughtn't to trust him simply because of that.

'Miss Hinchcliffe has been a bit overwhelmed, I think,' put in Susannah, 'by all the money we've been spending on her. I keep trying to persuade her into satins and gauze, but she would much rather stick to her boring old kerseymere and calico.'

His eyes sharpened. 'You cannot possibly go into a ballroom in a gown made up of calico.'

'She was joking,' Rosalind replied on a surge of resentment. Did he really think her so foolish that she would attempt to do such a thing?

Probably. After all, he'd caught her trying to run off in the dead of night in the belief she'd killed a man with a copy of *Sense and Sensibility.*

Which was typical of her. She had a terrible tendency to act first, then regret what she'd done later. Over the last couple of years, while she'd been trying to persuade Susannah that it might be a good idea to try to control *her* temper, she'd thought she'd cured herself of that besetting fault as well. But had she?

'Ah, I can see the waiter coming with your chocolate cake,' said Lord Caldicot. 'So I shan't keep you ladies from your innocent pleasures any longer.' He tipped his hat and made to move away from the carriage.

'I wonder,' said Susannah as he strode off, 'where he is going. And how he is planning to spend his day.'

'I have no idea,' Rosalind replied, a little stung by the statement he'd made about their pleasures being innocent. Because it implied that his weren't.

Was there some lady, waiting for him in a discreet little... love-nest? Men of his rank kept such ladies, didn't they? In luxury.

Oh! How could she be sitting here thinking about a man with his mistress with anything but...disgust? How could she feel even a touch envious of whichever woman he might be spending an afternoon kissing and caressing? In return for financial gain? Had her wits gone wandering? Not to mention her morals!

'You look rather warm, Miss Hinchcliffe,' Susannah observed as she dug her fork into her slice of chocolate cake. 'Is the heat too much for you?'

'Um...yes. Yes, it is rather a warm day,' she said, flustered to have been caught out entertaining the most inappropriate thoughts. 'But I have a fan with me...' Lowering her head, she opened her reticule and avoided Susannah's perceptive gaze by becoming busy with locating, spreading and then employing her fan.

While Susannah enjoyed her cake, she mulled over the entire situation again, in the light of the revelation she'd just had. About the way Lord Caldicot made her feel. As if she might, just might, cast all her morals to the winds, for a chance to...to...

She snapped her fan shut. She already suspected she might,

just might, have made a mistake in believing Mr Baxter was evil and Lord Caldicot a paragon. She might well have been as mistaken as...as Susannah had been, taking the word of who-ever it was who'd told her that she'd enjoy lavender ice cream. But then, how could any female make a sensible decision based on someone else's word, rather than on experience?

It was about time she started looking for some first-hand evidence regarding Mr Baxter, to observe him, if she had the chance, so that she could make up her own mind.

Because if Susannah really loved him, and he truly loved her, then what right had she, or anyone else, to keep them apart?

Chapter Nine

Michael shut the door on his study and went over to the table where Timms had thoughtfully set out a decanter of good brandy and some glasses. He felt as if he was going to need it, if he were to survive yet another evening as Susannah's escort.

To think that only two weeks ago, he'd frowned upon the amount of drink that men of the class he now inhabited consumed. Now, he could completely understand what drove them to do it. Since the night Miss Hinchcliffe had thrown Baxter off the balcony and they'd agreed to take turns guarding Susannah from any further approaches from undesirables of the same sort, he'd attended what felt like nineteen balls, twenty-four Venetian breakfasts and, worst of all, an entire evening during the course of which his ears had been assaulted by harpists, pianists and at least a brace of out-of-tune sopranos. One after the other. Relentlessly.

He poured himself a medicinal measure of brandy into the bottom of the glass. A finger to fortify himself against what lay in store for him that evening was one thing, but he needed to keep his wits about him.

It wasn't so much the watching of Susannah that was proving so difficult. The mere fact that he was in the ballroom, or drawing room, or wherever, was enough to deter the sort of men like Baxter, who looked upon green girls with large fortunes as pigeons for the plucking. While he was around, the kind of men who asked her to dance, or if they could fetch her glasses of lemonade or ratafia, were the kind who were her social equals and who seemed to genuinely find her appealing.

No, it was the matchmaking mothers who were making him feel as if he'd rather march over the Pyrenees, in the dead of winter, than stay in London during the Season. Because they kept on flinging their daughters in his path. Girls who were barely out of the schoolroom, for the most part, who didn't have a single opinion in their heads, or, if they did, took care not to let him suspect them of having any.

No, they all agreed with everything he said, looking up at him as though he was some sort of oracle.

He rather thought he was supposed to feel flattered by the way they gazed up at him and treated his every word as though he'd said something wonderful. Instead, it made him feel as though he was getting old. He much preferred the way Miss Hinchcliffe told him exactly what she was thinking. When he could get her alone, that was.

In company she was as dull and decorous as any debutante. Well, apart from the occasional quirk of her lips, or slight lift to the eyebrows which was far more eloquent than any amount of so-called conversation he'd had with any of the so-called eligible girls he met.

He finally tossed back his drink in one go, moodily placing the empty glass back on the tray, when he heard the sound of female footsteps and feminine giggles descending the stairs. Because he was a man of duty and was determined to do his duty by Susannah, no matter what it cost him, he strode over to the study door and flung it open.

And came to a halt at the sight of not only Susannah and Lady Birchwood standing in the hall, fussing with cloaks, but also Miss Hinchcliffe, garbed from head to toe in a variety of shades of blue.

He'd never seen a more welcome sight.

'Miss Hinchcliffe! You are coming with us tonight?' What a stupid thing to say. Of course she must be, or she wouldn't be wearing a gown that revealed so much of her arms. And moulded her breasts, rather than disguising the fact that she had any, the way her workaday clothes did.

'Doesn't she look lovely?' gushed Susannah.

She certainly did. Now that she wasn't swathed from neck to ankle in something shapeless and unflattering, he could see that she had a splendid physique. Not all flabby and dimpled, like so many society ladies, but slender and toned. Though he might have guessed as much from the ease with which she'd knocked Baxter off the balcony, with only a book to use as ammunition.

'I look,' she said gloomily, 'like a scarecrow got up in the vicar's wife's cast-offs.'

'No, no, you don't,' said Susannah, in exasperation. 'Tell her, Lord Caldicot, that she looks fine as fivepence!'

'You look...' He sought for some appropriate words. But all of a sudden, all he could think was that if she had on a helmet and carried a spear in one hand and bore a shield over the other, she'd resemble the Greek goddess Athena. 'Formidable.'

'Thank you,' said Miss Hinchcliffe drily. 'Just what every woman wishes to hear.'

She looked so very much as if she was experiencing the same sort of feelings that he'd been suffering alone in his study just now that he took the cloak, which Timms was holding out to her, and went to place it round her shoulders himself, while Susannah's and Lady Birchwood's maids performed the same office for them. He might have nobody in whom to confide, but at least he could provide some support for a fellow sufferer.

'Isn't that the aim,' he reminded her, softly, in the hopes that the others wouldn't be able to overhear him, 'of this venture? Don't you want to be able to repel curs like Baxter with one withering glance?'

'You know, it's funny,' she replied, in a murmur to match his own, 'that the very first time I clapped eyes on my reflection, when wearing this turban, I was reminded of the myth of the Gorgon.'

Her response made him feel, for the first time since the night they'd concealed the fate of Baxter, as if he had a comrade in arms.

'Then you shall be the perfect chaperon,' he said. 'Which

means that I will no longer have to endure many more evenings such as the one we are about to undergo.'

For a moment, he thought he could detect a look of panic in her eyes. Her breathing quickened. Was she going to beg him not to abandon her, on her first foray into society? He wanted to tell her that he had no intention of doing anything so shabby, no matter how tempting it might be.

But then she lifted her chin.

'You are making me feel so much better about going out this evening,' she replied, tartly. 'Should it be as tedious as you clearly expect it to be, I shall be able to alleviate my boredom by turning random young men to stone, with one glare.'

Oh, how he admired her pluck. She was clearly nervous, but she wasn't about to admit it, or betray it, to anyone. Instead, she was going to brazen it out, by making caustic comments such as that. Or self-deprecating ones about herself.

'Oh, how I wish,' he told her, 'you *did* have that power. Not that I particularly wish any of the young men any ill will, but there are one or two of the young ladies…who *giggle*,' he concluded on a shudder.

'How very irritating for you,' she replied with false sympathy.

Timms chose that moment to fling open the front door, through which he could see that the carriage stood waiting. And somehow, although only moments ago he'd thought he would seize upon any excuse to avoid going to Lady Templeton's ball tonight, now that he had the perfect one, in that Miss Hinchcliffe would be in attendance, he found himself taking her by the arm, and escorting her out of the house and into the carriage.

He liked Miss Hinchcliffe, he reflected as he took his seat beside her, facing his cousin's sister and his cousin's daughter. *She* didn't make him feel as if he was an elderly, wealthy, mark for marriage-minded schoolgirls. But like…well, himself. Or a version of himself, anyway. The one he really was deep down inside. Not the one he had to pretend to be now he was trying to behave like a marquess.

'Miss Templeton,' Lady Birchwood said to him, with a titter, as the carriage set off, 'will be *so* thrilled to see you tonight.'

'Why,' he replied, 'would that be?'

'Well, because of the particular interest you have shown her,' said Lady Birchwood archly.

'Have I?' No. He couldn't have done. He couldn't even recall what she looked like.

'Every time you have attended a ball,' put in Susannah, smoothing a tiny little wrinkle from her gloves, 'you have made sure to ask her to dance. Every single time.'

That was news to him.

'Everyone has noticed,' put in Lady Birchwood. 'Especially since you have not danced with any other young lady more than once.'

'Are we,' asked Susannah mischievously, 'to expect an announcement?'

'Because I happen to have danced with some chit, whose face I cannot even recall, more than once?' He shook his head. 'Don't talk such nonsense.' He was going to have to be more careful to mind who, exactly, he asked to dance if the fact that he'd inadvertently favoured one above all the others was causing comment.

'She's the *pretty* one,' said Susannah, looking a bit annoyed.

'Wealthy, too, don't forget, dear,' added Lady Birchwood. 'We don't blame you for preferring her to some of the others, if that is what has put you in a pelter.'

'That Lady Susan Pettifer, for example,' said Susannah, with a moue of distaste.

Ah, now, at least he could recall exactly who Lady Susan Pettifer was. 'I don't believe that saying her name is cause for you to pull that face, young lady,' he snapped. 'She, at least, has the virtue of being able to hold a rational conversation.' It was the one thing that made her stand out from the crowd. That, and the fact that she was clearly a little older than most of the others.

'Rational?' Susannah shook her head in mock pity. 'That girl has a tongue like a rapier. She enjoys nothing more than cutting everyone around her down to size!'

Well, he knew *that*. He hadn't said he *liked* her, had he? Only that he remembered who she was.

'It doesn't do to speak ill of another lady,' said Lady Birchwood, shooting Susannah a look of reproof.

'Even though,' Susannah argued, 'it's true?'

'Not if that lady may well become your guardian's wife,' said Lady Birchwood, giving him an arch look.

Susannah pouted, but fell silent. And thankfully before anyone thought of any more fatuous comments to make, they drew up outside Lord Templeton's London house.

He got out first, so was able to perform the service of helping all three ladies alight.

But the moment they'd gone to the ladies' cloakroom, to put off their shawls and put on their dancing shoes, he made a beeline for the card room.

Because, now that Miss Hinchcliffe was here, he could rely on her to look after Susannah's best interests. Besides, the only way to make sure he didn't raise false hopes in any female breast would be to keep well away from the lot of 'em.

Which suited him perfectly.

Chapter Ten

Rosalind watched him go with a sinking heart, for he'd led her to believe he'd be there to support her.

'See what you've done with all your teasing, Susannah?' Lady Birchwood said waspishly. 'You have made His Lordship run away to hide in the card room, just when I had such high hopes of seeing him come up to scratch.'

Run away? Was that what he'd done?

No! Whatever else he might be, he was no coward.

'I don't see why that has anything to do with me,' Susannah retorted. 'Besides, you spend most of the time, when we go anywhere, in the card room yourself!'

'That,' said Lady Birchwood loftily, 'is different. *I* will be going to the card room to catch up with my dearest friends. *I* am not hiding from anyone, or anything!'

And to the card room she went, leaving Rosalind and Susannah standing side by side at the edge of a room that seemed, to Rosalind, to be teeming with well-dressed, bejewelled, confident people. The cream, in fact, of society.

'I cannot believe,' said Susannah indignantly, 'that she just scolded me for making His Lordship uncomfortable, when *she* was the one who brought up the topic of him raising expectations in Miss Templeton's breast! But, oh, it is *just* like her! Like *all* my aunts, in fact. They…they start conversations and then, when I join in, they *rebuke* me. For agreeing with them! Oh, they make me so angry sometimes I could—'

'I shouldn't think,' Rosalind interjected, soothingly, 'you made His Lordship uncomfortable at all. He probably just enjoys playing cards.'

Susannah gave a derisive little laugh. 'Not he. Whenever he's been at a ball with us before, he's always gone straight over to the group of prettiest, most eligible girls, and systematically danced his way through them all.'

It was stupid to feel sad to hear that. She ought to feel pleased that she'd distracted Susannah before she'd descended into a fully-fledged tantrum. And of *course* Lord Caldicot would be looking for a wife. He had a duty to produce heirs to ensure continuance of his line. He might have *said* that he was only going to balls, et cetera, to keep a close watch on Susannah, since he clearly couldn't trust Lady Birchwood, who was much more concerned with her own enjoyment than keeping Susannah safe. But if that were the whole truth, he wouldn't need to ask so many girls to dance, would he? He could just stroll round the edge of the room, glowering at importunate suitors.

There! She'd made the same mistake again. Believing what he said, *completely*. Without question.

And yet…

'So, he doesn't appear to prefer any one of them,' she said, with a small flicker of hope, 'above any of the others?'

'Not *one*, no,' Susannah mused. 'I would say that at the moment there are three front runners. Miss Templeton, who you saw standing with her parents in the receiving line…'

The stunningly pretty, dainty girl who'd given Lord Caldicot a positively languishing look as he'd bowed over her hand.

'And Lady Susan, who I mentioned in the coach.'

The one with a spiteful tongue. Surely, he would not be seriously considering marrying someone like that?

'And then there's Miss Eastwick. Not as pretty as Miss Templeton, but her father is as influential as Lady Susan's and she is nowhere near as nasty.'

'Oh,' said Rosalind faintly, that brief glimmer of hope flickering and dying.

'But never mind *him*,' said Susannah, linking her arm through Rosalind's. 'Let's go and find you a seat with the other chaperons.'

As they made their way across the room, she couldn't help noticing that Susannah was looking round at the other guests as though she was searching for one particular person. By the time they reached a group of chairs, stationed so that the occupants would have a good view of the dance floor, Susannah was looking rather woebegone.

'Miss Hinchcliffe,' she said, as Rosalind took a seat right at the end of the row, 'do you think I may have been mistaken? About Cecil? He has not made any attempt to see me since Lord Caldicot forbade the match. And surely, if he really loved me, he would not just...run away with his tail between his legs?'

What an opportunity! Now that Susannah had begun to express doubts about Mr Baxter, Lord Caldicot would, no doubt, expect her to deal the death blow to Susannah's infatuation. By implying he was a coward, or unworthy in some other way.

The trouble was, Rosalind knew *exactly* why Mr Baxter had not been to any balls or tried to see Susannah since that night. And it had nothing to do with how he felt about Susannah. It was because she, Rosalind, had injured him. Possibly seriously.

She glanced up at Susannah's unhappy face and discovered that she knew just how the poor girl must feel. Because she, too, was wondering if the man she admired so much was worthy of her total devotion. And, in her case, *knowing* that he was looking elsewhere, rather than merely suspecting it, might be the case.

'Perhaps,' said Rosalind, 'something has happened...not connected in any way with Lord Caldicot and what he said, or anything to do with his feelings for you...to prevent him from attending balls, or trying to contact you.'

'You mean, he may be unwell?'

Rosalind flinched. Mr Baxter was certainly very unwell. She could easily imagine him lying on a bed of pain, somewhere, as he recovered from his injuries.

But before Susannah could notice her uneasiness and she

had to give an explanation for it, a group of young men came over, practically jostling each other out of the way as they vied for Susannah's attention.

It was exactly what Susannah needed. As the girl looked from one eager face to the other, all the misery and doubt she'd been expressing slid from her shoulders as though it was as insubstantial as a gossamer scarf.

'I will dance first,' she said, holding out her hand to a serious-looking dark-eyed man, in what looked like a naval uniform and whose face was disfigured by a couple of livid scars, 'with you, Lieutenant Minter.'

His jaw dropped. But after only a brief moment of looking as though he couldn't believe his luck, he seized her hand and tucked it possessively into the crook of his arm.

'And before the rest of you even ask,' Susannah added, 'Lieutenant Minter will be my partner for the supper dance, too.'

Susannah had mentioned this Lieutenant Minter once or twice when telling Rosalind about the balls and parties she'd gone to before Rosalind had been expected to attend as well.

And for a moment, Rosalind felt rather proud of Susannah, for what looked like an act of kindness. For thinking that since she couldn't dance with the man she really wanted to, she might as well spend her evening cheering up that disfigured veteran of the war with France instead.

But only for a moment. Because, as he led her on to the dance floor, she caught an expression on the girl's face that looked suspiciously like defiance.

Defiance? Oh, dear. What game was Susannah playing now? Was she trying to rebuff one of her other suitors, who were all watching her taking her place in the set, with varying degrees of disappointment? Or did she have something else in mind?

She watched the couple dancing keenly, in case she could detect something, anything that might give her a clue as to Susannah's motives in favouring him above the others. And began to wonder if it was simply that Susannah needed someone like Lieutenant Minter to gaze at her as though she was a goddess, far beyond the reach of a mere mortal man. Because that was what he was doing. Rosalind didn't know how he managed to avoid bumping into the other dancers, so reluctant was he to tear his gaze from Susannah's face for even a moment.

Rosalind sighed. It must be balm to Susannah's wounded pride, to have someone adore her so blatantly. None of the other men who danced with her, after that set finished, had anywhere near the intensity. They charmed, they flirted, they showed off their physical stamina and dexterity with all the leaping and hopping that most of the country dances demanded. But not one of the others gazed at Susannah with such a potent mixture of adoration and despair. As though she was a prize beyond his reach.

When it came time to cease dancing, and go in to supper, Rosalind also discovered that Lieutenant Minter was a very correct sort of young man. Because, rather than bearing Susannah into the supper room and taking advantage of the chance to snatch a few moments with her away from prying eyes, he brought her over to where Rosalind was sitting and held out his arm to offer his escort for her, too. And when they reached the supper room, once he'd found them a good seat, he fetched her a plate of delicacies, as well as serving Susannah, even though she worried that half of it was going to end up on the floor, so often did he glance over to where they were sitting, as if to make sure Susannah didn't disappear.

He had barely taken his own seat at their table when Lady Birchwood appeared, lured from the card room by the promise of refreshment, no doubt. Naturally, he stood up, as it was the polite thing to do. But then, to Rosalind's surprise, instead of greeting him, or acknowledging him in any way, Lady Birchwood waved him away with an impatient gesture of her fan. And took his chair. She had a smile on her face all the while, but Rosalind could tell from the glitter in her eyes that she was, for some reason, furious.

Susannah was smiling, too. But she was smiling in a way that put Rosalind in mind of a cat that has just caught a mouse in its paws.

The only person who looked as though he was not trying to pretend to feel something he didn't was Lieutenant Minter.

He had taken his dismissal with a sort of grim resignation, as though it was exactly what he'd been dreading all along. Then he slouched out of the room in dejection.

Lady Birchwood shot Rosalind a look of barely repressed annoyance, although the smile returned almost at once, because, she suspected, a couple of Susannah's previously rejected suitors came over to set up a flirtatious conversation.

For the rest of the evening, Susannah danced every dance, with a fixed, yet to Rosalind's eyes, rather strained smile on her lips.

At long last, both Lady Birchwood and Lord Caldicot emerged from the card room, signifying it was time to return to Kilburn House. As they climbed into the coach Lady Birchwood finally let her smile drop. But when she glared at Susannah the girl returned a smile that was not only genuine, but also full of the same sort of defiance she'd displayed when accepting that dance with Lieutenant Minter.

Lady Birchwood sucked in an outraged breath.

Lord Caldicot, looking from one to the other, took in a breath of his own as though about to ask a question, then appeared to think better of it. In the end, the four of them conducted the entire journey home in a tense, simmering sort of silence.

When they reached Kilburn House, Lady Birchwood tottered, as though with extreme fatigue, to the foot of the stairs and took hold of the newel post.

'That girl,' she said to nobody in particular, 'will be the death of me.'

The girl in question flounced past her and ran up the stairs, presumably, by the sound of a door slamming, going straight into her bedroom.

'Miss Hinchcliffe,' said Lord Caldicot, 'would you mind attending me in my study before you retire?'

'Not at all,' she replied with alacrity. Apart from anything else, if she didn't, everyone would expect her to follow Susannah upstairs, and *'deal with'* her mood. So, she turned to follow

Lord Caldicot as Timms went over to lend Lady Birchwood his arm to help her up the stairs to her own room.

'What,' said Lord Caldicot, the moment they reached the sanctuary of his study, 'has provoked the latest skirmish between my ward and her aunt?'

'You did.'

'I? I did nothing!'

'No, instead of dancing your way through all the prettiest debutantes, as is apparently your custom,' she said, allowing bitterness and disappointment to rule her tongue, 'you ran away and hid in the card room, just when Lady Birchwood had high hopes of you *"coming up to scratch"*. She said it was Susannah's fault for *"teasing"* you and Susannah said that was unfair since she'd started it.'

'And that,' he said with incredulity, 'kept them going all night?'

'Well, no, I think the quarrel might have languished had Susannah not flaunted Lieutenant Minter in Lady Birchwood's face.' Which, she was pretty sure by now, from Lady Birchwood's reaction to finding the young man sitting down to supper with them, was what Susannah had done. 'And I'm sorry,' she added, 'if Lieutenant Minter is another fortune hunter, from whom I should be protecting Susannah. And I don't know why,' she said, flinging decorum to the four winds by going over to the sofa and, without asking his permission, dropping heavily down on to it, 'you thought I could be of any use. I *liked* Lieutenant Minter,' she said defiantly. 'He seemed perfectly respectable to me. But what,' she said, tartly, 'do I know?'

She leaned her head back on the cushions and closed her eyes in a mixture of despair and exhaustion.

'At least *you* did not desert your post, no matter how hard you found your duties,' said Lord Caldicot, making her open her eyes and look to him with a slight lessening of the inadequacy she was feeling. 'From what I've been able to gather, this past couple of weeks, Lady Birchwood seems to think she has done enough by depositing Susannah among a group of equally silly girls and leaving them to their own devices while she goes off and enjoys herself. Which may well be how Baxter managed to get so close to Susannah.'

'Oh, dear.'

'Quite,' he said with feeling. 'Furthermore, it is only Lady Birchwood who considers the Lieutenant ineligible, not I. Well, not *completely* ineligible. He is, as I am sure you have gathered, a half-pay officer in the navy. With the war at sea faltering, it means he has few prospects of further promotion, or prize money. You know that promotion in the navy comes through merit, rather than purchase?'

She nodded.

'But worse than that, in her eyes, is the fact that he does not come from some old, or aristocratic, family, but merely from gentry stock.'

'But...that does not bother you?'

'Not, perhaps, as much as it should,' he mused, 'since my own mother was merely a doctor's daughter. And the thing is, not only is his service record exemplary, but, try as I might, I have not been able to find anything to his detriment, regarding his character or behaviour, since he's been on the town. Which is more than can be said for most men of his age.'

He held out a glass of brandy to her, which he must have poured while she was leaning back with her eyes closed.

'So, I need not,' she asked, as she accepted the glass, 'forbid Susannah from dancing with him?'

'Not on my account.' He swirled his own drink around, looking into his glass rather than starting to drink it. 'But if she really doesn't care for him, it might not be kind of her to encourage him too much. For if I'm not mistaken, he likes her rather too well. I would not approve of her carelessly breaking young men's hearts for sport.'

'No,' she said with conviction. 'Nor would I.'

'I suppose,' he said, 'that I need not ask you if *you* enjoyed your evening?'

'Enjoyed it?' She shuddered. 'Though I suppose,' she added morosely, 'at least I didn't have to dance, on top of everything else.'

'You don't like dancing? What an unusual young woman you are.'

She eyed him with some resentment. 'I have only really danced while having lessons, at school, which wasn't so bad. But I certainly don't think I would enjoy the kind of dancing I watched tonight. It was...relentless. All that skipping and hopping, and smiling at people over your shoulder to make your current partner jealous. I don't have the stamina for it,' she admitted. 'Nor the dexterity. And as for this turban...' She put her hand up to touch it, briefly. 'It wouldn't have stayed in place for five minutes. Perhaps that is why,' she mused, 'they make chaperons wear such ridiculous headgear. To remind them of their place, should they be tempted to join in the fun which belongs by rights only to the young.'

'You *didn't* enjoy the ball,' he said, with a chuckle, 'did you?' His face sobered. 'Look, if you really don't want to continue acting as Susannah's chaperon...and really, it was rather unfair of me to ask it of you. I mean, I employed you to be her teacher, originally, didn't I, not her chaperon?'

'Oh,' she said, a wave of gratitude washing over her. How *kind* he was. How *considerate*.

'And it wasn't just the dancing,' he added, 'was it? Something else has upset you.'

'What makes you say that?'

'You said, *on top of everything else*,' he reminded her. 'So, what is it? What is troubling you?'

That, she sighed, was what made her like him so much. The way he noticed her. The way nobody else did, or ever had done. And was interested enough to ask her what troubled her, when nobody else cared.

It tempted her to confide in him. Though not, naturally, about how it hurt to think of him marrying one of those eligible girls. Or about wondering if he had a mistress in keeping, who he visited in the afternoons while innocents like she and Susannah went shopping and ate ices.

'I feel guilty,' she blurted out, while still in the throes of that heady mix of gratitude and yearning to be able to share *some* of her feelings with him.

'About what?'

'Not being honest with Susannah,' she admitted. Only then she remembered that he was the one who'd started her on this course, when he'd told her Susannah must never find out she'd caused Mr Baxter to fall from the balcony.

'Even though,' he said with a perplexed frown, 'it is in her best interests?'

'I know, I know,' she said, shaking her head over the brandy glass she still held in her hands, of which she hadn't taken one sip. 'Deep down, I do know it is best for her. It is just that the poor girl is under the illusion that Mr Baxter has just walked away without making even a single attempt to defy you. Which makes her fear he might be a coward. Or that he doesn't love her enough to fight for her.'

'So?'

'Well, it isn't true, is it? He did try to fight for her. He climbed in through my window...'

'The act of a rogue. You'd never catch a man like Lieutenant Minter climbing in through a girl's window. He'd stand outside, clinging to the railings, and just gaze at her as she went out, if he'd been forbidden from speaking to her.'

'Yes, but she doesn't know that. And even now, she thinks he is avoiding her, when really, he must be lying in a bed some-where, nursing his injuries. Injuries that I caused...'

'Well-deserved injuries. If a chap tries to sneak in, what can he expect but a spirited rebuff?'

'Yes, but...oh, you are not even trying to understand!'

'I do understand,' he said more gently. 'You have a delicate conscience. It is to your credit that you are so sympathetic to the girl, but you are only doing what you need to, to protect her.'

Was she though? What if Mr Baxter was no worse than, say, Lieutenant Minter? What if Lord Caldicot's objections to that young man were no more substantial than Lady Birchwood's to the impoverished naval officer?

And how could she possibly find out?

Chapter Eleven

Rosalind didn't think she'd be able to get a wink of sleep, she had so many conflicting thoughts swirling round in her head at the same time.

But it seemed as though staying out so late at night had tired her out. For when the maid, Constance, came in to open her curtains she sat bolt upright, her heart pounding, with a bewildering sense of having only just laid her head upon the pillow.

When she looked at the clock, it informed her that it was almost midday.

'What?' she said in a hoarse voice that had her reaching for the glass of water at her bedside. 'Why have I been allowed to sleep in so late?' She flung aside the covers. 'I should have been about my duties hours ago.'

'Oh, it was His Lordship's orders,' replied Constance. 'He said as how you wasn't used to keeping late hours and we was to let you sleep as long as you needed.'

She was just starting to feel grateful for his consideration, when it dawned on her that she hadn't actually been allowed to sleep as long as she needed, or Constance wouldn't be in here drawing curtains and generally bustling about.

'So, why are you here? Not that I'm not grateful…'

'Coz Lady Birchwood wants to have a word with you,' she said, with a grimace.

Ah. She was about to be told off for allowing Susannah to dance twice with poor Lieutenant Minter, she suspected.

She was proved correct when Lady Birchwood launched into a long, involved account of why the Lieutenant was not a suitable person for Susannah to encourage.

Rosalind listened with her head bowed, her hands clasped at her waist. She made no excuses for not having tried to stop Susannah from dancing with whomever she'd wanted, the night before. For one thing, it sounded as though that was what the girl had been doing ever since the start of the Season, if Lady Birchwood was spending so much time in the card room with her own friends.

Once again, it made her understand just why Susannah lost her temper so often, when what little guidance she received from the people who were supposed to have her welfare at heart was so inconsistent. What was more, nobody had given Rosalind a list of those who might be welcomed and those who were not. The only person she'd known for certain ought to be prevented from getting anywhere near Susannah was Mr Baxter. And he hadn't put in an appearance.

Eventually Lady Birchwood ran out of complaints and said, 'Well? What have you to say for yourself?'

'I shall,' said Rosalind meekly, 'have a word with Susannah about Lieutenant Minter.' She'd intended to, anyway. Because she was pretty sure that although the Lieutenant looked upon Susannah with stars in his eyes, Susannah had encouraged him mostly because she'd known it would annoy Lady Birchwood. Which wasn't fair on the poor man.

'And perhaps,' Rosalind suggested, 'you could furnish me with a list of who is, and who is not, an acceptable partner, so that I do not make the same mistake again.'

'How tiresome,' sighed Lady Birchwood, closing her eyes for a moment or two as though the notion of picking up a pen and finding a sheet of paper had already exhausted her. 'But I suppose I shall have to do something of the sort, since you don't come from the kind of background where you would instinctively *know* a good catch from an ineligible partner.'

And nor do you, Rosalind silently seethed as Lady Birchwood waved a languid hand in dismissal. *Or I wouldn't have had Mr Baxter climbing in through my bedroom window.*

Rosalind set about finding Susannah at once and eventually found her in the drawing room, sitting at the piano, shuffling through some sheet music in a distracted manner.

'How lovely to see you practising your piano pieces,' said Rosalind bracingly, hoping that leading with a compliment would put Susannah in a receptive mood.

Susannah, however, shot her a suspicious look. 'I haven't even begun yet.'

'No, but you were about to. Or at least, you were thinking about it, without me having to remind you, which is most commendable. In fact,' she added, shutting the door softly behind her, 'I am, on the whole, extremely pleased with your progress. *And* your behaviour...'

'But?' Susannah sat up a little straighter and lifted her chin.

'Well, it isn't my opinion, really. It is Lady Birchwood. She is very cross with me for allowing you to dance, twice, with Lieutenant Minter last night.'

'Good!'

'You wanted her to be cross with me?'

'What? Oh, no! I didn't mean for you,' Susannah said, with contrition, 'to get into trouble. I just wanted to annoy her.'

'I thought as much. And, though I sympathise with you, because, really, the way she spoke to you after the conversation in the coach, which, as you pointed out, *she* started...' She paused as she realised her sentence had become as muddled as the various sheets of music, which, as far as she could see, were all from different sonatas.

With a rueful shake of her head, she started again.

'That is, from observing Lieutenant Minter last night, I gained the impression that he rather...um...worships you. He looked at you as though...'

Susannah began to look confused as well. 'What are you trying to say?'

'Well, do you think…um…it is *kind* to use the poor young man to score points off your aunt, when he is so susceptible to being hurt?'

Susannah pouted. 'I won't hurt *him*,' she scoffed. 'I couldn't possibly. I mean, he is a hero of all sorts of battles at sea.'

'Oh, no doubt he is terrifically brave in *that* respect. But in matters of the heart, he may be, well, I mean, I don't suppose he has had the chance to mix with many pretty girls, with all the years he spent at sea. And he does appear to have fallen for you rather hard.'

Susannah plucked a random sheet of music from the pile on top of the piano and set it on the music stand.

'I don't want to be unkind,' she eventually admitted. Then sighed. 'I suppose I had better not encourage him to think he has any hope of me returning his affections, hadn't I?'

'I think that would be the kindest thing to do,' said Rosalind, with relief. 'If you don't think you can love him…'

'Well, how can I possibly? My heart belongs to Cecil!' She faltered. Blushed. 'That is, it *did*. But now I am starting to wonder if…if…much as I hate to say it, Lord Caldicot might have been right to say he is unworthy. I mean, if he really loved me, wouldn't he have…have walked through fire, just to catch a glimpse of me?'

Not if he was nursing half a dozen broken bones, no. Not that Rosalind could say that out loud.

'As I said last night, there could be any number of reasons why you have not seen him, which have nothing to do with anything Lord Caldicot has said or done,' she said. 'That is, gentlemen do go out of town, occasionally don't they, to attend race meetings, or…'

'Race meetings!' Susannah's eyes flashed dangerously. 'Are you suggesting that he would go off to a race meeting when things are at such a difficult stage in our relationship?'

'Well, no, I was just trying to think of some reason, of something that might have taken him out of town.' Which didn't involve admitting the truth. 'I mean, Lord Caldicot has to go off, at a moment's notice to attend to sudden pressing business on his estate, occasionally, doesn't he?'

'Cecil doesn't have an estate.'

'No? Does he—I beg your pardon, but I know so little about him, really.' And while Susannah was looking at him a bit more clearly, this could be the perfect time to find out more. To find out if he might be a struggling artist, for example, without having to mention the fact that she'd heard him muttering the word *turpentine*. 'Does he...work for a living?'

'Work?' Susannah looked shocked. 'Of course not! He is a gentleman.'

But even a gentleman might, discreetly, paint portraits though, mightn't he? To help eke out his slender fortune. Or even because he loved art.

'Although,' Susannah added, with a frown, 'he did mention something about having expectations, when he asked me to marry him. So I suppose he might have had to go and deal with some sort of business connected with that. Though why,' she said, standing up suddenly, scattering sheet music in all directions, 'he couldn't have at least *written* to me, to let me know...'

She paced across the room. 'Although I dare say Lord Caldicot would have prevented me from receiving any such letter.' She stilled. Turned. 'Has he, do you think...?'

'I am sorry, but to the best of my knowledge Mr Baxter has not made any attempt to get a letter to you.'

Susannah's face tightened. 'How he could have left me to worry about him...with things at such a pass...' She turned and paced back to the piano.

Rosalind supposed she ought to be pleased that Susannah had progressed from pining for Mr Baxter to becoming annoyed with him for disappearing, but watching those sheets of music scatter all over the carpet somehow made her think of him tumbling out of the window and landing in an untidy heap in the bushes. And all she could feel was guilt.

'If only,' said Susannah, striking one fist into the palm of her other hand, 'I could find out where he is and what he's doing!' She went very still. Turned to look at Rosalind. 'Miss Hinchcliffe,' she said.

Oh, no. She'd come up with another of her notions. Rosalind could foresee the girl using her pin money to hire someone to track Mr Baxter down. Which would mean it would all come out.

Luckily, before Susannah could get as far as telling her what idea it was that had struck her just then, someone knocked at the door.

'Beg pardon, miss,' said Constance, poking her head round the door. 'But Mr Timms said as how I was to let you know that you have some callers. And…er… Lady Birchwood hasn't come out of her room yet, so I was to check that Miss Hinchcliffe can be present to lend propriety to the proceedings.'

Susannah groaned. 'I don't want to see anybody.'

'Well, some of the gentlemen are very good looking,' said Constance, rather cheekily.

'Oh?' Susannah looked a little less bored.

'I expect it is some of the gentlemen with whom you danced last night,' said Rosalind. 'Don't they usually visit the next morning, with posies and such like?'

'Yes,' said Susannah pensively. And then looked thoughtful. 'Yes, they do.' She dashed over to the mirror, patted at her curls, tweaked the lace at her neckline, then took her seat at the piano. 'You may show them up,' said Susannah. 'For as you can see, Miss Hinchcliffe is already here, supervising me at my *piano practice*,' she said, giving Constance a meaningful look.

'Susannah,' Rosalind said as soon as Constance left the room.

'Not now,' Susannah snapped, spreading her fingers over the keys. 'I must start playing a few notes, at once, since Constance will be telling them I'm practising, so they must hear me as they come up the stairs, mustn't they?'

There was no faulting that logic. But Susannah's decision not to confide in her did not bode well for whatever it was that had come into her head before.

She couldn't shake off that sense of foreboding over the next hour or so, even though, on the surface, Susannah behaved like a young lady who didn't have a care in the world, and who was simply enjoying the attentions of all the gentlemen who came to pay their respects and deliver their posies.

She behaved with such propriety that all Rosalind had to do was to sit in a corner, watching them come and go.

Which only deepened Rosalind's unease.

Eventually, Lieutenant Minter came in. He clenched his jaw when he saw Susannah talking with animation to two other gentlemen, one of whom was Lord Wapping. And then, like a man resigned to his fate, he came to sit next to Rosalind and spent the half-hour of his visit struggling to make polite conversation with her. Which was more than any of the others had done, though his clumsy attempt to make small talk, along with his complete inability to stake any sort of claim on Susannah's attention, confirmed her suspicions that he was not very experienced with ladies. Only when it was time for him to leave did he approach the piano stool where Susannah was holding court and bow over her hand.

She pouted up at him. 'Oh, are you leaving already? How vexing! When I particularly wished to speak with you!'

'Well, I, well, you know,' he stammered. 'Half an hour is considered…'

'I tell you what you should do,' Susannah supplied, when it was clear that poor Lieutenant Minter was out of his depth. 'You should call and take me for a drive in the park later on.'

'Oh, I say,' cried several of the other men there. 'How unfair! When we asked you ourselves and you refused!'

'Ah, but you have all had plenty of time to talk to me and he has had none. You quite cut him out. Isn't that the correct expression,' she said, looking up at him and fluttering her eyelashes shamelessly, 'Lieutenant?'

'Ah, yes,' he breathed, gazing at her as though all his birthdays had come at once.

What on earth, Rosalind fumed, was Susannah playing at? Singling the Lieutenant out, again, when she'd promised she was not going to hurt him?

'He doesn't,' put in Lord Wapping, with disdain, 'even have his own carriage.'

'I can soon hire one,' the Lieutenant retorted.

His look of determination was so ferocious that for the first time Rosalind could see exactly how he'd had such a successful career in the navy. He would never consider any obstacle too great to overcome. He would always, to judge by the set of that jaw, come up with some stratagem to surmount it.

'There, that's settled,' said Susannah.

Making Rosalind's heart sink. As if injuring Mr Baxter, physically, was not bad enough, now it looked as though yet another young man was about to become a casualty of Susannah's Season.

Where was it all going to end?

Chapter Twelve

'It's no use looking at me like that,' Susannah protested as she stalked out of the drawing room once the last caller had left the house.

'But you promised,' Rosalind said as Susannah went into her room.

'If I am to persuade Lieutenant Minter that he has no hope,' Susannah said, tugging on the bell rope to summon her maid, 'then shouldn't I give him just one treat, first?'

'He isn't a dog, Susannah! You cannot talk of tossing him treats!'

'Well, not a treat, then,' Susannah replied as she went to her armoire and opened the door. 'I should have said, a proper explanation.' She pulled out a pale green spencer and began rummaging among her dresses, for, Rosalind presumed, the carriage dress that went with it.

'For I *do* want to explain things properly,' she said, abandoning her search through the dresses to pull out a hatbox, open it and take out a creation covered with a profusion of flowers and feathers. 'And for that, I need privacy. Which a girl can only get when out driving with a gentleman in something like a phaeton. I know you advised me that sitting at a piano would be conducive to a little privacy,' she said, discarding the feathered headdress and pulling down another hatbox from the top shelf, which meant she didn't see Rosalind flinch with a pang of guilt.

For she had, indeed, told the headstrong girl, when she'd declared she couldn't see the point of learning to play any musical instrument, that playing the piano would be a useful tool in the art of flirting with men. She'd reminded her that a potential suitor would be able to draw close enough to her to whisper things nobody else could overhear, on the pretext of turning the pages of music, for example. But she'd only said that because she couldn't think of any other way to get her to practise, not because she approved of flirting.

'But a piano,' said Susannah, taking out a bonnet with a pale green ribbon round the crown and smiling, since it was an exact match for the spencer, 'must always remain in a room, containing all sorts of people, so that any of them might overhear things I wouldn't wish them to know.'

'That's all very well, but…'

'Besides,' Susannah added with a mischievous grin, 'I don't want it to look as though I am obeying Aunt Birchwood's stricture straight away, do I? How tame would that appear? As though I have no backbone!'

'Nobody who knows you at all,' Rosalind observed, 'could possibly accuse you of not having any backbone.'

Fortunately, Susannah was in a sunny mood and chose to be amused by that comment, rather than annoyed.

'Now, since there will be no room for you in the phaeton,' Susannah continued, as Pauline came in, 'why don't you take the afternoon off?'

Rosalind could certainly do with a lie down in a darkened room, recouping her strength for the evening ahead. And, since there was nothing further she could say in front of the maid, she drifted out of Susannah's room and into her own, which was just next door.

On the table, she spied a sheet of paper, covered with Lady Birchwood's distinctively spidery handwriting. The list, she sighed, of the men that Lady Birchwood considered ineligible and whom she must therefore discourage.

She picked it up, sank to her reading chair and glanced

through the almost illegible list of ineligibles with a sigh. It looked as though she was going to have to acquire the skills of something like a tightrope walker, to be able to maintain the delicate balance between annoying neither Susannah, nor Lady Birchwood, and all while fending off hordes of importunate men clamouring for permission to dance.

She was definitely going to need some time to herself, both to decipher this list of names and commit it to memory, and to recruit some stamina for the ordeal that clearly lay ahead of her.

But then she changed her mind. It was as she was standing on the front step, watching the Lieutenant hand Susannah into a rather shabby little curricle while the groom he must also have hired from somewhere to lend propriety to the proceedings held the heads of a pair of dispirited-looking hacks, that it struck her that she'd never had the chance to just go out on her own since they'd come to London. Every single outing here had been in the company of Susannah, either as a chaperon, or as a puppet for her to dress up.

A delicious breeze was making the branches of the trees that grew in the square bob about almost as though they were dancing. The sun was shining. And she really did need to return the three volumes of *Sense and Sensibility* to the circulating library at some time. On reflection, she would much rather do so without having to explain to a third party just how volume two had ended up looking so battered.

It didn't take her long to choose a hat to go with *her* outfit. She had only the one for day wear, a serviceable straw bonnet which shaded her eyes, framed her face and covered her hair into the bargain. Having tied it securely under her chin, she picked up her books, informed the footman who was loitering in the hall where she was going and set off in the direction of Bond Street.

She had only walked for a few minutes, when she gave a huge sigh. She'd made the right decision to get outside for a walk, she decided, as she felt a huge great weight of care roll from her shoulders. She rarely had a moment to herself. She was always at someone's beck and call. So, to be outside, walking along, and at her own pace at that, felt like an immense treat, even if it wasn't to admire the bluebells in the woods that surrounded Caldicot Dane, or to pop into the village post office to collect letters from friends she'd made at school, who still corresponded with her.

Once she'd exchanged her books, if the librarian would permit her to take any more out, after returning the last set in such a state, she could…well, what could she do in London? She could stroll in a park, she supposed, though it wouldn't have the same soothing effect as the woodlands of Caldicot Dane. Or go to Gunter's for tea and cake, though she wouldn't know anyone to chat to, or just wander along the street looking into shop windows at all the fripperies she couldn't afford.

Oh, yes, that would be grand, wouldn't it? Knowing her luck, someone would mistake her for a woman of loose morals if she went strolling through a park and she wouldn't be able to find a table if she went to Gunter's.

Still, once she had a new book to read, she could travel into the realm of imagination, as she delved into the adventure of the heroine. Much better. And much safer.

The encounter with the clearly irritated and dreadfully patronising man to whom she had to return her books went about as badly as she'd expected. For one awful moment she even feared he was going to refuse her permission to take out any more. But she'd paid her subscription, or at least, Lord Caldicot had done so on her behalf, and was still, according to the rules, entitled to borrow six more books.

Having survived that encounter, Rosalind made her way to the reading room to browse the shelves. She could make her choice from the catalogue, of course, but it was so pleasant to wander along the shelves of books, dreaming of the endless possibilities for entertainment or enlightenment hidden within the covers.

What would it be like to have her own library, stacked from floor to ceiling with books she had chosen herself, rather than relying on the taste of the man who'd purchased them? So lost was she in daydreams of her own, personal, perfect library, while contemplating the pleasures and possibilities she had to look forward to from the one she was actually in, that before long she didn't notice anyone else was in the room.

That impression was shattered when, just after she'd pulled a book, intriguingly entitled *The Miser and his Family*, from the shelf, someone addressed her directly.

'Miss Hinchcliffe, if I am not mistaken?'

She looked up, startled to be addressed by name by what sounded to her ears like a total stranger. And saw a man whose face was a mass of greenish bruises and whose arm was supported by a sling, making her what she could only assume was an ironic bow.

'Mr Baxter?' Her stomach turned over with guilt to see him looking so bruised and battered.

Oh, dear. What could he possibly want?

Well, obviously, he must be furious with her for reducing him to this state.

Which thought made her cling a bit more tightly to the book she'd just selected, though she really hoped she wouldn't need to use it.

He followed the movement of her hand with a wry smile.

'My dear lady,' he said, in an oily voice, 'you have no need of a shield. Indeed, you never had any need to attempt to defend yourself from me. I mean you no harm. I never have. And I am only sorry that I startled you so badly last time I attempted to get you alone.'

What? Was he saying that he'd climbed in through *her* window, on *purpose*? That he hadn't mistaken his way to Susannah's room at all?

'I can see I have surprised you,' he said, looking terrifically pleased with himself. 'But don't you think we *ought* to be allies?'

'Allies?'

'Yes,' he said, shifting a bit closer and lowering his voice. Since Rosalind was already standing with her back to a bookshelf, she had nowhere to go. Which meant she'd have to listen to whatever he wanted to say. Unless she thwacked him with the book she was holding and made good her escape.

Only…hadn't she decided that acting before thinking things

through was generally a mistake? And that, moreover, she ought to find out if he really loved Susannah and try to discover what sort of man he was. For her own peace of mind. And what better chance was she ever likely to have?

Nevertheless, she was glad she had a hefty tome to hand. Just in case.

Mr Baxter took a quick look round the room, as if to make sure nobody could overhear what he was about to say. Which didn't bode well. But she'd decided to hear him out. She owed him that much, after injuring him so badly, didn't she? And Susannah, too. If they really loved each other...

'That night,' he hissed. Yes, hissed, in a manner that put Rosalind in mind of a snake. 'I had come to put a proposition to you. The family's opposition to the match is extremely stupid, don't you think? For it is based on foolish things like status. They don't really have Susannah's best interests at heart, do they? They take no account of how painful it is to be young and in love.' He then did something with his face that put her in mind of a spaniel. All sort of woeful and pleading.

'And look,' he continued, 'I know it cannot be easy for you, working for a girl of Susannah's temperament. Very few have stayed with her as long as you. Which means, I suspect, that you have no alternative. Or at least, that your options are limited.'

Surely a man who was in love would not speak in such a way about the object of his affections?

'Furthermore, once Susannah marries you will be out of even the job you have, is that not so? New husbands do have a tendency to dispose of women in your position as soon as they can. Especially if, as you have, they have gained a reputation for being a bit of a dragon. Out the door in a flash! And then you will have to go through the sordid process of seeking new employment.'

That was, of course, depressingly true. She'd been aware of it from the very start of Susannah's Season. Coming to London at all was only, to be honest, a sort of reprieve, because she really ought to have started looking for a new post the moment Susannah's family decided she had no further use for a governess. In fact, what she ought to have done with this unexpected afternoon off was to have gone back to the agency she'd signed on with before, to let them know she might soon be in need of a new position and to keep her name in mind should anything suitable turn up.

'But I think,' he continued, 'no, I *know* I can be of help there.'

'You know of some other family in want of a governess?'

He grinned. 'Better than that. If we put our heads together, I can make sure you will never have to work again.'

'How,' she said in disbelief, 'do you think you could accomplish anything of the sort?'

'Well, it would be a kind of quid pro quo kind of deal.'

'Deal?' She felt her hackles rise.

'Yes, shall I spell it out?'

'I think you had better,' she replied in mystification.

'It is simple, really. You have it in your power to either grant or deny me access to your charge. Once I regain my looks and can go about in public again, you need only ease my way into her orbit and I shall soon get my ring on her finger. And then...'

'And then what?'

'Well, once I get my hands on the prize, I shall be sure to share the loot with you. Set you up in a neat little cottage, with an annuity. No other suitor, may I add, would make you anything like so generous an offer.'

'I am sure you are right,' she said, stunned by the way his mind worked. For it would not occur to any man who genuinely cared for Susannah to think of her as a commodity he could do a deal over. 'But how can you speak of loving Susannah, in one breath, then speak of her in terms of a prize, in the next?'

His eyes narrowed, as though sensing, finally, that she wasn't as interested in his deal as he'd assumed she'd be.

'I think,' she said, 'that the only thing you love, or are capable of loving, is money.'

'That isn't true,' he retorted. 'I love Susannah with all my heart. And if my words are not those of a poet, it is only that I am a forthright sort of chap.'

'So forthright that you climbed in through a window of the house when you *knew* she was out,' she said, suddenly wondering why that hadn't occurred to her before, 'to attempt to strike a deal with the one person you know could really stand in your way.' Because Susannah listened to her advice. Because Susannah had learned that Rosalind wasn't put off by her moods. That, on the contrary, she understood and sympathised with what brought them about in the first place.

'It is all very well for you to be so high and mighty,' snarled Mr Baxter. 'You don't know what it is like to have to do without the necessities of life!'

'Fustian!' She'd wager he'd never spent time in an orphanage, fighting over the meagre rations available. 'Hardly high and mighty—what woman would choose to work for a living if she didn't have to?'

'But I am offering you the chance to retire! If you help me win Susannah's hand, I can make sure you can live in comfort and idleness for the rest of your life!'

She didn't want to live in idleness for the rest of her life, not if it meant betraying Susannah! The girl might be, on the surface, a bit selfish and thoughtless, but deep down she wasn't malicious, not in the way she sensed Mr Baxter was malicious.

Hadn't she agreed to stop fostering false hope in Lieutenant Minter's heart and seemed genuinely reluctant to hurt him? And, when he'd come to call in that shabby, hired curricle, even though wealthier men had offered to take her out in their smart phaetons, she hadn't shown any sign of disappointment or disdain, had she?

What was more, there had already been too many people who had professed affection for her, then shown it didn't run all that deep. One aunt after another had come to Caldicot Dane, showering Susannah with kisses and treats, only to walk away the moment she became what they called 'difficult'.

Oh, Rosalind knew only too well what it felt like to have family members tell her she was 'unmanageable'. Which was why she'd ended up having to work as a governess, instead of having a debut ball and hopes of marriage. Even when Susannah had deliberately provoked Rosalind, as though attempting to drive her away, she'd felt it was important to show her that at least one person didn't think she was as bad as so many kept telling her she was. That Rosalind, for one, wasn't even tempted to leave. That she didn't think Susannah was 'unbearable' in the slightest.

And she wasn't. Yes, she had a temper. Yes, she could be a bit wilful, but she most definitely deserved better than Mr Baxter.

Well, any woman did! *No* woman deserved a husband of the sort Mr Baxter would prove to be. A man who looked upon his bride in the light of a sudden windfall that would solve all his financial difficulties.

'I am sorry,' she said firmly, though it was a matter of form to say so. She was not the slightest bit sorry about what she was about to say. 'But I cannot help you.'

'You could if you wanted to!'

'Yes, but I don't want to.'

'Why not? I have offered you everything you want, in exchange for just a few moments of looking the other way...'

'Apart from any other consideration,' she said, 'I don't trust you. You may *say* that you would set me up for life, but from what I know of you...'

'You think I would go back on my word?'

She said nothing. Only gave him her sternest, coldest look.

She saw it have its effect. The spaniel look disappeared. And in its place came something rather ugly.

'You will be sorry you made an enemy of me this day,' he said. Rather dramatically.

'I don't think so,' she said dismissively and shoved at him, hard, in the stomach, with the book she'd been clutching.

And then, when he reeled back, winded, she stalked out of the room with her nose in the air, trying hard not to imagine the look of loathing he must be hurling at her back.

Chapter Thirteen

Michael drew off his gloves as he began to climb the front steps of the house he still thought of as belonging to his cousin, the Marquess of Caldicot, feeling the by now familiar weight of it all bearing down on him the nearer he got to the front door.

It was all he could do to keep mounting the steps, steadily, as though it was the most natural thing in the world, when what he'd much rather do was go back to the set of rooms he'd hired last time he'd been in London. Just off Half Moon Street. They'd been a bit shabby and a bit cramped, but he could just toss his gloves on to a table when he went into his front door and know he could find them still there when he wanted to go out again.

The man who'd served him there had looked after his clothes and whatnot, but not to the extent of taking them from him at the door and stowing them away somewhere he couldn't lay his hands on them at a moment's notice. And it was just the one man. Not a butler, half a dozen footmen, and a valet, not to mention the coach driver, grooms and what have you loitering about in the mews.

And that was before he got to the legions of female staff his cousin, Lady Birchwood, and her niece seemed to think were an absolute necessity. And here was one of them now. Marching along the pavement with a militant glint in her eye and her fists clenched.

Although the sight of *her* did not depress him. On the contrary. Of all the people he'd become responsible for, since stepping into his pompous cousin's shoes, she alone was always able to bring a smile to his face.

'Good morning, Miss Hinchcliffe,' he said as she began stomping her way up the front steps.

'Is it?' She shook her head.

It hadn't felt all that good before he'd seen her, but now he noticed that the sun was shining, there was a pleasant breeze stirring the air, and that all the trees sported leaves that reminded him of brightly dressed ladies in a ballroom fluttering their fans.

'Hmm, technically,' he said, drawing his watch from his waistcoat pocket, 'it is afternoon, I agree.'

'Hmmph,' she said crossly.

'Dare I ask where you have been, or what has happened to put you out of sorts?'

'As to where I have been…well, I went to Hookham's library.'

'And yet you have no books in your hand. I take it that they took umbrage at the state of the books you were returning and refused to let you borrow another one?'

She looked down at her hands, in a bewildered manner. 'I came out of the library without any books? Oh. That is the outside of enough! *That man…*'

He felt as if his ears pricked up, if such a thing could be said of a human being. 'Which man?'

She gave him a look heavily laced with revulsion. 'Need you ask?'

'I think,' he said, taking her by the elbow, 'that we had better take this discussion off the front steps and into my study.'

'I couldn't agree more,' she said.

His feet no longer dragged at the prospect of getting inside this house. Not with Miss Hinchcliffe on his arm. Not when he knew he was about to have a conversation that would neither bore nor irritate him.

'So,' he said, once he'd gone through the ritual of surrendering his gloves, hat and coat to Timms, listening abstractedly to the messages the butler wanted to give him and then explaining why he was not going to do anything about any of them until he'd attended to Miss Hinchcliffe, in his study, 'what did *that man* do? Surely, not all that much, in the hallowed precincts of Hookham's?'

'You would be surprised at the audacity he is capable of demonstrating,' she said darkly, before flinging herself down on the chair before his desk, her feet, rather shockingly, straight out in front of her rather than neatly tucked to one side. 'He accosted me in the reading room and made me a proposition that so... so angered me that I hit him with the nearest book to hand.'

He supposed he ought to go and sit behind his desk and make this like a formal interview. His cousin would certainly have done so, had he ever had a woman like Miss Hinchcliffe on her own in here. So naturally, he wandered over to the table under the window, where there were several promising-looking decanters and a matching pair of cut-glass tumblers set out on a tray.

'He accosted you? In the reading room? I would not have thought that possible. Was there nobody else there to intercede?'

He poured two drinks. Well, there were two glasses and two of them in here, and she certainly looked as though she could do with a drink.

'Oh, well, he was so...sneaky about it, that anyone watching us would probably have thought we were having an assignation,' she said, with a curl to her lip.

'So he didn't *physically* attack you.' He handed her the drink.

'Oh, no. I beg your pardon. Was that what you thought? No, he is far too...cunning for that,' she mused, taking the drink from him in an absent-minded way, as though she scarcely noticed she was doing so. 'No, it was, as usual, *I* who resorted to violence.'

'Well, with all those weapons to hand,' he couldn't resist teasing her, 'I am not surprised you made use of one of them.'

She took a swig of the brandy, then coughed. Reached into her reticule for a handkerchief and wiped her streaming eyes. 'One of the most annoying things about it was that I'd just decided to listen to him *calmly*.'

He shook his head in mock reproof as he propped himself against the front edge of the desk. 'Habits, once formed, are very hard to break, aren't they?'

She gave him a baleful look. 'Hitting a man twice with a book hardly constitutes a habit. Especially when the first time was an accident.'

'No doubt he fully deserved it.'

'Well, of course he did!'

'And would you care to tell me what it was he did, if he didn't physically assault you, that rendered him worthy of such treatment again today?'

She glanced down at the glass as if considering taking another sip. Grimaced, as though thinking better of it, and raised her head. 'Well, for one thing, he confessed that the reason he climbed in through my window was not, as we had supposed, to try to persuade Susannah to elope with him.'

'No?' He found that hard to credit.

'No.' She twisted her mouth as though tasting something unpleasant. 'He said that he wanted to speak to me, alone, in order to persuade me to take part in a...what he called a *deal*. To get Susannah to the altar.'

'Then all those flowers he had stuffed down his waistcoat were not a romantic gesture aimed at my ward?' No. If he'd had no intention of seeing Susannah that night, it meant he'd brought them for *her*. For Miss Hinchcliffe.

He didn't like the thought of that. He didn't like it at all. It was bad enough the fellow sneaking around after his ward, but to imagine him trying to...to *woo* Miss Hinchcliffe made him want to go straight round to wherever he was lurking, grab him by the neck and shake him until his teeth rattled.

'It was an attempt to butter me up, I dare say,' she said with revulsion. Completely refusing to regard the way that man had bought her all those flowers, and climbed up to her window, as romantic. Which most women probably would.

But she, to his approval, was frowning. 'Why mention those flowers, when I have just told you that he was going to attempt to...to *pay* me to let him get at Susannah?'

Yes. Why had he taken such exception to the thought of that man bringing her flowers?

Why had the whole day seemed brighter just because he'd caught a glimpse of her, come to that?

He pushed aside those stray thoughts, as the irrelevancies that they were.

'Well,' he answered her, 'I always did wonder why on earth he'd stuffed all those roses down the front of his waistcoat. And it seems even more peculiar now, if he was about to offer you money.' He gave a short, mirthless laugh. 'And what was he going to say he would pay you with? The man has so many debts I am surprised he is still at liberty.'

'Oh, he was going to use Susannah's money, naturally,' she said tartly, 'once he'd got his greedy hands on it.'

'Ah.' He shook his head. 'How very predictable of him.'

'Really? You knew he was the sort of man who would stoop to...sneaky, underhanded means to try to get his hands on Susannah's money?'

'Oh, yes. Which is one of the reasons I refused him permission to attempt to fix his interest with her in the first place. And told her in no uncertain terms that I would never allow them to marry.'

'Not because he is a...struggling artist?'

'Artist? Whatever makes you think he's an artist?'

'Well, I cannot think of any other reason why the first word he said when he began to recover should be turpentine.'

'Turpentine,' he said wryly, 'I have recently discovered, is the name of a horse which plodded home last even though it was firm favourite. I should imagine Baxter lost a great deal of money on it if it was preying on his mind to that extent.'

'And *he* said your objections were all based on, well, I suppose you'd call it snobbery! And after what Lady Birchwood said about him only being a younger son with no prospects and then how angry she became over the way Susannah favoured Lieutenant Minter, for a moment there, I almost believed him.'

Almost. But he was glad to see she was too intelligent to be taken in by a plausible rogue for very long.

'But it is because,' she said, 'he is addicted to gambling, then, isn't it?'

Not altogether, no, but he wasn't about to go into the other, more unsavoury aspects of the man's character he'd learned from asking around.

'Lady Birchwood,' he said, 'may dislike the notion of a union with Lieutenant Minter, but I would never forbid the match to such a man, if Susannah really felt something for him. I might try to warn *him* what *he* was getting into...'

'Susannah isn't as bad as you are making her sound,' she said with indignation. 'She may be spoiled and selfish, but she doesn't have a malicious nature. She would never set out to hurt someone deliberately, for fun, the way I've heard many society misses do. And when I pointed out that she ought not to toy with the Lieutenant, if she really couldn't see herself falling in love with him, she said she was going to stop encouraging him. Which she'd only been doing to annoy Lady Birchwood, you know. She had no idea the man was truly smitten.'

'Yet I saw her, not an hour ago, sitting up beside him in a curricle, going round Hyde Park, chattering away like a magpie, while he was gazing at her with such adoration I was surprised the horses didn't stray on to the verge.'

'Oh, dear. She said she was going to tell him that she couldn't return his feelings during this drive.'

'Perhaps,' he suggested, seeing her distress, 'she hadn't quite got round to it yet when I saw them.'

She sighed. 'Or perhaps she was enjoying herself too much to remember that she was supposed to be letting him down gently.'

'Were you,' he couldn't resist asking, 'tempted by Mr Baxter's offer? At all?'

She snorted with indignation. 'Absolutely not! Apart from anything else—' She stopped short, looking rather guilty.

'Please continue. You cannot leave me in suspense.' And he was pretty certain that he'd find whatever it was she'd hesitated to tell him vastly entertaining.

'Well,' she said grudgingly, 'it occurred to me that even if I had gone along with his plan, there was no guarantee that he would actually part with the unspecified sum of money he offered me. He is the sort of man who would say anything to get what he wanted. And then go back on his word without suffering a qualm.'

He couldn't help it. He burst out laughing. 'You are priceless, Miss Hinchcliffe!'

She drew herself up in her chair and attempted to look down her nose at him. 'If you are suggesting that, had he offered me a cast-iron contract, signed and witnessed by lawyers, I might have gone into partnership with him, you are very much mistaken. And it was only *after* I'd turned him down,' she added triumphantly, 'that I thought of how unlikely it was he would share any of the prize winnings, as he called them, with anyone, let alone me.'

'I beg your pardon,' he said, with a grin. 'But it is rather difficult to take you all that seriously when you are sprawled in that chair with a glass of brandy in your hand. In the middle of the afternoon.'

She glanced down at the glass in her hand as though only just noticing it.

'Well, you were the one who gave it to me,' she pointed out.

'Guilty as charged. But in my defence, you did look as though you needed some sort of…er…medicinal comfort. And also…'

'Now *you* must continue, if you please. It is not gentlemanly to leave a person in suspense, after dangling the hint of a confession in their ears.'

'Touché!' He flung up one hand in the gesture of a fencer, acknowledging a hit. 'It seems to me,' he added, 'that we bring out the worst in each other.'

Her face fell. She bent down to place the almost untouched glass on the floor, then sat up straight, tucking her limbs away neatly.

He could have kicked himself for blundering so badly.

'I didn't mean that the way it must have sounded,' he said.

She raised one eyebrow in a most quelling manner.

'No. I mean,' he said, feeling his cheeks heat, 'that just lately, whenever we get together, it feels as though I can be, well, *me*. The me I was before I became the Marquess of Caldicot, that is.' He ran his hand round the back of his neck. 'Before I had to conform to what society expects of me.'

She tilted her head to one side, as though considering his words. 'I see,' she said, giving a small nod, 'in part. Although I fail to see why you should behave in any other manner than you always have done, merely because you have inherited a title.'

'Oh, don't you?' He pushed himself off the desk and paced to the window. Leaned against the frame and glared out on to the view of the back terrace, beyond which lay the ornamental lawn and the path leading to the mews.

He heard her sigh. 'No, that isn't completely true. Not true at all. I know exactly why you put on…manners, like a suit of armour, whenever you are in the company of certain people.'

He whirled round, startled by the accuracy of her description.

'I do it myself,' she admitted, ruefully. 'Well, in my position, I have to. I mean, nobody would hire a governess unless they believed she was the epitome of discipline and etiquette, would they?'

It was why he'd hired her, in the first place, he recalled. Because with that nose, and those brows, she looked so stern. Like the kind of person who could bring some discipline into the life of his wayward, spoiled ward.

'And aren't you?'

'I am afraid not,' she said with a wistful smile. 'As well you know,' she added, glancing down at the half-empty tumbler at her feet.

'Let's make a bargain,' he said, turning to face her fully. 'Oh, not the kind that Baxter attempted to make,' he added quickly when he saw a suspicious look cross her face. 'I mean, let us promise each other to always just be…ourselves, when we are alone together. No pretence. No manners—'

'You mean you want me to be rude to you?'

'Well, yes, if I deserve it. Actually,' he said, a smile tugging at his lips, 'you already are, aren't you? Perhaps that is why I like you so much.'

Her cheeks went pink. 'Well,' she said, 'I don't think I can do otherwise, anyway. For some reason, as you said before, you do bring out the worst in me. Whenever we are alone, since the night I thought I'd killed Mr Baxter, I don't manage to behave with the slightest bit of propriety at all!'

All of a sudden a vision sprang to his mind of Miss Hinchcliffe behaving with the sort of impropriety which he was certain she'd never imagined. And everything in him strained towards her.

But that would not do. If he were to yield to the impulse to haul her out of the chair and kiss her, she'd slap his face. And he'd destroy all the camaraderie which, so far, they'd enjoyed during the course of their unorthodox friendship.

Besides, she was in his employ. Living under his roof. Only a seedy sort of cove would take advantage of a woman under his protection in that fashion. What was more, Susannah needed her. Not one of his predecessor's haughty sisters had stood by her, the way this plucky governess had. Not one of them had won her trust, to the extent that she'd begged to have her stay on rather than demand her dismissal, the way she apparently had with so many others.

'You know,' she said, with a slightly lopsided smile, 'I find that this is a bargain I am only too happy to shake on.' She stood up and held out her hand.

Bargain? Oh, yes, she'd promised to always be herself with him.

He extended his hand, too, and she shook it in a brisk, no-nonsense way. Which was just typical of her. And was, in part, why he liked her so much.

But already, only moments after suggesting the deal, he was regretting he'd suggested it. Because how the devil could he tell her that, out of all the women he'd met since coming to town on the pretext of searching for a wife, she was the first, nay the *only* one, he'd wanted to sweep into his arms and kiss senseless?

Chapter Fourteen

Rosalind knew she shouldn't feel insulted by the way Lord Caldicot suddenly started to attend balls whether she was going or not. He was looking for a suitable bride, wasn't he? But she couldn't help worrying that he no longer trusted her to keep Susannah safe. Did he know about Lady Birchwood's list? Was he watching to make sure she didn't allow any of the men on it to dance with Susannah?

Or hadn't he believed her when she said she'd turned down Mr Baxter's offer of money? When she'd told him about it, he *had* asked her if she was tempted and had then appeared satisfied by her denial. But if he believed it, then why was he... *watching* her? With that strange, irritated look in his eyes?

Not that he looked at her that way if he thought she might notice. But she caught it several times when she looked up suddenly, before he could rearrange his features into a calmer, less perturbed pattern.

But then didn't she do much the same? Follow him round the ballroom, or drawing room, or supper room, with her own eyes? Although in her case, it was yearning, and hurt that she had to try to keep from showing in her expression.

Oh, if only she wasn't merely a governess. If only she could hope he might ask her to dance, the way he asked so many younger, prettier, *eligible* females to dance. Or if only she didn't have to sit on the sidelines, watching while he selected his bride, if that was what he was doing. He certainly never looked as if he was really enjoying himself with any of his dance partners. She never saw him grin at any of them the way he did at her when they were chatting. Come to think of it, she never saw him chatting with any of them, either before, or during the dance. If she could discern any emotion at all, she would say it was boredom.

'Miss Hinchcliffe,' said a deep, hoarse voice at her ear, startling her out of her brown study.

She looked up, to see Lieutenant Minter hovering at her side. She felt an immediate pang of sympathy for a fellow sufferer of unrequited longing. His case must be very much worse than hers, though, because Susannah kept on giving him cause to hope, even though she'd said she'd explained that he must not. Whereas Rosalind knew there was *no* hope for her, unless one morning Lord Caldicot woke up and decided that she was the only woman for him.

Which would only happen if he suffered some sort of seizure during the night that rendered him both stupid and half-blind.

'Yes,' she said, in as friendly a tone as she could, considering how low she felt, 'Lieutenant?'

'May I have your permission to take Susannah out on to the terrace for some air? She appears to be…rather out of sorts tonight and I thought a stroll in the moonlight might…' He petered out, his cheeks flushing.

'That won't make her change her mind about you, you know,' she couldn't help warning him.

To do Susannah justice, when she'd returned from that curricle ride, she'd told Rosalind that she *had* told the Lieutenant that she'd only singled him out for attention in a spirit of rebellion, merely because her aunt had forbidden her to have anything to do with him. And had apologised for treating him so shabbily. 'But do you know what,' Susannah had said, looking a bit perplexed, 'instead of taking umbrage and walking away, he said that my honesty and penitence made him admire me even more!'

'Even if I may never win her heart,' the poor besotted young man was now saying to Rosalind, 'I can at least be there for her, when she needs...a friend.'

Oh, yes! That was just how she felt about Lord Caldicot. That she would rather suffer hurt while watching him look for a suitable bride than risk offending him by pointing out that none of the girls he danced with were likely to make him happy, not if they all made him look so bored.

'And,' Lieutenant Minter continued, 'since a friend is all I can hope to be, or would ever be permitted to be by her family, I would like to ask if you would accompany us outside as well. So that she may be easy that I have no intention of trying to declare love to her, or anything she wouldn't like.'

She had half a mind to tell him that the more faithful he was, the less Susannah respected him. That the girl seemed to have started regarding him in the light of a sort of devoted hound.

No, perhaps that was being unfair. Susannah had said that at least the Lieutenant listened to her, rather than trying to impress her with a lot of idle boasting, the way so many other young men did. That she felt comfortable with him. That she could be herself, rather than having to remember all the rules there were about how girls were supposed to behave around eligible men. Which, she'd said, her hands clasped to her bosom, was very hard to do when her heart already belonged to Cecil Baxter.

Rosalind sighed. 'I shall go and fetch my shawl,' she said. 'But I warn you, Susannah won't like having me spoiling your tête-à-tête.'

'That is a risk,' he said with a grin, 'that I am prepared to take.'

She went to fetch her shawl and was just making for the terrace doors when Lord Caldicot came bearing down on her.

'Where,' he demanded, 'do you think you are going?'

'Outside,' she replied, wondering what was making him so cross with her all the time. 'To chaperon Susannah and Lieutenant Minter,' she added, before he had the chance to remind her that she had no business going outside for a stroll for her own enjoyment, in case that was what he suspected her of doing.

He gave a brisk nod. 'It *is* stuffy in the ballroom. A breath

of fresh air is just what I need, too.' And then he moved so that
he was in step with her and crooked his arm for her to take.

'I am perfectly capable of keeping an eye on them,' she said,
stung by what appeared to be yet more evidence that he no longer trusted her capabilities.

'I don't doubt it,' he said. 'Nevertheless, I wish to go outside. As I said, I need some air that doesn't stink of stale per-
fume and hypocrisy.'

Well, that was a bit of a surprise.

'You don't...that is,' she amended, as she laid her hand on
his sleeve, 'you are not enjoying this ball?'

He snorted by way of response as he pushed open the terrace door. 'I don't enjoy balls at all. Any of them. At least...'
he mused as they turned to the right and began to stroll along
the paved area running the entire length of Birkbeck House,
'I haven't enjoyed one since I've become the Marquess of Caldicot.'

Strange...he pronounced his title as though it was something unpleasant.

'Um... Would you mind me asking why that is?'

They walked a few steps before he said anything. 'There
they are,' he said, pointing to a couple partially concealed by a
gigantic urn, apparently deep in conversation.

She supposed she had to accept that for some reason Lord
Caldicot didn't want to tell her why he didn't enjoy balls, since
he'd changed the subject so emphatically. But at least she had
reason to hope that perhaps he wasn't looking so cross all the
time because of anything she'd done. That he was just...cross.

'We had better not go too much further,' she said, feeling far
less unhappy than she had for some time, now that she knew
it wasn't entirely her fault he was looking so glum lately. 'We
don't want them to think that we are attempting to eavesdrop
on their conversation.'

'Don't we?' He gave her an indecipherable look. Of course,
that might have just been because it was rather dark out here,
in spite of the light spilling out from the ballroom windows and
the addition of strategically placed torches along the terrace.

'In my opinion,' he said, 'that girl needs to know that we

aren't going to let her get away with whatever scheme she's trying to entrap that poor defenceless young man into.'

She examined the way the couple were standing, and the gestures Susannah was making, and agreed that it did look as though she might be trying to persuade the Lieutenant to take part in some sort of scheme. For he had his arms folded across his chest and, though his face was in shadow, she could tell, from the angle of his head, that he was probably frowning.

'Nevertheless,' she said firmly, 'we are not going to approach one step closer.' To add weight to what she'd said, she removed her hand from his sleeve and turned as though to look out over the gardens.

'Why not, you infuriating creature?'

For some reason, the informality of the way he addressed her made any last, lingering worries that he was cross with her, or disappointed in her, take flight. 'Because,' she explained, 'if we don't allow her the illusion of privacy, then she is the kind of enterprising girl who will begin to devise ways of ensuring she really gets it. And then we wouldn't have a clue where she is or what she's up to.'

'Hmm,' he said thoughtfully, turning to stand next to her, but facing the house rather than the darkened gardens. 'That, I suspect, is how she became close enough to Baxter to receive a marriage proposal. Because when I asked Lady Birchwood about how she allowed her to associate with undesirables, she... well, after bursting into tears and having the vapours, and uttering a series of implausible excuses about what a good family he comes from,' he said with disgust, 'admitted that she'd had no idea Susannah had even been introduced to the rogue.'

Rosalind spread her hands wide, as though to say, *Exactly.*

He said nothing. Only folded his arms across his chest and heaved a sigh.

It was strange, but as they stood there, side by side, one facing the garden, and the other the house, she could almost imagine a kind of...well, not precisely a romantic atmosphere. She would have to be the kind of girl who believed in fairy tales to even begin to think that just because they were standing next to each other, in the darkness, with music playing in the background and the scent of roses and rosemary drifting lazily in the air, that *he* would be thinking anything romantic.

She also rather thought that she'd have to be able to see some stars, to create such an illusion. Or even a sliver of moon. But she could see neither, since clouds completely blanketed the sky. The best she could hope to claim, could *ever* hope to claim existed between them, was a sort of companionship. Not even true friendship, since their stations in life were so very far apart.

'What the devil,' he said, shattering the stillness in which she'd been basking, 'can you possibly be looking at so intently out there?' He turned to peer into the shadows cloaking what by day would probably be a very well-maintained area of grass and shrubbery, to judge from the hints of fragrance she could detect whenever the breeze blew.

'Um…' She glanced up at him. At the perplexed frown knitting his brows. At the aggressive slant of his shoulders. And remembered her promise to be honest with him. 'I wasn't *looking* at anything. I was just thinking…wondering…well,' she said, taking the plunge, 'worrying, actually, whether you'd stopped trusting me, since I told you about you-know-who offering me money to make it easier for him to get to you-know-who,' she finished saying, jerking her head in Susannah's direction.

'Whatever gave you that idea?'

'Well, because you have suddenly started attending balls, even on evenings when it has not been your turn. Even though I am there. As though…'

'It is most emphatically not because I don't trust you. Far from it!'

'Oh?'

He shuffled his feet. Looked down at them as though he couldn't fathom what they might be doing. Then gave a half-shrug. 'Well, you know, I am supposed to be finding myself a wife, am I not?'

Yes. That was just what she'd been telling herself, earlier.

'And this is the sort of event where one is supposed to be able to find one.' He raised his head and glared at the glittering wall of windows, through which he must be able to see the other guests dancing to the music she could hear.

'Oh.' Her heart sank. It ought not to have done. She ought to have been relieved to hear that he hadn't stopped trusting her. That he didn't feel obliged to check up on her.

Yet hearing that the change in his routine was all because he was trying harder to find a wife...

'Yes, I see,' she said. She was such an idiot. To think that not five minutes ago, she'd been pitying Lieutenant Minter for having some hope and congratulating herself for being sensible enough to know she had none. When all the time it looked as though, deep down, there must have been a tiny ember, stubbornly refusing to go out, because hearing him remind her that he was looking for a bride had felt as though he'd doused it with a bucket of icy water.

'Everyone keeps telling me,' he said gloomily, 'that it is one of the most important of my duties, now that I am a marquess. To marry and start filling the nursery. And having some woman, some properly reared girl, who would know how to do it, to act as hostess for all the...political meetings I am supposed to be hosting. To run all the properties for which I'm now responsible.' He kicked moodily at something by his foot.

'You don't sound,' she said, her foolish heart picking up speed, 'as though it is something you really want to do...'

'That is putting it mildly,' he said, turning his back on the house to gaze out across the darkened gardens with her. 'But the fact is,' he said, gripping the balustrade, which had the effect of making his shoulders hunch, 'that without a partner who... has been brought up to live at that kind of level, I...' He swallowed. 'I don't think I will be able to do it.'

'Do what?'

'Be a marquess,' he said through gritted teeth.

'But you *are* a marquess,' she pointed out.

'Only because my cousin didn't manage to marry again and beget his own heir after Susannah's mother died. Which is why all his sisters keep saying I need to stop hesitating and come up to scratch. Not to let some distant relation, who is even less worthy than I, take over if something should happen to me...'

She gazed up at him in astonishment.

'*Less* worthy? Oh, that means…' She felt herself swelling with rage. 'Who has dared to tell you that you are not worthy?'

He glanced down at her, his lips quirking in amusement. 'I don't think I should tell you. By the sound of it, you might go charging round there with a hefty book in your hand and give 'em what for.'

'I hit *one* man with a book and you seem to think I do nothing but go round whacking people!'

'Two books.'

'Nevertheless, that does not change the fact that whoever told you that you aren't worthy to hold your title needs a sharp set-down!'

'It wasn't only one of 'em,' he said, his brief flash of humour fading. 'The whole family thinks it.'

'But…*why*?'

He ran his fingers through his hair. 'Well, probably because they know me much better than you. They knew me when I was a wild boy, rampaging all over the estates I'm now responsible for protecting from youths like I was. And don't forget, rather than coming home and knuckling down when I inherited the title, I stayed with my regiment, rampaging all over the Continent *enjoying myself.*'

'And how, exactly,' she asked, looking rather puzzled, 'did you *enjoy yourself* while fighting for your country?'

'Well, to start with, I used some of the money I'd inherited to buy a promotion.'

'Because…you thought you could do a better job than your superiors?'

'Yes, by God! Although that's not saying much when you think of the shambles that was John Moore's retreat to Corunna.'

'It sounds to *me* as though your heart was set on defeating Napoleon. An enemy of our country. As though you regarded abandoning your regiment as a dereliction of duty. As though duty to your country, and your comrades, trumped duty to your family,' she said, burning with indignation that he should have had to contend with that sort of criticism. 'Besides, even though you didn't come home, you made arrangements for your ward, Susannah, and all your properties to be taken care of in your absence. I mean, I haven't heard that they've all gone to rack and ruin, or anything like.'

'No, well, I have good, experienced men overseeing everything. The credit for which can be laid firmly at my deceased cousin's door. He left things in such good heart that I didn't feel as though, even if I did come back, I would make any difference. So what would have been the point? Then again, nobody ever dreamed I'd inherit anything, least of all me. So I didn't have any training in land management. Or wielding influence in political circles.'

'But you were in charge of men when you were in the army, weren't you? In the midst of war. Surely that was at times harder than running estates that are prosperous and thriving?'

'I told you. I have no training...'

'On the contrary, you have had plenty of training. You have experience in leading men. Which is what, by the sound of it, you still need to do with the ones put in place by your late cousin. You don't need to do their jobs for them.'

'Indeed, I couldn't if I wanted to.'

'Oh, stop harping on what you cannot do and think about what you can! If you want to make a difference, as you put it, I don't see any reason why you shouldn't. You have every right to make changes from the way your predecessor decreed things should be done. To have things done *your* way. I am certain you could inspire your employees to bring your vision of how things should be to fruition if you can lead men into battle.

'As for politics, well, if you have no ambition for yourself to rise through the ranks of any particular party and reach a position of power within government, then that leaves you free to vote according to your conscience on matters which really mean something to you. I wouldn't be a bit surprised if you didn't hold some very decided opinions when it comes to military matters and would enjoy weighing in behind, for instance, Lord Wellington.'

He turned so that he was facing her. 'In all the years since I've inherited, nobody has ever spoken to me with such...*sense*. All I've heard is that I cannot fill my cousin's shoes with any degree of success unless I change my ways. Settle down. Marry some...' He waved to the ballroom windows in a dismissive manner.

'Yes, and that's another thing,' she said. 'How old was Susannah when her mother died? Two? Three? And how old was she when her father died? Ten! In all that time, why do you suppose he never bothered to remarry, if it is so important to maintain the illustrious title of Caldicot? Why? Because he already had an heir. You! And if he didn't think it was imperative to father a son of his own, then *he* must have felt you *were* worthy to step into his shoes, mustn't he? What is more, if he was content to have you succeed him, then he should have jolly well made sure you had the training you feel you need!'

'Miss Hinchcliffe,' he said, taking hold of her shoulders and gazing into her eyes as though she was something...extraordinary. 'In a few short, pithy sentences, you have just blown all the arguments that have been flung at me about the extent of my failings and as to what my future plans should be to smithereens. Do you know,' he said, with a slow shake of his head. 'I could kiss you?'

He could...what?

Kiss?

Her?

Could he hear her heart pounding above the noise of the orchestra?

Could he feel her trembling?

Could he tell that she was hardly able to breathe for anticipation?

It would certainly explain the sudden change that came over his face.

Because of course he hadn't meant that he really wanted to kiss her. It had been a figure of speech. She'd just helped him to deal with a massive burden of self-doubt with which he'd been grappling ever since, by the sound of it, he'd unexpectedly inherited his lofty title.

And in that rush of relief, he'd said something he hadn't really meant.

How...mortifying that he must be able to tell that she'd taken him literally. Thank goodness it was so dark out here that he couldn't see the flush of shame that made her face feel as if it was on fire.

She took a hasty step back, before she could complete her humiliation by flinging herself on to his chest, or saying something like, *Go on, then, kiss me!* She moved so suddenly that his hands dropped from her shoulders.

He took a step back, too.

Then they just stood there. She, looking at the stone flags beneath her feet, and he, she rather thought, anywhere but at her.

She didn't know how long they might have stood there, neither of them knowing how to deal with their mutual embarrassment, had not Susannah and Lieutenant Minter come sauntering over, arm in arm.

'Oh, Miss Hinchcliffe,' said the Lieutenant, 'there you are. We could not see you for a moment...'

'Lurking behind the planter,' put in Susannah mischievously.

'We were not lurking,' said Lord Caldicot, irritably, 'behind anything.'

For the first time Rosalind noticed that they were, indeed, standing in the lee of another of those large urns containing trailing plants, which would have partially concealed them from the younger couple.

Oh...no! She glanced up at Lord Caldicot. Could he possibly suspect that she'd had an ulterior motive for choosing to stand just here, other than it being a matter of chance? Could he think she'd deliberately...enticed him there, in an attempt to force some sort of intimacy that might result in a kiss?

'I... I...' she said, wondering how to explain herself without coming across as a complete zany.

'No need to counter Susannah's ridiculous remark, Miss Hinchcliffe,' Lord Caldicot said sternly. 'Just because she chooses to lurk behind planters does not mean that every other person who has come out here to take the air would do the same.'

Rosalind glanced swiftly along the length of the terrace, at the other couples who were outside. A few of them were strolling along. But the ones who'd chosen to stop had all done so in the shelter of one of the urns. As though they were deliberately seeking whatever slim chance of privacy they could find.

Her heart sank further.

'And as for you, Susannah,' Lord Caldicot continued, 'can you not see you have put the poor woman to the blush?'

Susannah sighed. 'I beg your pardon, Miss Hinchcliffe. I was just teasing,' she said, coming up to her and putting one slender arm round her waist.

'Lieutenant,' said Susannah, over her shoulder. 'Why don't you cheer Miss Hinchcliffe up by asking her to dance? It sounds as if the current set is winding down, so there will be plenty of time to join the next. And I'm sure it must be very dull for her to have to trail about after me all evening and never having any fun herself.'

On the one hand, that sounded as though Susannah was making a very kind offer to make up for embarrassing Rosalind.

On the other hand, it could mean she wanted to make sure Rosalind was occupied, which would enable her to embark on some scheme or other.

'That,' said Lord Caldicot, before she could say something that would both express her thanks at what sounded like a kind offer, while making some solid excuse for why she could not possibly accept, 'sounds like a capital idea. Although...' he added, turning to Lieutenant Minter, 'I am sure that this young fellow would far rather dance with you, Susannah.'

'B-But,' stammered the young man. 'I thought that her family, that is to say you, disapproved of me.'

Lord Caldicot shrugged. '*I* have never had any objection to you, Lieutenant. And if you have any trouble from your aunt about this,' he said to Susannah, 'you may tell her that I engineered the situation with such fiendish cunning that you found yourself unable to wriggle out of dancing with him.'

'Oh.' Susannah stared at him wide-eyed. 'But...what about Miss Hinchcliffe?'

'Don't you worry about Miss Hinchcliffe. I shall take care of her myself.'

'You mean,' said Susannah, in surprise, '*you* are going to ask her to dance?'

No. That was not what he'd meant. Rosalind was sure of it. He was going to come up with some stratagem that would mean she'd be able to keep an eye on Susannah, and foil whatever scheme she'd been plotting.

'Of course,' said Lord Caldicot, 'I shall ask her to dance.'

He was? Oh! Her heart soared.

'Because I have no intention,' said Lord Caldicot to Susannah, drily, 'of permitting you to outdo me when it comes to scandalising your aunt.'

Her heart sank.

Of course. He was going to take her out on to the dance floor to divert Lady Birchwood's attention from Susannah's misdemeanour. And also shield her from censure. Because of course Rosalind could hardly forbid Susannah from dancing with Lieutenant Minter when Lord Caldicot had engineered it.

'And nothing, I am certain,' said Lord Caldicot, a slow smile spreading across his face, 'would scandalise her more than seeing me escort your lowly governess on to the dance floor in the face of all the ladies she considers more worthy.'

Which also made total sense. He was so sick of hearing how unworthy he was, and of being badgered into selecting a bride who would somehow make up for all his supposed defects, that she couldn't blame him for rebelling. With the most inappropriate woman in the ballroom.

'Lord Caldicot,' said Susannah, giving him an impish grin, 'if you carry on like this, I might one day be able to quite like you.'

He chuckled. Which made him look all the more appealing. And, oh, what did it matter why, precisely, he'd decided to dance with her tonight? That it wasn't really, truly romantic. The fact was that he had done so.

It was a dream come true. A legitimate opportunity to be closer to him. Even if only for half an hour.

And no matter how it had come about, or what his motives might be, she was going to seize her moment, with both hands.

Chapter Fifteen

Miss Hinchcliffe didn't look totally happy about the way he'd arranged things. In fact, he'd go so far as to say she had an air of grim determination about her as she laid her hand on his sleeve and began walking back to the ballroom.

Thank goodness he hadn't forgotten himself so much as to yield to that wild impulse to lean in and kiss her just now, then. Just imagine how she'd have reacted to *that*!

She didn't have any books to hand with which to...*whack* him, though. Would she, he wondered, have used her fists to express her outrage?

She would have had every right to do so. As her employer, he ought to behave with more...decorum. Only, whenever he got anywhere near her, decorum seemed to fly out of the window. Made him revert to the way he'd behaved before he became a marquess.

Made him feel like *himself*.

Although there was more to it than that, wasn't there? More than just...a feeling that he needn't pretend to be something he was not. She made him... He felt a frown furrow his brows as they reached the door to the ballroom.

She made him behave like a jealous lover, that's what she'd done tonight. When he'd thought she'd been about to go outside with that idiot boy, after he'd been leaning in and murmuring in her ear, he'd been so incensed that he'd stormed over and accosted her before she could get outside to take part in any sort of assignation.

Assignation? With the lovelorn Lieutenant? How could he have suspected any such thing? The boy only had eyes for his irritating ward, Susannah.

And as for Miss Hinchcliffe... He gave her a swift appraisal out of the corner of his eye, as she walked beside him, the picture of propriety. She would have been astonished had he told her what he'd thought. Astonished to think any man would take that sort of notice of her.

She genuinely had no idea how appealing she was. No idea that she stood out like a rose amid a field of cabbages, whenever she sat down on the bench with the other ladies performing the duties of chaperon. For though Susannah had crowned her with the dreaded dowager's turban, she'd also gowned her in materials and colours which served as a reminder to everyone how very young she truly was.

And the other dowagers resented her for it. He could tell from the way they eyed her askance and began gossiping among themselves in a way that excluded her. Every time he'd seen her sitting there, on that bench, with the older women who made such a point of snubbing her, he'd wished she could have a chance to get out on the dance floor and enjoy herself, instead of just watching the other young ladies.

The dowagers began elbowing each other and muttering to one another as he led Miss Hinchcliffe past them and on to the dance floor. It made him wonder if he'd done the right thing by compelling her to dance with him. She was going to pay for it later, by the looks of it. Society was full of the kind of women who delighted in tearing the weaker among them to shreds.

Not that anyone could describe Miss Hinchcliffe as weak. She'd survive whatever women such as those could throw at her. He was certain.

For one thing, she could claim, with total honesty, that had any other man ever invited her to dance, she would have refused.

She took her duties to Susannah too seriously to do anything as selfish as enjoy herself.

Unlike Lady Birchwood, who never did more than pay lip service to duty, before going off to gossip with her cronies, or play them for pin money in the card room. It had become increasingly clear to him, as the weeks went by, that the reason Lady Birchwood had been so keen to preside over Susannah's debut had less to do with any real fondness for her niece than because she'd wanted someone else to fund her own time in London. He didn't think her widow's jointure had left her uncomfortably off, financially, but she was certainly making the most of having the right to hang off his coat tails.

Whereas Miss Hinchcliffe played everything by the book. She'd only yielded to the opportunity to dance because he was her employer. And hadn't invited her so much as given her an order to do so.

He was jolly glad of the distraction created by walking on to the floor to join another two couples and making up a full set, because had Miss Hinchcliffe had the leisure to look at him too closely he was pretty certain she'd be able to tell that he was weltering in a slew of conflicting emotions.

For one thing, he'd lied to her, after promising that they'd always tell each other the truth.

But somehow, he just hadn't been able to admit that the reason he was attending far more balls than he needed to was entirely down to the fact that when she went out in the evenings, he...*fretted*. That was the word. He'd sit alone in his study, considering all the events to which he'd been invited, rejecting one after the other, knowing he would not enjoy any of them if she weren't there.

London wasn't so bad during the daytime. He could box at Gentleman Jackson's, fence at Angelo's, ride out on horseback, or drive his new team out as far as Richmond, if he wished. He could even enjoy the company of a woman, to judge from the lures that had been cast his way. The trouble was, none of the women who'd offered had tempted him for more than a moment or two. Either they laughed too often, or they couldn't respond with a swift put-down when he said something stupid. Or their eyebrows weren't full enough, or their noses were too small...

And when evening fell...

His eyes turned to her. The source of so much of his present turmoil. She was looking a little unsure of herself, he noted, now they'd formed an eightsome.

'I hope,' he said, thrusting his own dilemma aside as he bowed over her hand, 'that you have plenty of pins fastening your headgear on securely.'

Her hand flew, briefly, to her turban. Then she pursed her lips and shot him a look of annoyance. 'Thank you so much,' she said, as she swept him the requisite curtsy which heralded the opening figures of the dance, 'for giving me something *else* to worry about.'

He couldn't help chuckling at her quip. Oh, but it felt good to be with her, here, like this, even if he had been obliged to press her into dancing with him, under cover of...well, just under cover. She'd have been insulted, he would wager, if he admitted that he was here partly because he worried that the dowagers were being cruel to her. Or that Lady Birchwood was placing too much responsibility on her young shoulders, when it clearly needed at least two people to keep Susannah out of mischief.

No, that wasn't it, really, was it?

Was he lying to himself, now, as well as her?

The truth was that when she went out, he missed her. Simply missed her. He always wished he could be present at any event she attended, so that, even if he didn't get a chance to have any meaningful sort of discussion with her, he could at least *see* her. Even if, before tonight, he hadn't been able to come up with any scheme that would have broken down all her scruples and persuaded her to dance with him.

But far from looking as though she was currently suffering from the slightest twinge of guilty conscience at being his partner, she was clearly enjoying herself as she twirled round, retreated and clapped in time to the beat. She was still managing to hang on to her dignity, somehow, though, when so many other ladies he'd partnered could often resemble sad romps when performing a dance this energetic.

What a pity he hadn't timed it so that it was a waltz that had been starting up when they returned to the ballroom, he reflected, as he took her by both wrists to swing her round for the expected number of bars. For then he'd have had a legitimate excuse for keeping her in a hold for the entire dance, not just for the fleeting moments this particular country dance permitted.

For once he felt as if the musicians came to a halt all too soon, meaning all the couples in the set had to bow or curtsy to each other before leaving the floor.

Out of the corner of his eye he noticed the Lieutenant leading Susannah in the direction of the refreshment room. So he took the opportunity to stay close to Miss Hinchliffe by following suit.

'I am sure,' he said as he guided her into following the younger couple, 'you could do with a glass of lemonade after all that relentless hopping and twirling.' He paraphrased her earlier remarks about country dancing.

She looked up at him, her eyes sparkling. 'How thoughtful of you. I am quite sure your motives have nothing whatsoever to do with the fact that you do not wish to let Susannah and her partner out of your sight.'

'How could you suspect me of such a thing?' he asked with a grin.

She smiled back. But her smile dimmed as she caught sight of a wave of disapproving looks from the occupants of the various chaperons' benches.

'I fear,' he said, his conscience smarting, 'from the expressions on their faces, that you are going to pay for enjoying yourself this evening.'

'Much I care for anything they might say,' she retorted. 'And what can they do, other than talk?'

'You really are not angry with me for exposing you to possible censure?'

'Oh, no! Far from it. I have not enjoyed myself so much in an age. Besides, I can produce the defence that you compelled both Susannah and myself to do as you bid us. We are not responsible for your eccentricities, are we? It is for us to obey,' she said, lowering her head in a display of false meekness. And then ruining the effect by darting a look up at him that had a good deal of mirth in it.

'Nevertheless,' he said, 'Lady Birchwood will no doubt have the vapours when she hears what you both did. When, eventually,' he added drily, 'she emerges from the card room.'

'You need not worry,' she said in a reassuring tone. 'Her maid is an expert with the vinaigrette.'

'Yes, but her maid is not here.'

'Ah, but Her Ladyship won't indulge in the vapours while you are about, will she? She is bound to wait until she is safely home. With the trusty Throgmorton on hand to tend to her.'

He laughed. He couldn't help it. She had just summed up Lady Birchwood to a nicety. The woman knew that he would take no notice of her if she tried to play off her tricks. So she would, indeed, wait until she had a more responsive audience.

'But,' he added, 'don't let her bully you, will you? If she tries to do so, just refer her back to me.'

'But of course I will,' she replied, widening her eyes. 'Because it is, after all, entirely your fault!'

Chapter Sixteen

Rosalind floated through the next few days in cloud of something she'd never felt before in her life, but rather suspected was joy.

He'd danced with her.

Oh, only to annoy as many people as possible and to make a point about something or other, but that did not alter the fact that he'd done it. He'd taken her out on to the dance floor. And appeared to have enjoyed the experience. Why, she'd made him laugh out loud, when no other lady, from what she'd seen, managed to do anything but bore him. He'd given *no* sign that he was merely being kind to the poor, plain spinster governess, which was what some of the onlookers, those who had marriageable daughters, with ambitions to latch on to his title and wealth, chose to say about him.

The ones with nothing to lose said nothing bad about *him*, either. No, they chose to find fault with her instead. Saying that she was pushing, or brassy, and really quite ridiculous to think she could possibly interest a man of Lord Caldicot's calibre. Not to her face, since none of them ever deigned to actually talk to her, but loudly enough so that she would be sure to overhear.

And as for Lady Birchwood…oh, she'd been like a pot about to come to the boil all the way home from the ball. It had not been until they reached Kilburn House, as Rosalind had fore-warned Lord Caldicot, that she gave vent to her feelings.

'Have you,' she'd said to him, the moment they set foot in the hall, 'no sense of decorum? Or are you just ignorant of the kind of talk your behaviour tonight will have caused?'

'My behaviour?' Lord Caldicot had raised one eyebrow, then turned to hand his hat and gloves to Timms. 'I have been a model of propriety all evening.'

Susannah had made a noise that could have passed for a sneeze, but which was more likely to have been a stifled giggle.

'Not only,' Lady Birchwood had complained, 'did you cause speculation by partnering a mere governess in a set of dances, but worse, far worse, you permitted your ward to dance with a man who is completely ineligible in every way!'

'If you are speaking of Lieutenant Minter,' he'd said coldly, 'I have to inform you that I see no reason at all why Susannah should not dance with him. And further, it is a little late to make objections *after* the event.'

'Well, I couldn't say anything before, could I?'

'No,' he'd replied with a sarcastic smile. 'Because you were in the card room.'

Lady Birchwood had opened and closed her mouth a few times, but found nothing to say. Because the way he'd spoken had made it clear that he knew that if she really cared, she wouldn't be spending so much time in the card room, leaving the care of her niece in the hands of a paid employee.

His masterful set down had only silenced Lady Birchwood temporarily, though. The very next morning, she'd summoned Rosalind and Susannah to her room and, from the comfort of her bed and still crowned with her nightcap, let forth a stream of complaints. 'You both knew,' she said, 'that I frowned upon any association with Lieutenant Minter.'

'Yes,' Susannah had protested, 'but Lord Caldicot practically ordered me to dance with him.'

This retort had provoked a stream of reminiscences about times when Susannah had absolutely no qualms about disobeying orders from various members of her family.

'Yes, but,' Susannah had pointed out, 'Miss Hinchcliffe couldn't very well disobey him, could she?'

Lady Birchwood had flung herself back into the mound of pillows against which she'd been reclining, her mouth opening and closing again as words failed her. But, Rosalind suspected, clearly more furious about the whole episode than ever.

After a couple of days, during which Lady Birchwood had either made excuses for not coming to the dining table, or sitting there sighing and making use of her handkerchief to signify how upset she still was with them, Lord Caldicot took Rosalind aside and asked her how she was coping with the latest fit of the sulks.

Rosalind had shrugged. 'She will get over it, I am sure. And in the meantime, I can deal with her.'

'And Susannah?'

'Ah. Well, she *is* worrying me, rather.'

'I thought she seemed to be behaving rather better than usual.'

'Yes. Which is what is troubling me. Usually, if she is being docile, it means she is trying to lull me into a false sense of security, while she is hatching some scheme, only...'

'Only?'

'Well, I cannot put my finger on it, exactly. But if it weren't Susannah we were discussing, but some other, less spirited girl, I would describe her as...moping.'

'Or as though she's lost a shilling and found a farthing.'

'Yes! That's exactly it. And I very much fear...'

'What?'

'Well, I am wondering if she is pining for Mr Baxter.'

Lord Caldicot frowned. 'What, *still*?'

'You cannot expect her to give up on him just because he's playing least in sight, can you? A girl as stubborn as her? You know that she never gives up once she's got the bit between her teeth over some matter or other.'

Lord Caldicot sighed. 'Surely, by now, with all the other suitors clamouring for her attention and all the parties she attends...'

'No. A woman in love does not just forget the object of her affection if you dangle a shiny bauble in her face, you know. Once her heart is given, it remains true.'

She, for example, was never going to forget Lord Caldicot. The first man who had ever made her think about kisses in the moonlight. Though nothing could come of it, she'd never forget these precious, wonderful times when they spoke together as though they were almost equals. And especially not the evening when she'd danced with him, while every other female in the ballroom looked on with envy. Or at least, that was what it had felt like. It was what had enabled her to deal with the spiteful comments afterwards.

'Even though the fellow is not worth her devotion?'

'Well, they do say that love is blind, do they not?'

'It must be, in this case,' he snorted with derision. 'Either that, or the girl is an idiot.'

'I wonder...' she said.

'What do you wonder?'

'Well, if some of his allure isn't down to the fact that she cannot have him. That she has been forbidden to see him. I wonder if, had you allowed her to continue to see him, she might have seen through his smooth charm, to the snake he is inside.'

'May I remind you that it was not *I* who threw him out of a window? And put the fear of God into him?'

'You have freely admitted that you wished you had, though,' she retorted. 'But anyway,' she went on, having decided not to remind him that she hadn't *thrown* him out of the window and he jolly well knew it, 'as it is, she keeps on asking me where he can possibly be and why he hasn't made any attempt to see her. And does that mean he doesn't love her the way he said he did. Which makes me feel so...*guilty.*'

'Guilty? Why should you feel guilty? You have done that girl a true service in running off that bounder.'

'That's as may be. The fact is that I don't like seeing her so upset and not being able to tell her the truth. Which is that it's all my fault.'

'Oh, no, it isn't. If you hadn't broken a couple of his bones, I'd have come up with some way to see him off. In fact...' He pondered for a while. 'It wouldn't surprise me if he wasn't the sort of snivelling cur who would have been willing to have been bought off. If he'd seen that he had a real hold over Susannah and thought he could entice her into an elopement...'

'Yes. You are right. We have only done what we had to, to protect the poor girl. But... I just don't like seeing her so unhappy.'

'He would have made her unhappy no matter what steps we had taken, you know. Just think how much more she would have suffered had the affair continued to the point of marriage. She would soon have learned that he only cared about her money. And that, legally, she would have had little chance of escape. Or, supposing he had persuaded her to elope and she had to live with the disgrace. She enjoys being the belle of the ball too much to cope successfully with the way society would shun a girl who went that far astray.'

'Yes, you are right, of course. I must just keep reminding myself that I am doing what is best for her...'

'And I tell you what else. Any fellow who truly cared for her would try to win me round, by reforming his ways, or by showing his loyalty to her, even though his case was hopeless.'

'Like Lieutenant Minter?'

'Just like that. You wouldn't catch him climbing in through a girl's window, or steering clear of her whenever her disapproving guardian is about, would you? Or trying to strike a deal with her chaperon?'

Yes, it was a great pity Susannah didn't appreciate Minter's worth. Or find Lady Birchwood's aversion to him as tantalising as she'd found Lord Caldicot's aversion to Mr Baxter.

The thing was, though, now she'd spoken to Mr Baxter herself she could picture him putting on what she'd thought of as that spaniel face and doing his utmost to tug at Susannah's tender heartstrings. Whereas Lieutenant Minter, if put in a similar position, would square his shoulders, grit his teeth and generally behave like a gallant officer of His Majesty's navy.

She felt calmer about Susannah after that talk with Lord Caldicot. And, well, just happy for having that tête-à-tête with him. Even though they had not discussed anything personal between them, for of course there never could be anything of that nature between them, she basked in the feeling that he did trust her after all. Trusted her in a way he didn't seem to trust many other people. Certainly not females.

She was just congratulating herself for knowing that he, at least, approved of the way she was dealing with Susannah, and the whole Cecil Baxter episode, when Lady Birchwood summoned her to her room.

And ruined it all.

Chapter Seventeen

Michael had been spending a perfectly pleasant hour or so shooting wafers at Manton's gun range when he experienced one of those feelings he'd sometimes had just before walking into an enemy ambush. A sort of…not foreboding exactly, but as though he'd forgotten something. Or that there was something he should have noticed, taking place just out of the corner of his eye.

He looked round the gallery, but at this hour in the morning there were few other patrons. So it wasn't a literal ambush he had to worry about.

Probably.

He raised his arm to take another shot, but knew he would not take any more pleasure in practising his skill with that strange feeling nagging at him. Since it had saved his life, and that of his men, on several occasions, he'd learned to pay heed to it. And though he wasn't on reconnaissance on some barren gulley in the Pyrenees, he thought it was probably as important to pay attention in the refined atmosphere of London.

In the same way as he'd known he had to halt and take cover, when on active service, he knew he needed to lay down his pistol and return to base. That was where trouble was brewing. Now he came to think of it, there had been a distinct atmosphere at the breakfast table that morning. Though he couldn't pinpoint exactly what it was that was now making him feel he needed to return as soon as he could, he was going to trust his instincts. The worst that would happen, after all, was that he'd arrive to find absolutely nothing amiss. He'd feel like a bit of an idiot, and no harm done.

It didn't take long to walk there from Davis Street, and, as he rounded the corner into Grosvenor Square, it was to see the front door of Kilburn House open and Miss Hinchcliffe come striding out.

His lips were just starting to lift in a smile at the mere sight of her when he noted the case she was holding in one hand. A case he recognised, though this time there was no length of petticoat trailing from it. This time, it appeared she had taken her time to pack carefully.

Though why she should have taken it into her head to pack a case and leave, now, he couldn't imagine. She had no reason to leave, surely?

What was more, he was not going to permit her to do so. The very idea was…*abhorrent*. It was bad enough wondering where she would go and what would become of her when Susannah married and he'd no longer have any legitimate excuse to summon her to his study for a chat. But that day, he'd always thought, would be weeks away. Possibly months. He'd told himself he wouldn't need to worry about it until Susannah started to show a preference for one of her suitors. He certainly wasn't ready to face it today!

He strode out with even more urgency, reaching the foot of the front steps at the same time as she did.

'What,' he growled, leaning down and snatching the case from her gloved hand, 'is the meaning of this?'

She looked at him for a moment or two, her eyes welling up with an emotion that found an echo in his own heart, before replying.

'I should have thought,' she said, in a flat voice that didn't sound like her at all, 'it was obvious.'

'You are leaving me? I mean, leaving my employ? Is this such a bad post? I thought you were happy here.'

Her lower lip trembled. One tear spilled and ran down her cheek before she swiped it away, in a gesture that spoke to him of...defeat.

'I *have* been happy here,' she said, as a tear spilled from her other eye and ran down her other cheek.

'So why the devil are you running away?'

'I am not running away,' she protested.

He looked at the neatly tied bonnet, the coat buttons which were all fastened correctly, and realised that she had taken time over her appearance before walking out of the front door this time. As though she'd thought it all through and decided she'd had enough.

His heart plunged. The thought of enduring the rest of the Season without Miss Hinchcliffe around to make balls bearable by exchanging glances every now and then, or at musicales when someone failed to hit the right note...

The thought of enduring the rest of his life, in fact, without her...

'I won't allow it,' he said, taking her by the elbow.

'There is nothing you can do,' she said despondently. 'Lady Birchwood has made up her mind...'

'Lady Birchwood? What has she to do with this?'

Miss Hinchcliffe frowned up him, as though bewildered by the question. 'Why, it is she who has told me to leave. And...'

So she hadn't just decided to abandon him. That was, he hastily corrected himself, her duties as companion to his ward. She definitely didn't look as though she *wanted* to leave, either.

Good.

'Lady Birchwood has done what?' He'd expected her to be annoyed over the dance they'd all enjoyed at Birkbeck House. But he'd never dreamed the woman would go this far. For one thing, she had no right. 'How dare she? *I* am the one who hired you, who pays your wages. She has no right to turn you off!'

He tightened his grip on Miss Hinchcliffe's elbow, turned her round and marched her back up the steps once more. Timms opened the door to admit him so swiftly that Michael suspected he must have been standing on a chair, keeping an eye on proceedings through the fanlight.

'Lord Caldicot,' Miss Hinchcliffe protested, weakly, 'there is nothing you can do...'

'We'll soon see about that. Timms! Where might I find Lady Birchwood?'

'She is in the drawing room, having tea, My Lord.'

'Is she now?' He handed Miss Hinchcliffe's case to Timms. 'Have that taken back to Miss Hinchcliffe's room.'

'No!' Miss Hinchcliffe reached over and snatched it from the older man's hands. 'I will hang on to that, thank you. It is by no means certain that you will be able to persuade her to reinstate me.'

'She cannot reinstate you,' he argued, urging her up the stairs, 'since you have not been turned off. Not officially. Only *I* have the authority to do so.'

He thrust open the door to the drawing room and strode in, Miss Hinchcliffe's elbow still held firmly in his grip. Because, he found, he simply could not let go of her. No more than he could tamely let her go on Lady Birchwood's say-so.

She was, to his great annoyance, sitting on a sofa, calmly sipping tea and making inroads into a plate full of biscuits. Or scones. One could never be completely sure.

'What,' he growled, 'do you think you are about, my lady?'

She paused, a biscuit, yes, he'd give it the benefit of the doubt, halfway to her mouth, which hung open.

'I might well,' she said, rallying and adopting a forbidding air, 'ask you the same question. How dare you come in here incorrectly dressed?'

He was, he realised, still wearing his coat and hat. He'd been so angry and so determined to have things out with Lady Birchwood that he hadn't paused to take them off.

'And bringing,' Lady Birchwood continued, her nose wrinkling with disdain, 'that creature in with you?'

That creature?

'I have brought *Miss Hinchcliffe* in here,' he said, feeling as if he was hanging on to his temper by the merest thread, 'because I found her on the front steps, in some distress, telling me that you had so far forgotten yourself that you had taken it upon yourself to dismiss her. Without as much as consulting me!' To relieve his feelings, as much as to prevent the staff from overhearing the discussion, he kicked the door shut behind him.

'I suppose that is precisely the sort of behaviour I should have expected,' said Lady Birchwood with disdain, setting down her cup in its saucer, 'from a woman of her sort. Running off telling tales…'

'I only came across her by chance.' And thank heavens he'd listened to that prickle of premonition. If he'd shrugged it off and carried on testing out the new pistols he'd been thinking of purchasing, Miss Hinchcliffe would be heaven knew where by now. 'And the only thing she has told me is that you have had the audacity to dismiss her, without consulting me on the matter.'

'Surely the hiring and firing of female staff is in my remit, as your hostess in this house…'

'Yet I distinctly recall having to engage a companion for my ward, *myself*, because of your complete inability to choose one who had the nerve to remain in that post for more than a sennight.'

'That was years ago. And anyway…'

'You have no reason to dismiss Miss Hinchcliffe! She has not only been the only female with the backbone to stomach the kind of tantrums to which my ward has been allowed to indulge, but she has made positive progress. Before her advent, Susannah had no accomplishments, no manners. Now she not only manages to behave as prettily as any other well-born female when in company, but she can actually pick out a tune or two on a piano when occasion calls for it.'

At his side, he felt Miss Hinchcliffe attempting to tug her arm out of his hold. He supposed, if he deposited her on a chair and then took up a position by the door he'd kicked shut, she would not be able to escape.

So that was what he did. He led her to the sofa opposite Lady Birchwood's, made her sit on it, then went to the door to guard it.

'Nevertheless,' said Lady Birchwood, as Miss Hinchcliffe set her battered little case down at her feet, as though in readiness to snatch it up and run off with it at a moment's notice, 'I felt it my duty to remove this person from the house, with or without your consent. When I learned something…to her detriment.'

'What do you mean?' He leaned against the door and folded his arms across his chest, noting that Miss Hinchcliffe had bowed her head and that her cheeks were turning red.

'I have it on the best authority,' Lady Birchwood continued, darting Miss Hinchcliffe a disparaging glance, 'that she is prone to acts of violence.'

Good grief. Had someone seen her toss Baxter out of the window? No, they couldn't have. In fact, the only person who might have been able to tell Lady Birchwood anything about the events of that night was Baxter himself.

And he'd threatened Miss Hinchcliffe, hadn't he, when she'd refused to help him in his scheme to get his hands on Susannah's wealth? This was, by the sound of it, his notion of revenge.

'Someone has told you some fantastic tale,' he said witheringly, though his heart was beating rather fast, 'which they cannot possibly corroborate, and on that pretext you have taken it upon yourself to dismiss her?'

Someone, probably Baxter—yes, his money was on Baxter being behind this—must have handed her the excuse she'd been looking for ever since he'd danced with Miss Hinchcliffe at Birkbeck House. No, before that. She'd resented the way Susannah had insisted that the only way she would agree to having Lady Birchwood preside over her Season was if Miss Hinchcliffe stayed on and came to London with them. Lady Birchwood had argued in vain that Susannah no longer needed a governess. When Susannah made up her mind, nobody stood much chance of changing it.

And what he'd sensed over the breakfast table this morning, he perceived, had been the aroma of malevolent triumph, oozing from a woman who thought she was about to exact her revenge.

'On the contrary,' said Lady Birchwood, her own colour rising as her eyes flashed with anger, 'there are *several* persons who can corroborate the *tale*, as you deem to call it. You really should have looked into her references more closely.' She gave an arch little laugh. 'I mean to say, no person who spoke of a former employee in such glowing terms could possibly have wanted her to leave, could they?'

Her voice was rising to a squeal of such high pitch that it was a wonder she didn't set all the dogs in the neighbourhood to barking. 'And if you,' she said, jabbing one pudgy finger in his direction, 'had more experience in the hiring of governesses, or indeed, any at all, you would have smelled a rat at the time!'

That brought him up short. This wasn't about Miss Hinchcliffe ejecting Baxter from her bedroom window. She was referring to something that had happened before she'd ever come to work for him.

He turned to Miss Hinchcliffe slowly. She was hanging her head, biting down on her lower lip, her whole posture depicting a sort of defeated misery.

'Miss Hinchcliffe,' he said, his heart beating so fast now it was making him feel a bit sick, '*did* you gain employment with us by using false references?' If it was so, then she'd betrayed him. From the outset. And all the camaraderie that had sprung up between them, all the…affection he'd begun to feel for her, was all based on lies.

Chapter Eighteen

Rosalind couldn't bear the way he was looking at her. As though she'd betrayed him.

'Miss Hinchcliffe,' he said, in a rather cold voice, *'did* you gain employment with us by using false references?'

It was the way he put the emphasis on the word *did* that gave her the tiniest grain of hope. As though he didn't want to believe ill of her. As though he was hoping she could deny it. And so she lifted her head.

'No. Absolutely not.'

Lady Birchwood made a most undignified noise. If Susannah had made it, Rosalind would have accused her of snorting.

'Precisely what,' Lord Caldicot said coldly to Lady Birchwood, 'did you mean by that?'

'I have already told you,' she said, darting Rosalind a glance loaded with malevolence, 'that several persons can vouch for that creature,' she said, jabbing at her with the hand that was still clutching the thing that was masquerading as a biscuit, with the result that crumbs sprayed everywhere, 'who was dismissed from her last post for committing an act of violence!'

'You spoke,' he said in that same, cold, clipped tone, 'to these people, did you?'

'Well, no, not exactly. That is,' Lady Birchwood continued

when he raised one brow, 'I heard it from someone who has told me that there were several people who can corroborate the story.'

'So, in effect, you dismissed Miss Hinchcliffe on the basis of a rumour, repeated by one person, without checking with these other so-called witnesses.'

Oh. She could have hugged him. Because that was exactly what it had been like. Lady Birchwood had simply seized on the first excuse she could find to send her packing.

'May I ask who this person was?' said Lord Caldicot, his eyes turning cold and hard. 'Who related this absurd tale?'

'A most respectable person,' retorted Lady Birchwood. 'Who had it on the best authority...'

'Just as I thought,' he said drily. 'You listened to unsubstantiated gossip.'

'How dare you?' Lady Birchwood's jowls quivered with indignation. 'I did no such thing. I challenged Miss Hinchcliffe to give an account of herself and,' she concluded with triumph, 'she refused!'

He turned to regard her, solemnly. 'Is that true? Did you refuse to explain how such a rumour may have come about?'

Rosalind lowered her head and picked at a seam in her left glove with her right hand. Her bare right hand. Somewhere between the street, and this drawing room, she appeared to have lost her right glove.

'Miss Hinchcliffe,' he said. 'I am waiting for you to tell me what happened.'

Oh, how she wished she could tell him. But she'd made a promise. With a feeling of resignation, she lifted her head to look at him, probably for the last time. And this was not how she wanted to remember him, standing there, looking down at her so severely. She wanted to remember him laughing with her, talking to her as though their minds and thoughts matched. As though he respected her opinions and shared them. The man who'd asked her to dance and then looked as though he was thoroughly enjoying himself while he did so.

Had that version of him gone for ever?

'I cannot speak about it,' she said bleakly.

'Why not?'

To her relief, his voice was not harsh. He was not looking at her as though she'd committed some crime. He just looked... curious.

'Is it,' he persevered, gently, 'because you made a promise not to do so?'

'Yes! But how could you have known?'

He hadn't known. She could tell from the look of relief that wiped the lines of strain from his face. He'd *hoped* that it was something of the sort, that was what he'd done. He'd *hoped* she had a good reason for refusing to defend herself from Lady Birchwood's accusation and that was the only reason he had been able to come up with.

And it was the correct one.

'Miss Hinchcliffe,' he said, 'it is clear to me that nobody would have given you the kind of reference Lady Dorrington did had she dismissed you for committing some random act of violence. Besides, during the years you have been in my employ, you have proved yourself worthy of every encomium written in it.'

A little sob escaped her throat at this evidence of his faith in her. Because he knew very well that she did sometimes act before she'd thought things through. That she had caused Mr Baxter to fall out of a window and, more to the point, had hit him again when he'd accosted her in Hookham's library.

He could easily have believed whatever tale someone had told Lady Birchwood. Instead, he had brought her back into the house and given her a chance to defend herself.

'However,' he said, rather more sternly, 'for the sake of Lady Birchwood's nerves, I think it is time you put whatever promise you made aside, and tell us both, in confidence, what grounds your enemies have for spreading malicious gossip about you. Because it must be some enemy, must it not? Someone who wishes you ill and wants to see you humiliated?'

Oh. Yes, why hadn't she thought of that? As soon as he'd put the emphasis on the word *enemy*, her mind had flown back to Mr Baxter's threat that she'd be sorry she'd made an enemy of him.

But Lord Caldicot had recalled it at once. And seen this

whole episode for what it was. The attempt of a thwarted villain to exact his revenge.

'Pish!' Lady Birchwood threw the remnants of her biscuit back on to the plate. Which was probably the best place for it. 'A person of her sort doesn't make enemies. It is someone who is a true friend to our family who is warning us to beware of her, that is what this is!'

'Or someone who wishes to remove her, because she is doing such a sterling job of both guarding and advising Susannah. Have you forgotten,' he said, 'that you despaired of Susannah ever gaining any accomplishments before her Season? And how swiftly Miss Hinchcliffe persuaded her to practise at her piano? No other governess, nor any of her female relatives, was able to make her do anything she'd decided she didn't want to do, were they? In fact, I'd go so far as to say that nobody was able to as much as keep her in line, until I hired the redoubtable Miss Hinchcliffe.'

That was not a wise thing to say, to judge by the high colour which suddenly mottled Lady Birchwood's cheeks. It was a reminder that she'd failed to have any positive influence over her own niece whatsoever. That Susannah hadn't even wanted to go through her debut with only Lady Birchwood on whom to rely.

'Now, Miss Hinchcliffe,' he said in a rather more stern tone that he'd adopted during this interview so far, 'I really must insist that you tell us exactly why you left your former employ and how it came to be that you gave someone grounds for accusing you of acting in a reprehensible manner.'

She could refuse.

She could keep her promise to never speak of that day and just walk away, her conscience clear, knowing that he still had faith in her. That he'd perceived that this was the work of Mr Baxter, somehow.

Only, it would mean never seeing him again.

And she'd already spent most of this morning in an agony, believing that was exactly what was going to happen. She hadn't known how she would bear it. The pain of watching him cast his eye over prospective brides was as nothing compared to the prospect of never seeing him again. If there was a chance to prevent that happening, would it be so wrong to take it?

'I... I...'

'Look at her,' said Lady Birchwood scornfully. 'Struggling to come up with some story to excuse her behaviour!'

That did it. Before Rosalind could wrestle her conscience into submission, her temper flared, incinerating everything in its path, the way it so often did.

'I am not struggling to come up with a story,' she said indignantly, 'but with my conscience. It is not an easy thing to break my word, but now I come to think of it, somebody must have spoken out of turn, or you could not possibly have heard anything about my last day at Dorrington Hall. And we *both* promised. Both Lady Dorrington and I promised never to mention what her vile nephew had attempted to do to me...'

'Are you speaking, perchance,' put in Lord Caldicot, 'of Peregrine Fullerton?'

'Yes,' she said with loathing.

'Ah, yes,' he mused. 'I had forgotten the connection. Now it all begins to make sense.'

'What do you mean?' said Lady Birchwood querulously. 'What makes sense?'

'Only that Peregrine Fullerton has a reputation for being a... shall I say a rather unsavoury young man. Tell me,' he said to Rosalind, 'or rather, tell Lady Birchwood what he did, just to make things clear, although I have to say I have a pretty good idea.'

'It was my first post as a governess, you understand,' she said to Lord Caldicot, even though he'd urged her to explain to Lady Birchwood. But she no longer cared what Lady Birchwood thought of her. She didn't need to explain anything to her. She'd made an enemy of the woman the night she'd not only danced with Lord Caldicot, but aided and abetted Susannah to flout her authority by dancing with Lieutenant Minter.

No...actually...now Lord Caldicot had explained about the tension between the two of them, she could see that Lady Birchwood hadn't approved of her from the very moment she'd taken up the post as Susannah's governess. And that when they'd started making plans for Susannah's come out and Susannah had made her opinion of Lady Birchwood's dependability plain, in her typically heedless fashion, that disapproval had deepened into a dislike she'd been able to almost feel. And nothing she said or did was likely to change that.

But she did so want Lord Caldicot to hear it all. Even though he'd already reassured her that he had faith in her, she needed to...to confirm it. Oh, it was all so muddled in her head. Only one thing was clear. Whatever the outcome of this interview, she wanted to be able to look back on it, knowing she'd held nothing back from him.

'The family had young children, so were just beginning to need a governess rather than the education their nursery maids could provide. And I got the job through family influence, straight out of school. And I was...so *young*. So green.' She shook her head at how naive she'd been. She'd thought, because she was plain and bony, that no man would ever look at her in *that* way. And so she'd misunderstood the looks Peregrine had given her when he'd come to stay with his aunt and uncle. Had thought that he'd been mocking her.

'Which meant I hadn't taken sufficient care to stay safe. When he...erm...tried to take me in his arms, I was completely taken aback. And I acted on instinct. I...er...' She darted Lord Caldicot a look to see how he was taking it. To her surprise, she caught a look of what looked suspiciously like unholy glee before he swiftly straightened his face. Because he knew, or could guess, what was coming, the wretch!

'I punched him.'

'Where?'

'On the stairs. It wasn't even the back stairs, that was what shocked me so much...'

'No, I mean where, on his anatomy?'

'I don't see,' Lady Birchwood objected, 'what difference that makes.'

'I dare say it made a great deal of difference to *him*,' said Lord Caldicot. 'May I hope that it was somewhere particularly painful?'

'It was on the nose.'

'Oh,' he said, looking rather disappointed.

'But I rather think I broke it, because there was an awful lot of blood.'

'That's much better,' said Lord Caldicot with a nod of approval. 'And may we also deduce, since you were on the stairs at the time of the, er, altercation, that he fell down them?'

'Really!' Lady Birchwood was positively vibrating with disapproval. But Rosalind no longer cared. Because she could tell that Lord Caldicot was not in the least bit cross with her. That, on the contrary, he seemed to be enjoying hearing the story.

'Well, yes, he did tumble down an entire flight of stairs,' she said.

'Serve him right!' Lord Caldicot was actually grinning as he pictured the scene. 'Did he break anything else,' he enquired hopefully, 'on the way down?'

'No. He had a soft landing, you see. On the butler, who was hurrying up from the hall, to render, as he informed me later, what assistance he could.'

'That's a pity,' said Lord Caldicot, with a rueful shake of his head.

'Yes. For the butler's collarbone was broken. Peregrine was not what you would call a...a slender man.'

At that Lord Caldicot went off into a peal of laughter.

Which only served to inflame Lady Birchwood's sense of outrage even higher. 'This is no laughing matter! The fact is that after that...that outrageous display of...violence,' she said, shooting Rosalind a look of loathing, 'Lady Dorrington clearly had no alternative but to dismiss that creature, or heaven alone knows what kind of influence she would have had on her impressionable young offspring!'

'Actually,' Rosalind pointed out, 'Lady Dorrington did not dismiss me at all. It was I who *wanted* to leave. I found the whole thing very...'

'Yes, you must have done,' said Lord Caldicot, coming over to her sofa, sitting down next to her and taking her gloved hand in his.

Which sent Rosalind into a complete tizzy. For although it

was wonderful of him to display this kind of concern, it was only going to make Lady Birchwood even crosser.

'Everyone was, actually,' she said, keeping her gaze fixed on her hand, which he was now patting, as though to soothe her, 'very kind to me. A couple of the housemaids said they were glad to see him get his come-uppance. And when I left, they gave me all sorts of presents. Even the housekeeper packed me the most sumptuous hamper you could imagine, for my journey.'

'And the poor old butler?'

'Oh, he said it was a small price to pay. Particularly since Lord Dorrington gave him, so I understand, a huge amount of money, before sending him off to recover from his injury at Hastings, with a nurse in attendance and all expenses paid.'

'I am glad to hear it.'

'And when I sought another post, I deliberately looked for somewhere that there were no stray men lurking about the place. So, you see, no matter how much of a handful people keep telling me Susannah is, at least I have been...*safe* with her. From that sort of attention. Because she always stayed at Caldicot Dane and whichever of her aunts came to preside over the household, they never bothered bringing any of their husbands with them. Or encouraged unattached young men to visit. They were all, I suppose, looking out for her reputation, but I have to say it suited me very well.'

Lord Caldicot cleared his throat, hastily let go of her hand and stood up. Oh! Had he taken her statement as a hint he ought not to be holding her hand?

'And,' he said, once he'd removed to a suitably decorous distance from the sofa, 'the reference?'

'Well, you see, Lady Dorrington was terribly worried that if my grandfather ever got wind of the incident, he'd hunt Peregrine down and horsewhip him. I reassured her that she need not worry about Grandfather, because I never wished to have to speak to anyone about the whole sordid incident. And that prompted her to admit she'd feared I might demand some form of...compensation, or an inducement for keeping quiet, and she then became rather gushingly grateful that I didn't. So when she wrote that reference, she *may* have been in the sort of mood to, um, *exaggerate* my worth...'

'There! You see?' Lord Caldicot turned to Lady Birchwood. 'Miss Hinchcliffe did *not* leave that post under a cloud. If anything, the disgrace belonged to the family that had hired her and then failed to protect her from a man who is known to be a menace to females. No wonder they wanted to hush it all up.'

Lady Birchwood glowered at him. And then at her. Then harrumphed.

'I had no idea that Mr Fullerton was a menace to females,' she said, looking a little disconcerted. 'One can meet him anywhere!'

'That's as may be,' said Lord Caldicot, 'but chaps talk about him in the clubs. He's the kind of man that other men make sure to keep far away from their own daughters and sisters.'

'People should know about him, then,' objected Lady Birchwood. 'It makes no sense to keep that sort of information from ladies!'

'In general,' he said, 'the aim of most men is to make sure that their female relatives are shielded from any sort of unpleasantness. It is one of the reasons I decided I had to return to England once I heard Susannah was to make her come out. For the first time in her life, she really was in need of masculine protection. For the first time, there was something practical, as her guardian, I could do. Because there are many men of his ilk on the prowl for innocent females. Particularly females in possession of large fortunes. I wonder...' He gazed down at Rosalind for a moment or two.

'Lady Birchwood,' he said, turning to her as if he'd come to a decision. 'Rather than dismissing Miss Hinchcliffe, do you not think it would be better to use her experience to teach Susannah how to defend herself from predatory males?'

Lady Birchwood gaped at him. 'The very idea!'

'What?' said Lord Caldicot, smoothly. 'Do you think that females should remain helpless and unable to defend themselves when men of that ilk attempt to force their unwanted attentions on them? What if it had been Susannah, innocently walking down a flight of stairs, when some rake tried to push her into a corner and take liberties? Would you denounce *her* for punching said fellow on the nose? Or even pushing him down the stairs?'

'Well, that is a different matter,' said Lady Birchwood.

'Oh?' Lord Caldicot gave her a cold look. 'How, exactly?'

Lady Birchwood's mouth opened and closed a few times. It was, Rosalind thought, almost becoming a habit whenever she had to argue with Lord Caldicot.

'Do you think, because a woman is poor,' he said with a touch of disdain, 'she has no right to defend her virtue?'

Rosalind had the impression that was exactly what Lady Birchwood did think. Many of her class did. It was why all the housemaids at Dorrington Hall had been so glad when she'd punched the pernicious Peregrine and caused him to fall down the stairs. Because, for years, he'd been preying on them and nobody had done a single thing to stop him. Not Lady Dorrington, not Lord Dorrington, nobody.

'Very well,' said Lord Caldicot, turning to look at Rosalind, and clasping his hands behind his back. 'Not only will you *not* be leaving my employ, but as from tomorrow I would like you to start teaching my ward how to defend herself from importunate males. Just in case neither you, nor I, nor anyone else who cares for her welfare is on hand to come to her rescue.'

'That,' cried Lady Birchwood, 'is the most outrageous and ridiculous thing I've ever heard!'

'You forget, madam,' he said, 'that my ward is a considerable heiress. I have already noticed that she is attracting the attention of the very worst sort of men. Men who would not scruple to attempt an abduction.'

'No!' Lady Birchwood's hand went to her throat. And since she'd mangled that last biscuit so completely, the crumbs that had stuck to her fingers now found their way into the lace at her neckline.

'And anyway,' put in Rosalind, 'I don't really know anything that I could actually *teach* her. I mean, I just sort of…lashed out. In a panic. And got in a lucky punch. And if we hadn't been at the top of the stairs, I don't think I could have knocked him down, or anything like that.'

He gave her a searching look. 'In that case,' he said, 'you

will oblige me by accompanying me to my study, straight away, so that I may give you some pointers. And then you may pass on what you have learned, to my ward. For I have reason to believe,' he said to Lady Birchwood, 'that she is in particular need of protection.'

'Then we should hire someone...' said Lady Birchwood.

'And how would we explain that? Do you want to frighten the girl? Wouldn't you rather equip Miss Hinchcliffe with the weapons necessary to protect her, so that she may enjoy the rest of the Season without worrying about possible danger?'

Lady Birchwood scowled at him.

'I suppose,' she eventually said, though very grudgingly, 'that since Miss Hinchcliffe is the kind of person who *is* prone to violence,' she said, wrinkling her nose as though she'd smelled something nasty, 'we may as well put her proclivities to good use. Since you refuse to dismiss her.'

'It is the most practical solution,' said Lord Caldicot, smoothly.

Then he turned and, with his back to Lady Birchwood, winked at Rosalind.

Chapter Nineteen

He went to the door and opened it, and held it open until Miss Hinchcliffe got to her feet and crossed the room.

Beyond her, he could see Lady Birchwood subsiding into a mound of frustrated spite on her sofa. But there was nothing more she could do. Not today. He'd completely spiked her guns.

Miss Hinchcliffe kept her head down and said nothing all the way to the hall, where she paused and looked around frantically as though searching for something.

'My valise,' she said. 'I left it in the drawing room. I had better go back and get it.'

'No need.' More than that, he didn't want her going back and facing Lady Birchwood alone. 'I shall get Timms to take it back to your room. I dare say he will be only too glad to do so.'

She frowned. Her confused frown. God, he was starting to notice the difference between the degrees and intentions of those frowns of hers!

'Rather like the staff at your previous post,' he continued, brushing away that stray epiphany, 'the ones here won't want you to leave. Apart from anything else,' he hastened to add, when she gave a little shake of her head as though she wanted to contradict him, 'they know that if you leave, there will be nobody left who has the knack of calming her down when she flies into one of her pets.'

She said nothing, but only made a strange little noise, as though clucking her tongue at him. Which was better, to his way of thinking, than allowing her to sink into a slew of self-deprecation.

He went ahead of her, opened the study door and once again held it open until she'd taken the hint that she had to do as he'd bid her, in spite of her reservations.

'I cannot really teach Susannah how to defend herself, you know,' she announced, the moment he'd closed the door on them.

'I know,' he said gently, reaching for the ribbons of her bonnet to begin untying them.

She slapped his hand away. 'I am perfectly capable of undoing my own bonnet, thank you!'

'I know. But for some reason, the fact that you haven't yet done so gives me the uncomfortable feeling that you are still thinking of bolting.' And the fact that she'd lost her temper so far as to slap his hand cheered him no end. Because it meant that her spirit was recovering.

'I was not,' she said, yanking at the bows of her bonnet ribbon, *'bolting.'*

'Nevertheless, I feel easier in my mind now that you are removing your bonnet. It makes me more hopeful that you will not try to leave again. For any reason.'

She lifted it from her head and turned to set it on a table just inside the door. He would guess that this was as much to avoid having to look at him as for any real need to put it down in that particular spot.

'I... I must thank you for defending me from... Lady Birchwood's accusations,' she said, keeping her back to him. 'Even though you, of all people, must know that she had a fair point.' She turned to face him, her hands clasped at her waist, her brow furrowed, this time in...yes, contrition.

'I do have a tendency to resort to...to *violence*,' she said with a tremor, as though struggling with some strong emotion. 'I have a shocking temper...'

'Nonsense,' he said briskly. 'I have never met anyone with more patience than you! Nobody has ever managed to remain calm and unruffled in Susannah's orbit for long. If you really had a problem with controlling your temper it would have been Susannah you tossed out of the window.'

'I didn't *toss*...' she began to object, though, he thought, rather mechanically. 'Besides,' she added, wringing her hands, 'I have...sometimes...wanted to throw a glass of water into her face...'

'I am not a bit surprised. But you have never done so, have you? In fact, the only times you have ever resorted to any kind of action have been when you have been in danger. And then you have *defended* yourself. Not, I repeat, *not* gone on the attack.'

She considered what he said for a moment, her frown turning to one of consideration, as though she was running through all the instances of action she'd had to take. 'You make me sound...' she said.

'Spirited,' he declared, bracingly. 'And long-suffering.'

She frowned again, this time as though she disagreed. 'But, if you really believe *that* of me, then why did you...compel me to break my word to Lady Dorrington and speak of that... vile... *Peregrine*.' She spat his name out like a lump of unpalatable gristle.

'I had to get to the truth,' he said, a touch uncomfortably. He'd simply *had* to get to the truth. Because the thought that she'd lied to him, from the start, that his vision of her had been a false one, had been so abhorrent that, well, it had felt as though he'd run, full tilt, into a brick wall. A thing that hurt, particularly for being such a stupid thing to do. For what man in his right mind did such a thing as run into a wall? Only one who was an idiot. Or blind. And for a horrid moment or two there he'd suspected he might have been both, if he'd misjudged her so badly.

'And I only had to ask Lady Birchwood a few of the most rudimentary questions to see that she was just grasping at any excuse to be rid of you. She never approved of me hiring you, to start with. Then, when Susannah made it plain she felt she'd need you to stay with her during her Season, she must have felt it added insult to injury.'

'Not approve of you hiring me? But why? Susannah needed a governess, back then...'

'Yes, but up to that point, one or other of her aunts would have managed the business. They all regarded the fact that I stepped in and consulted an agency, rather than relying on someone in the family to recommend someone, and then proceeded to interview all the applicants myself, as a piece of impertinence. As interference in the management of family matters.'

'But...you are Susannah's legal guardian. How could she...?'

'It is probably largely because she's known me from my boyhood. She still sees me as an overgrown, impudent, jackanapes. Not only her. All her sisters cannot resist reminding me of how I invariably got into trouble on the few times I was invited to either this house, or Caldicot Dane, to pay homage to the venerable head of the family. Caldicot Dane, in particular, was run on such rigid rules that, well...'

'Yes,' she said with feeling. 'That was one of the reasons why I felt so safe there.'

'I can see your point. I cannot imagine anything havey-cavey ever going on beneath that particular roof. Which is a good thing. And something I wouldn't want to change when I eventually go down and take up the reins. But... I was just a scrubby schoolboy who would much rather have been out of doors shooting rabbits or climbing trees than sitting in a drawing room being told to mind his manners while all the adults talked and talked about...well...nothing I could ever get interested in.'

'Well, as someone who has climbed a few trees herself,' she said with a wry grin, 'I can see no reason why you should not have been allowed to do so.'

'Exactly! But the thing is, I got so bored that... Well, let me give you an example. I once spent a whole afternoon in the library, where I was supposed to be improving my mind, building a maze from the books for some rats I'd liberated from the rat catcher that morning. Only, being rather intelligent creatures, they spurned the sport I'd planned for them. The moment I let them out of their boxes, they went in search of something more to their taste, which just happened to be terrorising the people gathered in the next room drinking tea. All of whom were extremely dignified sorts. There was a general, I seem to recall, as well as a bishop and a Member of Parliament...'

To his relief, he saw her clap one hand over her mouth to suppress a spurt of laughter.

'The next time I went there, on the occasion of His Lordship's birthday, they made an attempt to keep me out of mischief, by effectively confining me to the schoolroom. Naturally I broke out, stole supplies from the kitchen and camped out in the grounds. It was only a day or so before they found me, that time...'

'That time?'

'Yes, the next time I went to Caldicot Dane I—' He broke off, aware that there were some sorts of mischief he was certain she wouldn't approve of. 'Suffice it to say that I continued to embark on adventures calculated to scandalise all of Susannah's aunts, which, erm, reflected my age and developing interests. So you see why,' he said, clearing his throat, 'she formed such a low opinion of my character and morals.'

'Yes,' she said, rather cautiously, 'you do sound as though you were a very...energetic sort of boy. And, having spent some time at Caldicot Dane myself, I can see how...stuffy it must have felt.'

'Precisely! Well, eventually one of them, probably one of the aunts, suggested that I was too much for my mother to manage—you see, my father had died by then and we were living in reduced circumstances, not that I really noticed. A great manager was my mother. I was never conscious of going without anything. But Lord Caldicot, that is, the previous one, arranged for her to go and live in a cottage at Weymouth and bought me a commission in a regiment serving overseas.

'In truth, he couldn't have done anything better for me. Army life suited me to a nicety. But I digress. I was supposed to be explaining why Lady Birchwood thinks so poorly of me and to try to help you understand why it infuriated her so much when you turned out to be such a treasure, instead of being totally wrong for the job.'

He went to his desk and leaned against it, spreading his hands on the surface behind him. 'She'd wanted you, I suspect, to be living proof that I am still irresponsible and useless. The dance last week was merely the last straw, causing her simmering resentment to come to the boil. It was entirely my fault,' he said ruefully, 'that she wanted to dismiss you. I deliberately provoked her, at that ball. Well, not just her, if you must know. I wanted to offend all of them!' He was sick of them all waiting for him to do something outrageous. Something that would prove he wasn't fit to hold the title that he'd inherited.

'All of...who?'

He pushed away from the desk and took a few steps across the room. 'Every last one of those matchmaking mothers,' he said as he reached the fireplace and braced one hand on the mantel, 'and their desperate daughters and the prosy old bores who pretend they have nothing to do with what their wives and daughters get up to, but who supply them with all the ammunition they need to gun down hapless men with titles and fortunes.'

That was the worst of it. They still wanted to marry their daughters to him, in spite of looking down their snobbish noses at him. Because of the title. They wanted the title for their daughters and the only way they could get at it was through him. 'It was a selfish act on my part,' he admitted, looking down into the grate. 'Because I exposed you to their spite.'

'Well, thank you for explaining all that to me. But it isn't the whole story, is it? I mean, I have made an enemy on my own account, haven't I? You reminded me, back there in the drawing room, when you spoke of an enemy spreading malicious gossip about me—who gave Lady Birchwood a mangled version of events surrounding the way I left my previous post?'

'Well, yes,' he said, straightening up and turning round, 'I do think that somehow Baxter was behind the unpleasantness you suffered this morning. However, he would not have had any success with Lady Birchwood had I not made you the target of some of the most spiteful people it has ever been my misfortune to meet.'

'I wouldn't wonder,' she mused, 'if he isn't just the sort of man who would be friends with *Peregrine*.' She said his name in that gristle-spitting way again.

'Or at least, the sort who frequents the same sort of hells,' he agreed. 'And they are both the sort of men who can charm a certain type of lady into believing in them. It was true, what Lady Birchwood said, about Fullerton being received everywhere. Just like Baxter, he comes from a respected family. So between them, they could have poured their poison into the ears of some female susceptible to their brand of charm, who could have run straight to Lady Birchwood to tell her the version of events *they* wanted known.'

'You know, in a way,' said Miss Hinchcliffe, going over to the chair before his desk, and sinking down wearily on to it, 'I can hardly blame Lady Birchwood for wanting to get rid of me. I am hardly a shining example of decorous female behaviour, am I?'

He went back to the desk, and hitched his hip on to it, as he'd grown into the habit of doing whenever they had one of their little meetings in here. He thought he'd persuaded her that she'd done nothing so very wrong. But her conscience was clearly still troubling her. There was nothing for it. He was going to have to tease her out of the sullens.

'I must admit,' he therefore said, 'that I am *shocked*, positively shocked, at the number of injuries you have done to men during the course of your young life.'

'No, you aren't,' she said, scowling up at him. 'You thought it was funny. You could hardly keep your face straight when I told you about punching Peregrine.'

He held up one hand, in a gesture familiar to a fencer, to acknowledge the hit. 'It was hearing how he landed on the butler that nearly did it for me,' he admitted. 'I could just picture it. That stout young rascal, tumbling head over heels, spraying blood all down the stairs, only to land on an incoming butler. Priceless!' It was what he'd been itching to do ever since he'd deduced that some rogue or other must have attempted something of the sort before she'd come to work for him.

'It isn't,' she said repressively, as he succumbed once more to the laughter that hearing the tale the first time had provoked, 'a laughing matter!'

'Oh, but it is. I could never have imagined how many adventures one innocent-looking governess could have. To think that when I left the army, I expected life to become a dull round of boring routine. And though mostly it is, I can always rely on you to relieve the monotony by doing something outrageous.'

'I don't! I mean, not on purpose.'

'Which makes it all the more delightful. Though I should love to know exactly how many bodies you have left strewn in your wake. I am sure the stories connected with each and every... *accident*...would be well worth the hearing.'

'None! I have not killed anyone!'

'I confess,' he said, with a rueful shake of his head, 'to being a trifle disappointed.'

'Well, I confess,' she said, her eyes narrowing, 'to thinking you can be rather...' She pulled herself up, biting down on her lower lip.

'Beastly? Yes, I think you have said so before. It comes, I dare say, of having been a serving soldier most of my adult life. I always had to do whatever was necessary, which meant there was no time to have scruples. Added to which, I am not the slightest bit squeamish. So, if there are no more bodies weighing down your conscience, you may freely confess to all the broken bones, lost teeth, bruises...'

She pulled her lips into a firm line, but to his concern, instead of scowling at him, she began to look rather upset.

'It isn't my fault. Things just happen...and when they do, though I have *tried* to curb my temper and behave in a more ladylike fashion...'

'Well, don't! Don't change anything about yourself!'

Her eyes widened.

'That is,' he put in hastily, wondering if he'd betrayed his feelings for her in too direct a manner, 'I mean, as I told Lady Birchwood, you need to be able to defend yourself against the kind of men who would take advantage of you. And if you didn't punch them, or kick them, or throw something at them, well, who knows what they might have done to you.'

She tilted her head to one side. 'Yes. That is a fair point. And thank you for saying it. But as for teaching Susannah how to fight...' She shook her head. 'I wouldn't know where to begin. You have been amused to paint me as some sort of...avenging harpy, going about fighting evil wherever I find it, but it isn't anything like so…noble. In fact, I think of the way I…lash out as something…instinctive. A habit. A bad habit, that I developed in the orphanage. You see, I hadn't been there for very long before I learned that if you didn't stick up for yourself, you would go hungry. Because the bigger children always pushed the smaller, weaker ones aside whenever mealtimes came round. And I was *always* hungry.'

'It is completely understandable,' he told her. 'I know just how hard it is to break habits developed in childhood. I can lecture myself until I am blue in the face, but I can never totally suppress that part of me which is still a little boy who doesn't want to sit in the schoolroom, who wants to break out and explore the world outside the stuffy confines of Caldicot Dane.

'You know, I didn't literally mean you should teach Susannah to box, or shoot, or anything of that nature. I was just trying to persuade Lady Birchwood that those very qualities in you she so dislikes could be seen as an advantage. Rather than just throwing my weight around and decreeing that my word in this house is law, which would have set her back up even more.'

'But your word in this house *should* be law.'

'You are just about the only person who thinks so,' he replied bitterly.

'I am sure that is not the case.'

'But Lady Birchwood makes it her business to undermine me at every turn! I shouldn't have let her take charge of hiring staff for the Season,' he mused, 'that was a mistake. It encouraged her to make out that she still has…rights over things here. She constantly reminds everyone how often she visited this house when her brother was the Marquess. And wastes no opportunity to bemoan the fact that I am only his uncle's son, rather than his own. A very inferior uncle at that, who married a woman of gentry stock!

'And do you remember how tediously she went on and on about her own come-out ball, which her father, the Fourth Marquess, threw for her, in this very house, while she was supposed to be welcoming Susannah's guests to *her* come-out ball?'

Rosalind nodded ruefully. On that occasion, she'd taken up a position on the landing, from which she could observe, without herself being seen, he recalled. And even back then, he'd wanted to invite her to come down and join in. Before he'd truly known what a delightful person she was.

'Well, never mind all that,' he said, pushing himself off the desk and walking over to the window. Because the way she looked at him, the way she spoke to him with such…trust, made him want to take her in his arms and kiss her. But if he did that, it would shatter that trust. She'd think he was just like all the other men who'd tried to take advantage of her.

And he'd be the next victim she felled with her powerful right hook. Unless she was left-handed.

He turned round. 'Are you left-handed, or right-handed?'

She frowned in confusion at the sudden change of subject. 'What has that to do with anything?'

'Only that I had a sudden…whim to know which arm you threw punches with.'

'I… Well, I write with my right hand,' she said. 'But I honestly couldn't tell you which hand I punched Peregrine with. It was so long ago, and I have tried to…to blot it out of my memory.'

'Stand up,' he said, suddenly seeing a way he could legitimately interact with her, in a physical way, right here, right now. He couldn't kiss her. After all she'd told him, that would be an act of sheer villainy. But he could spar with her. In fact, now he came to think of it, every encounter they'd ever had in private had been in the nature of a sparring match. Verbally, anyway.

She stood up, even though she still looked a bit confused, so he went round the desk to remove her chair, so as to clear a bit of floor space.

'Now, imagine, if you will, that I am Peregrine,' he said.

She pursed her lips. 'Really, my lord, I don't think this is the least bit appropriate.'

'Haven't you learned by now that I don't enjoy doing what is appropriate? Being appropriate is no fun.'

'And pretending to be a man like Peregrine is?'

'Just humour me,' he said. 'I suspect you must have a powerful right hook if you managed to knock a man right down the stairs. Let alone another one out of a window, just by throwing a book. And I'd like to feel it.'

'I couldn't punch you!'

'Well, no, of course not, not if you haven't any science. I box regularly, so I know how to block any attack you might make.'

'Then what is the point?'

The point was...to hell with what the point was! He couldn't do what he really wanted with her. And he couldn't dance with her, in here, not without benefit of music, she'd think he'd got windmills in his head. But this sort of flowed on from the conversation they'd been having.

'Now,' he said, stooping into a crouch, 'I am creeping up the stairs, trying to get you into an alcove,' he said, inching closer and spreading his arms wide as if to catch her. But instead of raising her fists, she just began to breathe more deeply. And her lips parted.

'This isn't going to work, Miss Hinchcliffe,' he warned her, 'if you look at me like that.'

He stepped right up to her. He was so close now that the toe of his boot slipped under the edge of her skirt. As she breathed out, her scent brushed his lips. The look of intensity in her gaze took his breath away.

She was blushing. Breathing heavily, but making no attempt to repulse him.

He began to bring his arms round her. He ought not to do it. He knew it was wrong. But the temptation was so great...

And then she moved. Her hand shot out so swiftly that it took him completely by surprise as she gave him a hefty shove in the chest. Then, her face flaming, she whirled round and fled from the room.

Leaving him standing there, staring at the open door and rubbing at his breastbone where he felt certain, by tomorrow, there would be a bruise.

He was, most definitely, a marked man.

But, since he'd been gazing into her eyes, or at her lips, he still had no idea whether she'd led with her left or her right.

Chapter Twenty

Rosalind ran all the way upstairs and didn't stop until she'd reached her room, gone in and slammed the door behind her.

She'd almost let him kiss her! What had she been thinking!

That she'd *wanted* him to, that was what. So much so that she'd just stood there, willing him to come closer, though how he could have done so when their breaths had been mingling in a way that, had it been any other man, she would have thought it indecent.

Why didn't she think it was indecent with him? What was it about him that overturned all her ingrained dislike and distrust of men and made her wish she was eligible and pretty, and, oh, all the things she was not?

She slumped against the door, letting it take her weight.

Would he believe the excuse that she'd been grateful to him for the way he'd come to her rescue? For persuading her that she *didn't* have trouble controlling her temper? For the way he'd… teased her, rousing her temper so that she'd started to feel more like herself than the weak, wilting watering pot she'd become when she'd thought she'd have to leave Kilburn House for ever. And never see him again.

For saying that he didn't want her to try to change herself. Which had meant that he liked her just as she was.

For confiding in her about his youth and his own background which wasn't all that dissimilar to hers, since his mother was from gentry stock, and his...struggles to fill the shoes of the former Marquess, who sounded to her like a complete fathead.

But none of that was the complete truth. She just...wanted him. In a way she'd never felt about any other man. Indeed, in a way she'd never thought she possibly *could* feel about a man. She'd always thought men were best avoided. They let her down, or caused trouble, or were just generally unreliable. But somehow, Lord Caldicot had crept into a category all his own. She couldn't see him letting her down, or causing her trouble, or being unreliable...

How on earth was she going to get through the days ahead, feeling the way she did about him, and, worse, knowing that he must know how she felt? He must think she was a sad, desperate, spinster, that was what. He must *despise* her.

It turned out that she managed to muddle through by never looking him in the eye. By making excuses about being too busy whenever he requested another private discussion about Susannah, so that she could avoid ever being on her own with him. And by forbidding herself from gazing at him, whenever they were in the same room, in case anyone else noticed her feelings. Because she was sure they must be written on her face.

It was hardest when they went out to a ball. Tonight, for example, she'd found it well-nigh impossible not to watch whatever he was doing. Whether it was talking to the other men present, or dancing with eligible debutantes. No matter how hard she tried to keep her eyes on Susannah, they just kept on straying back to him.

It was a huge relief when Lieutenant Minter came over to ask permission to take Susannah out on to the terrace, while new sets were forming up on the floor.

'You are not going to dance, then?' Rosalind looked from the Lieutenant, to Susannah, who was already taking his arm, with a determined look on her face.

'We would only annoy Lady Birchwood again, wouldn't we,' Susannah pointed out. 'And she would take it out on *you*, like she did before. I was so upset when I heard that she tried to dismiss you, it made me...' She bit down on her lower lip, then tossed her head as though casting whatever thought had troubled her to one side. 'But nobody could object to us going outside for a stroll, provided you accompanied us, could they?'

Rosalind pursed her lips, because she thought that people would probably think the exact opposite. That a man could not get a girl into trouble on a dance floor, the way he could if he took her outside. Even if he did make sure he had a chaperon in attendance. It hinted at...intimacy.

Nevertheless, she never could find it in herself to be unkind to poor Lieutenant Minter. And going outside would also mean she wouldn't have to sit watching Lord Caldicot dancing with Lady Susan Pettifer. Out of all the girls with titles, wealth and connections, why on earth did he seem to spend so much time with one who was renowned for her spiteful tongue?

But, perhaps most crucially, Susannah now had the kind of mulish set to her mouth which meant she'd made up her mind. And even though she'd just said she regretted acting in a way that had contributed to Rosalind almost losing her job, that was no guarantee her mood of contrition, and thoughtfulness for another's welfare, would persist, if Rosalind attempted to thwart her will. So, taking all things into consideration, she might as well accept the inevitable.

So, outside the three of them went. It was a mild night, so she did not need to go and fetch a shawl first. And the sky was clear. She went and leaned against the parapet separating the terrace from the grounds, while the younger couple kept on walking. It was a night with far more opportunity for romance, she reflected, than the last time she'd come out on to a terrace very similar to this one. Not only were the stars twinkling enthusiastically, but the moon was also smiling down on the scene.

She sighed. If only Lord Caldicot...but no. If he were to come out here, she'd have to *talk* to him. Which she'd successfully managed to avoid doing ever since the almost-kiss in his study. And if they talked, he'd probably get her to admit how she felt. And then he'd have to point out, in the kindest way possible, that she could never be anything more to him than...

She tilted back her head, blinking furiously up at the moon which was wavering before her watering eyes.

No, he wouldn't be kind. He'd be direct. Forthright. And wasn't that what she liked about him? No…flummery.

He…wait a minute, what on earth was the matter with Susannah? She appeared to be shouting, or at least, speaking to Lieutenant Minter in an agitated manner. Rosalind stepped back from the parapet and turned to look at the young couple.

Lieutenant Minter was glowering at Susannah. Glowering!

While Susannah had her hands on her hips, and was pouring out a torrent of words that, although she could not overhear them, sounded…indignant.

Oh, dear. Rosalind had been so wrapped up in her own concerns that she'd entirely neglected her charge. And it looked as if the young man must have overstepped the bounds of propriety, because all of a sudden Susannah stopped berating him, slapped his face, turned on her heel and came marching back along the terrace, tears streaming down her face.

'I want to go home,' she sobbed, flinging herself on to Rosalind's chest.

'Yes…yes, of course,' Rosalind murmured soothingly, as she wondered how on earth she was going to remove a sobbing girl from a ballroom without raising eyebrows.

Lieutenant Minter came over. 'I shall order your carriage and collect your cloaks,' he said grimly, before marching back into the house, solving Rosalind's concern without her having to ask for his help.

Susannah sobbed a bit harder and buried her face in Rosalind's neck.

'There, there,' she said, helplessly, patting Susannah's heaving shoulders. And then, 'I must say, I am surprised by the Lieutenant. I never thought he would step out of line. I thought he respected and admired you too much.' She'd begun to think that Lord Caldicot might not be the only man in the world who could treat a woman with respect.

'He is a beast!' Susannah raised her tear-stained face to Rosalind's. 'I never want to see him or speak to him again!'

At which precise moment, the Lieutenant appeared, carrying their cloaks. And though he must have heard Susannah, he took no notice of her outburst, merely draping her cloak round the girl's shoulders.

'The carriage should be ready by the time you reach the front steps,' he said woodenly. 'You can reach it by going along the terrace, down the steps, and through the servants' hall. Nobody needs to see her in such distress. I know it would pain her for anyone to see her when she is not in looks.'

Which she wasn't. Susannah didn't cry prettily. When she cried, she gave it her all. Which meant that her complexion went blotchy and her nose went red.

'Ooh!' cried Susannah, stamping her foot and whirling round indignantly. 'Must you be so…hatefully…*organised*? And how…ungallant of you to mention my looks!'

He looked down at Susannah's furious little face, pain etched across his features. 'I will inform our hosts that you have taken Lady Susannah home as she is suffering from a sudden headache,' he said to Rosalind. He reached out his hand, as though to touch Susannah's hair, then withdrew it, balling it into a fist.

'I *am* suffering from a headache,' Susannah spat, raising a resentful face to his. 'Thanks to you!'

Rosalind didn't think this was the time or the place to find out precisely what the Lieutenant had done to upset Susannah so. Nor to point out the fact that not two minutes after she'd said she never wanted to speak to him again, she'd done just that. As she'd learned from her own grandfather, when a person lost their temper, consistency, along with logic, frequently flew out of the window.

When they reached Kilburn House, Susannah went flying up the stairs to her room, scattering a trail of gloves, scarves and one dancing shoe in her wake. Rosalind trailed behind her, picking up each item and following her to her room. From beyond the closed door she could hear the sound of furious weeping.

Taking a deep breath, she knocked, then, without waiting for an answer, she went in.

Having dropped the bundle of random accessories Susannah had discarded, in a pile by the door, she crossed the room and sank down on her usual chair.

After only a short while, Susannah raised her head from the pillows and turned her tear-stained face in Rosalind's direction.

'Go away,' she sobbed. 'I do not want one of your...uplifting homilies! I do not want to be coaxed out of the sullens as though I am a child! My heart is broken—*broken*, do you hear me? And there is nothing anyone can do about it!'

'Oh, dear,' said Rosalind, inadequately. 'Should I perhaps ring for Pauline, then, to help you undress? And bring you some warm milk?'

'I just told you,' Susannah screamed. 'I am not a child to soothe with glasses of warm milk! Leave me alone!' she sobbed.

'Very well,' said Rosalind, getting to her feet. To be honest, she didn't feel up to dealing with Susannah tonight. She already had enough to perplex and trouble her on her own account.

Although, she mused, as she made her way next door to her own room, not once had she felt the slightest bit angry with the girl. Or inclined to slap her, or throw something at her.

Perhaps Lord Caldicot was correct about her. Perhaps she wasn't as bad-tempered as various people, throughout her life, had told her.

In some surprise, she sank on to her favourite chair, at which point she realised that Susannah was not the only one with a headache. She rubbed at a spot above her right eye, where it felt as if someone was stabbing her with a red-hot needle. How long had this been coming on? Days, probably. She'd put her general feeling of malaise, and her low spirits, down to a combination of all that crying when she'd thought she'd lost her job here and then the overwhelming humiliation of almost letting Lord Caldicot kiss her.

But now she wondered if she was, in truth, sickening for something. She felt...hot. And cold at the same time. And a bit...well, queasy.

She went over to the balcony to open the doors, wondering why it was that the maids insisted on shutting them every time she turned her back. There was little enough fresh air in

London at the best of times, but sometimes, in the evenings, a slight breeze did get up and made the rooms feel a bit fresher.

She was walking away, wondering whether to return to the chair from where she could reap the benefit of what air was coming into the room, or go over to the bed and flop on to it and pull a pillow over her head to muffle the pain which was starting to build and spread across her whole forehead, when she heard a sound that made a chill run down her spine.

The sound of something grating against her balcony railing.

Followed by the muffled grunt of someone clambering on to it.

She whirled round, her heart pounding, knowing that there was only one person who would use this route to gain entry to the house, rather than knocking on the front door.

And she was right.

It was Cecil Baxter.

Chapter Twenty-One

Mr Baxter looked rather the worse for wear. That was Rosalind's first thought. His hair needed cutting and the attention of a comb, and his clothes should have gone to the laundry at least a week ago.

But it was his face that really alarmed her. His complexion was mottled purple, his eyes glittering strangely.

Instinctively, she took a step back, her eyes scanning the room for something she could use as a weapon. Although hadn't she vowed to stop acting without thinking first? Especially when a man was poised on the edge of a balcony. If she rushed over and pushed him off, which was what she wanted to do, who was to say he wouldn't land on the terrace, rather than in the shrubbery this time?

She'd felt dreadful when she'd thought she'd killed him. She hadn't meant to hurt him at all, only to…to…well, she didn't know what she'd thought. She'd just *reacted*, as Lord Caldicot had said, to what had felt like a threat. It hadn't been, but how was a girl to have known that? Well, what was a girl to think when a man sneaked into a house through a window, at night, rather than entering through the front door, at a respectable hour for visiting?

But anyway, after hesitating this long, she would never be

able to claim that she hadn't *meant* to hurt him, would she, if she ran over and pushed him off the balcony now? She wouldn't just be lashing out in self-defence.

'You...' he breathed, as he finally got both feet on to the balcony, so that she no longer had much of a chance of ejecting him right back out the way he'd come in, anyway. 'You...jade.'

'No flowers to offer me this time, Mr Baxter?' she found herself saying, rather absurdly.

'Flowers are wasted on your type,' he hissed, prowling towards her in a way that made her retreat even further from him.

The backs of her legs connected with her reading chair. Unwilling to be trapped in it, with him looming over her, she skirted round it, so that it became a barrier between them.

'You have a mean, twisted heart,' he snarled, 'that no man will ever be able to melt. And what man would want to?'

She found herself unable to answer that, since she agreed with the second part of it, if not the first. Though her heart was not twisted, she suddenly saw very clearly, but already melted.

'Nothing to say?' Mr Baxter bent slightly, took hold of one of the arms of her chair, and then flung it aside, his face twisted into an ugly sneer.

'I don't know what you hope to gain from coming in here, being nasty,' she said, taking a couple of hasty steps away from the overturned chair, to avoid tripping over it. She tried to move away from the window, which had already proved to be the most dangerous place to linger. But something about the look on his face when she did that made her heart speed up uncomfortably. And about the same time, it occurred to her that he was deliberately herding her in the direction of the bedroom part of her room.

'Well, you'll soon find out,' he sneered, making her feel more frightened than she could ever recall feeling in her life. 'You have thwarted me from the start. Caused me bodily injury. And kept me from the one sure way out of my difficulties. I had that little pigeon,' he said, waving one arm in the direction of her bed, though she thought he probably meant to indicate the room which lay on the other side of the wall beyond it, which belonged to Susannah, 'ready for the plucking, until you shoved your oar in.'

'It is my job,' she protested.

Oh, dear, why had she ever thought it would be a good idea to try talking her way out of trouble? Every time she said something it only seemed to make him angrier. Though at least she'd refrained from pointing out his use of mixed metaphors, which she was certain would have enraged him. Men detested having their defects pointed out to them by women.

But his response was not encouraging. 'Hah!'

He was so close to her now that the explosive bark of cynical laughter blasted her face with the mingled fumes of stale beer and onions. And she'd retreated so far that there was nowhere else to go. One more step and her back would be pressed against the bedpost.

All sorts of thoughts flitted through her mind.

Lord Caldicot saying she'd never be able to land a punch on him because she had no *science*.

Her earlier declaration that if a woman showed weakness, a certain type of man would take advantage of it.

The knowledge that when the family went out for the evening, most of the servants leaped at the opportunity to do so as well, so that even if she should scream for help, the chances of anyone hearing her and rushing to help her were slim.

'Mr Baxter,' she said, as calmly as she could, all things considered, 'you can gain nothing by coming in here and threatening me. You really should leave, before somebody discovers you.'

'And who is to discover me, eh? The last of the menservants on the premises took himself off to join the others at the Jolly Footman as soon as he'd let you in...'

Just as she'd thought!

'And if I know anything about female staff, they will all be up in the attics, tucked up into their snug little beds...'

Yes, she'd thought the same, which was why she'd hesitated before ringing for Pauline, assuming she'd be taking the opportunity to snatch a well-earned nap.

'And I have learned from you,' he said with a sinister chuckle, 'that a person can get away with murder in this house, when the master and his family are out at a ball. After all, that is what you tried to do, isn't it?'

Then, just as she was opening her mouth to retort that she hadn't got away with murder, because here he was, large as life and twice as nasty, he reached out to grab her neck.

Rosalind just had the time to let out a brief scream before his dirty fingers closed round her throat, choking it off.

She clawed at his fingers, but they were stronger than hers.

She clawed at his face, but he didn't seem to care, which was probably because she kept her nails so short that they couldn't do much damage.

Finally, she thought of using her legs, to kick out at him, but all that achieved was to put her off balance so that they both tumbled to the floor on to the rug she kept next to her bed. His grip on her neck slackened slightly as they fell, but only briefly. And every breath she struggled to take now was rancid with the odour of greasy clothes and stale sweat.

Why on earth hadn't she just pushed him off the balcony when she'd had the chance? Lord Caldicot would have dealt with the body, even if he had fallen on to the terrace...

'What on earth,' cried the last person Rosalind might have expected to come to her rescue in the nick of time, 'is going on in here?'

'Susannah,' cried Mr Baxter, whipping his hands away from Rosalind's throat, though he still straddled her body, keeping her firmly pinned to the floor. 'She...she tried to kill me, my darling. What else could I do?'

'*She* tried to kill *you*?'

Rosalind tried to turn her head far enough to be able to look at Susannah, who still seemed to be hovering in the doorway. Or to speak, but it was all she could do to breathe, let alone force any words through her throat. And because of the angle at which she was lying, all she could see was the coverlet, hanging down from the side of her bed, and her slippers, set neatly side by side.

'I cannot,' said Susannah, in a bewildered voice, 'believe that. She wouldn't!'

'You don't know her,' said Mr Baxter. 'You don't know what violence she's capable of!'

'I didn't know you were capable of violence either,' said Susannah, sounding shocked. 'Especially not to a woman.'

'She's no woman, she's a hellcat!'

'Cecil,' said Susannah, in the petulant tone that usually came just before she lost her temper. 'Let go of Miss Hinchcliffe at once and get up off the floor.'

Amazingly, he did as he was told, and as he began to get to his feet, Rosalind rolled to one side, her hands to her bruised throat as she sucked in air greedily.

Mr Baxter stepped over her and she heard him scamper over to where Susannah was still standing, by the open door.

'My darling, I came to take you away from this place. To free you from her toils. So you can escape from the repressive rules that tyrannical guardian has set over you.'

Susannah made a strange sound. 'Cecil, you...smell awful!'

'I am sorry, my love,' he said in that oily voice he'd used on Rosalind in the library. 'But they have made things so hard for me, lately, that I've been unable to live as I would wish.'

'You have debts, then?' Susannah's voice sounded strained. 'You *have* been hiding from your creditors?'

'How clever of you to work that out.'

Rosalind began to feel as if she could sit up, now, if she did so very slowly and carefully. So she tried it, and, though the walls seemed to be rippling in and out of her vision and the floor heaved in an alarming fashion, she managed to get into a position from where she saw Mr Baxter take hold of Susannah's hand.

'Our only hope now,' he was saying, tugging Susannah away from where Rosalind lay on the floor, in the general direction of the window, 'is to elope. I know it is not the done thing, but can you not see that my case is desperate? They have kept me from you ever since your guardian refused me permission to marry you. You cannot imagine what lengths they have gone to, to keep us apart.'

'Elope? No,' said Susannah, trying to pull her hand free. 'I don't want to elope. It would be most uncomfortable.'

So, she *had* taken in some of the practical problems Rosalind had spelled out to her, when they'd been discussing eloping before, she reflected with satisfaction, as she got to her hands and knees. Whatever else she might be, Susannah was by no means stupid.

'It is the only way we can be together,' said Mr Baxter, getting one arm round Susannah's waist and compelling her in the direction of the window.

That, Rosalind reflected, was a mistake. The moment anyone attempted to compel Susannah to do anything, she invariably dug in her heels.

'I am not,' said Susannah, beginning, as anyone who knew her well would have known she would, to struggle in earnest, 'going out of that window!'

'I have provided a ladder,' said Mr Baxter soothingly. 'Surely a girl with your pluck can manage to climb down one little ladder.'

Not, Rosalind reflected, shuffling forward, a girl who was as scared of heights as Susannah.

'I am not going down a ladder,' said Susannah, 'and if you really loved me, you wouldn't ask it of me!'

'Then I will just have to carry you,' he said, stooping down to take Susannah by the knees and tipping her over his shoulder.

Susannah let out a piercing scream. One that he couldn't stifle, since both his hands were occupied in keeping her in place. And as he began to walk over to the window, the source of Susannah's terror, her screams became louder and she struggled more frantically.

Rosalind could see that if she didn't do something to stop him from getting to the ladder, they were both likely to end up plummeting to the terrace. And though it would serve Mr Baxter right, she could not allow him to harm poor Susannah.

She dismissed the bizarre notion of chucking her slippers at him, which were the only throwable objects in reach. She needed something much harder.

Underneath the bed, she knew, was a very hard object indeed. Her chamber pot.

She groped blindly for it, grasped it and, with her other hand, grabbed the bedpost, somehow managing to pull herself to her feet.

Then, with the last of her strength, she tottered across the room, her porcelain weapon primed for action.

Just as she raised it, to strike in the general direction of the back of Mr Baxter's head, he flinched and turned. He must have caught sight of her reflection in the glass panes of the window, Rosalind realised, as he swiped at her, the same way he'd swiped at her armchair before. This time, he knocked the chamber pot clean out of her hand. It flew across the room and smashed to pieces when it struck the wall.

But at least he'd slackened his hold on Susannah when she'd obliged him to use one of his hands to defend himself. He now held her with only one arm.

And Susannah was so determined not to go anywhere near that window that he had no hope of restraining her any longer. She squirmed out of his hold and landed on her hands and knees on the floor.

Leaving Mr Baxter standing right by the open balcony doors, glaring from one to the other of them, swaying first one way, and then the other, as though he couldn't decide which of them to deal with first.

Just like, Rosalind thought, rather hysterically, a bull being baited by two small, but determined terriers.

Chapter Twenty-Two

Michael was getting that feeling again. The feeling that something wasn't right.

It had started as soon as he'd noticed that both Miss Hinchliffe and Susannah had disappeared. When he'd asked a flunkey where they were, the man had told him that they'd gone home because the young lady had the headache. By that, he'd meant Susannah. But that didn't ring true. If anyone had reason to have a headache, it was Miss Hinchcliffe. She'd been looking distinctly peaky for the last few days.

Ever since he'd nearly lost his head and almost attempted to kiss her, damn fool that he was. She'd trusted him so much that she'd just stood there, allowing him closer. Which had shocked her. So much that she'd fled the room.

She'd been avoiding him ever since. And he couldn't blame her. Hadn't she just told him all about how she'd treated that pestilential Peregrine? She'd knocked *that* scoundrel down the stairs. He was lucky that shoving him away was the worst she'd done to *him*. She ought to have slapped his face, at the very least.

If only she wasn't his employee. If only he had the right to kiss her! He wouldn't even dislike attending balls so much if he could dance with her, without raising eyebrows.

But anyway, he was now getting the horrid feeling that this

headache they'd come up with between them was just a smoke-screen. That if he didn't get back to the house and put things right between them, he'd find her packed and gone.

And this time there might be no stopping her.

Although...wouldn't that solve the problem caused by her being in his employ? Yes! For once she was a free agent, he could...court her without any nasty overtones of impropriety. Which was exactly what he wanted to do, he realised. Court her.

She'd taken the carriage to convey Susannah back to Kilburn House, naturally. Not that he cared. It would be as quick to walk there, particularly as his state of mind was not going to allow him to stroll. Because, once Susannah had married and Rosalind was free, he would not have to stay in London, dancing attendance on women he could not imagine spending five minutes alone with, never mind the rest of his life!

Nobody answered his knock when he went up the front steps. He frowned. Lady Birchwood didn't seem to have hired a particularly reliable set of servants for this London Season. According to his account books, he paid a man a generous wage to act as night porter, so the fellow ought to be there to let him in. But from what he could tell, it looked as though the whole house was deserted. He wouldn't be a bit surprised to learn that all the staff had sloped off to the pub, just as they'd done the night Baxter had tried climbing in through a balcony window and received his just deserts. Though, if that was the case, how had Miss Hinchcliffe and Susannah fared when they got home? Where could they have gone if they hadn't been able to get in? If Miss Hinchcliffe had been in charge of this household she'd have kept the staff up to the mark, he was sure. In fact, she wouldn't have hired this motley crew in the first place.

Michael scowled at the infuriatingly unopened front door as he wondered how *he* was going to get in. Then, taking a step back, he noticed a light glowing through the window of the basement area. Might he be able to get in through the kitchen door?

The level of indignation he felt as he began to go down the area steps made him wonder if he finally *was* settling into the role of Marquess. After all, when he'd been merely Major Kil-

burn, he wouldn't have thought twice about going into anyone's house via the servants' entrance. And, though this was
the first time he'd tried to enter this particular house by way of
the kitchen door, he certainly wasn't unfamiliar with the areas
below stairs, was he? As a boy he'd felt more at home down
there, where the cook would give him biscuits and the grooms
would let him look at the horses, than above stairs where his
aunts and uncles, as well as his parents, would all expect him
to sit still and *behave*.

Nobody answered when he knocked on the kitchen door, either, dashing his hope that there might at least have been a cook
enjoying a doze before the fire, whom he could rouse. But when
he tried the handle, it turned easily and the door swung inwards.

And now he wasn't sure whether to be relieved he'd managed
to get in, or annoyed that *anyone* might have done the same.
Baxter, for example. In spite of it all, his lips quirked into a wry
grin. If only the fellow had known how lax security was in this
house, he could have saved himself a great deal of effort, not to
mention serious injury, last time he'd been here.

He stood for a moment or two, looking round the kitchen.
It looked like the same table where the old cook, Mrs Watson,
had plied him with biscuits, though she was long gone. On that
table stood the lighted lamp he'd glimpsed from the front steps.
A kettle was simmering on the stove, steam dulling the surfaces
of the copper pans hanging from the overmantel.

The staff who had deserted their posts, he reflected sardon-
ically, would be able to make themselves a lovely hot drink
when they got back.

He wondered whether he ought to have a word with Lady
Birchwood about the staff. Or speak to Timms, perhaps, he reflected as he walked across the room to the door leading to the
hall, about the non-existent security arrangements in place. He
could accept that staff hired for a Season couldn't be expected
to feel all that much loyalty for employers they might never see
again, once they'd returned to their own estates for summer. But
to all go out like this was practically an invitation to the local
housebreakers to walk in and help themselves.

On the other hand, if he made too much of a fuss, that same

lack of loyalty might induce them to simply seek employment elsewhere. And then they'd have to go through all the inconvenience of hiring new people, which could be rather tricky since they'd probably have gained a reputation for being difficult employers. He tossed his hat on to the nearest table he found once he was in the hall and was just pulling off his gloves when he heard from an upper floor the sound of a blood-curdling scream, followed by the crash of breaking crockery, then a series of muffled thuds.

All thoughts of staffing problems vanished. For it sounded as though it was not merely from any part of the upper floor, but from Miss Hinchcliffe's very room that those ominous sounds had come.

He took the stairs two at a time, his heart thudding painfully.

He threw open the door to Miss Hinchcliffe's room, not knowing what horrors might be waiting for him on the other side, only to see his worst fears made flesh.

Miss Hinchcliffe was lying, half on one side, unmoving, beside an overturned chair.

And Baxter was stalking steadily in Susannah's direction, though she was darting about in her attempts to evade him. She was the one he'd heard scream, he realised as she did it again.

Later, he supposed he should have gone straight to Susannah's aid, but at that moment, all he could think of was Miss Hinchcliffe, lying so still. So pale.

He went to her, bent over and saw livid marks on her neck. Marks that showed Baxter had throttled her.

He couldn't let the cur get away with that!

Rising to his feet, he crossed the room in two strides, grabbed Baxter by his collar, yanked him back, turned him round and punched him, hard, in the face.

He went down in an untidy sprawl of limbs.

'Lord Caldicot!' Susannah bounded over, wrapped her arms round his neck and burst into tears. 'You...s-saved m-me!'

'Yes, yes,' he said, impatiently removing her arms from about his neck. 'I only wish to God I'd been in time to save Miss Hinchcliffe, too.'

'She was so...so brave,' sobbed Susannah, dropping to the

floor the moment he let go of her, as though she had no bones in her legs. 'When Cecil tried to...to make me g-go out of the w-window,' he dimly heard the chit say, as he sank to his knees next to Miss Hinchcliffe's unnaturally still body, 'she w-went under her bed and g-got the chamber pot.'

Which was so typical of her. She wouldn't have thought twice about using whatever weapon she could get her hands on to save an innocent girl from the depredations of an ugly fellow like Baxter.

'She would have brained him with it, I think,' Susannah said, as he slipped one arm about Miss Hinchcliffe's shoulders, raised her limp form across his lap, and tucked her against his chest, while gazing into her deathly white face, 'only that he smacked it out of her hand, then made as if he was going to strike her.'

'Did he? Did he dare to strike her?' If he had, then he was a dead man.

'N-no. He would have done, I'm sure, only that she fainted just as he lunged at her.'

At that, Miss Hinchcliffe's eyes flew open. 'I did not faint,' she croaked, indignantly. 'I *never* faint. I tripped over the chair.' Then her hand flew to her neck. Her poor, bruised neck.

He wanted to cheer. She wasn't, as he'd feared for a few dreadful moments, dead. Even though her face was a ghastly shade that reminded him of finest hot-pressed writing paper.

'I b-beg your pardon, Miss Hinchcliffe,' said Susannah, while he was swallowing back a most unmanly rush of tears, 'but it wouldn't have been surprising if you had, after his attempt to throttle you. Indeed, it was very brave of you to try to go and fetch a weapon with which to brain him, when you could hardly breathe...'

'He tried to throttle you?' With hands that trembled, he brushed a stray lock of hair from her forehead.

As she nodded dumbly, Susannah took up the tale once more. '*He* said *she'd* tried to kill him when I came in and discovered him with his hands round her neck. I think...' She swallowed back a sob. 'I think he must have gone mad!' And then she began to sob in earnest.

He didn't have the time, or the patience, to deal with hysterics. Not when Miss Hinchcliffe was lying, unmoving, in his arms, looking up at him so...passively.

She must be seriously injured to be lying there, making no attempt to struggle, or slap his face, or utter a stern rebuke, or anything.

'Susannah,' he said curtly, 'I know you've had a shock, but Miss Hinchcliffe is in a far worse case. So I want you to pull yourself together, run down to my study, and fetch some brandy. Mixed with a little water it might just help to revive her.'

'Oh,' said Susannah, switching off the flow of tears and sitting up straight. 'Yes, poor Miss Hinchcliffe. But for her...' She wiped her face with the back of her hand. 'Though wouldn't it be better if *I* sat with her, while you went and got the brandy?'

No! There was no way he was going to let go of her and run the risk of her slipping from this life while he was away. And just to confirm him in his conviction that he ought not to leave her, Miss Hinchcliffe slid one hand up the front of his waistcoat and curled her fingers into his lapel.

Nothing that any woman, no matter how experienced in the arts of love, had ever done had moved him so much as that timid little gesture of appeal.

'You need to distract yourself from the unpleasantness you suffered at that villain's hands,' he said to Susannah without taking his eyes from Miss Hinchcliffe's face. 'I promise you, running down the stairs, and back up, while doing something to mend matters, will do you a whole lot more good than sitting there working yourself up into hysterics.'

'W-working myself up?' Susannah scrambled to her feet. 'She is right,' she said, pointing to Miss Hinchcliffe. 'You *are* beastly. But I *will* go and get some brandy. For *her*,' she snapped, whirling out of the room in a froth of expensive lace and pique.

'I thought I'd lost you,' he said, his voice hoarse with emotion, 'when I saw you lying there so still.' Then he took the opportunity of being alone with Miss Hinchcliffe to rain kisses across her forehead and cheeks. He would rather have kissed her on the mouth, but she was having enough trouble breathing as it was without him blocking up that essential lifeline.

'I'm sorry, but I cannot help kissing you,' he managed to say.

'Slap me, if you like. I deserve it for taking advantage when you are so weak and helpless.'

'Not weak,' she croaked. Then gave a funny sort of smile. 'Safe,' she mouthed. And then, with a little more conviction, *'Safe.'*

'Are you telling me I make you feel safe? Is that it?'

She nodded, shyly.

'You don't mind me holding you in my arms? You don't want to push me away, as you've done to every other male who's had the temerity to make an attempt on your virtue?'

She raised her brows, as though he'd said something extremely stupid.

'Does that mean what I think it means? That you...that you...' He gazed down at her, his heart racing. She just looked back up at him...with what looked like affection shining from her eyes. 'I *will* keep you safe from now on,' he vowed. 'Always, do you hear me? If you'll let me.'

She looked up at him then, a question in her eyes.

'What,' she whispered, 'are you trying to say?'

'That I want to marry you, of course!' He stroked her cheek, noting that it wasn't so dreadfully pale any longer. In fact, there was a distinct flush to it. 'I don't know why it hasn't occurred to me before. No other woman measures up. And I don't want any other woman the way I want you.'

'Mad,' she whispered, raising one trembling hand to briefly press her palm to his cheek. 'Quite mad.'

'Madly in love, I think,' he agreed.

'Excuse me,' came Susannah's petulant voice from the hall doorway. 'I have brought the drink you ordered, so you need to put Miss Hinchcliffe down so that I can help her drink it.'

'Don't be so silly, Susannah,' he replied curtly, reaching out his hand for the glass. 'I am perfectly capable of getting that brandy down Miss Hinchcliffe myself.'

'It isn't proper,' Susannah pointed out. 'Nor is kissing her the minute my back is turned. You have no right to...to make free with her!'

'Of course I do,' he said impatiently. 'I'm going to marry her.'

'Oh!' Susannah was so surprised to hear this that she lowered the hand which was holding the glass just enough that he was able to snatch it from her and raise it to Miss Hinchcliffe's lips.

'I cannot possibly go on calling you Miss Hinchcliffe if we are going to be married,' he remarked as he started tipping the contents of the glass into her parted lips. 'What is your given name?'

'Rosalind,' she whispered, between sips.

'And you must call me Michael,' he said.

'Lady Birchwood,' said Susannah, with what sounded to him like relish, 'is going to be livid!'

'That I am going to marry the lowly governess,' he replied, 'or that we are going to have to get the governess off a murder charge not one week after she attempted to throw her out of the house on the charge of excessive use of violence.'

'It wouldn't be murder,' Susannah objected. 'Besides, she never got near him with the chamber pot. I can vouch for that. It was you who knocked him down.'

'Yes,' croaked Rosalind, 'but he isn't dead.'

As though to prove her point, Baxter chose that moment to let out a moan.

All three of them turned to look at Baxter's body, with varying degrees of disgust.

Rosalind made as if to sit up. 'I am feeling stronger now, I should...'

He tightened the hold of his arm round her shoulders. 'You should stay exactly where you are, for now. While we decide what to do about...*him*.'

Susannah gave a little sob. 'Lieutenant Minter will never forgive me!'

'For what, precisely?' he said, wondering why on earth the girl should bring that name into this situation.

'For saying he was lying to me, in order to make me forsake what I thought was my true love,' she admitted, flicking her eyes briefly at Mr Baxter, who'd gone quiet again.

Rosalind must have seen the confusion on his face, because she explained, 'Susannah told Lieutenant Minter he was wasting his time courting her, because her heart was already engaged.' She paused and swallowed. 'To a man forbidden to her by her family. And the Lieutenant declared he would be content just to be her friend.' Her voice, at first rather raspy, began to fade away entirely. So he lifted the glass of brandy to her lips again.

'Yes, and then,' Susannah chipped in, since Rosalind seemed to need to rest her voice, 'when I became so worried about not seeing Cecil, Lieutenant Minter agreed to find out if some ill had befallen him. And then tonight, tonight...' Her face puckered. But instead of giving way to tears, this time she took a deep breath, swallowed hard, and continued.

'He told me that Cecil had run up debts all over town, and fobbed off his creditors by saying he was expecting to come into money. By which he meant, the Lieutenant told me, marrying me and gaining control of my fortune. But since word had got out that you had forbidden the match, he'd gone into hiding, so that his creditors wouldn't find him and have him thrown into prison for debt. I... I accused the Lieutenant of making it all up! I said if he thought he could make me forsake Cecil by making up a lot of lies, so that he could win me over, he had another think coming!'

'Ah,' said Rosalind. 'That was what you were arguing with him about tonight.'

'Yes,' said Susannah miserably. 'But now... But now...' She gulped. 'Oh, I would never have thought he could be so...' she looked at the still, unkempt, bloody form of Mr Baxter '...so downright nasty!'

'He revealed his true colours,' Michael told her gently. 'Even I had no idea how, er, *nasty* he really was. I only knew he had a reputation for being, er, unsteady. And I thought you deserved someone better. Someone who would care for you for your own sake, not for your money.'

Susannah, scrambled in a most undignified manner over to where he and Rosalind were sitting and flung her arms round his neck. Again.

'I am so sorry I didn't trust you!'

'Er...there, there,' he said, wishing he had at least one hand free to push her away. But he wasn't prepared to let go of Rosalind, not now he had her in his arms.

'How could you trust His Lordship,' said Rosalind, having

apparently recovered her voice again, 'when you didn't know him? And all your life, your various aunts and cousins had been telling you what a selfish, irresponsible person he was? Not a patch on your father.'

Susannah sat back, suddenly. 'Yes. They *did* do that. So that when he finally did come home, and was so…cold and distant with me, when he wasn't being stern and disapproving, I… I… Well…' She petered out, looking up at him with chagrin.

'It is hard,' put in Rosalind, 'knowing who to trust, isn't it?' And then she looked up at him, with a wry smile. 'I have never been able to rely on any of the men in my family, nor the ones I've met during the course of my work. Until I met your guardian.' She sighed then, gazing up at him with what looked like…worship. 'Men of his calibre,' she added, 'are very thin on the ground.'

'But I *should* have trusted you,' said Susannah, sitting back on her heels. 'And Lieutenant Minter. You are both…so…' she screwed up her face '…honourable. I thought that meant dull. But…'

Michael realised that if he didn't put a stop to this flow of confidences, they were going to be stuck on the floor all night.

'Glad though I am that you have finally realised the worth of a man who only wants the best for you, we have got to decide what to do with the *un*worthy one lying in a pool of his own gore over there.'

Susannah gave a disdainful sniff.

'And you don't need to worry about Lieutenant Minter too much, you know,' added Rosalind. 'He is fathoms deep in love with you. You will only have to apologise and tell him that you have seen his worth, and he will be so happy that he will probably burst his waistcoat buttons.'

'Oh, I wish he was here now,' cried Susannah. 'He would know just what to do! Why, he is always talking about the sort of stratagems he's had to adopt to defeat the enemy, you know, when at sea.'

Michael toyed with the idea of telling her that officers in His Majesty's army had to do that sort of thing on land, as well. But thought it was probably better not to dampen her enthusiasm for the fellow, now she'd decided to have some.

He was on the verge of telling her that one of them was going to have to go and fetch a constable, or something of the sort, when he became aware of the sound of muted voices, coming from the other side of the bedroom door.

Female voices.

'If I am not mistaken,' he said, 'it sounds as if some of the maids who have been asleep in the attics have woken up and come to find out what is going on in here. So we'd better come up with a story, quickly, unless you want everyone to know that this fellow almost abducted you?'

But it was too late. The door burst open and, with an air of valour, three housemaids came tumbling into the room, two of them brandishing pokers and the other one, a silver hairbrush.

Chapter Twenty-Three

'Oh, miss!' cried Susannah's maid, Pauline. 'Oh, miss!'

She had been taking a nap, Rosalind could tell, because she'd evidently put her hair in curling papers. There was still one tangled in a strand of hair that had escaped her cap.

The other two maids, who'd ranged themselves behind her, peeked over her shoulders, their eyes widening as they saw, well, an apparently dead body on the floor by the window and their master clutching the skinny, plain governess in his arms. It was hard to tell, as their heads swung from one tableau to the other, which they found the most shocking.

'If we'd only known it was a housebreaker,' said Constance, stepping round Pauline to take a closer look at Mr Baxter's body, 'we would have come sooner. Only when we first heard the screams, we just thought—' She broke off abruptly as Pauline dug her sharp elbow into the girl's ribs.

Yes, Rosalind could easily guess what they'd thought. That Susannah had been brought home early, because of some misdemeanour, and that the screams were just her indulging in a fit of bad temper. Also, they'd taken their time making themselves presentable. To try to look as though they'd been sitting up, patiently waiting for their mistresses to come home, and hadn't needed to tidy themselves up after lying on their beds.

'A housebreaker,' said Lord Caldicot, looking across at Baxter's form, thoughtfully. 'Yes. That is exactly what this is.'

'Oh, but...' said Susannah.

'And he tried to choke Miss Hinchcliffe to stop her calling out for help,' he continued, cutting through whatever Susannah had been about to say and shooting her a warning look while he was at it, 'when he climbed in through the window, not expecting to find anyone at home. Though why,' he continued, in withering accents, 'he went to all the trouble of procuring a ladder and climbing in by this window I cannot imagine. He might just as well have strolled in through the front door, since the night porter, a man I pay to be at his post to prevent such things, is conspicuous by his absence.'

'I suspect,' said Throgmorton, the third of the trio, with a disapproving sniff, 'they all went to the Jolly Footman.'

'Well, may I suggest,' said Lord Caldicot, in that same magnificently disdainful tone, 'that one of you go straight there and fetch some of the jolly footmen back? And dispatch at least one of them to fetch a constable, who can dispose of this... miscreant.'

All three maids dispersed at once, practically tumbling over each other in their eagerness to be the first to report on all the excitement the men had missed by going out.

Susannah gave an impatient huff, planting her hands on her hips.

'They've just gone off and left us to deal with...him,' she complained.

'It seems to me that you two are extremely capable,' Lord Caldicot said, giving Rosalind a bit of a squeeze, 'of dealing with anything or anyone who attempts to cross either of you.'

Susannah tilted her head to one side. 'Lord Caldicot,' she said with a shake of her head. 'It almost sounds as though you are *proud* of me!'

'Don't let it go to your head,' he said, though he was smiling as he said it. 'I dare say you will do something to make me cross with you again directly.'

Susannah chuckled. 'Or you will come over all tyrannical again and make me cross as crabs with you.'

Although Rosalind was glad the pair of them were getting on so well, she couldn't stop worrying about what Mr Baxter might do when he woke up.

'I hate to have to remind you both,' she therefore said, 'but Mr Baxter is still lying there.' And might wake up at any moment.

'I think,' said Lord Caldicot, 'that when the authorities come, it may be as well to go along with the suggestion the maids gave. After all, if the truth were known, that he'd tried to abduct Susannah, people will really enjoy making a scandal broth of it. Susannah, I know you haven't always trusted me, but trust me on this. That is *not* the sort of story a girl wants hanging over her head like the stench of bad fish.'

She pouted. 'I want him punished for this. For hurting Miss Hinchcliffe, too!'

'So do I,' said Lord Caldicot, grimly. 'But I think once he is taken into custody, there will be plenty of other people clamouring to press all sorts of charges. And that we could keep your names out of it.'

'That's not enough,' she said. '*I* want to...to *hurt* him!' She strode over to the body and glared down at it, her fists clenched.

'No, Susannah,' said Rosalind, stretching out her hand. 'If you gave in to the urge to have your revenge, you would be as bad as he is.'

'I would not!'

'In fact,' added Rosalind, 'what we really ought to be doing is fetching a doctor.'

'Oh, no, you don't,' said Lord Caldicot hastily. 'Not after what happened last time,' he added, lowering his voice so that Susannah, who was standing with her back to them as she glared down at Mr Baxter, could not hear. 'I am not going to give him the chance to escape a second time.'

'I know,' said Susannah, suddenly. 'We should tie him up.'

'That,' said Lord Caldicot, 'is an excellent idea.'

'I will go and find some ropes with which to bind him,' said Susannah, rather gleefully, and darted from the room.

'At last,' said Lord Caldicot, gazing down into her face. 'I thought we would never have any peace. How are you feeling, now? Can you breathe any better yet?'

'Yes, much better, thank you. And really, he only got his hands round my neck briefly. Susannah must have heard the sound of him throwing the chair across the room, and, knowing it was not the sort of thing I'd do, came to find out what was going on—'

'I don't care why she came in here,' he broke in.

'But...'

'Please, stop talking. Though I am glad you are able to, of course. But what I'd really rather be doing is kissing that mouth, not listening to what it can say.'

'What, like this? I mean, with Mr Baxter lying over there...'

'Absolutely! In fact, it is rather fitting, since the very first time I wanted to kiss you was the last time you rendered the blighter unconscious.'

'You...you wanted to kiss me...then? But...but why?'

Instead of explaining, he simply lowered his head and did what he'd been threatening to do. Or promising to do, she wasn't sure. She only knew that she'd never expected the evening, which had started out so badly, could have ended like this.

She felt as if she was floating. She felt as if she was dreaming. She was just plucking up the courage to raise her arms and link her hands behind his neck, when the door burst open. Again.

'What,' came the aggrieved tone of Lady Birchwood, 'is the meaning of this?'

Lord Caldicot groaned. And lifted his head.

'I heard all sorts of garbled talk,' continued Lady Birchwood, 'from Throgmorton as she went dashing out of the house just when she ought to be attending to *me*,' she said indignantly, 'about housebreakers and scandalous conduct, but never, ever, could I have imagined that you would be so shameless as to fling yourself at His Lordship like this. You, Miss,' she cried, pointing at Rosalind, 'are a disgrace!'

'No, she isn't,' said Lord Caldicot, getting to his feet, while keeping his arms firmly round Rosalind, with the result that he lifted her off the floor and held her in his arms, cradled to his chest. 'On the contrary, she saved your niece from being abducted by that villain.' He jerked his head at the body lying on the floor.

At that moment, Susannah came bounding back in, with what looked like the tasselled cords from all her bedroom curtains. 'It's true,' she said, skipping over to Mr Baxter. 'Even though he tried to strangle her, she went for him with the chamber pot.'

'The chamber pot?' Lady Birchwood looked even more appalled than ever as her eyes lit on the shattered pieces of the offending item.

'Come and help me tie him up, Aunt Birchwood,' said Susannah, dropping to her knees. 'If you know how to tie knots? Do you?'

'I?' Lady Birchwood reached out and took hold of the door frame as if she needed something solid to hang on to. 'Why on earth would I know how to tie knots?'

'Do you,' Susannah asked Rosalind, hopefully, 'know how to tie knots?'

Rosalind was about to answer that of course she could, when Lord Caldicot let out a low sort of growling noise.

'You are going to have to manage him on your own,' he said firmly. 'Miss Hinchcliffe has suffered enough. I am going to take her away.'

'Yes,' said Susannah with a grin. 'So you can kiss her more thoroughly, I dare say.'

'I have hardly managed to kiss her at all,' he said, sounding aggrieved, as he shouldered his way past Lady Birchwood.

Lady Birchwood let out a shriek. 'Put her down! This is scandalous!'

'No, it isn't,' he replied. 'I'm going to marry her.'

'Marry her? You can't! What will people think?'

'I don't care.' He came to a halt and gave Lady Birchwood a level look. 'Ever since I sold my commission and returned to England, I have been trying to atone for the mistakes my predecessor made. *He* was the one who was gudgeon enough not to remarry and secure the succession after Susannah's mother died, yet *I* have been the one trying to find what people term a *suitable* bride to fill the position. Mainly because you all made me feel that, since I was not fit to fill his shoes, I should at least find a woman who could make up for my deficiencies. But do you know what?'

He didn't pause to allow Lady Birchwood to make any response, but plunged straight on. 'Your brother was *not* the paragon you all made him out to be. And *I* am the Marquess of Caldicot now. And I am going to be a marquess on my own terms. Starting with marrying the one woman with whom I can see myself spending the rest of my life. The woman, in fact, that I love.'

'Bravo!' cried Susannah, though Lady Birchwood made a sort of choking noise, and tottered away to sink despondently on to a chair.

'The family honour...' Lady Birchwood began to wail.

'Oh, for heaven's sake!' Lord Caldicot turned to her, with Rosalind still held in his arms. 'It's not as if I was threatening to marry an opera dancer! Miss Hinchcliffe comes from a decent family, even if she has fallen on hard times. Her grandfather is General Smallwood! Not that it makes any difference to me, my darling,' he said, looking down at her with a slight frown. 'I don't want you thinking that...'

She reached up and placed one finger over his lips.

'I think,' she suggested, 'that you had better not waste your energy on arguing. Not right at this moment. I am not a small, delicate wisp of a woman. And since you seem so reluctant to put me down...'

'Good point! I can deal with Lady Birchwood's arguments later.'

With that, he turned from the room, strode along the landing, went down the stairs and into his study.

Even once there, he did not let her go, so that when he sat down on the chair in front of his desk, she ended up sitting on his lap.

'Now,' he said, studying her face intently. 'Where were we before we were so rudely interrupted?'

'You...' she said, her cheeks growing rather warm, 'had just declared your intention to marry me, in spite of what anyone might think. You had also said,' she reminded him hopefully, 'that you were planning to kiss me.'

He sucked in a sharp breath, looking rather alarmed.

Got to his feet, then set her down on the chair and began pacing back and forth, running his fingers through his hair.

Why, in heaven's name, why? Was he having second thoughts about her? Had he just said all those things about marriage, and kissing, to annoy Lady Birchwood? And was only now realising what it would really mean if he carried through on his threats to scandalise her?

All of a sudden his expression cleared. He went to the desk, picked up one of the ledgers, came back to her and held it out.

'Here,' he said. 'Take this.'

'Why?'

'So that you can hit me with it, of course,' he said, as though it was obvious.

'Why would I want to do anything of the sort?'

'Because I am about to attempt to take liberties with you,' he said. Then frowned. 'Actually, no, I'm not. It has just occurred to me, you see, that I *told* you I wanted to kiss you and that I told everyone else that I intended to marry you. Without once, ever, asking you what you want. Perhaps,' he said, eyeing the ledger warily, 'you ought to just whack me with it anyway. I fully deserve it after the way I…mauled you about and dragged you down here, not to mention the way I kissed your face when you were in no fit state to defend yourself…'

She stood up so abruptly that the ledger fell to the floor, reached out for the lapels of his coat and tugged, hard.

'I am *never* too weak to defend myself,' she declared. 'Could you not tell that I had no objection to anything you were doing, or saying?'

'Well, I…er…*hoped* you didn't. But then I wondered if I was just fooling myself, because it is what I want, so much.'

She shook her head. 'It is what I want, too.'

'Really?' His face lit up.

'Don't you remember, we made a deal to always be honest with one another?'

'I certainly do.' A brief shadow flitted dimmed his expression. 'Only, I haven't always kept to that deal. I never admitted, for instance, how much you were becoming to mean to me…'

'Never mind. I concealed my growing feelings for you, too.'

'So you have them? Feelings for me, that is?'

'How could you doubt it?' she asked, nudging the accounts ledger aside with one foot, then running her hands up his lapels until they rested on his shoulders.

'Last chance,' he said with a rather wicked looking grin, 'to escape.'

'I don't want to escape,' she breathed, her heart hammering in her chest as he lowered his head, purposefully. 'Never, ever... Mmm...'

She couldn't say any more—because he was, at last, kissing her in earnest. And suddenly she no longer felt headachy, or queasy, or as if she was sickening for something. On the contrary, she felt wonderfully, vibrantly alive, for perhaps the first time in her life.

Dimly, in the background, she could hear the sound of someone pounding on the front door and booted feet running across the hall and up the stairs, but Lord Caldicot, no, Michael—she could hardly think of him by any other name now that he was holding her like this, kissing her like this—paid no heed. So she decided it would be rude to suggest he ought to be overseeing whatever was going on.

Besides, she was rapidly losing the ability to think. Michael's kisses were unleashing feelings she'd never dreamed she could feel.

She needed to get closer to him. She wanted to feel him, every bit of him. His shoulders, his sides, even his legs. She didn't have enough hands! She'd have to run her own legs up and down his, she supposed, to satisfy that particular craving...

All of a sudden there came the sound of someone knocking, rather insistently, on the study door.

'What!' Michael lifted his head to glare at the door, only to see Timms peeping round it.

'Begging your pardon, my lord, but I thought you would wish to know that the...er...felon has been removed from the premises.'

'I don't know what the devil gave you that idea. If I cared two pins for that heap of refuse I would have overseen his removal myself!'

'Yes, my lord. Indeed.' Timms inclined his head. 'And may I be the first to congratulate you,' he said, his eyes sliding over Rosalind's dishevelled form. 'On behalf of all the staff, Miss Hinchcliffe,' he added with a decided twinkle in his eye.

'Yes, well now you've said your piece you can take yourself off,' said Michael, rather ungraciously.

'Really,' Rosalind protested, as Timms retreated, shutting the door behind him. 'The poor man was only doing his job.'

'It is a great pity,' he said bitterly, 'that he wasn't doing it earlier, rather than enjoying himself with his underlings, in that pub.'

'But if he hadn't neglected his post,' Rosalind pointed out, 'we might never have reached this point.'

'Hmmm,' he said, as though considering the rights and wrongs of it all. 'Well, never mind what *might* have happened,' he said, testily. 'The fact is, I've had enough of interruptions for one night. I feel as if I've wasted *weeks* trying to persuade people I don't really care about that I'm fit to inhabit the role that has been thrust upon me. Now that I've got you in my arms, that's all I care to think about. Just you. And me.' He hugged her tightly.

And kissed her again.

They managed another few moments, during which time his shirt became detached from the waistband of his breeches and his knees buckled, and somehow they ended up tumbling to the hearthrug, which, she discovered, was every bit as soft as she'd suspected when she'd watched Susannah employing it, before there was another knock on the door.

'What is it now? Whoever it is, they had better watch out,' he snarled, striding to the door and flinging it open.

Susannah stood there, a broad smile on her face. 'I've just had the most wonderful idea,' she said.

'Don't want to hear it. Can't you see I'm busy?'

She peeped round him, to where Rosalind was desperately trying to rearrange her clothing so that it didn't look as if he'd just been ravishing her on the hearthrug.

She giggled. 'You aren't setting me a very good example, are you?'

'Much you would care if I was,' he snapped, 'you minx.'

'Yes, but I was thinking, you will want to throw an engagement ball, won't you? And I have seen the most ravishing outfit...'

Michael dealt with her by shutting the door in her face, then turning the key in the lock.

'What are you laughing at?' He looked at her in confusion.

'Because it has just occurred to me, that the only way we are going to get any privacy to indulge in...' she felt her cheeks heat '...anything truly scandalous is to elope. And that, for once, Mr Baxter has done us a good turn.'

'He has?'

'Yes. Don't you remember? He left a ladder propped up outside my window!'

'No eloping for us,' he said firmly. 'I am going to throw you the most extravagant and public wedding money can buy, so that nobody can doubt how proud I am to have you as my bride.'

'Are you? Truly?'

'How can you doubt it?'

'B-Because there are so many prettier, more eligible women you could have chosen.'

'That's as may be,' he said, stalking over to where she was sitting, in a confusion of blushes and dishevelled clothing. 'But none of them dared argue with me the way you do. None of them could make me laugh. Or keep me wondering what audacious thing they might do or say next. None of them,' he added, sinking down beside her with what looked like a purposeful glint in his eye, 'made me long to throw propriety out of the window and kiss them senseless.'

'No other man has made me feel the way I feel about you, either,' she confessed shyly. 'But...'

'But what?'

'Well, I haven't been raised to fill a position in society...'

'I sincerely hope you aren't going to tell me that you have no idea how to be a marchioness.'

'Well, no, I don't.'

'May I remind you of what you said to me, when I admitted I didn't feel capable of being a marquess? You said that I was one and so other people would have to get used to me being a marquess my own way.'

'No, I didn't!'

'Well, words to that effect. Which is why I'm going to say them to you. Once you are my marchioness, people will have to accustom themselves to you doing things your way. One thing you've taught me is that you need not change to try and fit in with what you think other people expect of you. In fact, I expressly forbid you to change at all. I love you just as you are!'

And then he put paid to any further arguments by kissing her again.

And all at once she stopped caring about what anyone else thought. Michael loved her just as she was! And as long as *he* loved her just as she was, nothing else mattered.

* * * * *

The Earl's Marriage Dilemma
Sarah Mallory

MILLS & BOON

Sarah Mallory grew up in the West Country, England, telling stories. She moved to Yorkshire with her young family, but after nearly thirty years living in a farmhouse on the Pennines, she has now moved to live by the sea in Scotland. Sarah is an award-winning novelist with more than twenty books published by Harlequin Historical. She loves to hear from readers; you can reach her via her website at sarahmallory.com.

Books by Sarah Mallory

Harlequin Historical

His Countess for a Week
The Mysterious Miss Fairchild
Cinderella and the Scarred Viscount
The Duke's Family for Christmas
The Night She Met the Duke
The Major and the Scandalous Widow
Snowbound with the Brooding Lord
Wed in Haste to the Duke

Lairds of Ardvarrick

Forbidden to the Highland Laird
Rescued by Her Highland Soldier
The Laird's Runaway Wife

Saved from Disgrace

The Ton's Most Notorious Rake
Beauty and the Brooding Lord
The Highborn Housekeeper

Visit the Author Profile page
at millsandboon.com.au for more titles.

Author Note

This book started life with a trip to my home city, Bristol. I wanted to walk around the city dockland. In 1816, when my story starts, Bristol was a bustling port with ships sailing off from there to around the world—and that was what I needed for the start of my story.

In the heart of the harborside is Queen Square, its Georgian houses surrounded on three sides by the River Avon, and I decided it was the perfect place for Conham, the Earl of Dallamire, to meet Rosina, who is fleeing for her life.

Conham has inherited a mountain of debt from his father, and it is his job, his duty, to put it right, so he must marry a fortune. Rosina spent years helping her father run the family estate and knows only too well what is required of a responsible landowner.

A friendship develops between Rosina and Conham, but even when it threatens to turn into something stronger, she knows nothing can come of it. She must fend for herself and maintain her independence. Unless, of course, she and Conham can find a way out of their dilemma...

Writing Conham and Rosina's story has been a complete joy, and I do hope you enjoy reading it as much as I enjoyed creating it!

To Sue, who is not only an excellent host
but a great tour guide, too!

Chapter One

She refused. She refused me!

The words pounded through Conham's head as he strode out of the house. He had come to Bristol solely with the intention of proposing to Alicia Faulds, and she had turned him down.

She had been his mistress for six months and he had thought they were ideally suited. She was a widow, experienced, entertaining and witty. She was also very wealthy. As the Eleventh Earl of Dallamire, he had an impressive lineage and a large house in Berkshire, together with extensive estates around the country. True, he was sadly short of funds, but he had never made any attempt to hide the fact from her.

He had barely stepped out of the house when the door closed behind him with a thud. That was it. He was done with the rich Mrs Faulds. He almost winced as he recalled how she had laughed at him when he had admitted that his fortune was somewhat depleted.

Depleted? My dear Conham, it is nonexistent! The Dallamire estates—those that are not entailed—are riddled with debts. And you greatly misled me with talk of your latest inheritance, I have seen it. An insignificant property in the wilds of Gloucestershire and a ramshackle collection of run-down buildings on

*a few acres of land to the north of Bristol. Ha! There is noth-
ing there to tempt me.*

Suddenly, the lady he had thought might make him a good
wife had been more like a stranger. She had travelled ahead of
him to Bristol in order to assess the properties his godfather had
left him. Confound it, he had not even seen them for himself yet!

A chill breeze sprang up, rousing Conham from the useless
reflections. He looked about him. He had planned to escort
Alicia to a masquerade tonight, but that was clearly out of the
question now. He would not go alone, but neither did he want
to go back to his rooms at the Full Moon just yet. He felt too
tense, too restless, and it was more than likely Matt would still
be awake. He would want to know why Conham was back before daybreak and what had put him in such a foul mood.

*That's what comes of bringing Matt Talacre with me on this
journey*, Conham thought irritably. It was impossible to snub a
man who had fought beside you at Waterloo.

Across the street, Queen Square silent in the moonlight, and
the walks dissecting the lawns were deserted. It was an ideal
place to collect his thoughts and cool his temper. Conham threw
the domino around his shoulders to keep out the chill of the
November night and crossed the road. After jumping over the
low wooden rail and onto the grass, a few steps took him to
the gravel path that ran around the square beneath the trees.

It was very quiet, although he could hear faint noises from
the floating harbour that surrounded Queen Square on three
sides. Shouts and thuds drifted over the terraced houses that
separated the elegant square from the docks, and he guessed a
ship was getting ready to depart and catch the tide. From the
clear sky, a full moon shone down through the bare branches
of the trees, casting dappled shadows on the path. By the time
Conham began a second circuit of the square he could feel his
mind settling.

He could not deny that Alicia's rejection was a disappointment. She was a luscious brunette and knew how to drive a
man wild with desire. She also possessed a considerable fortune, but he had genuinely thought marriage would suit them
both. It would not be a love match, but they liked one another

well enough, which was as much as Conham expected from a wife. As an earl, marriage was a duty and, in his case, a rich bride was a necessity. However, it appeared the wealthy widow valued her independence above a title.

Conham could not blame her. He *was* impoverished, and a fool not to have done something about it. He had received the news of his father's death shortly after Waterloo, but had gone on to Paris with the Army of Occupation, believing there was no immediate need for him to rush home. However, when he had returned to England some six months ago, he discovered that the old earl, an inveterate gambler, had left him neglected estates and a mountain of crippling debt.

True, the Berkshire property was extensive, but years of bad management had left Dallamire Hall in a poor condition, and the combined income from all his lands was barely enough to provide for his stepmother and his two half-sisters, who were still in the schoolroom.

'Damme,' he muttered. 'I should have quit the army and come back earlier. I always knew Father was a gambler. I should have made more effort to keep an eye on him before he gambled away almost everything!'

The pill had been somewhat sweetened by the acquisition of his godfather's properties, which had been held in trust for him until his twenty-eighth birthday. That event had occurred in August, and was the reason Conham had come to the West Country, to inspect his inheritance.

The news that Alicia had gone ahead and rented a house for herself in Bristol he had taken as a good sign, until she had dashed all his hopes tonight. He flicked his cane at an errant weed in the grass. What was it she had called it? *Another ramshackle property.* From his lawyers' cautiously worded report, he suspected Alicia's description would prove to be correct.

He sighed and stared up at the moon. Well, what was done was done. His years in the army had shown him that a fellow must be philosophical about these things. There were any number of people who depended upon the Earl of Dallamire for their livelihood and he could not let them down. He must now look elsewhere for a rich bride. It shouldn't be too difficult. There were numerous tales of rich men willing to settle a fortune on their daughter in return for a title.

'*Oof!*'

His meanderings were cut short as a body cannoned into him, knocking his ebony cane from his hand. Instinctively, he grabbed the culprit.

'Oh, no, you don't!'

He expected oaths and curses from his struggling attacker. Instead, a soft female voice begged him to let her go.

'What the devil!'

Conham swung his captive into the moonlight and found himself looking at a pale, heart-shaped face set about with an untidy mass of fair curling hair. She wore no coat, but the sleeves beneath his hands felt very much like silk. At that moment he heard shouts coming from the Grove.

'Please, sir. They must not see me!'

A pair of wide eyes gazed anxiously up at him and he pulled the girl back into the shadows just as four men came running into the square.

'Too late for that,' he muttered, shrugging off his domino. 'Here, put this around you.' He threw the cloak around her shoulders and lifted the hood over her fair hair. 'Now, put your arms around my neck.'

And with that he bent his head and kissed her. She froze, but did not push him away. Instead, she clung tighter at the sound of boots pounding along the path. Someone was approaching at a run. Conham raised his head.

'Stay close to me,' he whispered.

He turned, keeping the woman behind him, in his shadow. The men had split up and only two were coming towards him. He moved forward, one hand pretending to straighten the fall flap of his breeches as he hailed them cheerfully.

'You are in the devil of a hurry, sirs. Are the pressmen abroad?'

The men stopped.

'And who might you be?' demanded one.

'I am Dallamire,' he said, with a touch of hauteur. 'The Earl of Dallamire.'

He saw them eyeing him, taking in the black woollen evening coat with its gilt buttons embossed with a coat of arms, the tight-fitting black trousers and dancing shoes. The second man touched his forelock, clearly impressed.

'No, my lord, not the press gang. We're after an escaped prisoner. But 'tis only a whore who slipped off the ship,' he added when Conham feigned alarm. 'Have you seen or heard anyone go past you?'

'Well, no.' Conham pulled his cloaked companion into his side. 'But as you can see, I have been rather…occupied.'

The man laughed coarsely. 'Aye, well, we'll not keep you from your pleasures, my lord. Come on, Joe!'

Conham watched the sailors until they were out of sight and he and the woman were alone again in the square.

'Well, now,' he said, 'I think you had best tell me what this is all about.'

'And I think you should let me go,' she retorted, struggling against his hold.

He tightened his grip. 'But I have yet to be convinced that you are innocent.'

'How dare you!'

'And besides that,' he said as she continued to fight him, 'it is not safe for a young woman to be wandering around unattended. We are in the docklands, there are some very rough characters abroad.'

'I am well aware of that!'

'Not me, you wildcat,' he exclaimed, catching her free wrist before she could claw at his eyes. 'There are those in the alleys around here who would kill you for the clothes on your back. And then there are your pursuers.'

She stopped struggling and eyed him resentfully. He went on.

'That's better. Let's go to an inn and you can tell me your story. Who knows? I may even be able to help you.'

For a moment she was silent. Then, 'Very well, I will come with you.'

'Good.' He retrieved his cane, saying, 'You had best keep my domino about you, too.'

'But it is far too long,' she objected. 'It will drag in all the dirt.'

Her concern for his property surprised him but he merely shrugged. 'Better that than you freeze to death.'

He heard a faint chuckle. 'Very true.'

'Come along, then.'

Conham pulled her hand onto his sleeve and set off, very much aware that she was not putting any weight on him at all. They had not gone far before she stumbled and he quickly put his arm around her.

'I beg your pardon,' she muttered. 'I feel a little dizzy.'

'It's not far to King Street. You will feel better once you are sitting down. And then you can tell me what all this is about.'

They had reached the edge of the Square when he saw the sailors coming back. He glanced down at his companion, to assure himself that the voluminous hood of the domino concealed her face. She had hesitated at the sight of them, but Conham put his hand on her arm, where it rested on his sleeve, and kept her moving. He addressed the men as they drew nearer.

'No luck finding your quarry?'

'There's no sign of the wench.' A rough curse followed the words. 'And we dare not wait any longer to cast off or the lock gates will be closed against us.' He spat into the gutter. 'She's disappeared into the stews. She'll not last long there.'

'No. Good night to you, then.' Conham touched his hat and strolled on, whistling nonchalantly and resisting the urge to look back until they had reached the corner of King Street.

'Have they gone?' came a whisper from beside him.

'Yes. They are scurrying back to their ship. You are safe from them now.'

'Thank goodness,' she said, and with that she crumpled against him.

As Conham swept her up into his arms, the hood slipped back and her fair hair cascaded over his sleeve like silk. Her eyes were closed and he gazed down at her, taking in the straight little nose and a mouth that he had already discovered was eminently kissable. Under the flare of the street lamp she looked older than he had first thought, but still defenceless. And far too young to be abroad unprotected.

'Oh, Lord,' he muttered. 'What the devil am I going to do with you?'

Chapter Two

Rosina stirred. Her head ached prodigiously and her mouth felt very dry. She was in bed, the covers pulled up snugly around her shoulders. She opened her eyes, wincing at the light from the unshuttered window. This was not her bedchamber. A chill ran through her as she began to remember parts of her ordeal.

She looked up at the plain wooden canopy above her head, then at the furniture around the room. Finally, her eyes came to rest upon the man standing by the hearth, looking down at the fire. He was tall, with broad shoulders and chest that tapered down to the flat plane of his stomach. A sportsman, perhaps, his glossy red-brown hair curling down to his collar like the drawings she had seen of fashionable Corinthians. He was not wearing a coat, and snowy white shirtsleeves billowed out from a fine silk waistcoat. That and his black trousers suggested evening dress, even though it was now full daylight.

As if aware of her gaze he turned to look at her and she noted a strong face with an angular jaw and piercing, grey-green eyes. She did not recognise him as her rescuer, but then the night had been fearsome, all blue-grey moonlight and dark shadows. However, when he spoke, his smooth, deep voice was familiar.

'So, you are awake at last.'

'How long have I been here?'

'Since midnight.'

'Midnight.' She frowned, struggling to remember. 'You are an earl...'

'Conham Mortlake, Earl of Dallamire, yes.'

He rose and came across to her, picking up a glass from the table beside the bed, but as he came closer she shrank away.

'Don't be afraid. It is only water.'

'Of course, but I can hold it for myself,' said Rosina, fighting down her momentary panic.

She reminded herself that this man had helped her, but even so, her hand was shaking when she reached out for the glass.

The earl laughed, but not unkindly. 'I think you should let me help you.'

He sat on the edge of the bed and slipped one hand behind her shoulders, the other holding the glass as she took a few sips.

It *was* water. No unpleasant taste or pungent smell; no one was trying to drug her now.

'Thank you,' she said. 'Where am I?'

'In my rooms at the Full Moon.' He arranged the pillows behind her so she could sit up more comfortably. 'You collapsed as we were leaving Queen Square and I thought it best to bring you here. You have slept the morning away. That was probably the result of all the laudanum you had taken. I could smell that, or something like it, on your breath.' He straightened. 'There, is that better?'

'Yes. Thank you.' Rosina realised she was only wearing her shift and she pulled the sheet up to her chin.

'The chambermaids undressed you, not I,' he told her. 'Unfortunately, the inn is full and they had no choice but to put you in my bed. No need to look so startled. I had another bed made up in my companion's bedroom. I came in here only to build up the fire. I am sorry if I woke you.'

He paused, but she was still too dazed to make a sensible reply, and after a moment he continued.

'I have to go out. I will send up a maid with some tea and bread and butter. Anything else you need, just ask her. This room and the adjoining parlour are at your disposal for as long as you need it. No one will disturb you, unless you ring for a servant.'

'Thank you.' She looked up at him, then said in a rush, 'You will come back?'

'Of course.' His crooked smile was kind, reassuring. 'I shall be gone for a few hours but I will look in on you when I return. Oh, and I have told everyone here you are a cousin of mine. A Mrs Alness. I said that your carriage overturned and all the trunks fell into the river, which accounts for your dishevelled state and lack of baggage. They may not believe that, but they will accept it, trust me.'

'Because you are an earl?'

'Because I am an earl.' He was still smiling, but she thought there was a hint of derision in it now. 'May I know your name?'

'Rosina.'

He waited, but she closed her lips, unwilling to give him any more information, and at length he nodded.

'Very well, Rosina. I will bid you *au revoir*.'

When Lord Dallamire had gone, Rosina lay back against the pillows, trying to put her thoughts into some order. When she had collided with him last night, she had been flying for her life. He had saved her; there was no doubt of that. And strangely, she had not been frightened when he kissed her. It had been shocking, very much as she imagined it would feel to be struck by lightning. But it had been energising and exciting, too. No one had ever kissed her like that before, so she had no idea if it was always that way.

Last night she had been wary of the earl, afraid he might be helping her for his own ends, but it seemed he had taken care of her. She closed her eyes. She had no idea what she was going to do, but for the moment she felt safe. Her arms were bruised, but that was the rough treatment of the sailors and from… Rosina shuddered. She did not want to think of how she had come to be on the ship. Not yet.

She threw back the covers and swung her legs to the floor, standing up cautiously. She felt a little dizzy, but her legs supported her. She did not want to lie in bed any longer. Carefully, she walked over to the bell-pull and tugged at it.

It was late afternoon and growing dark when Conham returned to the Full Moon and the landlady told him his cousin was waiting for him in the private parlour. He went upstairs to find the room glowing with candlelight and Rosina standing before the fire, warming her hands. For a moment he had a clear view of her profile, that glorious hair piled up loosely, one or two golden tendrils hanging down around her face, the dainty nose and chin and sculpted lips that looked made for laughter but were now drooping slightly.

Then she turned to look at him, and Conham's breath caught in his throat.

'You are dressed.' He said the first thing that came into his mind.

'Yes.' She glanced down at her skirts. 'The maid cleaned my gown as best she could and found me a brush and pins, so I could tidy my hair.'

Despite her shy smile, she still looked pale and drawn.

'Are you feeling better?'

'Very much so, my lord, thank you.'

'And have you eaten?'

'Yes, thank you.'

'How much?' he asked, giving her a searching look.

'A piece of bread and butter.'

'That is hardly enough to sustain you.'

An uneasy silence fell and his glance went to the small purse on the table. He had left it there deliberately, half expecting her to take the money and leave.

'I thought you might have gone by now.'

'You wanted an explanation.' Her shoulders lifted slightly. 'I owe you that much.'

He nodded. 'I will ring for refreshments.'

A servant entered and Rosina studied the earl as he gave his orders. He was no longer wearing his evening clothes but was dressed in pantaloons and Hessians, with a blue coat over his dove-grey waistcoat and snow-white linen. She had rarely seen such well-fitting clothes outside the pages of a fashion journal. Her brother Edgar's finery, the nipped-in waist of his coats, the high shirt points and pomaded hair, had always struck her as rather flamboyant. Edgar assured her it was the height of fashion but she had always thought he looked a trifle ridiculous.

There was nothing ridiculous about Lord Dallamire. The shoulders of his coat required no additional padding, while the flat plane of his stomach and muscular thighs hinted at a body honed by exercise. Not at all like Edgar or the friends he occasionally brought to the house. They were without exception overfed and overdressed, their faces already showing signs of dissipation. Just the thought of them made her shudder.

'Well, madam, is my presence here so offensive to you?'

The servant having withdrawn, the earl had turned back towards her and was regarding her coldly, his brows raised. He must have seen her look of revulsion and thought it was directed at him! Rosina felt the heat of a blush burning her cheeks.

'No, no, I was just...' She stopped and tried again. 'Your clothes. That is not what you were wearing when I saw you this morning. I did not expect...'

'I slept in my evening dress.' The icy look had gone and his lips twitched. There was even a gleam of amusement in his eyes as he explained. 'I knew I would be looking in on you several times in the night, and thought you might be alarmed if you woke and saw me dressed in a nightgown.'

As he pulled out a chair for her at the table, she suddenly remembered the domino he had wrapped around her.

'Oh, you were on your way to a ball last night! I beg your pardon, I am very sorry if I ruined your evening.'

He sat down opposite her, waving aside the apology. 'It is not important, I had already decided not to go. But let us return to the matter in hand. Why were those men chasing you? And no lies now!'

Rosina bridled a little at his tone, but decided it was a perfectly reasonable question. When she thought of how she must have looked, with her dusty gown and untidy hair, it was quite understandable that he should be cautious. But she needed to be wary, too.

'Forgive me, sir, but how do I know you are who you say?'

He took out a silver case and extracted a card for her.

'That will have to suffice for now,' he said. 'Until six months ago I was with the army in France.'

The entry of a servant with a tray caused a diversion. Rosina read the card and set it down while Lord Dallamire was pouring wine for them both. When the servant had retired again, she accepted a glass from the earl, but refused the sweet biscuits.

'Were you at Waterloo, my lord?'

'I was.' A shadow crossed his face, as if he found the memories disturbing. 'It was hailed as a glorious victory, but it was the end of so many good lives.'

'I am very sorry.'

He acknowledged her words with a nod, but said briskly, 'Now, are you going to tell me your story?'

Rosina sipped at her wine, trying to decide what to do. She was in a fix, and instinct told her she could trust this man.

'My name is Rosina Brackwood,' she said at last. 'My father was Sir Thomas Brackwood, of Brackwood Court in Somerset. It is some miles south of Bristol.'

'I do not think… Wait, I heard the name Brackwood recently in town.' He frowned. 'But that was a young man.'

'My brother Edgar.'

'Ah, yes, that would be it. I came across him once or twice, at the gaming tables.'

Her lip curled. 'That does not surprise me. He lives only for pleasure. While Papa was alive Edgar rarely visited Brackwood, except when he had outrun his allowance. He was at home when Papa died in April and when he stayed on, I thought it was to take up his responsibilities at last, but he was only interested in releasing funds from the estate to pay his debts. He has no interest in the people or the land, but my father did! Papa cared passionately. As do I, having lived at Brackwood all my life.' Her little spurt of defiance faded and she sighed. 'I had grown accustomed to running Brackwood as if it was my own. I suppose it was inevitable that Edgar and I would quarrel when he came home.'

She took another sip then put the glass down. She felt a little light-headed, and she needed to keep her wits about her if she was to explain everything.

'My father was concerned about what would happen to Brackwood when he died, so he drew up new agreements with some of the villagers and tenant farmers, giving them more se-curity. When Edgar tried to force them to leave, I made sure they knew he could not do so without due compensation. He has also tried to borrow money from Papa's friends, which I knew, as well as Edgar, that he would not be able to repay for years. If ever.' She glanced across at the earl and noted the slight frown on his brow. 'I did nothing illegal, merely told our friends the truth. Papa would have wanted them to know the risks. Edgar did not like that. He said I was interfering.'

'I can imagine.'

Conham remembered his own homecoming earlier in the year. Having been assured by his stepmother that they were managing very well at Dallamire, he returned to find that was very far from the truth.

'Do you think I was wrong?' she asked him. 'My father was an honest man, he would be ashamed of Edgar's duplicity to-wards our friends. As for the villagers, they are mostly poor people and ill-educated. What will become of them if they are turned out of their houses? Where could they go? My brother's actions would have ruined their lives, and all for a short-term gain because he wants to sell the houses and the unentailed land.'

'It is understandable that your brother will have his own ideas about his inheritance,' he replied, thinking of his own predicament.

'But he should be *protecting* it! Papa bought the extra land to help ensure Brackwood can survive and profit. If Edgar would only implement Papa's plans, then, in time, everyone would benefit. The farms would be improved, yields increased.' She went on, warming to her theme, 'I used to help my father with the estate business and before he died, he shared many of his ideas with me. He knew they would take time, of course but—' She stopped. 'You look sceptical. Do you not believe me?'

He said, gently, 'I believe you mean well, Miss Brackwood, but perhaps you do not understand the situation.'

The wine appeared to have put some heart into his companion.

'Lord Dallamire, I am five-and-twenty, four years older than my brother, and I understand the situation very well,' she said, sitting up very straight. 'I began helping my father before I left the schoolroom and when he discovered I had an aptitude for figures and for dealing with legal matters, too, he passed even more of the work over to me.'

'Did you not have a season in London?'

'I never wanted one. I was quite content looking after Brackwood.'

'But if you had married, you would have an establishment of your own.'

'That would be my husband's property, never mine.'

'Ah. Very true.'

He smiled and saw a shy twinkle appear briefly in those blue eyes, then she grew serious again.

'I *would* have stepped back and let Edgar take control of the estate, my lord. If only he had shown the slightest interest. Papa was deeply disappointed when my brother said he wanted to see more of life before settling down. He went off to town again and we rarely saw him after that.'

'You can hardly expect me to condemn him, Miss Brackwood. My own father died more than twelve months ago, and I have only just taken up my inheritance.'

'But you were in the army, my lord. You had responsibilities. My brother had no such claims upon his time. He only ever came home when he was obliged to do so, to escape his creditors. While Edgar was in London, squandering his allowance, I was working with Papa, discussing the improvements he wanted to make, drawing up plans and working out the costings. In fact, for the last year of my father's life, when his health was failing, I looked after everything for him.'

'Very commendable.'

She went on eagerly. 'Some of Papa's improvements have already been implemented and are bearing fruit, like the drainage of the long meadow and encouraging the farmers to use the Scotch plough on the heavy soils. Then there is the crop rotation—'

Conham threw up his hands. 'Enough! There is no need to go on. I stand corrected, you understand these things far more than I!'

Rosina saw the amusement in his face and sat back, chuckling. 'I beg your pardon. I do tend to get carried away once I begin talking of these things!'

'But your brother wants none of it.'

Rosina shook her head, all desire to smile gone.

'That is very sad, ma'am, but if he is master now, it is surely his choice what is done.'

'I know that, I had accepted it. I did not argue when he sold off the fields to the north of the village, nor the three houses in Wood Lane.' She drew a breath. 'But when it comes to our friends, I could not let Edgar dupe them into lending him money. He told them it was for improvements to Brackwood, but that was a lie. He needed it to settle the most pressing of his gambling debts!'

'And he was angry because you intervened.'

'More than angry.'

Rosina clasped her hands tightly in her lap. Lord Dallamire wanted the truth and she owed Edgar no loyalty now. Rosina felt a little sick as she uttered the next words.

'He had me abducted.'

The memory came flooding in on her, the images sharp and clear in her mind: returning the evening before last to find Brackwood Court unnaturally quiet, discovering Edgar had turned off her maid, given the rest of the servants a day's holiday and brought that awful woman, Moffat, into the house.

They had strapped her to a chair, Edgar laughing at her furious protests.

You have been a continual thorn in my flesh since our father died, dear sister. Overriding my orders, speaking out of turn. I have had enough of you and your interfering ways, madam!

She closed her eyes, trying to blot out his cruel voice.

I am the owner of Brackwood now and that is the end of it.

And it is the end of you, madam. I am sending you away where you will trouble me no more. Hold her!

She remembered Moffat's strong hands keeping her head still while her brother poured the sleeping draught into her throat, the woman's warning that it would be dangerous to administer too much of the drug and Edgar's callous response.

Do you think I care? It matters not to me if she is dead when she boards the ship.

Rosina had felt the blackness closing in. Her brother's voice was getting fainter and she heard only one more thing before her world went dark.

Just as long as she never leaves it alive!

Chapter Three

Conham jumped up and caught Rosina as she toppled from her chair. Gently, he lowered her to the floor, kneeling and cradling her head and shoulders against his chest.

She regained consciousness almost immediately and began to struggle against his hold.

'No, no, don't fight me. You are safe now.'

She grew still and opened her eyes, looking up at him blankly at first, but then with recognition, and one dainty hand clutched at his coat.

'You are safe,' he repeated. 'You fainted.'

She put her free hand to her head. 'I should not have drunk the wine.'

'You should have had more to eat!' He helped her into an armchair beside the fire. 'Sit there while I order something for you.'

Rosina obeyed, if only because she did not think she could move without assistance. She sat very still and took a few deep breaths while Lord Dallamire went out. She was mortified to have lost consciousness, to have shown such weakness over something that was nothing more than a bad memory.

She said, when the earl returned, 'I beg your pardon. I am not usually such a poor creature.'

'You are in shock. I have witnessed such things in my men, after they have seen action.' He dropped his hand briefly on her shoulder before returning to his own seat. 'The landlady is bringing you something to eat, then you shall go back to bed.'

'I need to tell you what happened.'

She put her elbows on the table and rested her head on her hands. It felt important to explain, to make him understand the enormity of what Edgar had done.

He filled a glass with water from the pitcher on the tray and pushed it across to her. 'Very well. I am listening.'

Rosina sat back and stared at the glass, but did not touch it.

'Edgar drugged me and hired a woman to bring me to Bristol and put me on board a ship bound for America. Boston.' She shivered and crossed her arms. 'He was going to put it about that I had used the money Papa left me to go travelling, but in fact, he had arranged for me to meet with a…an accident at sea.'

It all sounded quite outrageous and she had no idea if the earl believed her. His countenance was inscrutable. She drank a little of the water and went on.

'I regained consciousness as I was being carried below deck, but I pretended I was still asleep. That was when I heard Moffat talking with the captain and learned what was to happen to me, once they were at sea.'

'But you escaped.'

'Yes.' Rosina cradled the water glass between her hands to stop them shaking. 'Moffat bound me, hand and foot, once we were in the cabin and away from any witnesses, but she had been imbibing gin liberally during our journey to Bristol and made a mull of it. I managed to free myself and when she fell into a drunken stupor I slipped out of the cabin. It was dark by then. Everyone on deck was busy preparing to set sail, but thankfully, the gangplank was still in place.

'No one noticed me leaving the ship, but on the quay, I was accosted by a…a man. One of the ship's crew saw us scuffling and raised the alarm. I fled.' She paused, recalling the fearful thudding of her heart, the sudden terror when she heard the shouts and knew she was being pursued. 'Then I bumped into you.'

'That is a fantastical tale, madam. You were fortunate to get away.'

'You do not believe me.'

'I *do* believe you.' He reached across the table and caught her hands, turning them palms up to expose the angry red marks on her wrists. 'I saw these marks last night when you were sleeping. If this was your brother's doing, he deserves to be flogged.'

'But he won't be. He prefers to pay others to carry out his foul deeds. He did nothing himself, save to pour the sleeping draught down my throat.' She sighed. 'It would be my word against his. Edgar will have paid his villains well to swear I went on board that ship willingly.'

'They would have little choice,' he remarked. 'For the crew to say anything else would implicate them in your abduction.'

He had been absently rubbing his thumbs gently over her skin, causing little darts of heat to flow through her. She was hardly aware of how calming, how beguiling it was until he released her hands and she had to swallow a little mewl of protest.

She was grateful that the entrance of the landlady caused a timely diversion.

'Here we are, Your Lordship, supper for the lady.' She put down a tray with a steaming bowl of soup in front of Rosina, and drew her attention to the bread and butter and the large piece of cake. 'And if there is anything else you'd like, ma'am, all you have to do is ask.'

'Thank you. We will ring if we need you.' The earl dismissed the landlady with a smile and turned back to Rosina. 'Now, you will eat that before we continue.'

She complied, relieved not to have to look him in the face as she tried to decide just what she was feeling. She was not uncomfortable in his presence, even though he was sitting so close, drinking his wine and watching her. It was as if they had known each other forever.

When she had finished the soup and the bread she pushed the tray away.

'You have had enough?'

'Yes. Thank you.'

'Will you not try the cake?'

He broke a piece off and held it out. Rosina hesitated, then took it from him and popped it into her mouth. It was very good and she allowed him to feed her another small piece, and another. It was an unfamiliar sensation, having someone looking after her like this, but not unpleasant.

At last, she put up her hands. 'Thank you, I enjoyed the cake, very much, but I have had enough.'

He nodded. 'There is a little colour in your cheeks now. Would you like to try the wine again?'

'No, I shall drink the water.' She met his eyes across the table and returned his smile 'But thank you.'

'Very well. When you are ready to retire, the landlady will send up a maid to help you into bed.'

Rosina felt much better after her meal and not in the least tired. There was also the very real fear that the memories of her ordeal would return to haunt her dreams.

She said, 'I should like to stay here a little longer, my lord, if you do not object?'

'Not at all. Let us move to the chairs by the fire, I think they will be more comfortable. Then you can tell me how I may help you.'

She looked at him, confused.

'Do you have family or friends who will take care of you?'

She shook her head. 'There is no one. I have no family, save Edgar, and no friends apart from those who live near Brack-wood. My brother has demonstrated that his violent temper knows no bounds. To contact any one of them might put them in danger.'

'Then what do you intend to do?'

Rosina had been asking herself that very question. She had never visited Bristol before; it was a strange city to her. She had no money and there was no one she could call upon. At least, not yet. She glanced at the man sitting opposite. She *thought* she could trust him, but in truth, did she really have any choice?

'First of all, I need to quit Bristol,' she said quietly. 'Then I must find a way to support myself. As a companion, or a governess, perhaps. I want to be independent and will take any honest work. But finding any respectable position will be impossible without a character reference.' She bit her lip. 'Would you... I mean, could you, perhaps, write one for me?'

'My dear Miss Brackwood, I am not married. You must know as well as I that a reference from me would hardly benefit you.'

'Oh. Yes. Of course.'

'However, there are other ways.'

'No!' Her heart plummeted and she recoiled, lifting one hand to silence him. 'Pray, say no more!'

The very thought of him suggesting that she might sell herself in exchange for his help made her want to weep, but her distress turned to anger when she saw his look of amusement.

'You have no idea what I am going to say.'

'Oh, but I do!' She pushed herself to her feet. 'That is, I can guess, and I am grateful for your help in rescuing me, my lord, but I think I should go now.'

His hand shot out and caught her arm. 'Sit down and listen to me.'

His grip was so firm she knew there was no escape. She hesitated for a moment, then sank back onto the chair.

'That's better,' he said, releasing her. 'Now, madam, listen to me. I am not proposing to make you my mistress. I am on my way to Gloucester in the morning to inspect a property. The estate has been in trust for the past five years and the steward was recently turned off for mismanagement and neglect of his duties. I have no idea what condition it is all in now, but from everything you have told me, you appear to know more about these matters than most. You could come with me to see it and give me your opinion.'

'Me?'

'Why not? It would get you out of Bristol. And if you are as experienced in land management as you say, your advice would be very helpful to me.' He sat back in his chair. 'Well, Miss Rosina Brackwood, what do you say?'

Chapter Four

Conham waited for Rosina to speak. What the devil was he doing, offering to take her to Morton Gifford? Goodness knows what the staff there would think. But if what she had told him was true, if she had indeed spent several years working with her father on his estates, then she must know something about the running of a large house and its land, and that could prove very useful.

She said, 'But surely, you must have a steward for Dallamire. Why did you not bring him with you?'

'He already has more than enough to do in Berkshire. Unlike your father, Miss Brackwood, mine did not leave his land in good heart. My intention is to sell the Gloucester properties and invest everything in restoring Dallamire, but I cannot do that until certain legal matters have been settled. That will take a few months, possibly longer, and in the meantime, I would rather not leave Morton Gifford to deteriorate even further. Naturally, the Dallamire estates must take precedence over my time, but I should like to know someone I can trust is looking after my interests here in Gloucestershire.'

'I do not understand,' she said, her blue eyes fixed upon his face. 'Are you saying you want me to work as your steward?'

He considered it. 'Why yes, I suppose I am.'

'You want to *employ* me?'

There was disbelief in the candid blue eyes she fixed upon him, and he could not blame her. It was almost unheard of, a female land steward, but somehow, now the idea had occurred to him, it was not easily dismissed. He tried to explain it to her.

'You said you wished to support yourself, but without a sponsor, or a character reference, that is not possible. I do not anticipate keeping either of the Gloucester properties any longer than necessary, but that should be long enough for my man of business, or perhaps Mrs Jameson, the housekeeper at Gifford Manor, to provide you with a suitable reference.'

'I... I do not know what to say. You would trust me to look after your lands?'

Her astonishment made him smile. 'As an officer I was accustomed to quickly summing up a man's character. Gifford Manor is not an extensive property and from what you have told me, I believe you might be capable of running it. Also—' he nodded towards the purse, which was still lying on the table '—I left four guineas in there. More than enough to take you far away from here, if you had so wished.'

'But then I would be a thief, as well as a runaway.'

'Exactly.'

He held her gaze, the candlelight reflected in his grey-green eyes, and Rosina felt something stir inside. A slight flutter of hope and excitement.

'Will you do it?' he asked. 'Will you take the position?'

'I fear people would look askance at a female steward. Unmarried, too. Some might even refuse to do business with me.'

'It is not unheard of in France for a woman to be steward, so why not here? You might pose as a widow, if you are afraid of the gossip.'

'I will not do that. I abhor pretence.'

'Then keep your own name, if you wish. We must be some thirty or more miles from Brackwood and in another county. I think it unlikely your brother would search for you here. And as for anyone not dealing with you, you could appoint an assistant to act for you, if that situation arose. One of the servants, perhaps.

'I would pay you the same as the previous steward,' he went on, naming a sum that made her eyes widen. 'And I believe he had the use of a lodge in the grounds. That would be at your disposal. I will ask Mrs Jameson to provide a maid to live there with you, to make everything perfectly respectable.'

Rosina put her hands to her temples. Only two days ago she had been at Brackwood, sitting in her favourite chair by the fire, working on her embroidery. She closed her eyes. Best not to think of that. Everything had changed now and she could not go back, only forward. She looked up at the earl.

'Will it, my lord?' she asked him. 'Will it seem perfectly respectable if I arrive at Gifford Manor, without warning and in this shabby dress? I know what *I* would think if a gentleman brought a lady to my house in such a manner.'

'You are right, of course. It would be far better for you to remain in Bristol tomorrow and purchase the necessary accoutrements of respectability. Will one day suffice?'

'Why, yes, I should think so…'

'Good, then I shall send my carriage to collect you the following morning.'

Rosina shook her head at him. 'Does nothing ever throw you off balance, Lord Dallamire?'

He grinned. 'I am a soldier, Miss Brackwood. I am accustomed to overcoming every obstacle.'

A laugh bubbled up. 'Then it is no wonder we beat the French!'

Her eyes met the earl's and something sparked between them, a moment of understanding, of connection. So strong it took her breath away and did strange things to her heart, setting it beating most erratically.

A soft knock at the door broke the spell and Rosina turned towards the fire, hoping any observer might think the heat accounted for the flush on her cheeks.

The landlord appeared. 'Beggin' your pardon, my lord, but will you be wanting dinner this evening? Only 'tis growing late…'

'What?' Lord Dallamire sounded distracted. 'Oh, yes, I must have dinner. Will you join me, Cousin, or do you still wish to retire?'

Rosina remembered she was supposed to be his unfortunate relative, involved in a carriage accident, but the events of the past half hour had set her mind buzzing, and she knew it would be hours before she could sleep.

'The soup was very good, but I do not think it will sustain me until morning. A small meal would be very welcome.'

'Then it is settled,' the earl declared. 'You may serve it in here in, say, an hour. Will that suit you, Cousin?'

She summoned up a smile.

'Yes, an hour will suit me perfectly, my lord.'

Rosina went into the bedchamber and closed the door, standing for a moment with her back pressed against it.

'What on earth am I doing?'

She wondered if she had escaped from one peril only to fall into another. Conham Mortlake, Earl of Dallamire, appeared to be a gentleman, and she felt very at ease in his company, but what were his motives in carrying her to Gloucestershire? His arguments for offering the post of land steward had sounded so logical, so reasonable at the time, but she could not believe he was serious.

And yet, he had looked and sounded perfectly serious. She shook her head. It made no sense, but then, nothing had made sense since Edgar had drugged her and sent her off to her death. Lord Dallamire had rescued her from a hideous fate and she was grateful for that. Rosina decided she would trust him for a little longer, if only because she had not fully recovered from the effects of the laudanum, and the thought of leaving his protection was too daunting to consider.

An hour later she returned to the parlour, having tidied herself as best she could. Sadly, the black silk gown was showing distinct signs of wear. The lace at the neck was torn and there was dirt on the skirts. However, she had washed her face and brushed and re-pinned her hair. That would have to do.

The table had been set for dinner but there was no sign of Lord Dallamire and she went over to the mirror and tucked a stray curl back into place. She was on edge, the assurance she had felt when she agreed to dine with him having quite disappeared.

When he came in, she summoned a smile before turning to face him. His own black evening clothes looked so immaculate that she instinctively made a little curtsy.

'No, don't do that,' he said quickly. 'You are supposed to be my cousin. People will be suspicious if you do not treat me as an equal.'

He came to hold out a chair for her and she said, as she sat down, 'I feel very *un*equal, especially in this gown.'

'I asked Matt to speak to the landlady. Having explained that you are in a strange city, she understands that you need someone to show you the best places to quickly replenish your wardrobe. I shall provide you with the money to purchase whatever you need. You are not to worry about the cost.'

'But I do worry, my lord,' she told him, mortified. 'It goes very much against the grain to be beholden to any man. I prefer to be—'

'Independent,' he interrupted her, smiling. 'I know that. You can give me the receipts when you reach the Manor and I shall deduct what you owe me from your salary.'

'And if I do not take the position?' she asked. 'I do not know when I will be able to repay you!'

'I shall hold the debt until you can.' He looked at her, a teasing smile in his eyes. 'I shall have no need of your finery.'

Rosina felt the tension draining away. Somehow, nothing seemed quite so bad when Dallamire was teasing her.

It was almost as if she had found a friend.

They settled down to their dinner with Rosina far more at ease than she had expected. They conversed easily, and the earl was such excellent company that she accepted a second glass of wine and asked him about his plans for the future.

He sat back to consider. 'My first concern is for those who depend upon Dallamire for their existence. My father left his estates in a parlous state, barely paying their way. There are also any number of outstanding debts. He had hoped to settle those with his winnings from the gaming tables.'

'I believe it is always thus with true gamblers,' she said carefully. 'My brother is the same, always believing his bad luck is about to change, but even when he is successful, he continues to play until he has lost it all again.'

'You understand,' he said, a faint smile in his grey-green eyes. 'So you see, my first concern must be to repair the family fortunes.'

'Are they very depleted?' she asked him.

'Nothing that a prudent marriage won't resolve.'

'You mean an heiress.'

'I do. Are you shocked?'

'Not at all,' she replied. 'A rich wife would be just the thing for you.'

He smiled. 'What, no romantic notions of love?'

She pulled a face. 'I have never had any time for romance. That is for silly females who have too little occupation.'

'You are very harsh upon your sex.'

'Most young women emerge from the schoolroom with little thought except to catch a husband. And from what I have observed, most of them are disappointed, even when they achieve their dream.'

He sat back in his chair. 'And have you *never* thought of marriage, Miss Brackwood?'

'I have considered it, naturally, but I have never yet met a man I should *like* to marry. Not that I have had very many offers.' She chuckled. 'My brother says that is because I am too clever. But surely, no sensible man would be discouraged by an intelligent woman. You would not be, I am sure!'

'No, as long as she is rich.' He refilled their glasses. 'I could not marry a woman I actively disliked, but I think it more important to have a partner one can respect. As for love, that is for fools and poets. It is an indulgence few of us can afford.'

'I agree,' said Rosina.

She raised her glass to him, happy to find herself in such accord with the earl.

* * *

They finished their dinner and Conham did not linger over his port. He bade Rosina good-night and carried the bottle and glass off to the bedchamber he was sharing with Matt Talacre. He found his friend occupying one of two armchairs placed on either side of the hearth, sitting at his ease in his shirt and waistcoat, ankles crossed and his stockinged feet stretched out towards the fire. He was sipping a glass of wine and looked up as Conham came in.

'Oho! Did she throw you out?'

'No, she did not, damn your insolence.' Conham poured himself a measure of port wine and sat down. 'I am sorry to inconvenience you, Matt, but I shall be sleeping in here tonight.'

'Then I shall have to make do with the truckle bed again. Does the lady know the inconvenience she is causing, making you share a room with your servant?'

'She does not, and I'll thank you not to tell her!' Conham retorted. 'Miss Brackwood finds herself in unfortunate circumstances and she is embarrassed enough as it is, having to accept my charity. Which reminds me, have you arranged everything for tomorrow?'

'Aye. I have ordered a carriage to be at Miss Brackwood's disposal, plus the landlady has an acquaintance who has agreed to accompany her; a retired lady's maid who knows the best places to shop in the city.'

'Excellent work.'

'I know. Surely you would not expect anything less of me?'

Conham scowled at him. 'If you had any respect for your betters, Talacre, you would be fully dressed and serving my port, not leaving me to pour my own!'

Matt Talacre was not noticeably cast down by this rebuke and merely grinned.

'Is that what you want, someone to bow and scrape to you? You chose the wrong man for that, my lord!'

'Not sure I chose you at all, Captain. I found myself saddled with you!'

'Ha, so I *asked* you to come back and search the battlefield once you had routed the French, did I, Major?'

Conham grinned. 'You had saved my life more than once, and I would have been beholden to you forever if you had died at Waterloo. Couldn't have that!'

A companionable silence fell and Conham thought back to that final battle, when they had fought together. The friendship forged in war had lasted into the peace, and once Matt Talacre's leg wound had healed sufficiently, Conham appointed him as his batman while he was with the Army of Occupation in Paris. Then, when Conham returned to England in May this year, Matt had come with him.

'I'm sorry,' he said abruptly. 'If I had known the dire state of my finances, I would never have suggested you should stay on as my aide-de-camp.'

'What else is there for me? I may be a gentleman by birth, but one with no fortune, and a cripple, too! Who else would employ me?'

There was a bitter note in Matt's voice that Conham rarely heard. His friend was generally very cheerful, but although it was seldom mentioned, Conham knew he found his lameness galling.

He said now, 'The doctors have all said you should make a full recovery, in time.'

'Aye, I know that. It's just, sometimes…' Matthew drained his wineglass and said irritably, 'Enough now, or before we know it you will be feeling sorry for me!'

'Not me, my friend. I was just wondering how much longer I must wait for you to bring the warming pan for my sheets. Damme, man, what do I pay you for?'

'To fetch and carry for you and put you to bed! Which I will do, if you can curb your impatience while I pull on my boots!'

When Rosina went downstairs the following morning Lord Dallamire was standing in the doorway, talking to a dark-haired gentleman in a black greatcoat. As she approached, the man went to move away but the earl detained him.

'No, don't go, Matthew, I must make you known to, er, my cousin.'

Rosina stopped, hoping she looked more at ease than she felt at the subterfuge.

'Mrs Alness will be following us into Gloucestershire to-morrow,' the earl went on. 'This, Cousin, is Matthew Talacre. He was a captain in my regiment and now acts as my aide-de-camp.'

'Jack-of-all-trades is what he means, ma'am. I take on every-thing no one else wishes to do! I have been acting as his valet, too, but thankfully, that will end once we reach Morton Gif-ford, where I hope the estimable Dawkins has already arrived with His Lordship's dressing coach!'

Rosina smiled politely, all the time wondering how much this man knew about her.

'Lord Dallamire explained how you had come to lose all your possessions, madam,' Mr Talacre went on, as if reading her mind. 'Very unfortunate for you, *Mrs Alness.*'

The way he said that name and the understanding in his eyes told Rosina that Matthew Talacre enjoyed the earl's con-fidence and she felt herself relaxing. She had two allies now in this strange adventure.

Shortly after Lord Dallamire had left for Gloucestershire, Ro-sina set off on her shopping trip. The retired lady's maid hired to accompany her was an excellent guide and they went first to a discreet house in King Square, where Rosina purchased a selection of evening gowns, day dresses and shoes, as well as a serviceable pelisse in dove grey and a warm cloak of blue wool for travelling. The gowns needed a few slight alterations but the helpful lady serving them assured Rosina the work could be completed in a trice, and everything would be delivered to the hotel by four o'clock. A trunk was added to their purchases and they spent the rest of the day visiting any number of milliners, haberdashers and hosiers to buy undergarments and matching accessories. By the time they returned to the Full Moon, shortly before the dinner hour, Rosina was confident she had sufficient clothes to present a decorous appearance, and that would have to do until she had the means to buy new.

It wasn't until she was alone in her room, with all the boxes, parcels and packages spread out over the bed, that Rosina was assailed by doubts. With no money of her own, she'd had no choice but to allow Lord Dallamire to pay for everything, and only women of loose virtue would accept such gifts from a man who was not her husband or a relative.

On the other hand, she told herself, one must be pragmatic. Tomorrow the earl's carriage would take her into Gloucestershire, and whether or not she remained at Morton Gifford, it was imperative that she looked as respectable as possible.

Chapter Five

It was just gone noon when Lord Dallamire's travelling carriage drew up at Gifford Manor for the second time in as many days. Conham heard its approach and hurried out to meet it.

'Miss Brackwood.' He helped her out of the carriage. 'How was your journey?'

'Excellent, my lord, thank you. Your carriage is very comfortable.'

He noted with approval her warm cloak and a poke bonnet that was very fetching, despite its modest brim.

'What a charming building,' she exclaimed, looking up at the Manor. 'Is it Jacobean?'

'Yes. Built of the local Cotswold stone. But let us go in out of the cold. Allow me to escort you to the parlour, ma'am. We can talk there.'

He led Rosina into the small porch, where an elderly butler was waiting to greet them.

'This is Jameson. He and his wife have been running this house for many years and will be an invaluable source of knowledge for you about the Manor and its lands, I am sure.' The old retainer bowed and Conham added, by way of explanation, 'I have invited Miss Brackwood to consider the post of steward here, Jameson.'

'Mr Talacre has already apprised me of the situation, my lord. I shall endeavour to be of assistance to Miss Brackwood and I have sent people down to the steward's lodge to make sure it is habitable.'

'Thank you,' said Conham.

'And wine and cakes have been set out in the green parlour, my lord,' the butler went on. 'At Mr Talacre's suggestion.'

Conham nodded.

'Matthew has not been idle,' he remarked as he guided Rosina through the screens passage and across the great hall.

'He sounds like an excellent assistant.'

'He is.' Conham ushered her into a square, wainscoted room with a blazing fire. 'I shall miss him when he is gone.'

'Oh? Is he leaving your employ?'

'No, not yet, but he will. Once his leg improves, Matt will want to make his own way in the world, not live on what he sees as my charity.'

'Talking of charity, I must thank you for loaning me the money for my purchases yesterday.'

'Think nothing of it. I hope you found everything you required?'

'Why, yes,' she said, untying her bonnet and putting it down on a side table. 'I had a very successful day. I have discarded the black gown and have moved into half mourning. It is a year since my father died. I do not think there can be any objection.'

She had removed her cloak and he glanced down at the skirts of a white muslin gown showing beneath a dove-grey pelisse.

Conham smiled. 'No objection at all, Miss Brackwood. In fact, I think—'

He stopped. He was about to say how well the military-style pelisse fitted her admirable figure. Then she looked up at him and all coherent thought had fled when he gazed into those cornflower-blue eyes.

'Yes?' Her delicate brows went up slightly. 'What were you going to say, my lord?'

'Nothing.' He turned and walked over to the side table. 'It was nothing of moment. Will you take a glass of wine?'

'Yes, if you please.'

He took his time filling the glasses, trying to work out what had just happened. She had quite taken his breath away, but that must have been the surprise of seeing her in her new clothes and with her hair properly dressed. He had not imagined the bedraggled creature he rescued from Queen Square could look so, so beguiling.

His years in the army had taught him a great deal, but very little about women. For all he knew, Rosina Brackwood might be an adventuress. He had no real proof of who she was, or if what she had told him was true, and yet he had given her money and was even proposing to trust her with the management of his property. Was that wise, when his finances were in such a perilous state? He could hardly afford to throw his money away on a whim.

And he certainly could not afford to lose his head over a pretty face!

'I hope you will keep a reckoning of everything I owe you, sir.' Her soft, determined voice broke into his thoughts. 'No more than Mr Talacre do I wish to be beholden to you.'

Taking up the two glasses, he turned back. Rosina's dainty chin was tilted up slightly and there was a stubborn look on her face. Conham's doubts vanished like smoke on a windy day. Unlike Alicia who, despite her own wealth, had taken every penny he had lavished on her as her right, he knew in his bones that Rosina Brackwood would do her utmost to repay him every last groat.

He said, gravely, 'I shall make an exact note, ma'am.'

Rosina took the proffered glass and sat down. The earl took a seat opposite, stretching out his long legs in their glossy top boots. He was wearing country dress, but the cut of his tailed topcoat and buckskin breeches was the work of a master. They fitted his lithe, muscled figure to perfection. She suddenly felt shy, and a little vulnerable, alone in this room with a man she barely knew. She sipped her wine and tried to think of something to break the silence.

'This looks an interesting house,' she said, admiring the polished wainscotting and elaborate plasterwork on the ceiling. 'It belonged to your godfather?'

'Yes, Hugo Conham.'

'You are named after him? You introduced yourself as Con-ham Mortlake,' she reminded him, then flushed, remembering that she had been lying in his bed at the time.

'Ah, yes. Of course. I am sure Mrs Jameson would be delighted to give you a tour of the house. As a boy I thought it a splendid place, all those suits of armour and the weapons covering the walls in the great hall.' He smiled, settling back in his chair. 'It was paradise for a young boy. Hugo taught me to shoot here, and we went riding in the park or up on the hills. In the evenings he would tell me tales of his days fighting the French.'

'And is that why you joined the army?' she asked. She had seen the way his eyes softened when he spoke of his godfather.

'In part, although I was already army-mad. My father refused to buy me a commission, and at the time I thought it was because he disapproved. Now I realise it was because he could not afford to do so. Hugo, too, said he could not support me if my father was against the idea.'

'What did you do?'

'I scraped together enough to buy myself a captaincy.' His smile was replaced by a brooding frown and he stared into the fire. 'If I had known then the true state of affairs at Dallamire I would not have joined up. I would have done my duty by my family. Not that anyone ever reproached me.'

'I should hope not,' she replied, wanting to say something to dispel the sadness that had enveloped him. 'I am sure you did your duty for your country.'

Her words had some effect. The earl's countenance lightened a little.

'I did my best. I made major before Waterloo.'

'Your family should be proud of you.'

He shrugged. 'Hugo had been dead for four years by then and my father never mentioned my promotion, although he did write to me, some weeks before Waterloo, to wish me well. That was his last letter to me. He broke his neck in a riding accident a few weeks later.'

'I am so sorry.'

They sat in silence for several moments. Then the earl finished his wine and jumped up.

'They should have set the steward's lodge to rights by now. Shall we go and see it?'

Conham escorted Rosina out of the house and to the far side of the stables and kitchen gardens, where the lodge was situated. It was of much more recent date than the Manor itself, a neat little ashlar stone building with a good view out over the park. He had never been inside before and was pleased to discover it was well appointed, with everything Rosina might need, including the maid sent to wait upon her until such time as she hired a servant of her own.

'I hope you think it sufficiently comfortable,' he told her, when they had finished their short tour and returned to the little sitting room. 'Your office is in the Manor, and you will take your meals there, too. Unless you prefer to dine here, in private.'

'Thank you, but that would necessitate more work for everyone. I should be very happy to join the upper servants in the house.'

He frowned at that. 'I do not consider you a servant.'

'But that is what I will be, sir, if you employ me.' She laughed. 'Pray, do not look so concerned! As steward, it would be very useful to sit down to dinner and talk with those who work at the Manor.'

'Very well, but when I am in residence you will dine with me, starting with this evening,' he said firmly. 'Matthew will join us, too. He has an excellent mind for business and there are matters about your new role that we need to discuss.'

He watched her as she walked around the room, running her hand along the back of a chair, inspecting a watercolour on the wall.

'I have not yet accepted your offer,' she reminded him.

'But you will?' he pressed her. 'You would be doing me a service.'

Rosina did not answer immediately. What choice did she have? The idea of being out in the world, without money, or protection, was too alarming to contemplate.

'At least stay until Lady Day. Four months. By then I should know what I am going to do with my godfather's inheritance. And you will be in a better position to decide upon your future.'

'There is that,' she agreed. 'Very well, I will stay until March, and I thank you, my lord. I hope I will not disappoint you.'

'Oh, I doubt that,' said Conham, relieved beyond measure. She would be safe here. He could protect her.

Not that she was his primary concern. It was purely the Manor and estate that he was thinking of. Nor was he worried he might lose his heart. He had seen plenty of pretty women in his time and never yet lost his head over any of them.

He pulled out his watch. 'I shall leave you now. I expect you to present yourself in the green parlour a good half hour before dinner. Matthew will do the same. I shall stand upon no ceremony here. There are decisions to be made and at a time like this a man needs his friends around him!'

With that, he strode back to the Manor, not allowing himself to consider why he should be so pleased that Rosina Brackwood had agreed to stay on.

Rosina stared at the closed door, listening to the earl's departing footsteps. Friends! She shook her head, suppressing the burst of elation that had swept through her when the earl had said that word. He was referring to Matthew Talacre, of course, she knew that. It would be foolish to think anything else. But a tiny seed of pleasure had been planted and it refused to go away.

She crossed her arms and hugged herself. A few days ago, she had been running for her life with no one to help her. Now she was in this cosy house with a maid to wait upon her and an earl who called her his friend and who was offering her the prospect of gainful employment. She looked around the room and smiled. Suddenly, the future looked a little brighter.

Chapter Six

For dinner that evening, Rosina chose to wear the finer of the two evening gowns she had purchased in King Square. It was a grey silk, trimmed with a thin band of white lace at the neck and cuffs. A white muslin fichu fulfilled the double purpose of keeping her warm and providing a modest covering for her neck and shoulders. Five minutes before the appointed time, she took a final look in the mirror, threw her cloak about her shoulders and made her way to the Manor.

Rosina had mixed feelings about the forthcoming dinner, but any awkwardness she felt soon disappeared. Both the earl and Matt Talacre were eager to put her at ease and by the end of the meal, Rosina was far more comfortable in their company.

When the covers had been removed and dishes of nuts and sugared almonds put on the table, Rosina announced she had arranged for the housekeeper to show her over the house the following morning.

'I hope you will not be disappointed,' said the earl. 'Since my godfather's demise five years ago, only the Jamesons and a couple of servants have been living here.'

'True, but I believe Mrs Jameson has done her best to keep the house in order. From what I have seen so far everything has been very well maintained with hard work and beeswax.'

'I wish the same care had been taken with the land,' muttered the earl.

'Ah, yes, the rascally steward, Frumald.' Matthew Talacre pushed a dish of marzipan fruits towards Rosina. 'How long was he here?'

'About three years, I believe. The trustees appointed him when Hugo's steward became too old to continue. I understand that in the end Mrs Jameson wrote to the trustees to inform them Frumald was a miserly fellow, and that he was lining his own pockets rather than spending anything on maintaining the land or buildings. Once they started to investigate, it did not take them long to ascertain that she was telling the truth.'

'Damn his eyes,' declared Matthew. 'I hope they clapped him up for it!'

The earl shook his head. 'The fellow ran off as soon as the trustees began investigating. I called in at one of the farms on my way here yesterday, to see the old gamekeeper, whom I remembered from my previous visits. He gave me the word with no bark on it. Frumald was a sly dog, apparently. Slight increases in the rents, instructions for the odd wagon to be sent off to a different market. Nothing to cause an outcry, although it did raise suspicions.'

'Well, thank goodness you now have control of the place,' said Matthew, rising to his feet. 'You will soon have everything put to rights. Now, if you will excuse me, I am for my bed. Although I shall seek out Dawkins on my way, to make sure His Lordship's sheets have been warmed satisfactorily.' He winked at Rosina. 'Proper application of the warming pan is one of His Lordship's little foibles!'

'My little—! Take your sorry carcase out of here, Talacre, before I throw you out!'

Matthew went out laughing, and Rosina stifled a giggle.

'Insolent fellow,' drawled the earl. 'I should turn him off.'

But she had seen the twinkle in his eyes and knew he was not really offended. She drank the last of her sweet wine and pushed the glass away.

'I, too, should retire,' she said. 'It has been a tiring day.'

'I shall escort you back to the lodge.'

'There is no need, my lord.'

'Perhaps not, but I am going to do so.'

He picked up her cloak, which she had left across a chair at the side of the room, and put it around her shoulders before guiding her out of the house.

'You really do not need to come with me,' she repeated as they stepped out onto the drive. 'There is more than enough moonlight for me to see my way.'

He pulled her hand onto his arm before replying.

'But I want to see you safely to your door. Call it one of my, er, little foibles.'

Rosina gave in. She could not deny it would be pleasant to have his company for the short walk to the steward's lodge, although she cautioned herself not to think it anything more than gallantry. She walked beside him, feeling the strength of his arm beneath the fine woollen sleeve, breathing in the faint scent of his cologne.

He said, 'Mrs Jameson is showing you over the house to-morrow, I believe?'

'Yes. After breakfast. I believe she is vastly relieved that you are come, my lord. She thinks that now everything will be well.'

'I am very much afraid that is not the case. I hope she will not be too downcast when I sell the Manor.'

'You must, of course, do what you think best.'

'Your tone suggests I should keep it.'

'Not at all,' she said quickly. 'I understand that Dallamire must come first. It is, after all, your principal seat.'

'Yes. Although I should like the land and the house here to be in good condition before I sell. I think I owe that to my godfather.'

'And it would also increase the selling price.'

'Undoubtedly. Which is why I need a good steward for the land.'

Rosina bit her lip. 'Yes.'

'Do you think it beyond your abilities?' he asked her.

The black outline of the lodge was ahead of them, a soft glow shining from one of the windows as well as from the fanlight above the door. Brackwood Court now belonged to Edgar. There was no going back, and this small, compact little building represented a sanctuary. Suddenly, she wanted to stay here; she was eager to take on the challenge of running Morton Gifford.

'That remains to be seen,' she said briskly. 'The first thing to be done is to become acquainted with the estate. I should like to make a start as soon as possible. You said there is a gig I may use, my lord?'

'There is, but you will hardly go out alone.'

'No, I shall take one of the servants with me. One who knows the area and the people.'

'Then I suggest you take Fred Skillet, the head groom here. He was born in the village and knows everything there is to know about Morton Gifford. I will tell him to put himself at your disposal.'

'Thank you. Once I have some idea of what is required, I shall be able to tell you if I think I can make a difference here.'

They had reached the door and as they stopped, the earl released Rosina's arm. She turned to look up at him, but with the moon behind him she could not see his expression. She had no idea if he was satisfied with her answer.

'I am confident you can do this,' he said, sweeping away her doubts. 'There is a great deal of work to be done here, and I shall be glad to know you are in charge, Rosina. Now, why do you look at me like that? What have I said?'

She hesitated. 'You used my first name.'

'Did I? I didn't notice.' He took a step away from her. 'Don't fret, I have no designs upon your virtue.'

His calmly uttered words should have been reassuring, and Rosina was surprised by her sharp response.

'I am very glad to hear it! Good night, my lord.'

And she *was* glad, she told herself firmly as she went inside and handed her cloak to the waiting maid. She had no wish to become the object of any man's desires.

Although it was very lowering to think the earl found her so unattractive.

Since the weather was dry, Rosina spent the next few days travelling around Morton Gifford. She was accompanied by

Fred Skillet, who had worked on the Gifford estates since he was a boy. Not only was he knowledgeable about the estate, he was also known and trusted by everyone who lived or worked there. They might look askance at the young female calling upon them, albeit a gentlewoman with a friendly and engaging manner, but if Fred said she was Lord Dallamire's steward, come to make things right, and that they should open the budget to her, then they would do so.

When Rosina sat down to dinner with the earl and Mr Talacre three days later, she was able to explain to them just what had been going on at Morton Gifford.

'Since your godfather's death, everyone has been nervous for the future, not knowing if or when the estate was to be broken up and sold. Then Frumald, that awful steward the trustees appointed, frightened them all with threats of eviction and rent rises. Is it any wonder that your tenants had no interest in improving their homes or their businesses? The shopkeepers and millers I have spoken with see no point in expanding, while the farmers have little incentive to make changes or bring in new stock, since they will get no reward for their hard work.

'However,' she concluded, 'the land here appears to be fertile, my lord. If we can assure the farmers that they have security of tenure and bring in a fairer system of rents for everyone, it will pay dividends almost immediately. Morton Gifford need not be another drain on you, Lord Dallamire. Quite the opposite. I think it will soon be turning a small profit.'

'How soon?' Matt Talacre asked her.

'Next year, perhaps, if the harvest is a good one. Everyone agrees the weather this year has been particularly bad.'

They continued to discuss the matter while the meal progressed, and by the time the covers were removed, and the small dishes of bonbons, nuts and sweetmeats had been set on the table, Rosina had answered all their questions as honestly as she could.

'By Jove, Conham, I believe the lady really does know her business!' declared Matt Talacre, sitting back in his chair and grinning.

Rosina was pleased with the compliment, but it was the earl's verdict she needed.

At last, he nodded. 'Very well, Miss Brackwood. Leave your report on my desk, facts, figures and projections. I shall study them and then I may, perhaps, reconsider my decision to sell.'

Conham saw Rosina's look of surprise and delight and smiled to himself. She could not know that he was already minded to keep the property. He had spent some of his happiest times here as a boy and the house had quickly wrapped itself about him, just as it had done all those years ago. The furnishings might be faded and a little tired, but there was no doubting the Manor's comfort. He felt more relaxed here than he had at any time since returning to England.

'I have always felt at home here,' he admitted, when the servants had withdrawn. 'It would be somewhere to escape from the duties and grandeur of Dallamire.'

'Good idea, if you like it so much,' said Matthew. 'But what of this rich wife you intend to find? She may be like your stepmother and prefer to live in your stately pile.'

'Then she may do so.' Conham reached for the wine to refill everyone's glass. 'My wife may have parties and balls at Dallamire to her heart's content. Or in the London house, but not here. Gifford Manor is too small to accommodate more than a few friends, and that will suit me perfectly!'

'But will it suit your countess?' murmured Rosina.

The question was out before she could stop herself. The earl glanced at her in surprise.

'Damme, madam, you are growing as impertinent as Talacre!'

She blushed fierily, but Matthew came to her defence.

'No, no, Conham, don't fire up, 'tis a fair question.'

Rosina caught her breath, astonished at the informality between master and servant. She waited for Lord Dallamire to make some angry retort, but he merely grinned.

'Aye, she is, and I appreciate that.' His glance shifted to Rosina and she felt her pulse quicken at the smile warming his eyes. 'The advantage of a marriage of convenience, Miss Brackwood, is that both parties understand they will not be obliged to live in each other's pockets. I am sure my countess and I will both appreciate a little time away from one another.'

'How very civilised,' drawled Matt Talacre. 'I do not think I would want such a union.'

Conham almost retorted that he would rather not have to make such a marriage, but he didn't.

'You have always been such a romantic, Matthew. You know as well as I that many women would be only too happy to have the power and position that marriage can bestow upon them. Once they have it, they will want to go their own way.'

'Power and position?' Matt sat back, twirling the stem of his wineglass between his fingers. 'Then why did a certain rich widow in Bristol turn you down recently?'

A frosty silence met his words. Rosina felt the change and glanced at the earl, whose countenance had become stony. It was as if a sudden blast of arctic air had filled the room.

She put down her napkin. 'I think perhaps it would be best if I withdrew.'

Lord Dallamire put out his hand to stop her. 'No, no, Miss Brackwood, there is no need for you to go. It is Talacre who needs to apologise.'

'I'm damned if I will apologise! What, for challenging your absurd notion that every woman wants a man solely for his title, for his position in society? You don't really believe that, Conham.' He turned to Rosina. 'And it ain't the case, is it, ma'am?'

'Having never been to town, I do not feel qualified to answer. But for myself, I would say no, it is certainly not the case.'

'Then you are the exception, Miss Brackwood.'

'And what of Mrs Faulds?' Matthew persisted. 'She must be an exception, too, since she preferred to keep control of her own fortune rather than hand it over to you.' He gave the earl a quizzical look. 'Be honest now, man. Do you really blame her?'

Rosina waited, expecting an eruption of anger, but once again the earl surprised her. He relaxed.

'No,' he said, smiling slightly. 'I don't blame her for refusing me.'

Rosina had never experienced such a dinner before, where men spoke so freely, so openly. At Brackwood her neighbours and her father's friends had always behaved circumspectly before her. As for Edgar, he had shown nothing but contempt in her company. This free and easy banter was something new to her. It was slightly alarming, but hugely enjoyable, and she ventured a question of her own.

'Were you very disappointed, sir, when the lady refused your offer?'

She half expected him to cut her down with a withering reply. Instead, he shrugged.

'It was never a love match, but I thought we liked one another well enough. I believed we might rub along comfortably together. However, it would seem the lady prefers her independence to a title.'

After a moment's silence he lifted his glass to study the contents.

'But that is by the by,' he said lightly. 'My stepmother would never have approved of the wealthy Mrs Faulds and that could have made life very uncomfortable for everyone. Fortunately, there are many other young ladies that *do* meet with Lady Dallamire's approval, heiresses who—whatever Matt might think—would be only too willing to become my countess. Almack's is full of 'em!'

'Well, what you lack in funds you make up for in appearance,' retorted Matt outrageously. 'You are a handsome devil, Conham. Don't you agree, Miss Brackwood?'

Rosina answered cautiously.

'Handsome is that handsome does.'

'Aye, well, Dallamire scores on that point, too. There is no one I would trust more with my life or my money, if I had any. His is chivalrous to a fault!'

'Enough, enough, damn you!' exclaimed the earl, frowning. 'Shut up and refill the glasses, Matthew!'

'Very well, my friend. But I wish you luck finding a wife who will make you happy as well as rich.'

'Oh, I don't think that will be difficult,' drawled the earl, a glint of self-derision in his eyes.

Matthew gave a shout of laughter. 'Of all the conceited—'

'No, no, Matt, just practical.' Conham grinned. 'As soon as I leave here on Tuesday, I shall start my search!'

'You are leaving Gifford Manor next week?' said Rosina. 'So soon?'

'Yes. I only ever intended staying until I could appoint a land steward to manage the estate. I have pressing matters to deal with at Dallamire and then I shall return to town.'

Conham wondered again if perhaps this was too much of a risk, leaving a woman he barely knew in charge. But he squashed his doubts. Hugo, his godfather, had always considered Fred Skillet to be an excellent judge of people, and the elderly head groom had been surprisingly complimentary when Conham had spoken to him earlier.

'Miss Brackwood knows what she's about, my lord,' Skillet had told him. 'She has a friendly way with her, too, that puts people at their ease. Not like t'other bag o'wind who was here before, all smiles to yer face but ready to take the bread off yer plate if he thought he could get away with it.'

That was enough for him, for now.

He said, 'I do not intend to return here until the spring, but I will expect regular reports from you, Miss Brackwood. Send everything to Dallamire and it will find me, wherever I am.'

'Yes, my lord.'

'But what of Bellemonte?' demanded Matthew. 'Are you not going to see that before you leave Gloucestershire?'

'No. I shall instruct my lawyers to sell it.'

Conham frowned. Matt had already mentioned Alicia, damn his eyes, and now her scathing comments about Bellemonte came back to him. She had called it a collection of run-down buildings, and he already had enough of those at Dallamire.

'Excuse me.' Rosina sat forward. 'What is Bellemonte?'

'Part of my inheritance from my godfather. Land and buildings in the south of the county, close to Bristol. Hugo bought it as a business venture but sadly he died before he could do anything with it.' His mouth twisted. 'From the reports I have had, the buildings are dilapidated and it would require a great deal of money to put it right.'

'But surely you should at least look at it,' she persisted.

'Putting Dallamire in order must be my priority.'

'Of course, my lord, but to sell it without even seeing it...'

She stopped and looked at Matt, who said, 'You have to admit, Conham, Miss Brackwood has a point. We are here for another week yet. What harm would it do to visit Bellemonte?'

'I have not yet seen all the estate here,' he pointed out.

'That should not take more than a couple of days,' said Rosina. 'Three, at most.'

Conham found two pairs of eyes upon him and felt himself weakening. Perhaps it was the wine, but his mood had lightened. Alicia might be wrong about the state of his inheritance. After all, she had been very dismissive of Morton Gifford, calling it a few insignificant acres, and yet Rosina thought it could return a pretty profit, under the right management.

He threw up his hands. 'If you are going to unite against me, what can I say? Very well, I will send word to Bellemonte tomorrow that I will be visiting the property. But I insist you both come with me.'

'Oh.' Rosina looked startled. 'But it cannot be necessary for me to go, my lord.'

'Nonsense. I told you a man needs his friends about him at a time like this. You and Matt will accompany me and give your opinion of Bellemonte, since you both know as much about the matter as I. Besides,' he said, a mischievous smile growing inside him, 'I do not intend to be the only one wasting my time on what I have no doubt will be a wild-goose chase!'

Friends. There was that word again. Rosina turned her attention back to her meal. There was no doubt she felt valued here, in this unfamiliar house, miles from the home she had known all her life. Not only was the earl going to pay her to maintain and hopefully improve Gifford Manor, but she was also accompanying him and his aide-de-camp to Bellemonte. How long was it since someone had asked her opinion of anything?

She felt confused, dazed at the sudden change in her fortunes. Her comfortable existence had ended almost a year ago, when Papa had died. Since then, life had become ever more of a trial. Her brother had rebuffed all her attempts to help him manage

Brackwood. Remembering their last, violent encounter sent a shudder down her spine.

'Are you cold, Miss Brackwood?' the earl asked her.

'No, not really.' She looked up, surprised to find the meal was over and the servants had come in to remove the covers. 'A little tired, I think. I beg your pardon, it is very late and I should retire.'

When she rose, the gentlemen stood, too, and the earl walked over to the door.

'Good night, Miss Brackwood,' he said. 'You will find a servant waiting for you in the hall. I have ordered him to escort you back to the lodge.'

Rosina stopped.

'I am five-and-twenty, Lord Dallamire. I no longer require a chaperone.'

'At your advanced age, perhaps not,' he replied gravely. 'However, I insist you allow him to light your way, through these darker months.'

She was touched by his concern and looked at him, torn between amusement and exasperation.

'Another of your little foibles, my lord?'

'Precisely.'

A smile warmed his eyes and Rosina felt the heat rising to her cheeks. Quickly, she bade both men good-night and hurried out of the room.

Chapter Seven

Two days later Lord Dallamire's carriage set off for Belle-monte just as the sun was burning off the morning mist. Winter had not yet taken hold and Rosina gazed out at the passing landscape, enchanted by the rich autumn colours of the trees on the far hills, their yellow and gold leaves glowing even in the weak sunlight. She was now familiar with the lanes immediately around the Manor, but as they drove south, she recognised very little. On her previous journey, when she had first come to Morton Gifford, she had been too anxious to take in very much at all about the landscape. Now, at least for the present, she was safe, but if Edgar should discover her whereabouts, or if the earl withdrew his support, what then?

Best not to think of that, she told herself firmly. She could not change the past and must look to the future.

In due course they arrived at a straggling village and turned down a lane past a dilapidated inn to a large cobbled square.

Conham jumped out and gave a cursory glance around. Theirs was the only vehicle and there was no one in sight, save a ragged man, asleep against the wall of the inn. They had stopped outside a large building where a faded sign announced it as The Grand Pleasure Baths. Before them was a substantial house, once a gentleman's residence, but now unoccupied, its windows shuttered and boarded. Finally, the western side of the square was defined by a set of rusty railings with large gates at the centre. On the rising land behind the gates, he could see an avenue of trees cutting through the ragged and overgrown shrubbery.

Conham was unable to keep the sarcasm from his voice as he turned back and gave his hand to Rosina.

'Welcome to Bellemonte, my grand inheritance!'

'How…how interesting.'

'Is that what you call it!' He grimaced. 'A decrepit ruin would be more accurate.'

'The park beyond the railings looks very inviting.'

'If you like neglected gardens!'

Matthew had climbed out of the far door and chuckled as he limped around to join them on the footway.

'You are determined to find fault, Conham. It is far bigger than I anticipated. Does your inheritance include the pleasure baths, too?'

Conham cast his eyes towards the large wall that had presumably been built to preserve the privacy of the bathers.

'Aye, it does, although heaven knows what state it is in,' he muttered, glancing up at the weathered sign with its peeling paint. 'Now, where is the fellow who is to meet us?' He looked around the square. 'Ah, this might be he.'

A tall individual was hurrying towards them, wiping his mouth with a large spotted handkerchief in a way that suggested he had just come from the inn. He was dressed in a puce-coloured coat with wide padded shoulders and a nipped waist. Despite the cold weather, the coat was unbuttoned to show a garishly patterned waistcoat and a cravat so intricately tied and folded that it frothed beneath his chin, while the shirt points were so high they covered his cheeks.

'Lord Dallamire. Good day to you, m'lord.' The man swaggered up, removing his hat to expose a head covered in improbably black curls as he made a low bow. 'Josiah Hackthorpe at your service!'

He gave Rosina and Matthew a perfunctory nod when Conham introduced them, but quickly turned back to the earl.

'Your Lordship will be wanting to see Bellemonte. It will be my honour to show you everything, my lord!'

Conham was inclined to resent this slight to his companions, but rather than being offended, they were exchanging looks that were brim full of amusement as the fellow made another obsequious bow. However, he was reluctant to let such rudeness pass. He wanted to make a show of offering his arm to Rosina but as if reading his thoughts, she gave a slight shake of her head and turned to Matthew, tucking her hand into the curve of his elbow.

'Aye, lead on,' said Matt cheerfully. 'We are all ready now.'

Two hours later they were back in the chaise and bowling along the Gloucester Road.

'I beg your pardon,' said Conham, feeling obliged to offer Rosina an apology. 'I should never have taken you there.'

'But why not?' she replied cheerfully. 'I thoroughly enjoyed looking around Bellemonte.'

'Hackthorpe was unconscionably rude to you.'

'Aye, and you almost added to it,' Matt said bluntly. 'Having told the fellow that we were both in your employ, if you had offered your arm to Miss Brackwood there is only one conclusion he would have drawn from that.'

'Fustian. I was merely being courteous.'

'Hackthorpe wouldn't understand that. The fellow's a tuft hunter. He'd think you had brought your—'

'Yes, yes, no need to go on!' said Conham hastily.

'Mr Talacre is correct,' added Rosina. 'The man was only interested in one opinion, my lord. Yours.'

'Then he is a fool!'

'Undoubtedly.' Matt laughed. 'But we were both amused, watching the fellow bowing and scraping to you.'

The earl grimaced. 'Not an experience I enjoy. I would rather he had told the truth, that the place is beyond repair.'

'Oh, I wouldn't say that,' said Rosina. 'Although I have to admit the old house was in very poor condition. The nails and splinters were determined to catch at my skirts.'

'It was a waste of a morning,' he declared. 'The house is

nothing but a shell, stripped of all its furniture and fine panelling. The inn has become a common ale house, and as for the pleasure gardens, as they are named, it would require an army of gardeners to return them to order, despite what that rascally manager said!'

'But the baths are still popular,' Rosina pointed out.

'I applaud the philanthropic idea, to provide a bathing pool that everyone may use for a penny, but it barely brings in enough to cover its costs,' he replied. 'I shall write to my lawyers immediately with instructions to sell it all off as soon as may be. The whole place is beyond redemption.'

'Do you really think so? I think it has great possibilities.'

She was regarding him, her head on one side like a little bird. He laughed.

'You sound like the fellow my grandfather brought in to landscape the grounds at Dallamire.'

'Then I think you mean *capabilities*,' she corrected him, her blue eyes twinkling. 'Capability Brown. My father often said he would have liked to have him transform the park at Brackwood. Not that Papa could afford it, but as he said, one could always dream.'

She stopped, a small sigh escaping her, and Conham noted the sudden sadness in her eyes. He sought for something to distract her.

'Very well, tell me what *possibilities* you see at Bellemonte.'

'It was more a feeling than any fixed ideas. Let me see, it is on high ground, so the air is clear. And from the top of the hill, the views over Bristol and the countryside are very good.'

'Yes,' said Matt, 'and they would be even better if the overgrown bushes were cut back and the terrace on the ridge cleared of weeds.'

Rosina nodded. 'I agree. The same applies to the rest of the gardens. I do not believe they are beyond rescue, but there would be a cost, of course.'

'And therein lies the rub,' Conham retorted. 'Dallamire Hall needs a deal of work, and the land needs investment to improve it. I might be able to justify keeping Gifford Manor, if it pays its way, but Bellemonte must be sold.'

'Yes, of course, my lord.'

'But you will not be making any final decisions just yet,' said Matthew.

'No, not immediately, but I have the ledgers now,' he said, patting the heavy books piled on the seat beside him. I mean to take them with me to London next week. I shall have to take advice on the market price of such a property, but I hope it will provide something towards the restoring of Dallamire.'

Chapter Eight

Rosina spent the next two days exploring Morton Gifford with
Lord Dallamire. He told her it was ten years since he had stayed
here for any length of time, but when they drove around the
estate in the gig, she was surprised how many of the people he
already knew. From the conversations that followed it was clear
they remembered him fondly and she began to build up a picture of Conham as a schoolboy. Polite and friendly, interested
in people and eager to please.

Then there were the tenants who had come to Morton Gifford
in more recent years, to whom she could introduce *him*. They
were naturally cautious of meeting such a grand personage as
the Earl of Dallamire, but his easy manners soon won them over.

'You have made excellent progress in little more than a week,'
he said as she drove the gig back to the Manor on the second
day. 'I expected a great deal more resistance to the new ideas
you have proposed.'

Rosina flushed, pleased and gratified by his words.

'It was not difficult to persuade them that change has to
come, especially since they will benefit, as well as the estate.'

'I think you underrate yourself, ma'am. Local people are notoriously suspicious of newcomers.'

She laughed and shook her head. 'The previous steward made himself so odious that almost anyone would be welcome!'

'I don't agree, but let us not argue. Suffice to say that I am confident I am leaving the Manor in good hands.'

'Thank you. I only wish there was more time to show you some of the hill farms and hamlets further afield.'

'Yes, we would have covered more ground if we had been riding. What a pity there is no lady's mount in my godfather's stable.'

'Well, even if there had been, I have no riding habit.'

'Then that must be remedied before my next visit. Get yourself a habit and ask Skillet to seek out a suitable mount for you. Charge everything to the accounts.'

'Oh, no, I could not do that!'

'You can and you will.'

'But you are paying me so well. Far, far more than I would earn as a governess or a companion.'

'It is no more than Frumald was being paid, and now he is not here to cream off the profits from the estate, I hope to see far more going back into the coffers! And trust me, your salary will not go far once you have employed someone to look after the lodge for you.'

She bit her lip. 'My lord, I cannot thank you enough for giving me this opportunity.'

'Then don't,' he interrupted her, adding roughly, 'I needed a steward and if Edgar Brackwood could not see your worth then he is a fool as well as a villain.'

Rosina's thoughts had been far away from her brother, but her heart began to race with panic as the memory of his betrayal came rushing back. How he had sent her off to Bristol, to certain death. The horse jibbed as her hands tightened on the reins.

'I beg your pardon,' said the earl quickly. 'I did not mean to upset you.'

'No, no. I was not… That is…' She steadied herself and the horse. 'I was surprised by the recollections. I am so busy now, I rarely think of Edgar.'

'I am glad. He doesn't deserve that you should think of him.'

He reached out and briefly squeezed one of her hands. Rosina froze, her heart thudding so hard again that it was suddenly difficult to breathe. She kept her eyes fixed on the road, fighting for calm. What she was feeling now was nothing like her revulsion at the thought of her brother. This was entirely different. Her whole body felt alive with a sudden, blinding awareness of the man sitting beside her.

They had been driving together all day, chatting companionably, his shoulder sometimes rubbing against hers when the gig bumped over the uneven roads. It had been relaxed, enjoyable, but now she was almost overcome by unexpected sensations. A sudden tension inside her, a powerful yearning for him to pull her into his arms and kiss her, as he had done on their very first meeting. She had never felt such strong, primal feelings before and they frightened her.

'Are you ill, Rosina? Would you like me to drive?'

'No. Thank you, I can manage now.'

It took a supreme effort to drag her thoughts away from the desire pooling inside her but somehow, she succeeded. The earl had employed her as his land steward, a role normally performed by a man. To betray weakness, instability, would be disastrous. She could not afford to lose this position now. From somewhere deep inside she hauled up a smile.

'I was feeling a little homesick for Brackwood, that is all. I am quite well now, my lord.'

It was not true, but the earl would be leaving Morton Gifford in a few days. She would do her best to avoid his company and regain control of these foolish and unruly desires. They had no place in her new life. In fact, they could prove disastrous.

Rosina was a little quiet and withdrawn at dinner but Conham did not remark upon it. He blamed himself for mentioning her brother while they were out in the gig. It had brought back a host of painful memories for her. She had hidden it well and drove back to the Manor without incident, but Conham had been aware of a certain restraint afterwards, as if Rosina had withdrawn a little. She retired early, pleading fatigue, and on Sunday morning, as he waited in the hall for the carriage to take them all to church, he hoped she would not cry off.

In fact, it was Matthew who did that, joining him in the hall to explain why he would not be going.

'I have not attended a service for years and I'm damned if I will start now.'

'Well, most likely you are,' Conham replied. 'Damned, that is.'

A soft laugh made him look up. Rosina was coming down the stairs, dressed for the short journey in her grey pelisse and with the ribbons of her bonnet tied at a jaunty angle beneath her chin. His pleasure in seeing that she had quite recovered her spirits made him forget all about Matthew until he felt a quick dig in the ribs.

'That is not the sort of language to use in front of a lady, Conham!'

'I have heard far worse, from both of you,' she retorted, smiling as she came across to join them.

'My apologies, all the same,' said Matt. He gave a little bow. 'I shall leave you both to do your duty, and hope the sermon is neither too long nor too dull!'

Rosina's eyes twinkled merrily as she thanked him. 'And I shall say a prayer for your redemption.'

'I fear it will take more than one prayer for that rogue!' said Conham, watching Matthew limp away.

'Very likely,' said Rosina, a laugh in her voice. 'But I like him, all the same. The carriage is at the door now, my lord. Shall we go?'

After the service, there were any number of parishioners wishing to make themselves known to the earl, or to remind him of their acquaintance. As everyone milled around the church-yard in the weak sunshine, Conham noticed that Rosina, too, was busily engaged. She chatted with tenants and their wives, farmers and neighbours, always friendly, but with a quiet dignity that he thought could not fail to please. There was a rosy glow to her cheeks and he barely recognised the bedraggled waif he had rescued in Bristol.

'So she is your replacement for that rogue Frumald!'

The gravelly voice jolted Conham from his muse and he turned to find a portly, bewhiskered gentleman in a brown coat and bagwig standing beside him. It was Sir John Rissington, the squire.

'Yes, that is Miss Brackwood, Sir John.' He bowed, lower than necessary perhaps, but the last time they had met, he himself had been little more than a grubby schoolboy. 'Have you been introduced?'

'Aye. That is, she went out of her way to make herself known to me, when we met by chance. All very right and proper,' he added quickly, shooting a glance at Conham. 'She was with Skillet and he performed the introductions.'

This was an opportunity to spread word of Rosina's eligibility for the post of land steward, and Conham knew he must make the most of it.

'Miss Brackwood is highly experienced in land management, Sir John. She was running her father's estates in Somerset until he died last year.'

'Ah, that explains why she is so assured.' The squire nodded. 'Pity, though. A handsome gel like that should be married.'

'Perhaps she will be, one day. But for now, I have gained an excellent steward.'

The older man regarded Rosina, his bushy eyebrows drawn together. 'You know what everyone will think.'

'I am aware it is somewhat...irregular,' Conham replied calmly. 'However, she has her own staff in the steward's lodge, and until I decide what to do with the property, I need someone to manage the land.'

'And anyone would be better than that scoundrel the trustees put in charge! Well, well. She seems a very capable young woman. Has a good head on her shoulders, too. She asked if she might call on me for advice, if she needs it. I said yes, of course, but I'd be grateful if you will make sure she knows I meant it. Hugo Conham was a good friend. It has pained me to see his property so misused.'

With that, the squire walked off, leaving the earl to the mercy of another neighbour wishing to make himself known. By the time Conham had extricated himself from everyone who wanted a word, Rosina was already sitting in the carriage.

'I beg your pardon for keeping you waiting,' he said as he climbed in. 'I thought I would never get away!'

'Are you surprised?' she asked him. 'Everyone is eager to speak with the new owner of Gifford Manor.'

'And its steward,' he retorted, grinning at her.

'Well, yes, although I know a good number of your tenants now, and this is an excellent way to become acquainted with their families. It is early days, but I think most of them are happy to accept me as steward.'

'They are. Although one or two came to me with their problems today.'

'Oh, I am sorry.'

'No need for that. I instructed them to talk to you. Told them you have my full confidence. It is true, you know,' he told her, when she flushed. 'From what I have seen and heard thus far, I am happy to leave everything in your hands until Lady Day.'

'Thank you, my lord.'

He paused. 'And Squire Rissington tells me he will be happy to give you the benefit of his advice, which could be useful. He owns most of the land around Morton Gifford.'

'I know. That is why I thought it would be wise to make the acquaintance of Sir John and his lady.'

She turned to gaze out the window and Conham sat back, content to watch her. She had the most delightful profile, with its straight little nose and that dainty chin. How long would it be, he wondered, before someone paid court to her? She had insisted that she valued her independence, but that could change, if a suitor came along who was sufficiently rich and charming. He did not like the idea, but it was no business of his. Rosina had said she would stay until Lady Day, but after that... If he was going to sell the place it would not matter, but if he kept it, he might need to find a new steward.

When they reached the Manor Rosina went off to her office, saying she had unfinished business that required attention, and Conham was left standing in the hall. He felt restless, unable to settle to anything indoors. He glanced out the window then set off at a run up the stairs. There were still a good few hours of daylight left, enough time for a brisk walk to clear his head.

Having walked further than intended, Conham did not go down to the drawing room until shortly before dinner. He found Matt Talacre and Rosina already there and deep in conversation.

They broke off when he came in, Matt handing him a glass of wine and quizzing him for being late.

'How little faith you have in me,' Conham scoffed. 'And in my valet.'

'Oh, I have complete faith in Dawkins,' Matt retorted. 'The man is a saint, and can turn you out in style in the blink of an eye. Once you are present!'

He winked at Rosina, who chuckled, but since dinner was announced at that moment there was no time for more teasing exchanges. They went into the dining room, where conversation rambled over politics before touching on Conham's appearance at church that morning.

'I've no doubt that caused a flutter in the dovecot,' Matthew remarked.

'Not unexpected, but it proved useful.' Conham reached for the buttered parsnips and added some to his plate. 'Many of those I spoke with were glad I had taken possession at last.'

He passed the dish to Matthew, who said, 'But do they know you are looking to sell?'

'I am hoping now it need not come to that, if the new plans Rosina has in mind show progress by Lady Day.'

She looked up at that. 'You have read them already?'

'I have read enough to instruct you to make a start,' he replied.

'And what of Bellemonte?' asked Matt.

'The sooner that is off my hands the better.' Conham saw him exchange a glance with Rosina and put down his knife and fork.

'What?' he demanded. 'What have you two been plotting?'

Rosina shook her head. 'Not plotting, my lord. But Matthew and I have been *discussing* Bellemonte's future.'

'Oh, is that why you had your heads together when I came in? I call that plotting.'

'We had to talk of something, since you were so damnably late,' retorted Matt. 'Rosina thinks something might be done to improve the pleasure grounds at relatively little cost.'

Matthew? Rosina? Conham frowned. They hardly knew each other and were already on first-name terms.

He said, more sharply than he intended, 'I have already looked at the ledgers. The gardens are barely breaking even.'

'That is because they are so sadly run-down,' observed Rosina.

'As are the buildings. Everything at Bellemonte is beyond redemption.'

When she did not reply, Conham looked up and noticed the stubborn tilt to her chin.

'But you are not convinced.'

'No,' she said. 'I, too, have looked at the accounts, my lord. The baths are already breaking even and with a little improvement the income can be increased. I also think it is possible to revive the gardens.'

'You need to look into it, man,' said Matthew. 'Here, Rosina, let me help you to a little more of the fricasseed rabbit. It is exceedingly good.'

Conham frowned. 'I do not need to look into it. Bellemonte requires investment. Money that I don't have.'

'We should pay Bellemonte another visit, Matthew,' Rosina suggested as if he had not spoken. 'We need to look at it again, more closely. Mr Hackthorpe said they have a concert every Monday evening in the tea rooms. With supper, and all for the princely sum of threepence!'

Matt snorted. 'No wonder they are not making a profit.'

'It is so shabby that even threepence is probably too much!' muttered Conham.

'Yes, but that could be remedied, my lord.'

'Enough now, madam. Cease your funning and let's say no more about it.'

He frowned at Rosina, but Matt Talacre was not so easily silenced.

'Actually, I think it would be a very good thing to visit the gardens tomorrow night, Conham. To see just what it is you have inherited.' He grinned. 'And I am intrigued by the idea of your owning a pleasure gardens!'

'Well, you need not be, because I won't be their owner for long!'

'We shall go as paying customers,' Matt went on, ignoring him. 'What say you, Rosina? Supper and a concert, and perhaps a stroll about the gardens after.'

'In November?' protested Conham.

'Mr Hackthorpe said the gardens by lamplight are very popular,' Rosina reminded him.

'Aye, with the riff-raff from the surrounding villages! It would not be safe for you, madam.'

Her brows went up. 'How can you know that? Besides, I have no intention of wandering around the dark avenues *alone*, my lord.' She gave him a sunny smile. 'I shall not feel nervous with you and Matthew to escort me. Besides, as the owner of the gardens, my lord, you really should be aware of what the people are getting for their money.'

Conham found his resolution crumbling.

'Rosina's right,' Matt told him. 'Nothing like surveying the ground before taking action, my friend. You told me that, when we were in the army.'

Two pairs of eyes were fixed upon him and Conham capitulated.

'Very well,' he said with just the suggestion of gritted teeth. 'We shall go, but I shall not inform Hackthorpe. I do not want him fawning over us all evening!'

Chapter Nine

They arrived at Bellemonte to find only a few vehicles in the square, but any number of people were making their way into the gardens on foot. The earl surveyed the crowds through his eyeglass.

'A distinctly dubious assortment of customers,' he remarked. 'Are you sure you want to go in?'

Matthew was already opening the door.

'We are here now, we should at least take a look,' he said, climbing out.

They left the carriage and joined the throng filing through the gates.

'There is one of the reasons the receipts are so poor,' remarked Matt, glancing along the broken railings. 'People are slipping in through the gaps.'

The Pavilion was a large building that had clearly seen better days, and Josiah Hackthorpe had not taken them inside on their earlier visit. Now they went into the concert room. It was a large, airy space, in need of decoration but otherwise perfectly acceptable. The orchestra, when it began, was woefully under-rehearsed. After sitting through half an hour of poorly played chamber music, Conham could stand no more. He escorted his companions away to the supper room. There were large fireplaces at each end of this ornate chamber, but only one fire was burning and the air felt damp. They each took a glass of wine from a hovering waiter and made their way to where a cold collation was set out on long tables at one side of the room. The food was plentiful, but it all looked dry and unappetising.

'Oh, dear,' murmured Rosina, a laugh trembling in her voice. 'Mr Hackthorpe told us his suppers would rival the finest you could find in Bath.'

Matthew scoffed. 'He clearly did not expect us to come and see for ourselves.'

'No.' Conham had put aside his wine after only one sip. Now he raised his quizzing glass and surveyed the table. 'Mrs Jameson can provide us with a far superior meal. I think we should forego supper and take a stroll in the gardens before returning to Gifford Manor.'

His suggestion was readily accepted by his companions. They collected their outdoor clothes and went out to explore the gardens.

'It will be quicker if we split up,' said Matt as they moved away from the buildings. 'I am going to look at the boundary fencing. I want to see if it is all as bad as those railings at the entrance. Rosina, perhaps you and the earl can see if the lighted paths are as good as Hackthorpe said they would be.'

'Very well, although I do not hold out much hope of it.' Conham took out his watch. 'We shall meet back here in, say, an hour.'

'That will hardly give me time to walk the boundary,' Matt objected. 'Let's make it two.'

Conham was about to say he would be damned if he'd spend two hours wandering around the neglected gardens, but Rosina spoke first.

'I agree, Matthew. We need to spend a little time looking at everything we can. Lord Dallamire will not have another opportunity before he leaves Gloucestershire.'

'Confound it, I have already told you my opinion!'

'You have indeed, my lord,' she replied, 'But since we are here we might as well make a thorough inspection, don't you agree?'

He wanted to say no, he did not agree, but she was smiling up at him in a way that dissolved his rising temper. He contented himself with a scowl, which only made her laugh.

'Come along, then, my lord, let us make a start!'

Matthew limped away into the shrubbery and Rosina set off with the earl along the main walk, which was illuminated by numerous coloured lamps hanging from the trees.

'This is very pretty,' she observed. The earl did not reply and she glanced at him. 'I do believe you are sulking.'

'Nonsense!'

'You would rather be anywhere than this. Pray, do not be afraid to say so, Lord Dallamire.' She hesitated then added in a mournful tone, 'It would be the most savage blow to my self-esteem, but I shall bear it.'

'Witch!'

She laughed. 'No, no, merely trying to coax you out of the sullens, as any friend would do.'

'Ha, with friends such as you and Matt Talacre—'

'Yes, you are very fortunate, are you not, my lord?'

'That is not how I would put it. Quiet now. If we have to explore these damned gardens the least you can do is spare me your teasing.'

Having succeeded in coaxing him out of his bad mood, Rosina fell silent. For a short time.

'I have never visited Vauxhall Gardens, my lord. Is this very like?'

'Not much.' A small group of revellers came towards them and the earl pulled her quickly to one side.

'I suppose people there are better behaved,' she said, watching the little party continue unsteadily on its way.

'Not at all. Despite the higher ticket prices, and extortionate sums for what passes as supper, Vauxhall can be riotous, especially when everyone is masked.' He pulled her hand back onto his arm and set off again. 'However, it is in far better condition than this! For one thing, the Grand Walk is much wider, and has many more lamps.'

'I agree the foliage has seriously encroached on this path, but I think this has a certain charm.'

'If you say so, madam. *I'd* say it is beyond saving.'

'I noticed when we were here in daylight that there are recesses and alcoves on either side of the path.' She began to look around. 'They are all overgrown now, but I remember seeing a few stone figures…yes, there is one. I can see the head and shoulders rising above the shrubs. And on the other side there is a small colonnade. Look, you can just see the tops of the columns.'

'Yes, you are right. I think there are even more, up here.'

They continued to peer into the shadows at the side of the meandering main path, and even if Dallamire was not quite as eager as Rosina, at least she thought he was now showing more interest in the gardens. The ground had been rising steadily but soon they reached a bend, where the main route curved away and downwards, leaving only a narrow track leading up into the darkness.

Rosina stopped. 'Why, that is the way to the viewing terrace! Do you remember, Conham? We walked up there and looked out over Bristol.'

'Yes, I remember.' He pretended not to notice that in her excitement she had used his name. 'What of it?'

'We should walk up and look at the same view at night.'

'There is no moon.'

'There is a crescent,' she said. 'From the viewing point we should be able to pick out the river and the city.'

'But why would we want to do that?'

'Having looked out over Bristol by day, I should like to see the same view at night.'

She had turned to look up at him, the lamplight showing her hopeful expression. He sighed.

'Very well, if that is what you want.'

'I do,' she said. 'Who knows if I shall ever have the chance to do so again?'

'And I would by no means curtail any pleasure of yours,' he said politely.

She gave him a sunny smile. 'Thank you!'

She turned and headed towards the upward track. Conham followed, but they had gone no more than a few steps along the path before she stopped. He could see why. After the lamplight of the main walk there was nothing but impenetrable shadow beneath the close, overhanging branches. He remembered how they had pushed aside the untended plants on either side of the track when they had walked there in daylight. In the dark it would be almost impossible to negotiate.

More than enough reason to turn back, he thought. A perfect excuse to cut short this pointless exercise.

Instead, he reached up and unhooked one of the lamps from the nearest tree. Then, taking her hand, he set off into the darkness.

The single lamp gave them barely enough light to see their way, and Conham kept Rosina behind him to protect her from the worst of the overgrown foliage. Mostly it was just leaves, or stray tendrils of ivy, but the occasional small branch caught at their clothes. He stopped again.

'This is not sensible, Rosina.'

'Pho,' she answered him. 'It is only a few twigs. Besides, it cannot be far now, I can see the night sky. Look.'

It was true; there was a definite lightness ahead of them and in a very short time they stepped out of the constricting darkness of the trees to see the sliver of moon suspended high above them.

'There, you see?' she declared, moving ahead of him. 'It is light as day out here.'

It was a gross exaggeration, but Conham said nothing. He followed her up the winding path until they had reached the long terrace that marked the northernmost boundary of the grounds. Beyond was nothing but fields and a large wood, but Rosina had turned to look back over the gardens and towards the city.

'There.' She clasped her hands before her. 'I *said* it would be worth the effort!'

Conham gazed out at the view. Over the treetops he could see the pale outline of the lower gardens and the Pavilion. Beyond that, in the distance, were the roofs and spires of Bristol and the river winding in and around everything like a silver ribbon. He glanced at Rosina. Her eyes, her whole attention, was fixed on the distant city and something contracted inside him, like an iron band around his chest.

His years in the army had taken him to many countries. He had stood on hills and mountain ridges in Portugal and Spain, gazing down on cities far grander than Bristol, but here, now, sharing this moment with Rosina and witnessing her innocent pleasure, he thought this must be the most memorable of them all.

A sudden gust of wind raced across the terrace, icy and biting. It flung Rosina's blue cloak back from her shoulders. As if waking from a dream she started, her hands fumbling to reach the cape that was fluttering away behind her.

'Here, let me help you.'

Conham put down the lamp and caught the flapping material, stepping close to wrap the warm woollen folds about her. For a moment they stood thus, her back pressed against his chest and his arms around her. The strong wind had teased free several curls from beneath her close-fitting jockey cap, and the tendrils brushed his chin. His pulse quickened. He closed his eyes, imagining how it would be to turn her about, to feel her heart beating against his as he captured those soft lips beneath his own. To explore her mouth with his tongue and kiss her until she was moaning with pleasure...

'Thank you, Lord Dallamire.' She was gently pulling the mantle from his fingers. 'I have it now.'

He stepped back smartly, breathing in the cold air, fighting down the desire raging through him. What the devil was he doing? He picked up the lamp.

'We should get back.'

'Yes.'

She turned, avoiding his eyes and clutching her cloak around her as if it could defend her from far more than the weather. Confound it, had she guessed what was in his mind? It was not his way to tamper with innocents. Or to promise more than he could give. Conham reminded himself sharply that he needed to marry a fortune.

A flurry of snow whirled in from one of the small clouds scudding across the sky and he said, trying to lighten the mood, 'We are going just in time, I think.' He put out his hand but she did not move. He felt rather than saw her reluctance and let it fall again. 'Stay close behind me.'

They set off back down the path, Conham going ahead and holding the lamp high. Even so, he knew Rosina would be walking in his shadow. He could protect her from obtruding branches but she would not be able to see the rough, uneven path beneath her feet. He stopped.

'I'd be happier if I knew you hadn't tripped or slipped,' he said, without turning around. 'Take hold of my coat.'

He thought she might refuse, then he felt a slight tug as she clutched at his greatcoat. They set off again, Conham shortening his stride to make sure he did not outpace her.

By the time they reached the main path again, Rosina had regained her composure. Not that she would have lost it, if her cape had not flown open. If Dallamire had not stepped up so close. He had enveloped her, his broad chest against her back, his strong arms wrapped around her. Supremely warm and comforting yet oh, so very dangerous!

While the earl replaced the lamp on a branch of the nearest tree, she fidgeted, refastening her cloak. She needed to rid herself of the wicked thoughts and images crowding her head. They were turning her insides to water. For someone who prided herself on her common sense, she had shown a sad lack of it this evening.

Nothing to do with the earl's presence, of course. It was merely the moonlight and the dark sky with its scattering of stars. And the night air, she thought, a touch wistfully. It had been calm, almost balmy, before that wintry breeze blew in and whipped away her cloak. Heaven knew what might have happened if they had stayed there any longer, the earl with his arms about her, his breath on her cheek and her whole body crying out for him to kiss her.

Just the thought of what might have followed sent another delicious shiver down her spine and she was obliged to give herself a mental scolding. Conham had made her land steward of Morton Gifford with a salary she could never attain in more conventional female roles. She must never forget that. If she made a success of this and could keep her good name, then it might be possible to find a similar post elsewhere, to secure an independent future for herself.

When Dallamire offered her his arm she took it, head up, breathing steadily as they set off back towards the Pavilion. Being alone in the moonlight with a handsome man might be construed by many females as incredibly romantic, but Rosina had no time for such silliness.

The main path was far busier than when they set out, and Rosina guessed supper in the Pavilion was now over. She also suspected that many of those they passed were intoxicated. With Dallamire at her side Rosina felt perfectly safe, but it was clear that Bellemonte's visitors were far from respectable, as she observed to her companions once they were all safely in the carriage and on their way back to Gifford Manor.

'Precisely,' said the earl. 'I have neither the time nor the funds to turn the gardens around. Hackthorpe's contract runs out on Christmas Day, then Bellemonte will be put up for sale to the highest bidder, and that's an end to it!'

No more was said on the subject for the remainder of the journey. Rosina settled back in one corner, content to listen to Conham and Matthew talking in a desultory manner. It was clear to her now that they were more than just master and servant. There was a strong bond between them. She remembered Conham's words to her at the lodge, about having friends around him. With the loss of her father and Edgar's treachery still raw, it was no small comfort to think that these men regarded her as a friend.

And that, she told herself, was another reason to be thankful she had not made a fool of herself upon the viewing terrace tonight.

* * *

The carriage made good time returning to Morton Gifford, and when they reached the Manor, Rosina declared she had no appetite for supper, but would retire immediately.

'Then I will walk you to the lodge,' said the earl.

'Thank you, my lord, but your footman is already here and waiting to do so.'

'Then he can go away again.' He dismissed the man with a wave. 'I shall accompany you.'

Rosina gazed at him helplessly. He might call her a friend, but he was still her employer. How could she refuse?

'Besides,' he continued, 'it will give Matthew time to arrange for our supper to be brought to the library, and to make sure there is a good fire burning.'

'I should have known he would not let me rest,' declared Matt, grinning. 'I shall bid you good-night, then, Rosina. Sleep well.'

He lounged away and the earl turned to Rosina. 'Shall we go?'

She fell into step beside him on the drive, taking care not to walk so close that their arms might brush.

'Matthew and I are leaving in the morning,' he reminded her. 'I hope you will join us for breakfast. We can go over any last-minute details that might arise. About the estate.'

Rosina felt a ripple of apprehension at the prospect of being here alone, without the earl's presence. What if her brother found her? He had tried to do away with her once; next time she might not escape. She quickly shook off her fears. She was not alone here, there were any number of servants and she was well-known in the area. Edgar could not drag her away from Morton Gifford against her will.

'A good idea, my lord,' she said now. 'I will be there.'

'Good. And if you use the carriage while I am away, you must instruct the driver to bring you to your door.'

'Indeed I shall not,' she replied, indignant. 'I am not a guest here but land steward, at least until Lady Day.'

'I would have thought seeing Bellemonte tonight might have discouraged you from staying even that long!'

'But I have very little to do with Bellemonte, which is fortunate, since I shall be busy enough looking after Gifford Manor and its land. I do not want to let you down.'

'Somehow, I don't think you will do that.'

His smile and the warm tone he used sent a little flutter through Rosina, a warm mixture of pride and pleasure, and she was grateful for the darkness to hide the telltale blush upon her cheek.

It took only a few minutes to reach the lodge. Not long enough, thought Conham, as they approached the small building. He stopped and turned to Rosina.

'Good night, Miss Brackwood.'

'Thank you.'

His brows went up. 'What, for escorting you here?'

'No, not just that. For including me in your visit to Bellemonte tonight. For asking my opinion, even if you have already made up your mind to sell.'

He looked up to the night sky and sighed. 'I am not selling it through choice, Rosina. Heaven knows Bellemonte is in such a parlous state it will fetch little enough, but there is no alternative. Dallamire must be my priority. I need every penny I have to keep it in order. And more.'

'Yes, of course.'

The stars were twinkling above them, just as they had done at Bellemonte. He took a deep breath.

'That's why I must find a rich wife. You do understand that, Rosina?'

He dragged his eyes away from the stars and fixed them on her face. She nodded.

'To quote from one of Papa's favourite books, "Handsome young men must have something to live on, as well as the plain."'

She was looking up at him, her eyes reflecting the starlight, and he could not tear his gaze away. The air around them was thick and charged with electricity, like the prelude to a thunderstorm. One word, one touch, and he knew the storm would break. He felt suddenly awkward, off balance, but there was something he must tell her.

'Rosina—'

The lodge door opened with a creak and lamplight spilled out around the black outline of the maid. Conham could no longer see Rosina's expression, but he caught the slight lift of her shoulders and heard a murmured 'good-night' before she disappeared into the house.

He turned away, balling his hands into tight fists as he began to walk swiftly back to the Manor. Confound it, was the lady's position not precarious enough without his trying to take advantage of her at every opportunity? He was a damned rogue. She was in his employ, and she was also fiercely independent. Despite the strong attraction, he could not afford to marry her. He needed a bride with a substantial dowry. A great many people, including his stepmother and half-sisters, were depending upon him to repair the fortune his father had gambled away.

Reaching the house, he strode inside, but instead of making his way to the library he went up to his room, telling the butler, whom he met on the stairs, to make his apologies to Mr Talacre and say he would see him in the morning.

Chapter Ten

The earl went down to breakfast to find Matt Talacre alone at the table.

'My apologies for last night,' he said before Matt could speak. 'I found I was not hungry after all, just dog-tired.'

'Aye, so Jameson informed me.'

Conham saw the speculative gleam in his friend's eyes but willed himself not to react.

'Once I had handed Miss Brackwood over to her maid, I went straight to bed.'

Matt shrugged. 'No matter. I had plenty to occupy me.'

'Oh?'

'Yes. I sat down and wrote out my thoughts about Belle-monte.'

'Would you like to share them?' Anything, as long as it stopped Matt from talking of Rosina.

'Very well.'

Matthew paused while he selected another bread roll from the basket on the table.

'After I had inspected the boundary fencing last night, I went back to take another look at the Pavilion. It is not in such poor repair as I first thought. Nothing that a little paint and minor refurbishment would not remedy.

'So, before I went to bed, I fetched the ledgers and went over them. I think, no, I am sure, that with a little investment and some hard work, Bellemonte could begin turning a better profit by next summer.'

Matt stopped and looked at Conham, who nodded.

'Go on.'

'All the ticket prices need to be increased, of course. That would instantly bring more in from the baths, which could remain open for the present. As for the gardens, the bushes and trees require some attention, as do all the paths. And I think the main walks would be improved with new coloured lamps. All that could be done during the winter, ready for a grand reopening in May.'

'But at what cost?' asked Conham. 'As I told you, I have no money to invest in Bellemonte.'

'That is the point.' Matthew sat forward, his eyes shining. 'I am not asking you to put more money in. I would like to invest mine.'

'Yours!'

'The money I received when I sold my commission. I haven't needed it, since you are paying me a salary. I have checked all the figures and I think it will be enough to get things started.'

He broke off as Rosina came in. She greeted both men in her usual calm, friendly way, and Conham felt an intense relief that she was not offended or upset by anything he had said last night.

'Good morning,' he said. 'Did you know about this harebrained idea of Matthew's?'

'To invest in Bellemonte? Yes. Matthew came to my office before breakfast and we looked at the figures together. I believe it might work.'

He narrowed his eyes at her. 'And you told me you weren't plotting.'

'Not at all, my lord. Merely trying to help.'

'Conham, you have told me often enough that I would one day find something that interests me,' said Matthew. 'This does. With your permission, I would like to remain in Gloucestershire, oversee Hackthorpe's removal at the end of December—it is only a few weeks, after all—and manage the renovations myself. The public house will need a new landlord. I have no objection to locals drinking in the taproom, but the place was once a thriving inn for travellers and I think it could be again.'

'Yes,' added Rosina, 'and do not forget there are the gardens, too. The basic ground plan is still in evidence and that would be an excellent starting point for our improvements.'

'*Our* improvements?' Conham interrupted her.

She nodded. 'Why, yes. You will still be the owner, so it is in everyone's interests for this project to be a success.'

'I want to improve the path up to the viewpoint,' said Matt. 'Rosina has suggested we build a small circle of columns up there and call it the temple of... Which goddess was it, Rosina? What did you call her?'

'Selene, Greek goddess of the full moon.'

There was a slight blush on her cheek and she avoided his eyes, which made Conham wonder if she was thinking of that moment on the terrace. The midnight madness that had brought him dangerously close to doing something they would both regret. He had not forgotten it, his fitful, dream-filled sleep was proof of that.

'Yes, and in the summer we might have someone up there selling refreshments for those who make the climb.' Matt's voice interrupted his thoughts. 'Most of these ideas can be carried out at very little cost.'

'And quickly, too,' added Rosina, who had regained her composure. 'Matthew's idea is to have the gardens open again by the summer. More improvements can follow, when funds allow.'

Matt raised his coffee cup and regarded Conham over its rim. 'If you can hold fire on selling Bellemonte until Lady Day, I hope to show you some improvement in Bellemonte's fortunes.'

'You and Rosina appear to have thought it all out.' He paused. 'I suppose you would continue to live at Gifford Manor?'

'No, no. I shall put up at the inn until I can make a few rooms habitable in the big house.' He laughed. 'We learned how to make ourselves comfortable in veritable *ruins* when we were in the Peninsula, do you remember, Conham? In time, I want to renovate the whole place and turn it into an hotel, keeping the top floor for my own use. One of the first things I want to do, though, is to make the area more respectable. I plan to employ two or three watchmen, and to build a charley box.'

Conham looked up. 'A what?'

'A lock-up, where those intent on trouble can be left to cool their heels overnight. Once we have cleared the worst of the scoundrels from the area and increased the prices, the customers will come flocking in.' Matt went on, warming to his theme, 'There are plenty of rich merchants in Bristol willing to pay handsomely for their entertainment. And Bellemonte is only a couple of miles from the Hotwells and Clifton Village. Oh, I know the hot baths there are superior, but apart from the theatre and the assembly rooms, there is very little in the way of entertainment for those in residence.'

Conham sat back, considering, while the others waited expectantly.

'This is utter madness,' he said slowly. 'But it might just work.'

'It *will* work,' Matt was adamant. 'Of course, it is only the beginning. We shall need more investment in the future, but I thought we might sell shares—only in small amounts. I do not want to risk losing control of the project.'

Conham frowned at him.

'And just what do you want from me?' he demanded. 'Apart from my not selling Bellemonte, that is.'

'Your name. Once it is known the gardens enjoy the patronage of the Earl of Dallamire I have no doubt the crowds will come.'

Conham's fingers tapped on the table. 'We would need legal documents.'

'Of course, we will draw up an agreement for rents, and the division of profits. I want it to be watertight, Conham. As they say in these parts, shipshape and Bristol fashion. I will consult with Rosina regularly. She can act as your agent while you are away and keep you informed of progress.'

'You are already agreed on this?' Conham looked at Rosina.

'Yes, we discussed it earlier this morning. I know there is a risk but believe me, my lord, I would not lend my support to such a scheme if I did not think it could benefit you.'

Matthew leaned forward. 'Well, man, what do you say?'

Conham gave his attention to his breakfast, but his brain was working furiously. It was years since he had seen Matt looking so eager and enthusiastic about anything. He knew the man had a good head on his shoulders and he trusted him not to make a mull of it. Eventually, he pushed away his plate.

'Very well. If you think you can do this with no extra funds from me, I am willing to let you put your scheme into action. Hackthorpe's contract on the gardens and the inn expires on the December Quarter Day, but he has no legal hold over the old house or the baths, so you may do what you will with that now.'

'Thank you, I shall make a start, then.' Matt beamed at him across the table. 'I won't let you down, Conham!'

An hour later all three of them walked to the door, where the earl's travelling chariot was waiting on the drive. Conham turned to Matthew.

'We will look at this again when I return at the end of March, but until then any expenditure must come from your own funds.'

'Agreed!' Matt gripped his hand and pumped it. 'I think, between us, Rosina and I can make a success of this for you!'

Conham nodded and climbed into the coach. He looked back, his last view being of Matt and Rosina standing together on the drive, watching his departure. They were already very friendly. Who was to say where that would lead over the next few months, if they were working closely together? It was very likely that they would fall in love but that was no business of his. He hoped they would be very happy.

He shrugged himself into the corner and looked out at the bleak, wintry landscape. He must find himself a rich bride, that much was certain, and he had no right to be a dog in the manger where Rosina was concerned.

Chapter Eleven

Spring was bursting into bloom in the London parks. New leaf buds were appearing on the trees but it was still early March and the warm, sunny days gave way to icy nights. Consequently, the long windows of the ballroom overlooking Green Park had been firmly closed.

Conham stood by one of the windows, staring out into the darkness. It was near midnight and behind him, the dancing was continuing. He could hear the scrape of fiddles mixing with the chatter and laughter that filled the room.

By heaven, he was bored! He longed to be out of London. He would much prefer to be at Gifford Manor, sitting quietly by the fire in the drawing room and sharing a glass of wine with Matt Talacre. Perhaps they might even persuade Rosina to join them for a business dinner. Only it never felt like business when she was present. It was always far more pleasurable than that. They would sit at the dining table talking late into the night, and even if they disagreed it was never serious, they always found some common ground, something to smile about.

He tore his thoughts away from Rosina. She was his land steward and as unattainable as ever. By heaven, if only he had paid as much attention to his own land as she had to Brackwood, perhaps he would not be in this mess now!

'Dallamire, what are you doing, standing here all alone?' His stepmother's voice interrupted his thoughts. 'You must come and dance.'

'I have partnered more than enough young ladies for one evening, ma'am.'

'And did none of them take your fancy? If there is anyone in particular you would like to stand up with for the waltz, I am sure our hostess would oblige…'

'For heaven's sake don't suggest it,' he interrupted her. 'To dance the waltz with anyone would be as good as announcing our betrothal!'

'Well, that is what you are here for,' she told him. 'Dallamire, you have been dithering all winter! You need to find a bride, sir, and a rich one. You appeared to be getting on well with Miss Hewick. She's a very pretty behaved girl, she would make you a good wife.'

'Yes, if you like someone who agrees with your every utterance!'

The countess gave his arm a sharp tap with her closed fan. 'Pray, do not be so disagreeable, Dallamire. She has a fortune as well as birth and breeding.'

'But no brain!'

His stepmother's eyes snapped.

'I vow you are being odiously provoking this evening! If you had not stayed away in France for so long, if you had returned to Dallamire earlier, this might not have been necessary, but you know we are all depending upon you to restore the family fortunes.' She stepped closer. 'If you will not think of me, consider your poor half-sisters, reduced to penury by our unfortunate circumstances. If you do not stir yourself, Dallamire, they will end up old maids!'

Conham almost ground his teeth. 'Since they are still in the schoolroom, I cannot see the urgency!' He took a breath, fighting down his irritation. 'I have told you, madam, when the time comes the girls will be presented at court in a fitting manner.'

'And you will need to marry a fortune to make that happen,' she argued. 'Now. If Miss Hewick does not please you, there is another young lady here who might do so. Come along, I shall introduce you to Miss Skelton.' She tucked her hand in his arm and gave a little tug. 'Dallamire, will you come and do your duty?'

Conham looked down into the countess's lined, determined face and swallowed a sigh. There was no escaping his duty, so he had best get it over with.

'Yes, of course, ma'am. Lead on.'

He went back into the fray, smiling outwardly, while inside he felt all the enthusiasm of a man heading for the scaffold.

The sight of the blackthorn flowers in the hedgerows and primroses pushing up in the grassy banks cheered Rosina as she rode back to Gifford Manor. It was almost four months since she had arrived in Gloucestershire, and she had thrown herself into the work of the estate. She had blotted out her old life so successfully that now she rarely thought of Brackwood, or her brother. She had been accepted surprisingly well by her neighbours and the estate's tenants, in part because the squire's wife, Lady Rissington, had befriended her, but it also helped that the previous steward had been such a rogue that almost any replacement would have been welcomed.

However, the hard winter had seriously impeded Rosina's plans to improve the estate. She had made some progress, but not as much as she would have liked, and Lady Day was now only weeks away, when Lord Dallamire would return to judge her progress.

Conham was never far from her thoughts. She had written to him several times, reporting on estate matters and informing him of any changes she wished to make. The replies were always brief and often written by his secretary or the steward at Dallamire.

Did he ever think of her?

Rosina doubted it. Not only was he busy with affairs at Dallamire, he had also said he intended to find himself a wife, something she did not think would prove very difficult. She was forced to agree with Matt that, despite his lack of fortune, Conham was a handsome devil, with his auburn hair that fell across his wide brow, the crooked grin and strong jawline. Then there were those grey-green eyes that could light up with laughter in an instant. It was more than enough to send any lady's pulse racing. He was also tall, with broad shoulders that looked as if they could bear all one's problems.

No, she had no doubt there were any number of heiresses ready to snap up the Earl of Dallamire, and Rosina lived in daily expectation of hearing that he had contracted a brilliant alliance. Not that she could bear to read the society pages in the London newspaper that Squire Rissington insisted on bringing over to her, once he had read it, but Jameson scanned it eagerly, and she was sure the butler would waste no time in passing on the happy news, when it came.

Gifford Manor was in sight, rising above its surrounding trees, the honey-coloured stone warm and glowing in the sunshine. If Dallamire did find himself a bride, it was entirely possible she would persuade him to sell the estate at Morton Gifford. If that happened, Rosina could only hope she had done enough to convince the earl to provide her with a reference, and recommend to the new owner that she continue in the post.

As she trotted through the gates she saw a carriage pulled up at the door. A second glance and she saw the earl was standing on the drive, giving instructions to his driver. He looked up as she drew nearer and Rosina felt a wave of happiness surge through her body.

'We did not expect you for a week yet!'

'You have acquired a pony!'

They spoke at the same time, and both smiled self-consciously.

'Yes, this is Bramble.' Rosina leaned forward to run her hand along the mare's brown neck. 'Welsh-bred and chosen for her stamina and steady nature. Fred Skillet went to Painswick to buy her for me. She can carry me all day with never a stumble.'

'She is certainly a sturdy beast,' remarked the earl, rubbing the mare's nose. 'Although clearly not chosen for her looks.'

Rosina laughed. 'Hush now, I will not allow you to abuse her! She is proving very useful to me, since she is equally at home pulling the gig.'

'Then I will happily allow her space in the stables,' replied the earl, grinning. 'Is that where you are going now? I will have someone take the pony away and you can come into the house.'

He signalled to a hovering servant to take the mare's head and he stepped around to lift Rosina from the saddle. For a moment her heart took flight. She was suspended in his arms and her stomach flipped at the sudden feeling of helplessness, the sensation of being at the earl's mercy, totally dependent upon him. It should have been unpleasant, but it wasn't. In fact, she felt a definite disappointment when he put her down and she quickly busied herself, shaking out her skirts to hide her confusion.

Conham, too, was struggling to remain calm. His pleasure at seeing her and the easy way they spoke to one another—it was as if they had been acquainted for years. It had seemed the most natural thing in the world to lift her down from the saddle.

Until he was actually holding her, that is. A light but heady fragrance assailed his senses, summer flowers with just a hint of lemon, clean and fresh, and she was surprisingly light in his arms. Surprisingly *precious*. He did not want to let her go. The urge to kiss her was so strong that it shocked him, and it had taken every ounce of his self-control to set her on her feet. Now Conham looked about him, at the retreating carriage, at the house, across to the far hills. Anywhere but at Rosina.

He cleared his throat. One of them would have to break this awkward silence.

'Yes, well. Come into the house,' he repeated. 'I did not send word that I was coming today and nothing has been prepared. Mrs Jameson is making ready my room and then Dawkins will need to unpack. In the meantime you can tell me how you have gone on.'

'Then I suggest we go to my office,' said Rosina. 'If you were not expected there will be no fires burning in any of the other rooms.'

'Good point. Come along, then!'

Conham escorted Rosina into the house and held open the door for her to precede him into the office. It looked much as it had done when he had last seen it in November, dark wood cupboards lining the walls, a large desk in the centre of the room, yet something was different. It took him a few moments to notice the changes: a jug of early spring flowers on a table by the window and extra cushions on the steward's desk chair as well as the armchair in the corner. How odd that such tiny changes could make a room feel so much more welcoming.

'We will be more comfortable over here,' he said, pushing the armchair closer to the hearth and indicating that Rosina should sit down. She hesitated, watching him pull up a plain wooden chair for himself.

'Would you not prefer to use my desk chair?'

'No, no, you sit down, I shall do very well here.' He grinned as he settled himself on the hard seat. 'I want to know how my tenants feel when they come in here to see you!'

She smiled at that. 'They rarely come to the house. I prefer to visit them.'

'And how are you received? Answer me truthfully now.'

'In the main, my reception here has been very good.'

'And has there been any talk?'

'Talk?'

'Any gossip that you are my mistress?'

She blushed a little but answered him with equal frankness.

'Of course, at first. But the squire and his lady acknowledge me, which has helped a great deal.'

She could not help adding, with a touch of pride, 'I believe, however, my reputation as an experienced land steward is spreading. I have had more than a few letters now, asking for my advice.'

'That is a great compliment.'

'Yes, it is, although I hope word does not spread south as far as Somerset.'

'You are concerned your brother might hear of it?'

She shook her head. 'Not seriously concerned. I think it is the novelty of a female land steward that has engendered a little gossip within the area. It will die down soon enough.'

'And the tenant farmers, the local tradesmen—is anyone proving especially difficult?'

'No. That is, one or two tried to bully me at first, but I learned very early at Brackwood how to deal with that! I understand that it hurts the pride of some men to answer to a woman, but I have dealt with that problem, too.'

'Oh, how?'

'I have taken on a young man from the village. Davy Redmond, the vicar's son. He was at Oxford but has finished his studies now and is come home. Having been born and raised here, he is familiar with the life of a rural parish and is acquainted with everyone in the area.'

'That seems like an excellent plan. When will I meet this young man?'

'Tomorrow. He is taking several of the tenant farmers to Home Farm today, to show them the new drainage we have put in there. We are trying to persuade them that it is worth the effort to drain at least some of their lower meadows. My father did something similar at Brackwood, to very good effect. I have spoken to the squire and he agrees with me that these farms in particular would benefit from the investment.'

'And how much will it cost *me*?' Conham enquired.

'Very little.' She went across to the desk and pulled out a sheaf of papers from one of the drawers. 'These particular leases are due for renewal on Lady Day and I am hoping you will agree to maintaining the present rents and guarantee the farmers a full year's lease if they will undertake the improvements we have suggested.'

He took the papers she was holding out to him and glanced at them.

'I will need to study all this a little more before I can agree.'

'But of course. I would not expect anything else, Lord Dallamire.'

'Very well. Have all the ledgers and accounts brought to my study tomorrow and I will look at them.' He rose. 'I had best go and change. Will I see you at dinner?'

'I think not. I shall dine with the Jamesons, as I usually do.'

'We might continue discussing these new plans of yours.'

She smiled but shook her head. 'Tempting, but it will not do, my lord, and you know it.'

'I know nothing of the sort!' He frowned at her. 'I thought we were friends, Rosina. Why are you being so formal?'

'I have no choice. Can you not see that it must be this way? You made me steward here and I would like to remain in the post for some time yet. I am in your employ and cannot compromise my position by dining alone with you, even though a lady might risk it.'

Conham growled. 'You *are* a lady!'

'Thank you.' She smiled a little, but he could tell from her mulish look that she was not to be moved. He sighed.

'So be it. I know your reasoning is sound, but when we are alone you will call me Conham, do you understand? That is an order.'

'Yes my—Conham.'

Their eyes met and a giggle escaped her. The tension eased immediately and Conham went up to his room, still smiling, albeit a little rueful. He would miss her presence at dinner but he knew she was right. Any hint of scandal and it would be impossible for her to remain at Morton Gifford as land steward. And he really did not want her to leave.

Rosina carried all the accounts and papers to the earl's office very early the next morning, still unsettled by the see-saw of emotions she had felt when she had first seen him yesterday. She was pleased he was at the Manor and yet she knew she must be on her guard. It would be very easy to be too familiar, to tease him or touch his arm, or call him Conham in front of the servants. Just one slip would be enough to set tongues wagging. Not that she thought any of the servants would deliberately set out to destroy her reputation, but it would only take an ill-judged word and her position here would be untenable.

She was back in her own office before the earl had left the breakfast room and it was there that he found her some hours later. He came in just as she and Davy were poring over a large map of the estate, and she lost no time in presenting her assistant.

'I know your father, of course,' said Conham, giving the young man a friendly smile. 'I sat through any number of his sermons with my godfather as a schoolboy. You had no desire to go into the church?'

Davy shook his head. 'Alas, no, much to my father's disappointment, although he is far too good to mention it. He sends his regards, by the way.'

They chatted for a little longer before Conham turned to the subject of drainage on the tenant farms.

'I have read Miss Brackwood's report and looked at the plans this morning. And I believe you spoke with the farmers yesterday, Mr Redmond?'

Rosina was content to let them talk, knowing Conham wanted to discover if her assistant understood the matter in hand. Davy acquitted himself well, he was deferential and polite, but in no way intimidated. She thought Conham would like that and she was right, for he told her as much when she went with him to his study to collect up all the documents.

'I am glad you like him,' she said. 'He is already proving an asset to the estate, and keen to learn more.'

The earl was standing behind his desk, looking down at an open ledger.

'When exactly did you take him on?'

'At Christmas. Squire Rissington knew I was looking for someone and suggested Davy Redmond might be just the person.'

'And you have been paying him monthly.'

'Yes.'

Conham ran his finger down the entries in the ledger. He had already looked at them once, but he wanted to be sure.

'There is no mention here of any wages for an assistant.' He glanced up, and saw that Rosina was looking a little self-conscious.

She said, 'I was not sure the estate could bear the cost. I have been paying him myself.'

'How much?'

When she told him, he frowned. 'It will not do, Rosina.'

'But my salary is more than generous. Far more than I could earn as a governess or a teacher.' She raised her chin. 'And if, as a *woman*, I am not capable of fulfilling my role here, surely I should be responsible for employing someone to assist me.'

'We agreed a fair wage for the post, but it is not an excessive one. Frumald was a scoundrel and he was lining his pockets at the estate's expense with far more than you are paying Redmond.

'You will add the young man to the wages roll with immediate effect, do you understand?' He saw the stubborn look on her face and said again, more forcefully, 'Do you understand, madam?'

'Yes, my lord.'

'Oho! So we are back to being formal when we are alone.'

'*You* addressed me as madam.'

'That was because I was angry with you!'

She gazed at him, brows raised, and he laughed. 'What's sauce for the goose, eh?'

'I would not be so impolite as to suggest such a thing, my lord.'

She spoke coolly, but a twinkle lurked in those blue eyes. He grinned at her.

'Witch! No, no, do not fire up again. Here.' He closed the ledger and handed it to her. 'Take this away now. I have seen enough to know the estate is in safe hands.'

'Thank you, my—' She stopped when he threw a warning look at her. 'Thank you, Conham.'

There was a decided smile in her eyes now and he liked that, just as he liked the becoming flush that mantled her cheeks. He imagined himself moving around the desk and taking her in his arms, kissing her until they both forgot all about drains and ditches and debts. If only that were possible.

He turned his sigh into a cough and said brusquely, 'Very well. Off you go now. But you will dine with me tomorrow. A working dinner,' he added. 'I sent word to Matt Talacre and he is joining us. To discuss Bellemonte.'

He did not fail to miss the lightening of her countenance, or the sudden smile that curved her lips.

'Have you seen much of Matthew?' He was careful to keep his tone light, and held back from adding *while I have been away*.

'No, he has not called, although we have exchanged correspondence about Bellemonte. His letters and copies of my replies are here, somewhere...' She glanced down at the books and papers cradled in her arms.

'Ah yes, of course. I saw them. They make interesting reading.' The little demon of jealousy subsided. 'We can discuss everything tomorrow evening.'

She nodded. 'I shall look forward to it.'

'As will I.'

Their eyes met and held, as if neither of them wanted to move. Then Rosina hurried from the room and Conham was left standing by the desk, breathing in the fading traces of her scent.

Chapter Twelve

The sun was already climbing in the clear sky when Rosina left the steward's lodge the following morning. It was not only the prospect of a bright warm day that accounted for her sunny mood. The earl was back at Morton Gifford, and even the sight of him riding away across the park as she walked to the Manor did not dishearten her. Just the fact that he was in residence was enough to lift her spirits.

She spent an hour with Davy Redmond before he went off to see the gamekeeper, who had reported a spate of poaching in the home wood. After that she settled down to read through the new tenancy agreements Davy had prepared.

It was midday before she finally put them aside and rubbed her eyes, wondering what to do next. The sun was still shining, and she was tempted to take a walk. Then she noticed the large pile of books on the table by the window. They were in the main local histories, plus instructive tomes on farming practices and animal husbandry purchased by Hugo Conham. She had been studying them during her first weeks at Gifford, but now decided it was time they were returned to the library shelves.

Rosina collected up all the books and set off for the library. It was situated at the back of the house, with large windows that looked out over the rolling hills. It was a glorious spring day and she promised herself that as soon as she had put the books back in their proper place, she would collect her shawl and enjoy a brisk walk in the sunshine.

She had just pushed two accounts of local history back amongst their fellows when she heard the door open. She turned, thinking it must be a servant, but she gasped, her clutch tightening on the books in her arms, when she saw her brother's stocky frame filling the doorway.

'You!'

'Surprised, Sister?'

Edgar closed the door and stood with his back to it, his lip curled in a smile that chilled her blood.

'Who let you in here?' she demanded, trying to keep a tremor out of her voice.

'Some fool of a footman. I told him I was your brother and not to bother announcing me.'

The last time Rosina had seen Edgar he had been forcing laudanum down her throat while the hard-faced woman, Moffat, held her prisoner. She told herself he could not do that here. There were servants in the house, if only she could alert them. She glanced towards the fireplace and immediately he took a few steps forward. There was no way she could reach the door or the bellpull without his intercepting her.

Rosina fought down her panic. If she screamed there was a slight possibility someone would hear her, but she could not be certain and it might push Edgar into violence. All she could do for now was play for time.

'How did you find me?'

'Sheer chance. You will remember my good friend Alfred Tumby. He was an admirer of yours.'

'He was an odious villain,' she retorted. 'He tried to seduce me, and with Papa lying ill above-stairs!'

'Nonsense. If you hadn't been so starched up, he would have made you a fine husband. Not that any of that matters now. The thing is, he was visiting friends in Wales and stopped at Chepstow, where he heard a group of farmers talking of an estate in Gloucestershire that has employed a female land steward. Name of Brackwood.' His lips parted in another leering smile. 'That was very foolish of you, my dear. Should have called yourself something different.'

She put up her chin. 'Why should I? *I* have nothing to be ashamed of.'

'Instead, you would drag our name into the gutter.'

'It is you who has done that,' she shot back at him. She curbed her anger and went on, trying to sound nonchalant, 'But I am curious to know: did you think your plan had worked, that I had perished at sea?'

'I could not be sure. Moffat wrote to tell me she had fulfilled her part and left you on board the ship, but then I heard nothing. I thought the captain might have decided it was safer not to commit anything to paper, or that his letter had gone astray. I should have preferred to be able to announce you had perished at sea but that was a small matter. You were gone, out of my way.' He uttered a string of vicious curses that made her wince. 'Or so I thought, until I heard Tumby's story. Naturally, I had to investigate. And now I have found you.'

'Well, you can go away again,' she told him, trying to ignore the fearful thudding of her heart. 'I am no threat to you. I want merely to live my own life.'

His face darkened. 'Oh, no, dear sister, I cannot allow that. Not now.'

He came towards her, menace in every line. Rosina took a step back, but even as she was deciding if her energies were best used to scream or retreat, the door opened.

Conham had seen a gentleman's hat and gloves on the side table as soon as he walked into the Manor and did not stop to divest himself of his own, once he learned the visitor's identity. He rushed to the library and, stepping into the room, he summed up the scene at a glance.

Edgar Brackwood swung around to see who had entered and now glared at Conham. Rosina looked pale and defiant. She was clutching an armful of books like a shield, and Conham was relieved he had arrived in time to protect her. There was no longer any doubt in his mind about Brackwood's part in Rosina's abduction.

Beneath a thatch of fair hair, the young man's face was blotched an angry red. His fury was almost tangible, and Conham knew the situation was volatile. He must tread carefully.

'Sir Edgar.' Conham put his hat and crop on the side table and slowly drew off his gloves. 'To what do we owe the pleasure of this visit?'

His icily polite manner had the desired effect. Brackwood's fists were balled tight but he contained his anger and even managed a small bow.

'My lord. I wish to talk to my sister. Alone.'

'Ah, but does Miss Brackwood wish to talk to *you*?' drawled Conham, moving forward.

Rosina answered swiftly, her voice clipped and angry. 'We have nothing to say to one another.'

'There, Sir Edgar. You have your answer.'

'I will not leave without my sister. She must come home with me.'

'So that you can try to murder her again?' Conham saw the man's look of surprise and continued in a voice as smooth as silk. 'Oh, yes. Miss Brackwood has told me all about that.'

'She is lying!' Brackwood took a step closer. 'You cannot prove a thing against me.'

'Perhaps not, but I prefer to believe the lady.'

'Please, Edgar.' Rosina put down the books. 'I do not want to quarrel with you. I only want to be left alone to live my own life. Please go.'

'Not without you, madam!'

Brackwood lunged towards her but Conham was quicker. He stepped between them.

'You are not welcome in my house, Brackwood. It is time for you to leave.'

'Very well. If you are content to be a laughing stock, installing your whore as steward here, that is no business of mi—'

His last words were lost as Conham brought his fist crashing into Brackwood's jaw. The blow sent the man sprawling to the floor, where he remained, cringing in fear of a further onslaught.

'No, Conham!' Rosina rushed up and caught his arm. 'No more, please!'

'Don't worry, I am done. The man's a bully, and not worth the effort.'

He went across to the bell pull, where his violent tugging on the sash resulted in Jameson and one of the footmen hurrying into the room. They stopped and goggled at the figure cowering on the floor.

'Get him out of the house and into his carriage,' Conham ordered. 'Send a rider with him, to make sure he leaves my land. And Jameson, make it known that this man is not to be allowed on my property again. Is that understood?'

He waited while the men helped Brackwood to his feet and escorted him out of the room before turning to Rosina. Her eyes were fixed on the closed door, hands clasped in front of her as she tried to control their shaking.

'Well, that was diverting,' he remarked, strolling across the room to her.

'I b-beg your p-pardon.' She struggled to speak. 'I n-never thought he w-would f-find me.'

Conham pulled her gently into his arms as she dissolved into tears.

'Hush now. It was inevitable. I only wish we'd had the fore-thought to warn the servants to be on guard against the fellow. How did he discover you were here?' he asked, handing her his handkerchief.

'Farmers. T-talking of me in Ch-Chepstow.'

'Chepstow! By heaven, your fame has spread far and wide!'

'Pray, do not laugh. I should have known better than to come here! A female land steward was bound to cause a great deal of gossip.' She pushed herself away from him and wiped her eyes. 'It reflects ill on you, too. It was wrong of me to accept the post.'

'Fustian! No one here believes you are my mistress.'

'If they did, they would not dare tell you.'

He caught her arms and turned her to face him. 'That is be-yond foolish, Rosina. Your brother was goading you. Goading *us*. There was always going to be talk at first but that has died down now. You have earned your place here and I am content to have you remain, as land steward, for as long as you wish.'

'That is very kind, sir, but—'

'I am not being kind!' He gave her a little shake. 'You have a way with people, Rosina. At a time when many stewards are feared and even hated, *you* are respected and admired. I have heard nothing but good reports of you from everyone I have met since I returned. The job is yours. As long as you want it.'

Conham desperately wanted to kiss away the last of her tears, but that would not help the situation at all. He released her and stepped away.

'Now, dry your eyes, madam, and let's have no more of this nonsense. Matthew will be here soon for dinner and I would still like you to join us, if you feel well enough.'

'Yes, of course,' muttered Rosina, giving her nose a final wipe.

She said, with a fair assumption of calm, 'I had best go and change, if you will excuse me.'

She went to hand the mangled handkerchief back to him, then thought better of it and walked to the door, where she turned back.

'Will you tell Matthew about Edgar's visit?'

'He is likely to hear something of it from the servants, and if he does, I will explain. But you need not make yourself uneasy. Matt would not be surprised to learn I drove the villain from the house. He does know something of your story, after all.'

'Ah yes, of course.' She hesitated, wanting to apologise for all the trouble she had caused, for weeping over him like some feeble-minded female in a silly gothic romance. In the end she settled for a simple *thank you* before whisking herself out of the room.

Chapter Thirteen

Rosina had purchased a new evening gown from the local dressmaker, a celestial blue crape over a white satin slip, but after what had occurred, she decided to wear the grey silk she bought in Bristol for her dinner with the earl and Matt Talacre. She asked Mrs Goddard to dress her hair simply with a parting in the centre and pulled back into a Grecian knot, and then picked up her new shawl, a rose-pink cashmere she had found by chance in the village, on a market stall selling not-so-old clothes. She studied herself in the mirror and, once she was satisfied that she looked the very model of propriety, and that her dress could not be in any way construed as frivolous, she set off to walk to the Manor.

Conham was crossing the great hall when he heard voices in the screen passage. He grinned when Matthew Talacre walked in.

Conham stopped. 'Matt! It is good to see you. Come along into the drawing room.'

'Welcome back to Gloucestershire, my lord.' Matt followed him across the hall and remarked, once they were alone in the drawing room, 'I had not expected you for a week or two yet.'

'I had concluded my business in town. There was no reason for me to stay longer.'

'What, could none of the beauties there tempt you to stay?

I have been in daily expectation of seeing your betrothal announced in the London newspaper.'

'Then I am sorry to disappoint you.'

'Damnation, man, you told me you were going to London with the sole purpose of finding a rich wife.'

'I did. Sadly, I could not find a lady to suit.'

'What, not one?'

'No.' Conham shifted uncomfortably under his friend's scrutiny.

'Coming it too brown, my friend!' Matt exclaimed, with brutal frankness. 'I have it on good authority—my cousin Mildred, companion to Viscountess Wodington and an avid reader of the society pages!—that there were at least six very eligible females on the market this winter.'

'Confound it, Matthew, have you been discussing me with your cousin?'

'No, no, my friend, your name was never mentioned, so you can put down those hackles! Lady Wodington is in Hotwells to take the waters and I went over to call upon Mildy.'

'And you just happened to hit upon the subject of heiresses.'

Conham's sarcastic tone had no effect at all upon his old friend, who merely grinned.

'It came up, amongst other things. Let me see, did you meet Miss Throckley?'

'Yes. She has a squint.'

'Miss Jessop? My cousin told me she is the talk of the town. The family is from Yorkshire. Halifax, or Bradford, I believe. Rich as Croesus.'

'Aye, and very full of themselves. The father is aiming higher than a mere earl for his daughter.'

'Then what about Julia Hewick? Related to the Duke of Chandos.'

'Yes, I stood up with her a couple of times.'

'And?'

'No conversation.'

'And the celebrated Miss Kingston? Mildy wrote to tell me she is very pretty.'

'Perhaps, if you can ignore her constant giggles.'

Matt laughed. 'By heaven, my friend, you are very hard to please!'

'I am looking for a *wife*,' retorted Conham. 'I need to know that we can at least be comfortable together. And besides, I have no idea what these females really think of *me*. My impression is they would all of them marry an ogre just to become a countess.'

Matt sobered. 'I can tell your heart isn't in this, my friend.'

His pitying tone caught Conham on the raw.

He burst out, 'Damn it all, Matt, the Mortlakes have owned Dallamire Hall and its estates for centuries. It is my duty, as head of the family, to save the house if I can. I *must* marry money, if I am to restore Dallamire.'

Rosina's entrance put an end to their discussion, much to Conham's relief. After a few moments exchanging greetings, he shifted the conversation away from himself by asking Matthew to tell them how matters were progressing at Bellemonte.

'Very well. There is a great deal to do, but I am making good progress. My leg is healing, too, so I am now able to tackle much of the work myself.' He held up his hands, displaying the roughened skin. 'Although I can no longer pretend to be a gentleman!'

'One should never decry honest toil,' Rosina told him, smiling.

Conham agreed. 'Indeed not. I have read your letters, Matt. You are making good progress. An interesting idea of yours, bringing in some of your old regimental comrades to help you clear the pleasure gardens.'

'Many of them have been unable to find work since returning to England and are eager for the chance to prove themselves. They work hard, which pleases the gardener I have hired. He is confident now that we will be ready for reopening in May. I hope you and Rosina will both be able to attend?'

'I will do my best, but I cannot promise,' said Conham. He saw that Rosina was regarding him with a slight frown and he put up his brows. 'Is that not good enough?'

'No, my lord. Your presence will be necessary to ensure the opening is a success.'

'And I will need your support if I am to raise more funds for the next phase of the project,' added Matt. 'My reason for going to Hotwells was not only to see Cousin Mildred. I went to look at the spa. I talked to some of those taking the waters, and the doctors, too. Bellemonte cannot boast of hot baths, so it is not a direct rival, but we have the swimming pool and the cold bath, which are already gaining popularity, especially since I opened a private bath for the ladies and employed watchmen to ensure the streets are safe for visitors.'

Rosina turned to Conham. 'Did you note that the watchmen, too, are former soldiers?' she asked him. 'Trustworthy men, in need of employment.'

'Yes, I did. Since the end of the war I have seen far too many good men unable to find work to support themselves and their families. I am delighted that Matt is able to help some of them.'

'Aye,' put in Matt, grinning. 'Because of their regular patrols, Bellemonte is a positive haven of respectability these days.'

'What, even the tavern?' asked Conham, surprised.

'Not yet. It closed when the current lease expired, but I have a new landlord in mind, a captain of the footguards who is willing to use what is left of his funds to improve the inn. He is an honest fellow and his wife an excellent cook, so between them they will make a big difference, but I need to assure them they will be able to rent the inn from you for at least a year.' Matthew laughed. 'It is all part of my plans for Bellemonte, Conham. We need to talk about it.'

'Aye, but later,' said Conham. 'Here is Jameson come to tell us dinner is ready.'

They walked across to the dining room and no more was said of Bellemonte until the meal was finished.

'I should withdraw now,' murmured Rosina as the last of the dishes were removed.

But Matthew would not hear of it.

'We have not finished discussing Bellemonte yet.' He turned to the earl. 'Tell her she must stay, my lord!'

Conham was enjoying the evening. It was everything he had hoped for. He was far more at ease here than in town, where he was constantly on his guard against raising false hopes in matchmaking parents or their daughters. Even Dallamire felt cold and inhospitable without Matt's cheerful companionship.

As for Rosina, he very much wanted her to stay a little longer, although he refused to think too much about why that should be.

'Yes, you must remain,' he said to her now. 'To discuss Bellemonte. I should value your opinion.'

That becoming blush touched her creamy cheeks and she said, 'Then I should very much like to stay.'

Masking his inordinate pleasure at her answer, Conham turned to Jameson, the only servant left in the room.

'Bring an extra glass for Miss Brackwood, if you please.'

'And will Miss Brackwood drink *brandy*, my lord?' the butler asked him in repressive accents.

'I have no idea.' Conham's lips twitched. He looked at Rosina. 'Will you, ma'am?'

'No, not brandy,' she replied, trying not to laugh. 'Perhaps a glass of madeira?'

Mollified, the butler bowed and went out. Rosina shook her head, chuckling.

'Poor Jameson, I am sure he thinks we will be carousing late into the night.'

Carousing. The word sent Conham's mind careering away from business. He imagined himself dining alone with Rosina, sitting beside her and drinking sweet wines, offering up tiny slices of peach or pineapple and then leaning close to kiss the juice from her lips...

'Well, he would be wrong,' declared Matt. 'We are talking business and it would not be right to exclude you from that. You have been involved in the planning of this from the beginning. Besides, I shall need your help persuading the earl to lend me his support.'

Conham sighed and dragged his thoughts away from a very pleasant daydream.

'Very well, Matthew, tell me what it is you want of me. I will consider anything, except spending more money. You know all my unentailed land is mortgaged to the hilt.'

'Hardly your fault, my friend,' said Matt quietly. 'If you had been informed at the outset, you could have come home directly after Waterloo.'

'I have thought that myself, but it is too late now for regrets.'

Conham shrugged. 'The countess acted as she thought best in my absence. If I had not joined the army, if I had remained at Dallamire and shown more interest in the estates, then I might have seen how things stood. I might have been able to do something about it.'

'But you weren't,' growled Matt. 'You have been over that ground before, Major, and it does no good to fret over it.'

'I agree, you cannot change the past,' Rosina said, gently. 'It is what happens now that is important.'

'Yes, and I must decide what to do for the best.'

'Your stepmama and half-sisters,' she asked. 'Are they provided for?'

When Conham hesitated, Matt spoke up.

'He is too generous to say it, so I will. Lady Dallamire and the girls *are* provided for. The countess *could* move to the Dower House and live very comfortably within her means, but she prefers to remain at Dallamire, living in the grand manner, and expects Conham to resolve everything.'

'Oh, dear.'

'Selling my godfather's estates would not cover all my debts,' explained Conham, observing the anxious look on Rosina's face. 'Don't worry, I intend to keep Morton Gifford, if I can.'

'And Bellemonte?' she asked.

'Matt's plans have a fair chance of making money.'

And providing his friend with a much-needed boost to his funds and his confidence. Conham did not say this, but he knew from the look Matthew gave him that he understood.

'I believe it could do very well for both of us, but I need you to put your name to my proposals.' Matt leaned forward, elbows on the table. 'My plan is to open up the stables again. The yard and outbuildings are still there but derelict. They would service both the inn and the hotel, when it is finished. The project needs more funds but I believe I already know several possible investors, all trustworthy men. I want to keep their share of the business small, in order that the project is not at risk if any one of them should suddenly pull out.'

He paused as Jameson came in with the decanters. Once they

each had a full glass, Conham waved away the butler and waited until they were alone again before inviting Matthew to continue.

Rosina sipped at her wine and listened attentively while Matt Talacre outlined his ideas. The earl interrupted him occasionally to ask a question, but it was clear that Matthew had calculated the final costings quite rigorously.

'So you see, Conham,' he concluded, 'before I can do anything more, I need your assurance that you will not sell Bellemonte, at least for the next twelve months. After that I believe we may well begin to see a return on the investment.'

'I think I can give you that assurance, Matt. From your reports and what you have told me it is clear that you have considered this matter very thoroughly. I am also impressed with what you have managed to achieve in just a few months.' He turned to Rosina to refill her glass and added, 'What you have both achieved. Well done.'

It was his warm smile as much as the praise that sent a rush of pleasure coursing through Rosina. It was encouraging to have him acknowledge her hard work.

'All we need to do now is raise the funds to develop Bellemonte,' said Matthew. 'I do not think it will prove too difficult.'

'I wonder.' She swallowed nervously before posing her question. 'Would I be able to invest?'

Two pairs of eyes turned towards her. She took a deep breath and continued.

'The idea came to me this evening, while Matthew was outlining his plans. There is no longer any need for secrecy, now my brother knows I am here, so—'

'Wait!' Matt put up his hand. 'Your brother found you? When was this?'

'He came here today,' said Conham. 'Having heard of a Miss Brackwood making a name for herself as a land agent in Gloucestershire.'

'The devil he did!'

'I threw him out, and told him not to set foot on my land again.'

'Can you trust him to do that?'

'The servants know not to let him in the house again. Also,

I made him aware that I know of his part in Rosina's abduction, even if I cannot prove it. I hope that will be enough to keep him away.'

'I hope so, too, but that is not the point,' Rosina interrupted them impatiently. 'Now that Edgar knows I am alive, there is no longer any reason for me to hide. I can write to my family's attorney. Papa entrusted him with the jewels my mother left for me and I am going to ask him to release them. Not that I intend to wear them. I want to sell them.' She hesitated. 'I have no idea how much they will realise. I do not suppose it will be enough to make me a rich woman, but it should be sufficient to invest in Bellemonte.'

Silence greeted her announcement. Both gentlemen were staring at her.

Matt Talacre cleared his throat. 'I am honoured by your trust, Rosina, but are you sure about this?'

'Very sure.'

'Investments are always a risk, Rosina,' the earl cautioned her.

'I am well aware of that, but I have no need of the money, at least not yet. And I truly believe this can succeed. From what Matthew has said, the returns could be far better than investing in the Funds.'

Matthew laughed. 'By Jove, then I shall be very glad to welcome you as an investor, Rosina. Let us shake hands upon it!'

Smiling, Rosina reached out to take his hand.

'I shall wait to hear what your jewels will raise,' Matthew told her, sitting back again. 'If it is sufficient, we may be able to restore Bellemonte without the need for any other investors at present. Would that not be an excellent solution?' He lifted his glass. 'I propose a toast to our new adventure!'

Rosina raised her wineglass. Inside she was giddy with excitement, feeling there was now some real hope for the future.

'To Bellemonte,' she cried gaily.

'Aye, to Bellemonte,' said Matthew. He tapped sharply on the table. 'Conham? Come along, man, will you not join us?'

The earl was distracted, frowning slightly, but he looked up quickly.

'What? Oh, yes.' He saluted his companions. 'To Bellemonte.'

The toast drunk, they all repaired to the drawing room, but it was not long before Matthew announced it was time for him to ride back to Bellemonte.

'I want to make an early start in the morning,' he said. 'I am grateful for your faith in me, Rosina, and for yours, Conham, my old friend. Truly.'

He went out. In the silence that followed his departure, Rosina heard Matthew's footsteps fading away, and shortly after that the soft chimes of the hall clock filtered through the door. She counted them.

'Midnight,' she said. 'It grows late.'

Conham pushed back his chair. 'I will walk you to the lodge.'

Rosina did not demure as he draped the cashmere shawl around her shoulders. They stepped outside to make the short journey by the light of the moon, which was making fitful appearances between scudding clouds. Conham did not proffer his arm, and she thought he seemed a little distracted, but she was still fizzing with excitement and was content just to walk beside him in silence.

'I need to ask you something, sir,' said Rosina, when they were halfway to the lodge.

'Oh?'

'I shall need assistance to sell the jewels. I think it would be best done in London and I had hoped you would be willing to sell them for me. Or rather, to ask your man of business to do so. I believe that is the surest way to obtain the best price, if you have no objection?'

He did not answer immediately and she turned her head to look up at him, but it was impossible to read his expression in the dim light.

'It must be your decision, of course,' he said at last. 'But to put everything you have into Bellemonte… Is that wise, Rosina?'

'Why not? *You* have decided it is a sound enough investment.'

'Yes, but that is different.'

'Why?'

They walked several steps more before he replied.

'If Matt's plans fail, you could lose all your money.'

She laughed. 'But I do not believe he will fail. I have every faith in Matthew.'

'Ha! *That* is only too clear!'

The harsh response shocked her and she stopped.

'What do you mean? I thought you trusted him implicitly.'

'I do, but I also recognise that every investment carries a risk.' He hissed out a breath and began to walk on again. 'I suppose it is not my place to interfere.'

'Wait, wait.' She caught up with him and touched his arm. 'Conham, what is it? What is wrong with you?'

He swung around to face her.

'I do not want you to be hurt, that is all. Hell and damnation, Rosina, I care about you!'

'Then why are you so against me trying to secure my future?'

'I am not, I just…'

'Do you think it so very unwise for me to throw my lot in with Matthew's plans?'

Conham raked a hand through his hair.

'I think it would be better for the two of you to marry and have done with it!'

'*What?*'

She clutched at her shawl, her head spinning. She felt dizzy, uncertain. As if the very ground beneath her was crumbling away.

'Matt's a good fellow, Rosina. He'd make an excellent husband. In fact, it would be an obvious choice for you. You are already as thick as thieves together! He would always be on hand to protect you from your brother, too, which must be an advantage.'

Rosina stared at him. Her earlier elation had quite gone, replaced by a raging disappointment, which turned to anger as the meaning of his words became clear. How dare he suggest such a thing! She considered telling Conham that she could never marry a man she did not love. Or even better, scratching his eyes out.

In the end she settled for an angry laugh.

'I am well aware that *you* must marry, my lord, but *I* am not trammelled by any such necessity! I can assure you that I have no thoughts of marriage.' She drew in a breath and announced grandly, 'Now I have found my freedom, not even a man as rich as Croesus could persuade me to give it up!'

She turned on her heel and strode off towards the lodge, seething with indignation.

Conham fell into step beside her and they walked on in stony silence. He cursed himself, knowing he had erred, and badly, in speaking to Rosina of marriage and Matt in the same breath. He had been unable to help himself, unable to control the demon of jealousy that had been unleashed as he watched them throughout dinner, noting how friendly they were, how easy in each other's company.

He decided it was best not to risk saying anything further tonight. He might only make things worse. The demon was still there, subdued now but ready to roar into life again at the slightest provocation.

At the lodge door she bade him a frosty good-night and Conham turned and walked away. A good night's sleep, and then he must find some way to repair their friendship.

Chapter Fourteen

Rosina woke with a thumping headache. She ascribed it to the wine she had drunk, but in her heart she knew it was more likely caused by a lack of sleep. She had tossed and turned for most of the night, thinking that Conham would rather see her married to Matt Talacre than have her remain here as his land steward.

Did he not understand her at all? Did he not know that she had no interest in marrying a man merely for the protection of his name? That he could think she would even consider such a thing angered her and, having no wish to see or speak with the earl, she sent a message to Davy to say she would meet him at Burntwood Farm and went off to the stables to collect her pony.

A gallop across the park, followed by an absorbing day discussing with tenants the improvements she had in mind for the farms did much to restore her spirits. However, she was still too angry with Conham to want to talk to him. She took an early dinner alone at the lodge and spent the remainder of the evening writing letters.

Her attempts to avoid the earl the next morning were foiled when she heard him call her name as she hurried to the stables. She was obliged to stop and wait for him to come up to her.

'I am on my way to meet Davy, can this wait?' She hoped she sounded businesslike rather than angry.

'It will not take long. In case I did not make myself clear, I wanted to confirm that I will help you to sell your jewels. Of course I will. If that is what you wish.'

No contrition, no apology. She said coolly, 'I do wish it. I have written to Mr Shipton, my family's attorney, and I am awaiting his reply.'

'Very well. When you hear from him let me know. I will come with you to collect them.'

'Thank you, but there is no need. Mrs Goddard can accompany me.' She saw him frown and added, 'Mr Goddard, too, if you think I need more protection.'

'I will not allow you to make the journey without me.' He raised one hand to silence any further objection. 'I insist. It is not just the valuable items you will be carrying. I should not rest until I knew you were back here safely.'

With that, he turned and strode away, leaving Rosina to continue to the stables. As an apology it left a lot to be desired. But as an olive branch…well. A little smile was unfurling inside her. It would suffice.

It was a week before Rosina heard from Mr Shipton and another four days before she set off for his office to collect her jewels. The earl had insisted on coming with her, putting at her disposal his travelling chariot with postilions at the front and a guard sitting on the rumble seat.

'I want to leave nothing to chance,' he said as he handed her into the carriage. 'From what you have told me of your brother, I would not be surprised if he tried to waylay us.'

'If he hears of it,' she agreed. 'However, Mr Shipton has known for years that Edgar and I are not on the best of terms. I can only hope he did not feel himself obliged to tell my brother of our appointment.'

'Well, we shall see,' he replied, climbing in after her. 'Drive on, Robert!'

The chariot bounded forward and soon they were bowling along the lanes away from the Manor. Conham took out his watch.

'We should be at our destination by noon. What time is Shipton expecting you?'

'I told him I would call around two.'

'Then we have time to eat before we call upon Mr Shipton.' He grinned. 'Never wise to go into battle on an empty stomach.'

The journey into Somerset was uneventful. Once they had passed Bath they stopped at the Crown, a posting inn some two miles from Brackwood, which Rosina knew by reputation. They were shown into a private parlour and after removing her cloak, Rosina went over to the hearth to warm her hands at the cheerful fire.

'You have been very quiet this past hour,' Conham remarked. 'Are you anxious at returning to Brackwood?'

'A little,' she confessed. 'I have no idea what lies Edgar has spread about me. I admit I half expected to learn that he had somehow prised Mama's jewels away from the attorney.'

'But Shipton has confirmed that is not the case.'

'True. Or at least, not at the time of writing to me. In his letter, he merely said he was relieved to know that I was safely back in England, although he was sorry I was no longer living at Brackwood.' She smiled a little. 'One can have very few secrets from one's lawyer, and Mr Shipton was well aware that Edgar and I disagreed over how the estate should be run, so his answer was extremely circumspect. As for Mama's jewels, I can only hope that they are still safe.'

'We shall soon find out,' said Conham, pulling out a chair for her. 'Come and sit down.'

The meal put new heart into Rosina and when they resumed their journey, she looked with interest at the familiar landscape.

'I have always loved Somerset, especially in the spring,' she said, gazing out the window.

'Do you miss it?'

'Of course. I grew up here, I have so many happy memories of my life here. This is bringing it all back.'

She gave him a little smile before turning her attention back to the view outside the window. As they drew closer to the village, she could see changes that disturbed her. Farm buildings looking dilapidated, the remains of one barn standing stark against the sky, its roof torn off during the winter and never replaced. On the edge of Brackwood itself she noted with dismay that the labourers' cottages looked neglected. One or two, that she recalled had housed young families, were now standing empty.

'I am sorry, did you speak?' asked the earl.

'Only to myself.' She sighed. 'The village is looking very run-down.'

'Only to be expected after a harsh winter.'

'Yes, but…' She stopped, closing her lips on any criticism of her brother. Brackwood was no longer her concern.

At precisely two o'clock, the earl escorted Rosina into Mr Shipton's small office. The lawyer was a tall, spare man with thinning hair and a gaunt face, but his eyes, behind the spectacles, were kindly as he greeted Rosina.

'I am pleased to see you looking so well, Miss Brackwood.'

He turned his attention to Conham, bowing to him before fixing the earl with a mildly enquiring gaze. Rosina quickly introduced them.

'Lord Dallamire was good enough to escort me,' she explained. 'You were no doubt surprised when I wrote to tell you I was land steward at Morton Gifford.'

Conham did not miss the faint note of defiance in her voice. She had lifted her chin, challenging the attorney to think there was anything improper in this extraordinary news. The old man merely nodded.

'I cannot deny it, although I am sure the task is well within your capabilities.' He smiled slightly. 'I know I speak for many when I say that your talents are sadly missed here at Brackwood, ma'am, sadly missed indeed. Shall we all sit down?'

An hour later, Rosina stepped out onto the High Street. A leather box was clutched in her hands, but the success in obtaining her mother's jewels was overshadowed by the news Mr Shipton had imparted to her.

'Edgar, married! I cannot take it in,' she uttered as they

waited for the earl's travelling chariot to come up. 'I know Mr Shipton thought it was a kindness to keep the news until he could tell me in person, but it is still a shock.'

'I am sure it is,' said Conham. 'What would you like to do now?'

'I hardly know. I feel a little dazed.'

The chariot had come to a stop beside them, but Conham ignored it and looked about him.

'We could walk to the Red Lion and order coffee, or wine if you prefer?'

'No,' she said quickly. 'Thank you, but no. I do not want to see the landlord or anyone else in Brackwood today.'

'I can understand that.' He gave her fingers a slight squeeze before handing her up into the carriage. 'We will head back to Morton Gifford.'

'Except…'

'Except?' He was about to follow her but stopped, one foot on the step. 'Tell me what you would like to do, Rosina.'

'Papa's old valet. He lives with his widowed sister at the edge of the village. I *should* like to see them, and explain what has happened. Not everything, of course. Merely what I told Mr Shipton, that I changed my mind about going abroad and remained in England, and I am estranged from my brother.'

'Very well.' He gave his orders to the coachman and jumped in beside her. 'But why not tell everyone the truth? Brackwood deserves no loyalty from you now.'

'Perhaps not, but if Edgar will leave me to live in peace then I will do the same for him.'

'The world should know how badly he has behaved to you.'

'But there is no proof. Even if I were to tell the world, not everyone would believe me. There would still be doubts, questions.' The chariot slowed and she looked out the window. 'We have reached the Paxbys' house. May I ask you to take care of my jewel box, sir?'

'Of course, if you trust me to keep it safe for you,' he replied lightly.

She smiled, but when she responded, he heard the slight tremor in her voice.

'My friend, I have already trusted you with my life and my reputation. I am not anxious about a few little gems.'

He met her eyes, his heart contracting as he gazed into the blue depths. She had forgiven him; that silly quarrel was forgotten. It was only the trust she had just spoken of that prevented him from taking her in his arms and kissing her.

She called you her friend, man. You cannot let her down!

'Of course I will take care of it.' He took the box she was holding out to him and hid it in the small space behind one of the squabs. 'There. When do you want me to call back for you?'

Rosina knocked on the cottage door and it was opened by a plump, homely woman dressed neatly in a grey gown and snowy apron.

'Mrs Jones, good day to you.'

'Miss Brackwood! Well, bless me! Come in, ma'am, come in!'

She stood back, holding the door wide, and Rosina heard the carriage drive off as she stepped over the threshold.

'Good heavens, Jem will be that pleased to see you!'

At the sound of their voices, a querulous voice called, 'Martha, who is it, who's there?'

'It is I, Mr Paxby. Rosina Brackwood.' She moved further into the room and crossed to the fireplace, where her father's aged valet was sitting in an armchair, a patchwork blanket wrapped around his knees. 'No, no, sir, don't get up.'

She placed a hand on his shoulder before turning back to accept the offer of tea from his sister, then she pulled a chair closer to the old man's and sat down.

'I thought you had left us,' he exclaimed, his rheumy eyes fixed on her face. 'They said you was gone off to America.'

'I decided to stay in England, after all.'

'But not with Sir Edgar.'

'No. Not with him.'

'Can't say I'm surprised,' said Martha, bustling up with the tea tray. 'But it was a sad day when you left us, Miss. You know your brother's married now?'

'Yes, I had heard.'

'It is rumoured the lady's family had no choice,' she added, placing the tray down on a nearby table. 'It being what you would call a hasty wedding.'

'You mean...?'

'I do, Miss.' Martha rested her hands on her stomach and gave Rosina a darkling look.

'Seen her at church a couple of times,' muttered Mr Paxby. 'Poor little dab of a woman. Didn't look to be happy, but that's no wonder. Everyone knows he married her for her dowry.'

'Now then, Jem. We've no reason to think she's unhappy.'

Martha chided the old man as she handed him a cup of tea, but the look he gave Rosina was eloquent. He knew Edgar's temper as well as she did, although the valet had always been too loyal to Papa to speak ill of his son.

Rosina sipped her tea and encouraged the valet to talk about the old days. She was content to listen to his stories of Brack-wood Court when she was a child and he and Sir Thomas had both been hale and hearty. She was conscious of the time, and did not wish to tire the old man. At length, she finished her tea and took her leave, promising to call again.

'Thank you, ma'am. Your visit's done Jem the world of good,' Martha told her as she escorted Rosina to the door. 'He misses life at Brackwood Court something fierce and although he don't speak of it, I know he frets over what the new master is doing. Or rather,' she added, her homely face adopting an uncharacteristic frown, 'what he is *not* doing. It's been a tonic for him to see you, though, and to know you are well.'

Rosina heard the faint doubtful note in the widow's voice as she said this, her eyes on the handsome travelling chariot that had drawn up. She had explained that she was land steward at Morton Gifford, but she was well aware that many, including Mr Paxby and his sister, would find it hard to believe that a woman could hold down such a position.

Conham waited until Rosina had waved to Martha as the chariot pulled away from the little house, then he asked her what she would like to do next.

'There is still time to visit Brackwood Court, if you would like to see it?'

'Thank you, but no, I do not wish to see it,' she said emphatically. 'There is nothing for me there. I should like to go home, if you please.'

It cheered him to hear her refer to Morton Gifford as home, but the sadness in her countenance concerned him.

'Did your meeting with your father's valet bring back painful memories?'

'No indeed. We talked of happier times. But what I have seen here and what I have learned from Mr Paxby and Mr Shipton today suggest things are not being managed as they ought.' She stopped and shook her head. 'I keep saying Brackwood is no longer my concern, but it is so very hard not to care. But who knows, things may not be so bad as they seem. My brother is still learning how to go on here. Perhaps he will settle down, now he has a wife.'

'Perhaps he will.' Conham spoke more in hope than expectation.

'I had forgotten quite how many of Mama's jewels Papa had put aside for me,' said Rosina, changing the subject. 'Diamonds, too. I should be able to invest a useful sum in Bellemonte.'

'Yes.' He hesitated, not wishing to stir up their previous argument. 'I shall not try to dissuade you, but I hope you will consider putting some of it in the Funds. For a little security.'

'I believe Bellemonte is secure enough, is it not?'

'I hope so, but I am no expert. Far from it. In fact, you would do well to ignore any advice I may give. I know far less than you about these matters!' He turned to stare out the window, saying bitterly, 'Unlike your excellent father, mine did not always make the wisest choices where money was concerned.'

'Would you like to talk about it?'

Her voice, gentle, sympathetic, broke into his dark thoughts. Conham closed his eyes for a moment. He desperately wanted to tell her. Rosina already knew something of his debts, but would it sink him still lower in her estimation? He felt the gentle touch of her fingers on his arm.

'I am very willing to listen, if it would help. In confidence. We are friends, are we not?'

'Matt knows the whole sorry tale, so you may as well know it, too. My stepmother is an excellent woman in many ways. She gave my father two delightful daughters, whom he loved very much. When she wrote to me to tell me of my father's demise in a riding accident, she assured me there was no need for me to sell out immediately. She and the lawyers would deal with everything.

'However, she kept from me the fact that six years ago my father mortgaged all the unentailed lands at Dallamire. He was a gambling man, and not content with running up huge debts at the gaming tables, he speculated wildly with the money he borrowed, believing he could pay off all his debts and the mortgages, too. Of course, that never happened. Somehow, when he died, the lawyers managed to keep the creditors at bay while I was away. I was never informed of any of this. It was only when I came home that I discovered the true state of affairs. That I am now responsible for the repayments. I could sell some of the land, but even that will not be enough to cover all my commitments.'

'And would leave you with even less income.'

'Precisely.' His mouth twisted. 'I knew next to nothing about the responsibilities and obligations of my new position and I have had to learn very quickly.'

'Oh, Conham!'

'Aye. If Bellemonte does prove successful then the profit will help pay off the mortgages. However, if my business acumen is as poor as my father's...'

He trailed off, grimacing.

'But your father was following a gambler's instincts rather than any sound business plan,' she said, tucking her hand into his arm. 'Besides, this is not based on your judgement alone. Matthew and I also believe it will work. Which is why I want to invest in it. But I need not decide anything until the jewels are sold. Will you write to your man in London, and ask him to arrange it for me?'

Conham nodded. Somehow, just talking with Rosina, having her in his life, made the future seem a little less dark.

'Better than that. I will take them myself.'

'Oh, I would not want to put you to any trouble!' She removed her hand from his sleeve and rearranged the folds of her cloak. 'Although you will have to go back to London, will you not? To continue your search for a wife.'

'Yes.'

Her words were like a sudden drenching with icy water, but he could not deny the truth of them. He could not neglect his duty or Dallamire by staying any longer at Morton Gifford.

Chapter Fifteen

The day being far advanced, they decided to dine at the Crown and arrived at the hostelry just as the sun was setting. The travelling chariot came to a halt behind another vehicle and as Conham helped Rosina to alight, he saw a footman jump down from the larger carriage and open the door while gazing expectantly towards the inn.

'That augurs well,' he murmured. 'If the owner of that smart equipage is leaving, I have high hopes of there being a private parlour for us.'

Even as he spoke, a couple stepped out of the building. Conham felt Rosina clutch his sleeve as the gentleman glanced idly in their direction then stopped, glaring at them. She uttered one shocked, breathless word.

'Edgar!'

They were but yards away; there could be no avoiding a meeting, with the landlord and any number of interested servants looking on. Conham knew what must be done.

He nodded. 'Brackwood.'

He said it with a degree of hauteur that he hoped would evoke a polite response from the man, if nothing more cordial. Brackwood inclined his head.

'Lord Dallamire.'

'I believe I am to congratulate you, Edgar,' said Rosina, recovering a little.

'Yes. This is my wife. Harriet, my sister Rosina and her...' He met Conham's steely gaze and went on with only the faintest sneer. 'Her *employer*, the Earl of Dallamire.'

Conham watched the ladies exchange curtsies before he made an elegant bow.

'Your servant, Lady Brackwood.'

Edgar Brackwood clearly had no time for such civility and he scowled.

'What were you doing in Brackwood, Sister?'

'I called upon Mr Shipton.'

Rosina spoke calmly enough although her fingers clutched tightly at Conham's sleeve. He thought Brackwood would ask her reason for visiting the attorney but, glancing down, he saw that her chin was raised and he smiled inwardly. He was familiar with that rebellious tilt, and he could imagine the defiant look in her blue eyes. By heaven, she had challenged him with it often enough! He was not surprised that Brackwood remained silent.

'But let us not stand any longer in this chill wind,' she went on. 'I bid you good day, Edgar. Lady Brackwood.'

Conham felt the squeeze on his arm. He touched his hat and escorted Rosina past her brother and his wife and into the inn without another glance.

'Goodness, how, how unfortunate,' declared Rosina, once they were alone in a private parlour. She untied her cloak with hands that were not quite steady. 'I do not know which of us was most surprised, Edgar or me!'

'I thought he would have a fit of apoplexy,' remarked Conham.

'He certainly looked most put out! I felt sorry for his poor wife. I thought she might faint off at any moment, which would not be surprising, if she is indeed with child.' Rosina sighed. 'She is just as Mr Paxby described her. Small and mouselike. I am very much afraid Edgar will bully her. After all, we can be very sure it is not a love match, at least on his part.'

'I am in no position to criticise him for that,' said Conham, drily.

'No, but *you* will do all in your power to make your wife happy.'

Rosina uttered the words without thinking, but her heart took off at a gallop when she saw the look in Conham's hard eyes. They positively blazed, expressing feelings, passions that she recognised. That she shared.

Her heart was pounding, her whole body tingling with a sense of danger, as if the very air around them could ignite at any moment. She was painfully aware that they were alone. One gesture, one wrong word, and she knew, with devastating certainty, that he would cross the small space between them and drag her into his arms.

And oh, how she wanted him to do just that!

It would not stop at kisses. Rosina knew the emotions whirling about them were far too powerful. Conham filled her dreams, he was never far from her thoughts, and if he touched her now her fragile defences would crumble. She would throw herself at him and do everything she could to satisfy the aching desire she felt for this man. And that would be disastrous. She would face ruin in the eyes of the world, all hopes of respectable employment would be wiped out.

Or he would feel obliged to marry her, which would destroy all his family's hopes of restoring their name and house to former glory.

Quickly, she turned away, desperate to recover the situation.

She said, 'Seeing the new Lady Brackwood today has convinced me that marriage is a prison for women. I am right to make my own way in the world.'

She waited, half hoping that Conham would contradict her, but he said nothing and she went on with false cheerfulness.

'I hope they will not be long in bringing us something to eat. I am very eager to drive on to Morton Gifford and get back to my work. As I am sure you must be, my lord.'

Conham listened to Rosina with growing dismay. He had thought himself well under control but he knew that he had given himself away. Rosina had read in his eyes that he wanted her. Did she realise he would give up his life to make her happy?

Because that was what he must do. She was telling him, with awful, gut-wrenching clarity, that they could never have anything more than friendship.

They completed the journey in what could best be described as an awkward politeness, each sitting close to their corner, trying to avoid touching within the close confines of the travelling chariot.

Rosina wanted to weep, but she dared not risk Conham turning to comfort her. With a supreme effort she maintained her composure until they reached Morton Gifford, where the driver had orders to drive on to the lodge. When they left the main road and passed through the gates, Conham broke the silence.

'I would suggest you allow me to lock your jewel box in my strong room at the Manor.'

'Yes, thank you. It will be safe there until you can take the jewels to town.'

'Are you sure there are no pieces you wish to keep for your own use?'

'Perfectly sure. I have my pearls and a few trinkets.' She managed a small laugh. 'When would I ever wear diamonds or emeralds?'

To hear her talking like this was too much for Conham. She was trying so hard to be cheerful and her bravery tore at his heart. Something between a growl and a moan escaped him and he reached out, dragging her into his arms.

'Oh, don't…don't.'

But her protest was half-hearted and she clung to him as he covered her face with kisses.

'You *should* wear them,' he muttered. 'You deserve to be dressed in the finest silks and wearing a king's ransom in jewels. Every day!'

He captured her lips and Rosina gave herself up to his kiss. It was ruthless, demanding. Her skin tingled, her body was on fire with all the yearning desires she had so rigorously suppressed since he had first kissed her on that dark, wintry night in Bristol.

But it was the thought of that first encounter that now in-truded and a renewed sense of self-preservation brought her to her senses. However much Conham might want her, she knew they could never be happy together.

'Ah, no, we cannot. We must not do this,' she muttered, some-how finding the strength to push against him.

Conham released her just as the travelling chariot stopped outside the lodge. The blood was pounding through him; his breathing was ragged, painful. The new lanterns outside the lodge door sent a faint glow into the carriage, enough for him to see the tears gleaming in Rosina's eyes. The sight tore at his heart.

'What else can we do? I lo—'

'No!' She put her fingers to his lips. 'No. Please don't say it, Conham. That would only make things worse.'

'But I want to marry you, Rosina!'

'That can never be.' She drew in a breath, as unsteady as his own. 'You must marry well, for the sake of your family. I could sell my jewels and invest the money safely in government funds, but even with the money Papa settled upon me it would only bring in, what...a hundred pounds a year at most.' She pushed herself out of his arms. 'You need *thousands* to restore Dalla-mire and live as an earl should.'

'Dallamire be damned,' he said savagely. 'What is to pre-vent us going abroad?'

'Conscience.' She uttered the word flatly. 'Can you in all honesty tell me you could abandon your stepmother and your half-sisters, give up Dallamire and your good name? Could you truly do all that and still be happy?'

He wanted to say yes, that with her beside him he would think the world well lost, but something stopped him.

'You see?' She reached up and cupped his cheek. 'You are far too good, too kind, to turn your back on everyone who de-pends upon you.'

'Then be my mistress!' He caught her hand and pressed a kiss into the palm. 'I could set you up in your own establishment—'

'Paid for by your rich wife!' A bitter laugh escaped her and she pulled herself free. 'None of us would be happy with that arrangement.'

With a groan he sat back, rubbing one hand across his eyes. 'Confound it, what a damned tangle!'

There was an agonising silence. Then.

'I should leave. Go away somewhere…'

'No, that will not do!' Conham reached out for her, this time catching both her hands. 'I cannot bear to lose you. I have grown accustomed to having you here, to seeing you every day. I could not bear it if I did not know where you were. If I did not know you were safe.'

'Nor I you.' Her words were so quiet he almost missed them.

She pushed him away and sat up straight, folding her hands in her lap.

'There *is* an alternative, my lord. We can forget this moment, and carry on as we had planned. You will sell my jewels for me and I will invest in Bellemonte. It would be painful, but it is the only way.'

For a long time they sat there, side by side, saying nothing and staring into the darkness.

'You would stay on here, as land steward?'

'Having worked so hard to overcome everyone's initial doubts and prove myself, I should very much like to continue.'

'Another twelve months, then. Until Lady Day next year.' He uttered the words, even though it would be agony to have her so close, yet so unattainable.

'Yes, I will stay. Heaven knows I have nowhere else to go. Brackwood is lost to me now.' She spoke so softly he hardly heard those last words, then she seemed to pull herself together and said in a stronger voice, 'However, if Bellemonte is a success, my investment might provide me with sufficient funds to set up my own establishment.'

But that was a long way in the future, thought Conham. For now, she would be under his eye, somewhere he could look after her. Even if not in the way he would like.

He said, almost to himself, 'Do you think we could do this?'

'It will be easier when you are not here.'

Her frankness almost made him laugh, even as it sliced into his heart.

'Of course.' He closed his eyes, gathering himself. 'I bid you good-night, then, Rosina.'

He jumped out of the carriage and held his hand out to help her down.

'I plan to leave very early tomorrow. I shall not see you before I go. Write to me, if there are any matters that you cannot deal with yourself.'

She nodded. Her eyes were downcast and he caught the glint of tears on her lashes. Leaving her there and ordering the driver to take him back to the Manor was the hardest thing he had ever done in his life.

Chapter Sixteen

It was May. Rosina stood in the square at Bellemonte and gazed at the entrance to the gardens. The ironwork had all been repaired and the lettering in the metal arch that curved above the gates was freshly picked out in gold.

'Grand Pleasure Gardens.' There was no mistaking the pride in Matt's voice as he read the words aloud. 'It is only a week until the opening ceremony, Rosina! I admit, there were times I thought we would not be ready.'

She squeezed his arm. 'I never doubted you would succeed.'

'I could not have done it without you,' he told her. 'Your investment was most timely. I cannot thank you enough for that.'

'I am glad my small sum could be of use.'

'Two thousand pounds!' He laughed. 'A handsome sum, by anyone's reckoning. It meant we could begin on the renovations for the Pavilion without having to wait for new investors. By heaven, Rosina, everything has progressed a great deal quicker than I imagined it could! But are you sure this is what you want?' He turned to look at her. 'If you had invested elsewhere, in the Funds, for example, you could set yourself up in your own house, quite comfortably.'

'I know that, but I do not need the money at present, and

Bellemonte's returns should prove far more lucrative, in the long term.'

'You have no wish to move away from Gloucestershire?'

She had known Matt Talacre long enough to understand the concern in his eyes.

She shook her head. 'No, I cannot bring myself to leave Morton Gifford. Not yet.'

She had never told him how she felt about Conham, but somehow he knew, and it was a comfort.

'Then I am very grateful to you for your trust in me, Rosina. I hope it will be repaid a thousandfold!'

'Then we shall all be rich!' She laughed. His exaggeration had lightened the mood. She added with a smile, 'I have no doubt Bellemonte will be a success, my friend, although it might take a little while and I am glad for you. Truly.'

Rosina knew Matt had thrown himself into the work with a will, taking on physical challenges as well as dealing with the management of the project, and the change in him was noticeable. The exercise had helped to strengthen his wounded leg, so that his lameness was barely perceptible. His spare frame had filled out a little, too, and he carried himself more proudly. He looked like a different man and she could not wait to know what Conham made of the transformation in his friend.

Conham. It was six weeks since he had left for London and since then she had heard no word from him. His secretary had conducted all correspondence concerning the sale of her jewels, and the proceeds had duly been forwarded without any word from the earl himself.

Giving herself a little shake, she turned to look at what had once been the run-down tavern. It was freshly painted, the front step scrubbed and a new sign swung proudly above the door, proclaiming this was now The Dallamire Arms.

'And the inn, too, looks very grand, Matthew.'

'Aye. My new landlord is a very good fellow. It was his idea to ask the earl if he might change the name. By the by, talking of Conham, when do you expect him?'

'I know no more than you,' said Rosina. 'Mrs Jameson has had no word telling her to prepare his rooms.'

'And he has not written to you?'

'No. Why should he?' She forced herself to smile.

'No reason. I just thought...' Matt glanced at her again, then shrugged. 'Conham was never one for letter writing.'

It was not what he had been about to say, but Rosina let it go.

'You promised me a full tour of the gardens,' she reminded him, taking his arm.

'So I did! Come along, then. We only closed off sections of the grounds during the renovations, to keep interest alive, and I think it has worked. Tickets for the reopening are selling well. Once I have shown you around, then we will go into the inn. There is a very respectable private parlour in there now and I will treat you to cakes and wine before you leave. I shall introduce you to the landlord and his wife as my business partner!'

Rosina drove back to Morton Gifford late that afternoon, cheered by the progress at Bellemonte. It had helped to divert her mind from Conham, for a few hours at least. He was her first thought each morning, and last one each night. She did not admit to anyone how much she missed him, but it was a constant ache, almost physical at times.

Thus it was that when she reached the Manor, her heart began to beat just a little faster when she noticed signs of an arrival. She hurried into the house to find the earl himself standing in the hall, talking to Jameson while servants struggled up the stairs with several large trunks.

'You are here!' Even his frowning look as he turned towards her could not prevent the smile spreading over her face. 'Welcome back to Gifford Manor, my lord.'

'Thank you.'

'We had no idea when you would be returning,' she went on, peeling off her gloves. 'If I had known I could have postponed my visit to Bellemonte.'

'It was all arranged last minute.' It was hard to read the expression in his hooded eyes, but despite his polite tone, Rosina sensed he was ill at ease. 'I sent a rider on ahead of us early this morning, when we stopped to change horses at Bath. To prepare rooms for my visitors.'

Visitors! Rosina forced herself to keep smiling, conscious that Jameson was still in the hall and a footman was hovering, waiting to relieve her of her outdoor clothes.

'You have guests, my lord?'

A sense of foreboding was growing inside her.

'Yes. My stepmother, the Countess of Dallamire, is with me. And Lady Skelton and her daughter.'

'Ah.' Not by the flicker of an eyelid did Rosina show her dismay. What could this be but the visit of a prospective bride? 'Then I will not detain you, my lord. Excuse me.'

She handed her bonnet and pelisse to the waiting servant and hurried away to her office. Wild thoughts chased through her mind and she told herself not to jump to conclusions. It would be foolish to read anything into this. Why should Conham not invite his stepmama to stay? Or anyone else, for that matter. Lady Skelton might turn out to be an aged crone, and her daughter an elderly spinster. Although she could not bring herself to believe that.

Rosina closed the door and sat down at her desk, feeling a little faint. She dropped her head in her hands, berating herself for her weakness. She had known Conham was looking for a rich bride; why was she so surprised?

Because she had expected to read of his betrothal in the London paper. Or he could have stirred himself to write to her on estate business and added the information as a postscript. Instead, he had brought the lady here, to Morton Gifford, where she would be forced to witness their courtship. After all they had said at their last meeting, would Conham really be that cruel?

She pulled a ledger towards her and opened it, trying to concentrate on the figures, but the question kept forcing its way into her mind. It took every ounce of resolve not to go in search of Mrs Jameson to glean more information, but she hated the thought of listening to gossip and was determined not to leave her office until it was time to join the upper servants for dinner.

The time dragged. She wrote up a report on Bellemonte and made a note of questions and suggestions to discuss with Matthew at their next meeting. Then she set to work on her accounts until the chimes of the hall clock told her it was nearing the dinner hour.

She was just blotting the last row of figures when there was a knock at the door. Conham came into the room and she looked up, trying to ignore how handsome he looked in his evening clothes, the black coat fitting without a crease across his broad shoulders, his auburn hair gleaming red in the early-evening sunlight that blazed into the study at that time of day.

'I hope I am not disturbing you?'

'Not at all, my lord.'

'I wanted to explain. I had no intention of bringing anyone with me, but when my stepmother suggested it, I could hardly refuse. I should have written. I am sorry.' He was pacing the small room, reminding her of a caged animal. 'The countess is keen that I should marry as soon as possible. Miss Skelton comes from a good family. Excellent credentials.'

'Including a generous dowry?'

Heavens, how could she sound so calm, so practical?

'A *very* generous dowry.'

'Then you should offer for her with all speed.'

'Yes.'

He came to a stand before the desk and looked down at her, his eyes troubled. She looked away before he glimpsed in her countenance the seething mass of jealousy, rage and misery she felt inside.

Rosina closed the ledger. 'Thank you for informing me, my lord. Now, if you will excuse me, it is nearly time for dinner.'

He did not move. She added pointedly, 'Your guests will be waiting for you.'

She kept her eyes lowered and tidied the desk while the silence lengthened between them. Then, just when she thought she could bear it no longer, she heard him turn and leave the room.

Rosina exhaled, long and slow. He had apologised, removing her reason to be angry with him. The jealousy and unhappiness she must deal with herself. And now that first meeting was over, they could continue as master and steward. It would be difficult, but surely not impossible. She had thought herself prepared. She had known that at some point Conham would marry, but she had not realised the depths of despair that would engulf her when the idea became a possibility. If only she had known how painful it would be, then she would have taken the money she received for her jewels and run far away from Morton Gifford. From Conham.

She closed her eyes. The salary he was paying her was far higher than anything she could command elsewhere, and she had sunk all her money into Bellemonte now. She could not withdraw without jeopardising Matthew's plans, as well as the earl's. She had no choice but to continue.

Her spirits sank even lower when she joined the Jamesons for dinner that evening. She knew it was likely that the subject of the earl's visitors would come up, but when she learned that Mr Dawkins would not be joining them, it was inevitable. Mrs Jameson's housekeeping skills had not been tested very much over recent years and she was now relishing the challenge of having ladies in the house.

'This has always been a bachelor household,' she explained. 'Lady Dallamire has never been here before and not for the world would I have her find anything wanting. Thankfully, we only recently turned the house upside down. There is nothing like spring sunshine for showing up every speck of dust, is there, Miss Brackwood? As soon as Lord Dallamire's message arrived, I inspected every nook and cranny and was relieved to find them spotless. I have brought in two more girls from the village, though, just in case. With three ladies in the house there will be far more fetching and carrying to be done, I am sure.'

'I believe the earl has two half-sisters,' offered Rosina, trying to avoid mentioning Miss Skelton. 'Did the countess include them in the party?'

'Oh, no. They are still in the schoolroom at Dallamire, I believe, which is fortunate, since the house is now as full as it can hold. No, *this* visit has another reason altogether.' The housekeeper lowered her voice a little. 'Her Ladyship is matchmaking!'

'Now, now,' said her husband, frowning a little. 'We should not be gossiping about these matters.'

'Oh, pish, Mr Jameson, you are as bad as Mr Dawkins, not

wanting to talk about the master, but this is not gossip, for none of us would say anything outside these walls. And this may be our only opportunity. The ladies' maids are all so busy, I have had to send their meals up to them tonight, but tomorrow I shall invite them to dine with us. Very ladylike they are, too,' she added. 'The countess's maid is French, and inclined to turn her nose up at our country ways, which is not surprising, I suppose, if they are more accustomed to a grand house like Dallamire. However, Lady Skelton's and her daughter's maids are very pleasant and agreeable.'

'And did they say how long their visit is likely to be?' asked Rosina, curiosity getting the better of her.

'Only two weeks. Miss Skelton's maid told me they had planned to stay in London for the season, only then Lady Dallamire invited them to make a short visit here.' She chuckled. 'Well, we can all guess what *that* means!'

Mr Jameson looked up from his dinner to say firmly, 'Enough now, madam.'

His spouse, thus admonished, turned her attention to her dinner and Rosina was left to her own thoughts. With the reopening of Bellemonte's Grand Pleasure Gardens only a week away, did that mean Conham had changed his mind about going, or did he intend to bring his visitors? She could not decide which she would prefer.

When dinner was over, Rosina went to the great hall to put on her pelisse before walking back to the lodge. Jameson was carrying a tray of decanters to the drawing room, and as the butler passed through the open door, the sound of animated chatter flowed out. She heard Conham's deep voice, then the sweet, bell-like sound of a lady's laugh.

Matt would lose a significant opportunity to puff off his new project to his investors if Conham decided to stay away from Bellemonte. But she thought it most likely he would attend, accompanied by his guests. Rosina followed the footman with his lantern out into the darkness. Either way, her pleasure in the event was now sadly diminished.

Chapter Seventeen

Rosina kept herself busy for the rest of the week, the good weather giving her an excuse to spend more time out of doors, but she knew she could not avoid the earl and his guests forever.

The inevitable meeting occurred when she was riding back to the stables one afternoon. She saw the open carriage on the drive, Conham riding beside it on his black hunter. Her heart sank when they all stopped and waited for her to come up to them. Bramble was nothing like the beautiful horses she had ridden at Brackwood, and today's ride had been particularly muddy. She had taken a short cut across the meadows to reach one of the farms and she knew it wasn't just the pony's sturdy legs that were spattered with dirt. However, there was no avoiding the meeting so she squared her shoulders and approached, bidding the earl a calm good day.

Conham touched his hat to Rosina before presenting her to the occupants of the carriage. They responded, eyeing her with varying degrees of curiosity. She knew some of her hair had escaped around the edges of her riding hat, and that her skirts were liberally splashed with mud, but there was nothing to do but smile and brave it out.

'I have been visiting Valley Farm,' she told Conham, by way of explanation. 'Stratton has been reroofing his barn.'

'Ah yes, you wrote to tell me.' He nodded. 'I must go down and see it for myself. Although not today. I am about to accompany the ladies on a short tour of the park.'

'So, you are the new land steward here.'

Lady Dallamire's voice cut across them, thick with disapproval. She was a tall, thin woman, dressed in widow's weeds and with her dark hair sprinkled with grey. Before Rosina could respond, she turned away and addressed Conham.

'It is most irregular. I have never heard of such a thing.'

'Perhaps not, but Miss Brackwood has proved herself to be an excellent choice.'

'But surely you do not ride out unaccompanied, Miss Brackwood?' remarked Lady Skelton, a stern-faced matron in a walking dress and pelisse whose colour exactly matched her iron-grey hair. 'Is that wise?'

'There is little danger riding about the estate, or in the village.' Rosina answered her cheerfully. 'I used to do so on my father's estate, when he was too ill to go out himself.'

The youngest member of the party, Miss Skelton, was staring at Rosina with a look of awed fascination. She was a young lady of no more than one-and-twenty, her willowy figure clothed in a fashionable deep rose pelisse and with a matching bonnet, beneath which a mass of glossy black curls peeped out to frame a very pretty face. When Rosina gave her a friendly smile, she blushed rosily and looked away.

'I cannot think it a suitable occupation for a lady,' declared Lady Dallamire in repressive accents.

'It is, however, a *respectable* occupation, ma'am,' Rosina countered, more sharply than perhaps she should. 'And there are precious few of those open to ladies.'

'Miss Brackwood knows more about land management than anyone else who came forward for the position,' said Conham. He turned to Rosina and touched his hat to her again. 'But unlike those of us idling our day away in pleasure, I know you have work to do, 'ma'am. We will not keep you from it any longer.'

His smile took the sting out of the dismissal, and Rosina was grateful.

'Thank you, my lord.'

She nodded to the ladies and urged Bramble to walk on, feeling their eyes upon her as she rode away. She sat up very straight in the saddle, conscious that the Welsh pony was by no means an elegant beast. Rosina had no doubt she would be compared very unfavourably with the graceful Miss Skelton.

Rosina was dismayed but not surprised when Conham informed her he was taking his guests to Bellemonte's grand re-opening.

They were in her office and had just spent an hour on estate business, which, he had told her, was all he could spare.

'I understand,' she replied. 'You have guests, after all.'

'Yes.' He paused. 'I have invited them to come with us to-morrow evening.'

She nodded. 'Then if you will allow me to use the chariot, I shall go on ahead.'

'No, *I* will use the chariot. You will be more comfortable travelling in the landau with the other ladies.'

'Very well.'

She thought there would be nothing comfortable about sitting with the countess and Lady Skelton. Since that first introduction, whenever Rosina encountered the ladies in the house or grounds, they ignored her.

As befitted a servant.

Rosina presented herself in the hall at the appointed time the next evening, wearing her white cambric muslin, trimmed at the hem with a single flounce. Over this she wore a new pelisse of dark red velvet. It fitted snugly to the high waist, where it was confined with a narrow band of matching satin before falling down to her ankles in soft folds. She had trimmed a straw bonnet with red ribbons to match and, knowing the other ladies would disapprove of her presence whatever she wore, she had secured the bonnet with a defiantly jaunty bow beneath one ear.

The earl politely handed them all into the carriage and the ladies set off, travelling in a chilly silence that was finally broken by the countess.

'Really, I do not know why Dallamire should insist you

should come along this evening, Miss Brackwood. Surely there is no need for his steward to attend.'

'You are quite right, ma'am. I am not here in my capacity as the earl's land steward. I am an investor.'

'What!'

'Lord Dallamire owns the land, but Mr Talacre and I have invested in the development of Bellemonte.' Rosina could not suppress a smile at the look of shock and surprise on the faces of her auditors. 'You might say we are all, er, business partners.'

'Well, a lady involved in *business*!' exclaimed Lady Skelton. 'How extraordinary. I have never known such a thing.'

'Oh, I am sure you have, ma'am,' said Rosina. 'Think of the milliners and modistes you use, I am sure at least some of them are in charge of their own business. And my father often talked of Mrs Coade, who manufactures the excellent Coade Stone. He even purchased two of her sculptures for the gardens at Brackwood Court.'

Lady Skelton gave a little titter of disdain. 'Milliners, tradespeople,' she declared. 'Not the *haute ton*, at all.'

Rosina went on as if she had not heard her.

'And of course there is Lady Jersey, who has been a senior partner of Child's Bank for the past ten years.' She smiled. 'She is a patroness of Almack's, and I am sure you would be delighted to accept vouchers from her for Miss Skelton, would you not, ma'am?'

Lady Skelton looked nonplussed, but the countess gave a little snort of laughter.

'Very well, Miss Brackwood, you have made your point. But as for this business venture, well. Time will tell if my stepson was wise to keep Bellemonte.'

'It will indeed, ma'am.'

Rosina settled back in her corner, pleased that she had not allowed herself to be browbeaten, and satisfied that Lady Dallamire, at least, was looking a little less disapproving.

Matthew was waiting at the gates to meet them. He tenderly handed the countess out of the carriage, declaring what a pleasure it was to see her again.

'It has been too long, ma'am. And may I say you are looking as radiant as ever!'

'Enough of your insolence,' she scolded, although it was clear she was not displeased with Matt's form of address.

'No, no, I mean every word, Lady Dallamire. You cannot conceive how delighted I am to have you grace our celebrations with your presence.'

'Yes, well, I hope I shall not be disappointed,' she retorted sharply.

Rosina moved away a little and watched as the countess presented him to Lady Skelton and her daughter.

'I see Matt is working his charm on my stepmother and her guests.'

She turned to find the earl beside her. 'Yes, he is. Very much at his ease, and so confident! Have you noticed how well he is looking? He appears to be perfectly at home here.'

'Yes, I have.' Conham smiled as he observed his friend chatting to the ladies in such an animated fashion. 'This could be the making of him.'

There was no time for more. Lady Dallamire commanded his attention and he went off to give her his arm.

Matthew guided them all to the Pavilion, which was now resplendent with fresh paint.

'You see the card and tea rooms have been furnished in the very latest style,' he said, ushering the party through the building. 'Then we have the supper room, and the ballroom, which is also an ideal place to promenade during the day, if the weather is inclement.'

Conham had to admit he was impressed. Compared to his last visit, everything now looked new and elegant. Chandeliers blazed in every room, picking out the gilding on the plastered ceilings and casting a warm glow over the guests. Matthew suggested they should enjoy a light repast before venturing out into the gardens.

'I shall not be able to accompany you, alas,' he informed them. 'However, Dallamire has been here before. I hope he will tell you how much everything is improved.'

Conham grinned and waved him away. 'Yes, yes, you have

given us enough of your time. Off you go and do the pretty by your other guests.'

When Matt had gone, Conham escorted his party back to the supper room, where an impressive array of refreshments had been laid out on long tables covered with snowy white cloths. They found an empty table and the countess took charge of seating everyone. Conham found himself sitting between Lady Skelton and her daughter, and since his stepmother dominated the conversation, he had no opportunity to speak to Rosina until they were back in the vestibule.

She was the first to join him after the ladies had gone off to collect their cloaks, prior to visiting the lamplit garden walks, and he spoke without preamble.

'I am sorry, I hope my guests have not spoiled your enjoyment of the evening. It was never my intention—'

'You could hardly leave them at the Manor,' she replied. 'And it cannot be a bad thing that they are present. There are few people here with whom you are acquainted, but it will be widely reported that both the Earl *and* the Countess of Dallamire were in attendance.'

'Aye, Matt will make sure of it!'

'And why not? He wishes it to be known that Bellemonte is a very fashionable place.' She looked about her. 'Judging by those I have seen here tonight, I believe it has every chance of succeeding.'

'And that will benefit all of us.'

'Yes, although nothing compared to what you need to restore Dallamire's fortunes.'

'But it could make a real difference for you, as well as Matthew.' He paused, then added quietly, 'I hope it does, Rosina. I hope, eventually, you will achieve the independence you desire.'

'What are you saying, Dallamire? What are you and Miss Brackwood discussing?'

His stepmother came up and Conham reluctantly turned away from Rosina. It was time to do his duty.

'Nothing of moment, ma'am.' He smiled at Miss Skelton and her mother, who had now joined them. 'Shall we go and explore the gardens?'

The countess agreed, but insisted that Conham accompany Amelia. 'And you must escort Lady Skelton, too, Dallamire. I wish to talk with Miss Brackwood.'

Rosina hid her alarm at this news and fell into step beside the countess as they set off along the path, following the earl, who strolled ahead of them with a lady on each arm.

'Dallamire has told me of your background, Miss Brackwood. He says your father owned an estate in Somerset. I believe that is where you learned about land management.'

'Yes, ma'am, it is.'

'My stepson has been singing your praises.'

'Has he?' Rosina hoped she was not blushing. 'The earl is very kind, ma'am.'

'He is, but you must not expect anything to come of it.'

'I do not know what Your Ladyship means.'

'Oh, I think you do, Miss Brackwood. You are a clever woman, after all.' The countess waited, possibly expecting a modest disclaimer, and when nothing was forthcoming, she continued. 'Let me be frank. My stepson may be very impressed with your intellect but he will never marry you.'

'I do not expect him to do so,' replied Rosina, bristling.

'I am glad. I would not wish to see you disappointed. The Dallamires can trace their history back to the Conqueror. You may entice him into bed, but he will not forget himself so far as to marry a servant.'

'I am his *land steward*, madam, not his servant,' said Rosina, holding on to her temper.

'Which is even worse!' declared Lady Dallamire. 'You are associating with men of all ranks, sullying your hands with *commerce*. If he forgot what was owed to his name and married you, he would become a laughing stock. His peers would despise him for ignoring his duty to his family!'

Rosina drew herself up. 'The earl is not one to forget his responsibilities, my lady. It is not in his nature. He is the most honourable man I know.'

'Precisely.' The countess gave Rosina a pitying look, then she reached across to pat her hand. 'You may be a lady who has fallen upon hard times, but Conham is not your knight in shining armour, my dear. He knows it is his duty to take a rich wife. He has been bred to it.'

'Has he?' Rosina hid her anger beneath a derisive smile. 'You make him sound like a prize stallion.'

The countess's eyes narrowed, but then she laughed gently.

'Why, perhaps that is what he is,' she said. 'He certainly knows what is due to his rank and his name. His pride, his *conscience*, will not let him do other than provide for those of us who are dependent upon him. I shall say no more, Miss Brackwood. You are a sensible woman; I trust you will not make Conham's life more difficult than it already is.'

With that, she set off again and Rosina followed, curbing a sudden desire to storm off in the opposite direction. They soon caught up with Conham and the other ladies, who had stopped at a fork in the path to wait for them.

A short conversation ensued before the party moved again, strolling along the main path that Rosina recalled would take them back to the Pavilion. The earl and Miss Skelton were still leading the way, but Lady Skelton was now walking with the countess, and as they were both ignoring Rosina, she dropped back. She had no desire to listen to them discussing the best warehouses for bridal silks, as if a marriage between Lord Dallamire and Miss Skelton was as good as decided.

Which it probably was, she thought miserably. The countess had not told her anything she did not already know. She had merely confirmed that Rosina was wholly ineligible, compared to the rich Miss Skelton. Conham himself was aware of it, too. She had watched him earlier, doing his best to set Amelia Skelton at her ease. Even now, he was bending his head to catch her words, giving her one of his encouraging smiles.

Resolutely pushing her unhappiness aside, Rosina forced her mind to more practical matters. She had invested in these gardens; it was in her interests to look out for anything that might be improved. It would also be useful to note whether the majority of visitors were members of the gentry or well-to-do tradespeople.

Matt's voice broke into her thoughts: 'Have the fearsome matrons cut you out?'

She jumped and looked around. Smiling, he offered her his arm.

'Well, have they?'

'I chose to fall behind.' She slipped her hand onto his sleeve. 'I have been observing your customers.'

'That does not answer my question. Oh, no need to throw me that warning look, we are sufficiently far behind now that they will not hear us.'

She hesitated. 'They are intent on promoting a match for the earl. With Miss Skelton.'

He gave her a searching look. 'Would you mind that?'

Rosina laughed, pleased she could sound so carefree, so genuinely amused.

'Good heavens, no! Conham needs to marry well, we all know that. And Amelia Skelton is a sweet, biddable little thing. He could do far worse.'

'Damned with faint praise, then!'

She flushed a little. 'Truly, Matthew, it is not our concern, so let us not waste time on the matter. Tell me instead how you have gone on tonight. I must say there appears to be hundreds of people in the gardens.'

'There are, and they are still coming in! The notices in the newspapers, and the bills I posted around the hotels and shops have proved worthwhile. There are any number of people who have come to see what Bellemonte has to offer before committing themselves to a season ticket.' He stopped and took her hands, saying eagerly, 'I really think we can make a success of this, Rosina! There is a great hunger for more entertainment than the city can presently offer, and being only a mile or so from Clifton and the Hotwells, we are ideally placed to provide it.'

The excitement in his voice was unmistakeable and his eyes glowed in the lamplight. Rosina could not help but smile at his enthusiasm.

'I think you are right, Matt, but have a care,' she warned, squeezing his fingers. 'You must not overstretch your resources.'

'*Our* resources, m'dear. You have invested in Bellemonte, too. And don't forget it was you who thought to buy Mr Matthews's Directory and Guide,' he added, pulling her hand back onto his arm and resuming their walk. 'That has proved very useful in knowing where best to direct our advertisements.'

Ahead of them, Conham noted that the arbours to the side of the path had been cleared of foliage and new lamps hung within, so that the stone benches and figures could now be seen in all their glory. He turned to point out one particularly fine sculpture to his stepmother and as he did so he noticed Matthew standing with Rosina. They were holding hands and she was laughing up at him. Conham felt an unexpected stab of jealousy so strong that he stopped talking, midsentence. Until he heard the countess's sharp voice addressing him.

'Well, Dallamire, did you say something about a Rysbrack? Pray, continue!'

'What?' He dragged his wandering thoughts back to the ladies looking up at him expectantly. 'Ah, yes. Rysbrack.' He cleared his throat, hoping it would also clear his head. 'The goddess in the arbour over there, Matthew is confident it is by the sculptor. Of course he needs to have that confirmed, but it seems very likely, because there are any number of Rysbrack's works in and around Bristol...'

They moved on, Conham searching his memory to find things of interest to say about the gardens. His struggle was made harder because he could not stop thinking about Matt and Rosina. Were they still following? He kept his eyes resolutely on the path ahead, afraid that if he looked back he might discover they had disappeared, that Matt had whisked Rosina into one of the romantic arbours and was now making love to her.

Chapter Eighteen

For Rosina, the evening at Bellemonte was bittersweet. Watching Conham paying court to Miss Skelton was not easy, and the other ladies in the party didn't welcome her presence. She would have liked to wander off and explore the gardens alone but without a companion she knew that would have been most improper, not to say foolhardy. Matthew had other guests to attend and after he had left her, she trailed along at the back of the group, excluded from the matrons' conversation and trying not to heed the smiles that passed between Conham and Amelia Skelton.

By the time the carriage deposited them all at the door to Gifford Manor, she had a pounding headache and was glad of the short walk back to the lodge, accompanied by a footman who neither wanted nor expected her to talk to him.

Conham saw Rosina walk away. He wanted to stand there and watch her until the bend in the path hid her from sight, but it could not be. His attention was quickly claimed by the countess and he escorted his guests into the house. Lady Skelton carried her daughter away up the stairs, declaring they were both exhausted, and Conham was left to join his stepmother for her customary glass of claret in the drawing room.

'An interesting evening,' she declared, when they had been served with wine. 'I hope the venture will prove a success for you.'

'Thank you.' Her tone indicated that she did not believe this, but he let that go.

'However, I still believe you would have done better to sell Bellemonte and put the money into Dallamire. The roof on the west wing is leaking again.'

'I am aware of that, ma'am. The lead guttering has failed. I have already set men to work on it, as well as several other problems that need urgent attention.'

'The whole house needs urgent attention,' she snapped. 'Dallamire Hall is hardly likely to impress a future bride in its present condition.'

He smiled slightly. 'Is it too much to hope that a woman might like me for myself, rather than my houses?'

'Do not be so tiresome, Conham, this is not about you. I am thinking of the future of the family! Mortlakes have lived at Dallamire for generations.'

'And will continue to do so,' said Conham, refilling their glasses. 'My keeping Bellemonte makes no difference to that.'

'It delays refurbishment of your principal seat,' she retorted. 'I brought the Skeltons here to see you because I could not risk Lady Skelton discovering just how badly run-down Dallamire has become.'

She saw the flash of irritation in his eyes and had the grace to flush. 'I know it is not entirely your fault,' she conceded. 'Your father did nothing to the house. And he was far too complacent, believing he could restore our fortunes with a few successful nights at the card tables.'

'Then borrowing even more to cover his losses.'

'It was always a point of honour with your father to pay his gaming debts.' She pulled out her handkerchief. 'You cannot blame him for breaking his neck when he did!'

Conham watched her dabbing at her eyes. He had long ago given up arguing with his stepmother. What was done was done. It was his duty to put it right.

* * *

The countess and her guests remained at the Manor for another three full days, during which time Conham saw nothing of Rosina. Whenever he spoke with Davy, the young man told him that she was busy. One day she was visiting several farms, another riding out to inspect a new barn, and on the third she was in the village, helping the vicar to organise a widows and orphans fund.

The countess demanded Conham's full attention and he did his best to put Rosina to the back of his mind while he threw himself into playing host to his guests, until at last the travelling carriage was at the door, loaded and ready to carry them away to London.

'I trust we shall see you in town very soon,' said Lady Skelton as he handed her into the carriage.

Conham murmured something noncommittal and turned to take his leave of the countess. She, however, was not so easily dismissed.

'You must come as soon as you can,' she commanded. 'I had hoped to hear that there was a firm understanding between you and Miss Skelton by now.'

'I am sorry to disappoint you, ma'am.'

She said, bluntly, 'I can hold off the other suitors for a few weeks, perhaps, but a pretty girl with such a large fortune will not remain single for long.' Her fingers curled around his hand like claws. 'And you *need* a large fortune, if you are to rescue Dallamire. Remember that!'

'I can hardly forget it,' he replied, feeling the web of obligation tightening around him.

With his visitors gone, Conham needed an outlet for his frustration. He ordered his horse to be saddled and rode off cross-country to the high ground north of Morton Gifford. He rode for miles, soothed by the exercise but knowing he could not outrun the problems that beset him.

He returned to the stables, tired and muddy, with barely enough time to change for dinner, and had just handed his horse over to a groom when he heard a carriage. He looked around in time to see Rosina turning the gig into the yard.

He stopped to watch, drinking in the sight of her. She was dressed in her riding habit, the mannish jacket fitting snugly over curves that were anything but masculine, and she looked completely at home as she manoeuvred the vehicle through the narrow arched entrance. By heaven, he thought, as she drew up beside him, she was everything he wanted in a partner. Kind, intelligent and resourceful.

And out of your reach.

'You have been out riding,' she greeted him as he helped her alight.

'Yes.' He glanced down at his mud-spattered boots and breeches. 'My guests left early and it being such a fine day, I took the opportunity to ride to Gifford Hill.'

'How delightful that must have been! I have been to Belle-monte.' She pulled a small leather bag from the footrest. 'These ledgers need to go back into the office.'

'Then I will walk with you.' He fell into step beside her as they took a shortcut across the grass. 'How is Matt?'

'In high good humour,' she told him. 'We have been going over the receipts. The grand opening was a triumph. Ticket sales were excellent and he has already had more than a hundred requests for season tickets!'

'A good start.'

'Yes, very good. The baths, too, have become more popular, even though Matthew increased the price a little. And the wardens he employed are very successful at keeping out the less... er...*respectable* customers.'

Conham heard the laughter in her voice and swiped his riding crop at a thistle that had escaped the gardener's scythe. He knew he should be happy to find her in such good spirits, but for some illogical reason it irked him, and his irritation grew as she chattered on, describing the progress that had been made at Bellemonte and the success of its opening night.

'It helped a great deal that you were in attendance,' she told him, leading the way into her office. She laughed. 'One can never have too many earls at these events, you know!'

'I am glad an earl can be useful for something!'

'I beg your pardon,' she said quickly. 'I did not mean to be disparaging.'

She put the bag onto the desk and dropped her gloves on top of it before turning to him, smiling.

'Oh, Conham, Matthew is in alt about the prospects for Bellemonte, and so full of plans for the future! I have never seen him so happy. I wish you could have been there.'

'I don't believe that.'

'I beg your pardon?'

He felt a stab of guilt for his ill temper, but he could not stop himself from continuing.

'My presence would have sadly curtailed your chance to flirt with him!'

Her eyes widened in horror, which flayed his conscience even more, but the demon jealousy had not finished with him yet.

'Well,' he demanded savagely, 'has he kissed you? Is that why you are blushing?'

She slapped him, hard.

Conham reeled back, the shock of knowing he deserved it hurting far more than his stinging cheek.

'How dare you!' Rosina glared at him, her face as white as the cravat tied so neatly beneath her chin. 'How dare you even *think* I would… Matthew and I are friends, nothing more.'

Having done its work, the demon slunk away, leaving Conham full of remorse.

'Yes. Of course. I beg your pardon.' He added, as she walked to the door, 'Rosina, forgive me!'

She turned, her eyes stormy, and delivered a parting shot that hit him squarely in the gut.

'And if we were anything more than that, it would be no concern of yours, my lord!'

Rosina strode out of the Manor and hurried away to the lodge. Tears were not far away and she wanted to be alone when they fell. How could he think that she would flirt with Matthew? How could he say such things to her? But even before she reached the lodge door, she knew exactly why he had lashed out at her. Had she not felt the same illogical rage when she had seen him with Amelia Skelton? Had she not wanted to spit and scratch and tear?

By the time she had washed and dressed for the evening her temper had cooled, replaced by a dull ache of unhappiness. She could not face company, and sent word to the housekeeper she would take supper at the lodge. She was somewhat surprised when Mrs Goddard returned from her errand not carrying a tray, but a letter.

'An express has come for you, madam,' she said, holding out the sealed message. 'I thought I should bring it over to you directly rather than wait for Cook to put your supper together. I'll go back and fetch that now.'

'Yes, yes, thank you,' said Rosina, quickly breaking the seal.

She scanned the letter, barely noticing the servant's departure, nor Conham's entrance moments later.

'You have received an urgent message. Is it bad news?'

'Papa's old valet, Mr Paxby.' She did not raise her eyes from the paper. 'He has had a fall and taken to his bed. He wants to see me.'

She looked up, as if suddenly aware of his presence. 'Why have you come?'

'I thought you might need help.'

Of course. The earlier confrontation was forgotten. It was the most natural thing in the world that he should be here.

She turned again to the letter. 'It is from Martha, Mr Paxby's sister. She says he is asking for me and declares he will not rest until we have spoken. I fear he must be very ill. Excuse me, I must go to Brackwood.'

'I will come with you.' He caught her arm as she went to walk past him. 'But not tonight, there is no moon. We can leave as soon as it is light and be at Brackwood almost as quickly.'

'Yes. Thank you.'

When he had gone, Rosina sat down, still clutching the letter. She needed to pack, but not immediately. Conham would call for her in the morning. All she had to do was be ready to go with him.

Conham. He had offered his help and she had accepted, without a second thought. She closed her eyes. Their friendship was too deep, too strong, to be broken by a few hasty words. But when he married, as he must do, what would happen then?

Chapter Nineteen

They set off at dawn and by late morning, the earl's travelling chariot was bowling through Brackwood village. It pulled up at the small neat house and Conham accompanied Rosina to the door, prepared to support her if the worst had happened and they had arrived too late.

She knocked and was greeting the woman even before the door was fully opened.

'Mrs Jones, I received your letter and came as quickly as I could!'

'Oh, bless you, Miss Brackwood, Jem will be so pleased. He is recovering well from his fall, but he's been fretting so much about seeing you that he can't be easy. Come along in, ma'am. And you, too, my lord,' she said, when Rosina had introduced him.

'Thank you, ma'am, but I think it best if I do not.'

Rosina looked up at him. 'Please, stay. I have no secrets from you.'

Her words warmed his heart but he shook his head. 'Mr Paxby may want to talk privately with you. A stranger's presence could unsettle him. I will call back within the hour, will that do?'

Her answer was a smile and a nod. Conham touched his hat and went back to the chariot.

Rosina watched him go before stepping into the house. She remembered the one large room from her previous visit. It sufficed as a kitchen and sitting room, but now she saw that in the far corner a bed had been made up for Mr Paxby, who was propped up against the pillows.

'He's not so bad, ma'am. It's just a sprained ankle and a few bruises,' said Martha, a note of apology in her voice. 'But when I first put him to bed he wouldn't lie still until I had written to you. Making himself ill with it, he was.'

'And I am glad you did write to me, Mrs Jones.' Rosina gave her a reassuring smile before hurrying across to the bed. 'My dear Mr Paxby, I am sorry to see you like this. Is there anything I can do for you?'

'Ah, 'tis good of you to come, Miss Brackwood. There is something I need to tell you, while I still can. My memory isn't what it was, you see. I didn't even remember this until I was laid up here, in bed, and fearing I might not leave it again.'

'Now, now,' she chided him gently. 'You must not think like that. Your sister is taking the very best care of you.'

'She is, bless her, but when the Lord calls me, it will be too late, so I must tell you this now.' His thin hand plucked at the cheerful patchwork coverlet. 'You will remember when Sir Thomas sent you off to the north, to attend your aunt's funeral.'

'How could I forget? If I had known Papa would be taken ill while I was away I would never have gone.'

The old man wiped away a tear. 'Aye, ma'am, it was very sad, but he was adamant someone should go in his stead. It should have been your brother, of course, but he couldn't be persuaded.' The old man scowled. 'Not that he was much company for your father, even though he told you he'd look after him! But that's by the by, and Sir Thomas was content enough, while you were away.

'He spent every day in his study, working. Putting his affairs in order, he told me. It was as if he knew the end was near. And he was heartened, the day you left, by a letter from two old friends. They were visiting Bath and as they were little more than ten miles from Brackwood, they proposed to call.'

'Yes, I remember you told me. You said their visit had cheered him enormously.'

'Yes, it did. But I have been thinking on it since you last called and I wonder now, from something Sir Thomas said to me at the time, if they helped him to write a new will.'

Rosina froze. 'A…a new will?'

'Yes, ma'am. It was when I was helping your father into bed that night, after his visitors had left us, and he says to me, "I can rest easy now, Paxby, knowing Brackwood's future is secure." I thought no more of it, especially since he had that seizure the very next day, and we was all at sixes and sevens, but it's come back to me now.'

'But there was no new will, Mr Paxby,' said Rosina. 'The one Mr Shipton read out after the funeral was dated some four years earlier.' She paused, then, 'Did you ask him about it?'

'No. I did not think it important at the time, because the estate is entailed, so Brackwood is already secure. But then, the day after you came to visit, Sir Edgar called on me.'

'I'd gone shopping,' put in Martha, from the other side of the room. 'If I'd been here, he'd never have troubled Jem so. I'd have given him short shrift, baronet or no baronet!'

'I am sure you would,' said Rosina, smiling. 'Go on, Mr Paxby.'

'He demanded I tell him what we had discussed. I couldn't rightly say, because it was nothing of consequence, was it?'

'It was purely a social call, Mr Paxby. I came to see how you went on, as befits an old friend.'

'He wouldn't believe that, miss, no matter how many times I told him. He threatened me with dire consequences if I was to speak out of turn and I told him straight I would never do such a thing! Then, out of the blue, he asked me about your father's visitors. He demanded to know who they were, but I could tell him nothing, bar that Sir Thomas had mentioned one of them was groomsman at his wedding. Then Sir Edgar lost his temper,' said the old man, his voice rising. 'He suggested I had been gossiping about your sainted father's last days, and that I had told you he'd destroyed his father's new will, but I didn't, Miss

Brackwood, did I? I hadn't even considered the idea of a new will until he mentioned it!'

'Ooh, if that isn't Edgar all over!' declared Rosina. She reached over to take the old man's agitated hands between her own. 'Hush now, Mr Paxby, you must not upset yourself. You know as well as I that when Edgar is in a rage he quite loses his head and says the most foolish things. Now, I shall ask Martha to bring you some fresh tea.'

'It's already done, miss.'

Mrs Jones appeared at her elbow with a cup and together they calmed the invalid, plumping up his pillows and smoothing the coverlet before Martha helped him to drink his tea.

The cup emptied, the old valet lay back against the pillows and smiled at Rosina.

'Thank you for coming, Miss Brackwood. The matter's been troubling me ever since Sir Edgar came here. Perhaps I had it wrong and Sir Thomas wasn't talking about a new will, but whatever it was I feel sure now it must have been important to him. Do you not think so?'

Rosina hesitated, then she said quietly 'I do, Mr Paxby. I do indeed.'

Conham returned at the appointed time and Mrs Jones opened the door wide.

'Do, pray, step in, my lord. Miss Brackwood is just saying goodbye to my brother and won't be above ten minutes, I am sure. And I have tea brewing already, for it's all I can get Jem to drink now. But there is some of my cowslip wine, if Your Lordship would prefer?'

His Lordship did prefer, not trusting tea that might have been stewing for an hour, but knowing that to refuse everything would cause offence. Once his eyes had accustomed to the dim light, he could see Rosina talking quietly with an old, white-haired man lying in the bed at the far end of the room. He sat down and allowed his hostess to bustle about him, bringing his wine, which he pronounced excellent, but he refused a slice of cake, saying he was about to carry Miss Brackwood off to partake of a nuncheon before they returned to Morton Gifford.

Mrs Jones nodded sagely. 'Very wise, when you have a long journey ahead. It was very kind of you both to come today. Jem is tired now but Miss Brackwood's visit has done him the world of good. He thinks a great deal of her, my lord. He says she has a way of winning people's hearts.'

'Yes.' Conham watched Rosina taking her leave of Mr Paxby. 'She has a very rare gift for that.'

Not long after, they were in the travelling chariot and bowling back along the Bath Road. It was clear to Conham that Rosina was labouring under strong emotions and it took little prompting for her to tell him all that Mr Paxby had relayed to her.

'My brother has always been a hothead, and to frighten a poor, sick old man almost out of his wits was unforgiveable!' she said, when she had come to the end of her tale.

'And to mention destroying a will was downright foolish,' added Conham. 'It smacks of a guilty conscience.'

'Yes, I thought that,' said Rosina, frowning. 'But there is no denying that my brother often speaks without thinking.'

'You were not present when your father's friends called to see him?'

'No. Papa was too ill to travel to his sister's funeral but he was very anxious someone should represent him.' She hesitated. 'I know that might seem a little unusual...'

His lips twitched. 'But you are a most unusual lady, Rosina.' He noted the gleam in her eye. It was a moment of shared amusement, something to be cherished. He said lightly, 'But tell me, why did your brother not go?'

'Papa asked him, but Edgar had come home on a repairing lease and claimed he needed complete rest.'

He did not miss the scathing note in her voice.

She went on, 'However, he promised to look after Papa while I was away. When I got back, I discovered he had spent most of his time gambling and...and worse, at the local inns. Thankfully, my father had Paxby to look after him.'

'The important thing now is to ascertain if there is, or was, a new will,' said Conham. 'First, we will need to find your father's friends.'

'Mr Paxby did not know them, although he did say that one of them had been Papa's groomsman,' she replied, frowning a little. 'If so, that would be his great friend James MacDowell. Papa sometimes talked of him. He was a professor at Edinburgh, I believe.' A sudden smile smoothed the crease from her brow. 'I shall write to the university, and hopefully they will forward my letter on to him.'

The earl was crossing the hall the next day when he saw Rosina adding a letter to the notes already on the silver tray, ready to be taken to the post later that day.

'It is written, then?'

'Yes.' She did not pretend to misunderstand him. 'I must now resign myself to waiting for a reply.'

'If your father did write a new will, what would you expect it to contain?' he asked, following her into her office.

'Brackwood and its Home Farm are barely viable. The income is certainly not sufficient to pay for my brother's extravagant lifestyle without rents from the land and property that Papa purchased during his lifetime. My father never openly criticised Edgar, but he knew he was very wild and I think he may have put in place measures to stop my brother selling off the unentailed part of his inheritance, at least until Edgar is older and more settled.'

'As my godfather did with my inheritance.'

She sighed. 'Yes, but you were never profligate.'

'You think it will not answer?'

'One can only hope it does.'

'Brackwood means a lot to you, doesn't it?'

'Until a year ago, it was my whole life.'

'Rosina, I wish there was something I could say, or do—'

She put up a hand to cut him off. 'Thank you, but at present we do not know if my father *did* write another will.'

'But it seems very likely, given your brother's visit to the old valet.'

'Yes. Perhaps it is mere wishful thinking on my part. Mr Paxby may have misunderstood Papa.'

'Perhaps.'

Rosina was relieved he did not try to comfort her with platitudes. She fell silent, thinking wistfully of Brackwood and all she had lost.

'There is nothing to be done until I receive a reply,' she said at last. 'And that cannot be for some time, if ever. Thankfully, I have plenty here to occupy me.'

He did not respond to her attempt at a smile.

'I must leave for London at the end of the week,' he said. 'You will write to me, if you please. If—no, *when* you receive a reply.'

'As you wish, my lord.'

She saw him frown at the formality of her response but he made no comment, merely going out and leaving her to her thoughts.

Rosina did not have time to indulge long in idle speculation. There was plenty to be done at Morton Gifford and also at Bellemonte, where Matthew was continuing with improvements to the gardens. He had written to say he had secured more investors, which meant work could begin to turn the derelict house into an hotel.

She saw Conham only once more before his departure, when he returned the ledgers she had left with him for inspection.

'Your record-keeping is excellent, as always, and needs no clarification,' he told her, putting the books down on her desk. 'I leave tomorrow, at first light. You can write to me at the town house with any matters that require attention, I believe I shall be in residence for some time.' At the door he stopped. 'The countess expects me to remain in London for the rest of the season.'

Rosina knew he meant *The countess expects me to propose to Miss Skelton*, and could only reply with a little nod.

'Very well. I doubt we will meet again before I leave. Do not forget to inform me when you receive a response to your letter!'

And with that sharp reminder, he departed.

Davy was proving his worth at Morton Gifford, but Rosina remained as busy as ever. She was thankful for the occupation to pass each of the long days as June progressed. Yet, no matter how full her days, she still found time to scour the society pages of the London newspaper, looking for a notice of the earl's betrothal.

It was on Midsummer's Day that she returned to her office to find a letter from Edinburgh on her desk. She quickly broke the seal and spread the pages, but she had to sit down and read them twice more before the words actually sank in.

After expressing his condolences for her father's untimely death, Professor MacDowell confirmed that he and his friend had called upon Sir Thomas:

> *We declined his invitation to remain the night, not wishing to put him to the inconvenience at such short notice. However, we did stay to dinner, and it was after we had dined that Sir Thomas asked us to witness his new will, although neither of us more than glanced at its contents. They did not concern us. After all, we were merely obliging and old friend.*
>
> *When it was done, I recall that Sir Thomas placed the document inside a packet that he had addressed to his attorney and he added it to the rest of his correspondence, ready for his servant to deliver or to post for him the following day.*
>
> *I also remember that your dear father was quite insistent that we should sign a second copy that he had prepared and when we took our leave later that night, to return to our hotel, I distinctly recall that the copy was lying on the desk.*

Rosina read that line twice, then sat back and closed her eyes. Her thudding heartbeat began to slow. She still had no idea what was in the new will, but it seemed clear to her that the will, and its copy, had disappeared during the night.

For a long time, she remained in her chair with only the quiet chiming of the clock in the hall breaking the silence in the study. She did not weep, there was no point in that. Instead, she tried to consider what must be done.

Professor MacDowell had informed her he had written to a Mr Palmer, the second witness, but he thought the man had gone abroad and he could not be sure his letter would reach him. Even if Professor MacDowell and his friend could be summoned and provide statements, if neither of them knew the contents of the will, what good would it do? No good at all, was her conclusion. There was no one to share her disappointment and only one person with any interest at all in knowing what she had learned.

Sitting up, she pulled a clean sheet of paper from the drawer and began a letter to Lord Dallamire.

Chapter Twenty

'I hope you have not forgotten it is Lady Skelton's soirée tonight, Dallamire. You are escorting me.'

'I have not forgotten, ma'am.' Conham did not look up, but he knew the countess would be fixing him with a gimlet stare across the breakfast table. 'I have business in the city today but I shall be back in time to dine with you beforehand.'

'Make sure you are,' she told him. 'Lady Skelton said most particularly that she expects to see you there tonight.'

'I shall not disappoint her.'

The countess let out an exasperated huff. 'Really, Dallamire, you might at least show a little more enthusiasm! How can you be so tiresome, when we are all going to such lengths for your benefit?'

He looked up then, his brows raised.

'When you are going to such lengths to sell me to the highest bidder. Do you expect me to be grateful for that?'

'Yes, I do,' she told him. 'It is your duty to marry well. And if you will not think of yourself, consider your half-sisters.'

'I would remind you, madam, that my father did not leave them penniless. They have at least another two years in the schoolroom, and there is money held in trust for them.'

She scoffed. 'Barely enough for their dowries! And who is to pay for their presentation, pray?'

'*You* might do so easily, with a little economy!'

His sharp retort had the countess sitting up in her chair, nostrils flaring and eyes darting fire.

'How can you say such a cruel thing, Dallamire, would you have me live as a pauper?' She began to hunt for her handkerchief. 'W-would you have me d-disgrace the sainted name of your dear father?'

Conham held on to his temper, knowing this little display of sensibility would turn into full-blown hysteria if he challenged her.

'Of course not. Be assured, I intend to do my duty.'

'But *when*, sir? You must marry, and soon. Heaven knows I have done my best since you came home. I have presented any number of young ladies to you. All of them pretty and amiable.'

'And boring!'

'Nonsense. They may be biddable, but at least they all have impeccable lineage. Unlike that female you were making up to in the West Country.'

Conham tensed.

'And what *female* might that be?' he asked with dangerous calm.

'The widow you followed to Bristol. Mrs Fawkes, or Fowles, or something...'

He relaxed. 'You mean Mrs Faulds.'

'Yes, that was it. Very flighty piece. My heart sank when I heard your name was being linked with hers. Your father would not rest in his grave if you had brought her home as your countess!'

'But she was rich enough to refill the Dallamire coffers.' Conham felt a slight lightening of his mood; he had not thought of Alicia for months now. 'Would you have objected if I had used Mrs Faulds's money to pay off the debts my father left?'

The countess eyed him resentfully, but after holding her gaze for a moment he laughed.

'You should thank your stars then, dear Stepmama. She would not have me!' He pushed back his chair. 'Now, if you will excuse me, I have papers to go through before I leave the house. But pray, rest easy, madam. When it is time for my half-sisters to be presented, I will make sure it is done properly.'

'And you will come with me to the soirée? I have your word?'

'You have my word, ma'am.'

Conham went out, resisting the urge to run a finger around his collar. It might as well be a noose that was tied about his neck, not the finest muslin.

He could not blame the countess for trying to find him a rich wife. She had lived in luxury her whole life and wanted nothing to change. She complained constantly about Dallamire Hall although she refused to leave it, declaring that she would not quit that stately pile until he brought home a wife. He felt a sudden sting of grim humour. The prospect of seeing his stepmother and half-sisters move into the smaller but infinitely more comfortable Dower House upon his marriage was by far the most pleasant thought that had come to him all morning!

Conham went into his study to find his secretary had left a neat pile of papers on his desk. He quickly flicked through them. Bills, letters from tenants and stewards at his various properties requesting help, polite notes from charitable groups seeking his patronage. So many calls upon his time and his purse.

His thoughts changed abruptly when he picked up the next letter and saw Rosina's neat writing. Walking around the desk, he sat down and broke the seal.

...in conclusion, my lord, with the second witness gone abroad indefinitely, my enquiries regarding a new will have met with no success. If neither the original document nor the copy exists, then to pursue the matter further would only cause distress to everyone involved and be of no material benefit to anyone save, perhaps, the lawyers.

The letter continued with matters of business, a summary of the accounts for Quarter Day, questions about proposed new farming methods and a report on the efficacy of the new drains and ditches during the recent heavy rains.

He read to the end then lowered the paper and sat back in

his chair. Poor Rosina, she had been hoping that somehow, her father might have found a way to protect Brackwood from the ravages of his irresponsible son. Conham could admit now that he had been hoping for something more. In some wild, fantastical and quite illogical way, he had hoped Sir Thomas might have done something to protect his daughter, too. Increased the amount he had settled upon her. Sufficient, perhaps, for her to marry an impoverished earl...

With an oath Conham threw the letter aside. How shameful, how *contemptible*, to think of himself in all this. Rosina loved Brackwood. Even if she had inherited everything, she would not want to sell her old home in order to restore his crumbling house.

For now, she had no option but to continue as land steward at Morton Gifford. It was possible that in a year or two Bellemonte might be profitable enough to provide her with a comfortable income. Or it was not inconceivable that she might receive an offer of marriage. After all, she was highly respected in Morton Gifford.

That idea did not find favour with him but he could not deny it was a possibility, if she met someone she loved enough to give up her independence. He released a sigh, long and heartfelt.

'If only I was free! If only—'

Conham shook his head, determined not to think of what might have been. He picked up Rosina's letter again. There were estate matters here that needed a reply and he would dictate something to his secretary before going off to the city. Then he must put all thoughts of Rosina Brackwood from his mind and fulfil his destiny.

He must propose to Amelia Skelton.

Conham rubbed one hand across his eyes. The windows of Lady Skelton's drawing room had been thrown open but the night was sultry and with the candles adding to the heat, it was uncomfortably warm.

'It is gone eleven, Dallamire,' said the countess, coming up to him. 'Lady Skelton has sent Amelia off to the morning room.

She will be quite alone there.' When he did not speak, her fingers tightened on his sleeve. 'She is expecting you, my lord.'

The message could not have been clearer. With a little nod he walked off and went down the stairs to the morning room. There was nothing else to be done. Amelia Skelton had indicated she was happy to receive an offer and both families approved the match. All he had to do was make that offer. Just a few simple words and everyone would be happy. Miss Skelton would be a countess and he would have the means to protect his family home and keep the countess and her daughters in the luxury to which they were accustomed.

And Rosina could remain at Morton Gifford.

'I can do that much for her,' he muttered as he walked the final few steps to the morning room. Even though it would be torture for him to see her there, so near and yet quite, quite unattainable.

His first thought on entering the room was thank goodness it was bright with candlelight and not a soft, romantic glow, but his relief was quickly replaced by the feeling that something was not quite right.

Miss Skelton was standing on the far side of the room. She had her back to him and he had the impression that her shoulders were shaking, although she turned to face him almost as soon as the door opened. He looked at her closely. She was a little pale, but her voice and her countenance were welcoming.

'Lord Dallamire.'

'Miss Skelton.' He closed the door and moved further into the room. 'I am pleased to have this opportunity to speak with you alone.'

'Yes.'

He smiled, hoping to put her at her ease. 'Forgive me, I have not had much practice at this sort of thing.'

She blushed. 'Do go on, my lord.'

Her tone was inviting, a faint smile curved her lips, but he noticed that the knuckles of her clasped fingers were white. It could be maidenly nerves, but something in her demeanour told him it was more than that.

He said quietly, 'Is anything wrong, Miss Skelton?'

Her eyes flew to his face. 'Wrong?' She gave a little laugh. 'Oh, no, no! It is merely…excitement, my lord.'

Conham looked at her then. Really looked. Her pretty face was wreathed in smiles, but it was what he saw in her eyes that gave him pause.

Pure terror.

He had seen it before in the eyes of his soldiers, men as well as boys, when they were facing a cavalry charge, or before going into battle. Then he had been able to do nothing about it. They were at war; his men had no choice but to fight and he had no choice but to lead them. It was his duty.

It is your duty now to go through with this!

The countess's voice rang in his head but he ignored it.

'Amelia, we don't have to do this, you know.'

'Oh, but we do! Mama has set her heart on it.'

'But what of *your* heart?'

Her face crumpled. Taking her hands, Conham led her over to a chair and she sank quickly onto it, as if her legs would no longer support her. He pulled up another chair, close enough to talk, but not to intimidate. He regarded her bowed head.

'Why is Lady Skelton so set on this marriage?' he asked her.

'Because you are an earl. She says it was always Papa's dearest wish that I should marry well. And there are no dukes or marquesses available this season.'

His mouth twisted in disdain at her final remark, and he could only be thankful that she was hunting for her handkerchief and did not see it.

'I beg your pardon,' she said. 'That must sound terribly unfeeling, when you are being so kind to me.'

'Let us be clear, your mother and my stepmother hatched a plot to marry us off.'

'Yes. Mama made me promise I would accept you. And…' She took a deep breath. 'And I thought I could. Only, this evening, when she told me to come down here and, and *wait*, I knew…' She blew her nose and gave a shuddering sigh. 'Oh, dear. There is going to be such a fuss when she discovers I have refused you. She will accuse me of breaking my word!'

'We shall not give her the opportunity to do that. You cannot accept my offer until I have made it, can you?' He pushed himself out of the chair. 'I think the best thing is for me to go away now.'

'But she will know we have been talking!'

'Not necessarily. Leave it to me.' For the first time that day he felt like grinning and he did so. 'I hope that when Lady Skelton comes in, she will have nothing but sympathy for you. All the opprobrium will be heaped upon my head, and you will be the hapless victim.'

She jumped up, relief lighting her countenance.

'Oh, thank you, my lord! That is… I hope I haven't offended you?'

'Offended, no,' he said with perfect truth. His next words, however, were not nearly as sincere. 'I am disappointed, naturally, but that will pass.'

She went with him to the door but before he opened it, he stopped.

'Tell me, is there anyone else?'

Another blush touched her cheek, but this time it was accompanied by a soft glow in her eyes.

'There *is* a young man. William. He is a neighbour of ours, and we have known each other forever! But he is only a baronet, and not nearly lofty enough for Mama.'

'But you and he would like to marry?'

She nodded. 'Very much, only, he understands that Mama has such plans for me.'

'How old are you now, Amelia?'

'I shall be one-and-twenty in October. Mama would have brought me to town last season, only we were still in mourning for Papa.'

'Then let me give you some advice,' he said. 'In a few months you will be able to marry whomsoever you choose. In the meantime, you must make it clear to your mama that you do not wish to receive any more offers of marriage. You only have to be firm; she cannot force you. Can you do that?'

She nodded. 'I think I can now, my lord. After all, there are only viscounts and barons left to choose from.'

A shy twinkle appeared in her eye, and Conham had a glimpse of the charming young lady Amelia could be, when she was not being browbeaten out of her wits.

'Indeed! I am sorry if things are a little uncomfortable for a few weeks. Lady Skelton might even think it expedient to take you home.'

'Oh, I should very much like that,' she exclaimed, clasping her hands together, but this time in happiness.

Conham smiled. 'Remember that none of this is your fault. I am the one who did not come up to scratch.'

With that, he slipped out of the morning room and across the hall, which was empty save for the footman dozing by the street door. Previous visits to the house had shown him there was a small library on the far side. It was in darkness, but taking a candlestick from the hall he soon remedied that.

He needed to marshal his thoughts. Relief was uppermost. He had not realised how repugnant the idea of a loveless marriage was to him until this evening, and if Amelia Skelton had not shied at the last fence, they would even now be announcing their betrothal.

'Never again,' he muttered. 'There must be another way.'

Conham began to pace the room. He felt that he had been given another chance and he must take it. There must be some way to raise funds without selling himself to the highest bidder. He thought of Matt, throwing himself into restoring Bellemonte, and Rosina, who had already made a difference at Morton Gifford. The land was in much better heart and showing a return for all the changes she had made.

He stopped, saying aloud, 'If they can do it, why can't I?'

He set off again, a plan forming in his head. There were one or two properties he might sell. The town house, for example. It would fetch a handsome price and he could hire a residence if he wished to spend any time in London.

Conham heard the unmistakable sound of his stepmother's voice coming from the hall. No time to think any more about that now. He made his way towards the door, grabbing a book from one of the shelves as he passed and was in time to see the countess and Lady Skelton coming down the stairs, on their way to the morning room to congratulate the happy couple.

Opening the book, he strolled across the hall, pretending to be engrossed in the text. It took a moment for them to notice his presence.

'Dallamire! What on earth are you doing?'

The countess's voice floated down to him.

He looked up. 'Reading, ma'am. I have discovered the most fascinating book in the library. *The Principles of Morals and Legislation.*' Horror and confusion were writ large upon the ladies' faces and he smiled. 'I had not come across Jeremy Bentham's work before. Most enlightening.'

'But why are you not in the morning room?' demanded Lady Skelton, hurrying down the last few stairs.

'I was, er, distracted, ma'am.'

'Distracted, *by a book*?' She stared at him then looked at the countess. 'But it was all agreed, all arranged!'

His smile did not waver, but his voice contained an implacable note that he had seldom used since leaving the army.

'Yes, it was agreed between you and the countess, madam, *not* by me. In the end I thought better of it.'

'Conham!' Lady Dallamire shut her fan with a snap. 'You do not mean you have left that poor gel in there, waiting?'

'I fear I may have done so, ma'am.'

A frosty silence ensued. Lady Skelton flushed angrily, while the countess went by turns red and white as her emotions moved between anger and chagrin.

She drew herself up and declared in arctic accents, 'I think it is time we left, Dallamire.'

He bowed. 'I think so, too, ma'am.'

They took their leave of their hostess, who was clearly beyond anything other than a stiff nod of dismissal. Lady Dallamire waited in silence for her cloak to be fetched but once they had climbed into the carriage, she did not hold back.

She expressed herself fluently and at length, pouring scorn upon her stepson's ingratitude. Conham listened in silence while she talked herself almost to a stand, but when, after a few gusty sighs, she drew out her handkerchief and asked him in tearful accents just what he had been thinking of, he replied quite calmly.

'I discovered I did not like having my hand forced, ma'am.'

'But that poor girl. It was all decided!'

'Only between you and her mother. If Lady Skelton has been spreading it about, boasting of the impending match, then the best thing she can do is to take her daughter home until the matter is forgotten.'

'Yes, I have no doubt that is what she will do,' muttered the countess, dragging her handkerchief angrily between her fingers. 'And we must leave town, too. I will not remain here and have people laughing up their sleeves at me. And they will be, sir! Lady Skelton is not one to keep quiet about a thing like this. She will take great delight in telling all and sundry that you as good as jilted her poor daughter. And how, then, am I to arrange an advantageous match for you?'

'I do not want you to arrange any match for me.'

She sat up quickly. 'But you have to marry! How else are we to solve our predicament?'

'I do not believe our *predicament* as you call it, is as bad as all that. If we were to draw in the purse strings a little.'

'No, no, it is not to be borne!' The countess resorted to tears again. 'The shame of it, to be reduced to penury, at my age!'

'We are a long way from penury, madam!'

But she was beyond reason and continued to weep and bemoan the cruelty of Fate for the remainder of the journey. Only when they had reached their own entrance hall and Conham agreed to her pleas not to rush into any decisions did she manage to calm herself sufficiently to be delivered into the hands of her maid and helped up to her bedchamber.

Conham ordered brandy to be brought to him in the library and walked off. One problem had been resolved tonight, and although he disliked the thought of the talk and condemnation that would follow, in his eyes it was no worse than the gossip and sly remarks that would have arisen if he had married Amelia purely for her money.

He sat down and closed his eyes. He would far rather face the French cavalry than the tears and tantrums of his stepmother, or her constant reminders of how he had failed his father, but tonight there had been no other way to deal with a difficult situation.

Amelia Skelton was free to find happiness with her baronet and, although he dare not put too much store by it just yet, if the ideas now whirling about in his head were practicable, then he, too, might find a way to achieve his dreams.

As summer wore on, Rosina tried to occupy herself with the estate. She looked eagerly through the post each day, hoping for a reply from Conham. Her disappointment at the disappearance of her father's new will went much deeper than she had expected, and with no one but the earl to confide in, she was desperate to hear from him, to read a line or two of sympathy.

When at last a letter did arrive from London, her hopes were dashed the moment she saw that it was not the earl's bold handwriting but that of his secretary, and dealt only with matters pertaining to the estate.

For a while, she continued to hope that perhaps Conham would write to her privately, but when after a week no letter arrived, she knew it was time to put aside her foolish daydreams. The earl was too busy with his own affairs to spare any more time on hers.

Thankfully, there was plenty to keep Rosina busy into the autumn months. She decided to reinstate the harvest supper that Hugo Conham had always held for his neighbours and tenants, which proved to be a great success. Everyone lamented the fact that Lord Dallamire could not be present although Rosina had explained that the earl was exceedingly busy.

She had written to Conham, telling him of her plans, and was unsurprised to learn he would not be attending. However, he had written this letter himself; it was very brief but it ended with the words *warmest regards*, which gave her some comfort and she had folded it away for safekeeping.

A few weeks later, she added to it a letter that arrived from Mr Shipton, informing her that Lady Brackwood had given birth to a boy and that mother and baby were doing well.

Chapter Twenty-One

'Well, Conham, what do you think of Bellemonte now?' Matt Talacre handed his guest a glass of brandy. 'It must be, what, five months since you were last in Gloucester.'

'Yes.'

A full five months since Conham had seen Rosina, but she was never far from his thoughts. He had thrown himself into repairing his family fortunes, but even though it filled his days, Rosina was like a phantom, constantly at his shoulder. Sometimes he felt her presence so powerfully he thought if he turned his head she would be there, standing beside him.

He said, 'You are quite right, Matt. I haven't been here since May.'

Dinner was finished and they were sitting before the fire in Matt's rooms on the first floor of what had been the derelict house on Bellemonte Square.

'You have made great strides,' Conham remarked. 'Your plans for the hotel appear to be going very well.'

'Thank you. Only this wing is habitable at present, but I am glad to have my own apartment here now. I have good people working for me but I like to be on hand to look after the gardens and the baths. I like to help with the building work, too, where I can.'

Conham raised his glass in salute. 'Your efforts do you credit, my friend.'

They had spent the short November day touring Bellemonte and he was impressed by the improvement. Despite the wintry weather the pleasure baths were busier than ever under Matt's management. More walks had been opened through the gardens and there were new, rose-covered arbours designed for romantic trysts. The Pavilion was proving popular for its winter concerts and balls, as well as with patrons wanting to dine or sup there in the evenings.

'It is not only my efforts,' said Matt, pouring them both more brandy. 'Rosina has supported me throughout. She has an excellent grasp of business.'

'Has she now?' Conham interrupted him without thinking, then had to look away from his friend's knowing grin. 'I hope she has not been neglecting her own duties.'

'Of course she hasn't, you dolt,' retorted Matt with his customary lack of respect for his friend's rank. 'She has been far too busy looking after your interests at Morton Gifford to spare me more than a few hours, but her advice is always sound. She is a very intelligent lady.'

'I know it,' growled Conham.

Matthew laughed. 'You can take that frown from your face, Conham. Rest easy, I have no interest in Rosina, other than as a good friend.' He hesitated. 'Did she tell you her brother has had a son?'

'I had heard.' Conham was not going to admit, even to his best friend, that he scoured every letter from Rosina, reading it at least twice, even though he rarely penned a reply himself. He had resolved to keep their correspondence formal, businesslike, afraid that if he picked up the pen, he would not put it down until he had poured his heart out to her.

'Aye,' Matt went on. 'When Rosina and I last met she told me she hopes having an heir might be the making of Brackwood. Personally, I doubt it. From what she has told me, that brother of hers is bad, through and through. She is far better off making a life for herself, away from him.'

'My thoughts exactly.' Conham nodded, but he was not yet

ready to explain himself. He said instead, 'But enough of that, we were talking about Bellemonte.'

As he suspected, Matt was only too pleased to expound upon his plans.

'Yes, I was saying, Rosina has been very helpful, as have you, Conham! The patronage of the Earl of Dallamire has worked like a charm with prospective investors! I have secured funding to continue with the improvements next year, too. As we thought, those living or visiting Clifton Village and Hotwells are hungry for more entertainment. And I mean to extend the stables. I will need more room when the hotel opens, for those using their own cattle.'

Conham smiled. 'You have it all planned out.'

'I have indeed, but everything is costed, I do not mean to outrun my funds. I have worked out all the figures and I am confident the gardens will be making a small profit by Lady Day. And if things continue to go well for the next twelve months,' he added, with a grin, 'you will be able to increase my rent.'

'Not many tenants would admit to that!'

'No, but I know retaining Bellemonte was not your original plan, and with Dallamire in dire straits...'

'Actually,' said Conham, staring down at the golden liquid in his glass, 'things are not so dire as I first thought. Selling the town house and two of the hunting lodges in the north has allowed me to clear the remainder of my father's debts, and I have spent the past few months going over all the accounts with my man of business and we have negotiated better terms on a new loan. Not a fortune, but it will help. I now have a full programme of repairs for Dallamire Hall. It will take some time to complete, of course, but that was always going to be the case.'

'And what does the countess say to it all?'

'The ongoing building work has...er...persuaded her to remove with my half-sisters to the Dower House. With the countess now running and paying for her own household, matters have improved a great deal. I have promised her I will fund the girls' come-out, and I am already making provision for that. I have assured her I shall be able to do my duty by my half-sisters.'

'So, you have no need to marry an heiress.'

'No.' Conham was unable to hide his smile any longer. 'An heiress is no longer necessary.'

Matthew laughed. 'I know a lady who will be delighted to hear you say that, my friend!'

Conham felt the heat rising in his cheeks. 'Oh, I hope so, Matthew. I do hope so.'

The short November day was coming to an end as Rosina made her way back to the Manor. An icy wind was buffeting her and she was glad she had her mannish greatcoat to wear over her riding habit. She had ordered it from the village tailor and it was far more practical than a cloak, although even with the collar turned up and her wide-brimmed hat pulled low, the icy wind still managed to sneak in and sting her cheeks.

A storm was brewing, the heavy clouds threatened rain, or even snow, and she wanted to get back to the Manor before the weather broke. Bramble needed little urging to keep up a good pace. She was eager to return to her warm stall, and Rosina was happy to let the mare pick her way over the ground while she turned her own thoughts to a problem that had been nagging her all day.

She had seen nothing of Conham since May, when he had come to Gloucester for the reopening of Bellemonte Gardens, and she had no news of him, except that he had quit London in the summer and returned to Dallamire. Whether or not he had proposed to Miss Skelton she had no idea. Matthew had not said anything about it, when she had seen him at Bellemonte.

Neither had she seen any announcements concerning the Earl of Dallamire in the newspaper, although that was not surprising. Throughout the summer the news had been all about the crowds flocking to see Lord Elgin's Parthenon marbles, the opening of Waterloo Bridge and the introduction of the Sovereign coin, as well as speculation over Princess Charlotte's forthcoming confinement, and if the child would be a boy or a girl.

Then, last week, Mrs Jameson had received a note saying that the earl would shortly be returning to Gifford Manor. Four days later he had still not arrived and Rosina could not decide if she was most relieved or disappointed. She feared that this would be exactly like his last visit, when he had arrived so suddenly with Lady Dallamire and the Skeltons.

For the past year Rosina had thrown herself into work, determined not to allow her growing affection for Conham Mortlake to ruin the life she was making for herself. And yet, her pleasure in living at Morton Gifford was diminished. She still valued her independence, enjoyed her work and the estate was thriving under her management, but she was haunted by Conham's presence. There were constant reminders of him everywhere. Memories of discussing estate matters with him in her office or riding out together to visit tenants, the hours flying by, even though she could not remember what they found to talk about.

And every time she walked back to the lodge, she remembered him accompanying her to the door, remembered him kissing her.

Nothing could come of it. Conham must marry well, and Rosina was prepared for that. She was committed to remaining at Morton Gifford until Lady Day, but then she would leave. She could not expect to find another position as a land agent, but by March she would have saved enough of her generous salary to augment her own meagre inheritance and keep her for a few months, until she could find somewhere to live and some sort of employment. Perhaps she might open a school, or take in girl boarders.

'Or my investment in Bellemonte will come good,' she said aloud, determined to be cheerful, 'Who knows? The profits might soar and overnight I shall become a woman of independent means!'

It was a nonsensical idea but it made her smile, despite the icy weather and the lowering thoughts that threatened to depress her.

When she reached the stable yard, Fred Skillet came hurrying over.

'Here, let me take 'er for you, Miss Brackwood!'

'Thank you, Fred.'

Rosina handed Bramble's reins to the elderly stable hand and jumped down.

'No sign of His Lordship yet,' he remarked.

It was an answer to the question uppermost in Rosina's mind, but one she had been determined not to ask. She nodded to the old man, murmured another word of thanks and set off towards the Manor.

It was of no consequence to her at all when His Lordship should arrive, she told herself, not quite truthfully. Everything was in order. She was confident he would find nothing wanting in her accounting or the records she kept of estate business. She was his land steward and would meet him as such. His absence over the past months had made it quite clear that he required nothing more from her.

Sadly, her defiant thoughts could not dispel the gloom that descended over her spirits. A gloom that was never very far away these days. Martha Jones had become a regular correspondent, and while the news that Mr Paxby was recovered from his fall was cheering, everything else she wrote about Brackwood was not. Edgar was gambling heavily and had put much of the unentailed land up for sale. Much as Rosina told herself Brackwood was no longer her concern, she could not help feeling depressed at the thought of what was happening to her old home.

The butler was crossing the hall when Rosina entered, and he turned and came over to her.

'Miss Brackwood, you are back, and not a minute too soon, by the looks of it,' he said, taking her greatcoat from her.

'Thank you, Jameson. Yes, it is sleeting out there now and the wind is getting up. Is Mr Redmond still here?'

'No, ma'am, but he has only just left, so there is a good fire burning in your office and it won't take me a moment to relight the candles for you.'

'No need, thank you, I can do that.'

The old retainer wasn't fooled by her smile, which she had had to dig deep to find.

'Then perhaps you'd like Mrs Jameson to prepare some coffee for you, to warm you up?' he suggested.

His kindly look cheered her, and the smile became a little less forced.

She said, 'That would be very welcome, thank you.'

By the time the housekeeper arrived with the coffee, Rosina was putting the last of the ledgers away in the large bookcase.

'Thank you, Mrs Jameson, although I really should not have bothered you. Apart from a few letters that have arrived for me, Mr Redmond has left me with nothing to do today.'

The housekeeper chuckled as she put the tray down on the desk.

'Then you can sit by the fire and enjoy your coffee before you read your letters. You certainly don't want to be traipsing back to the lodge until this shower has passed. And the squire has sent over his London news sheet for you,' she said, taking the paper from under her arm and placing it next to the tray.

'How kind of Sir John. And it is kind of you, too, to bring me the coffee. I am very grateful.'

'Nonsense, it's the least we can do, when you are out and about in all weathers.'

When the housekeeper had left the room Rosina went over to the desk and picked up the newspaper. It was a little creased from having been through several hands, and she noticed that it was folded at one of the inner pages. The headline jumped out at her—*The Demise of Her Royal Highness, the Princess Charlotte*.

Forgetting her coffee and the wind howling around the house, Rosina turned towards the lighted candelabra and read the report of the princess's death, only days after giving birth to her stillborn son. The shock of this double tragedy brought on a wave of sadness that broke through the control Rosina had kept over her own feelings for so long. She put down the paper, leaned against the edge of the desk and let her tears fall unchecked.

Conham had hoped to reach Morton Gifford by early afternoon, but one of the glossy matched bays pulling his curricle cast a shoe and it was dark by the time he eventually reached the Manor. Gusts of wind were blowing sheets of sleety rain across the drive as he ran into the house. A footman was on hand to take his hat, gloves and greatcoat and he paused only to confirm that Miss Brackwood was in the house before hurrying to her office.

He opened the door, an apology for appearing in all his dirt already on his lips, but the sight of Rosina weeping unrestrainedly put to flight everything except the need to comfort her. He crossed the space between them in two strides.

'What is it? Rosina, what's wrong?'

With a sob she threw herself into his arms. He held her close, resting his cheek on her golden hair and murmuring soft words, but they were lost against the noise of the storm raging outside.

At last, her tears were spent and she muttered into his shoulder.

'I b-beg your pardon. I am not usually so lachrymose! You took me by surprise.'

'Thank goodness it was me, then, and not a stranger!' She gave a watery chuckle and he kissed her hair. 'Tell me who or what has upset you so?'

She pushed against him and he released her immediately.

'So silly of me,' she mumbled, searching for her handkerchief. 'It was the news, about P-Princess Charlotte. Heartbreaking, so soon after losing her baby.'

He frowned. 'I do not believe that is all, Rosina. You are not one to cry so easily. Tell me what has happened to upset you.'

'N-nothing!'

She jumped as the wind hurled rain against the window in a sharp tattoo and he reached out for her again, but she held him off.

'You can—you *should* go. Now. I am p-perfectly well.'

'Little liar.'

'Please, Conham, leave me.'

She ended on a sob, but her dainty hands were clutching at his coat and she did not resist when he put his arms around her.

'Look at me, Rosina.' He put his finger under her chin. 'Look up and tell me you want me to go.'

There was a momentary lull in the storm and his words

fell into the sudden silence. The air in the room was stifling, charged with tension, and Conham's heart pounded like a hammer against his ribs. Slowly, she raised her head and looked at him. Her eyes were bright with tears, but in their blue depths he saw a hunger and such fierce desire, that it took his breath away. His arms tightened and he lowered his head, capturing her mouth for a kiss that expressed all the months of pent-up longing.

Rosina responded eagerly, slipping her arms around his neck, her lips moving instinctively against his, and she pressed her body against him with an eagerness that shocked her, as did the hunger that consumed her. Every nerve within her was crying out for more.

He sighed, murmuring her name over and over as he planted butterfly kisses on her eyes, her jaw, and moved down to touch his lips to the erratic pulse in her neck.

'I have wanted this for so long,' she whispered, clinging to him. 'I have wanted *you*, Conham!'

His heart swelled at her soft words. He swept her up into his arms and when she laid her head against his shoulder and gazed up at him, smiling, a jolt of pure lust shot through his body.

'Oh, confound it, Rosina,' he muttered, his voice ragged, unsteady. 'I have never wanted anyone, anything, as much as I want you!'

'Then show me,' she whispered, her eyes glowing like sapphires. 'Take me to bed.'

Conham's heart soared. Holding his precious bundle he turned towards the door.

'Conham, the servants!' She clutched at his collar. 'We must be discreet.'

'Discretion be damned,' he said savagely, 'I am bedding my future wife and I don't care who knows of it!'

Rosina awoke slowly from a deep sleep. The storm had passed but it was still dark and very quiet. She took a moment to consider how she felt. Content. Happier than she had been for a very long time.

Everything came flooding back. Conham carrying her up to his room—quite fortuitously meeting no one on the way—the frantic kisses and caresses that accompanied their undressing and the delight of exploring each other's bodies.

Desire was pooling again, low inside her, as she remembered all they had done. The intimate caresses that sent her body out of control, the joyful ecstasy of their coupling, first on the woollen rug before the fire and later between the cool sheets of Conham's bed, where he had touched her as no one had ever done before, bringing her alive, awakening thoughts, feelings so new, so exciting, that she ached for more.

She dismissed his declared intention to marry her as the heat of the moment. Once he remembered his duty to his name, to his family, he would realise how impossible that was. Even if he did marry her, how long would it be before his conscience began to eat away at their happiness? She folded her arms across her breasts, as if trying to protect herself from the unpleasant truth. Everything was different, but nothing had changed between them. He still needed a fortune, which she could not give him. She knew him too well to believe he would be happy if he could not fulfil his duty to his family.

Conham was sleeping beside her and, seeking comfort, she turned towards him. She pressed herself against his naked body and closed her eyes. She was familiar with the hints of cedarwood and spicy cologne that clung to his linen, but now she breathed in the very male, musky scent of the man himself.

When he stirred and reached for her, she cupped his face in her hands and kissed him. As their kisses grew ever more urgent, she let her hands explore him, desire mounting as she smoothed her fingers over the muscled contours. Then she followed his lead, running her lips over his skin, exulting in her power to make him moan with pleasure at her touch even as he continued to caress her until they were both beyond thought and came together for a final joyous union.

Afterwards, Rosina lay in his arms, sated, replete, while silent tears spilled over her cheeks. The future could not be theirs, but she would carry the memories of this night with her forever.

* * *

As the first rosy fingers of dawn crept into the sky, Rosina slipped out of Conham's bed.

'Where are you going, my love?'

'Back to the lodge, before anyone sees me.'

'That no longer matters. We will soon be married.'

She pretended not to hear that and continued putting on her clothes. She walked over to the long glass and studied her reflection as she fastened her riding habit. Her clothes looked neat enough, but there was little she could do about her hair, save to use what few pins she could find to put it up in a knot.

'You are really going?'

Conham's deep voice came from the shadows of the bed and she went over to him.

'Yes, I am really going.' She kissed him briefly. 'Now, go back to sleep.'

He sat up and caught her hand. 'But you will marry me?'

'I must go back to the lodge and make myself respectable. Then I will come back to my office and we can talk.' She squeezed his fingers and slipped quietly out of the room.

Conham lay back against the pillows, his hands behind his head. Last night had not gone as he had expected. He had wanted to explain to Rosina about the changes he was making and his plans for the future. For *their* future. It would be slow work and hard, too, rebuilding Dallamire and reviving the estates from their previously dire position, but he did not think she would mind that. With Rosina at his side, working with him, he knew they would succeed.

Finding her in tears had thrown his thoughts into disarray. He had taken her in his arms, all his carefully worded speeches replaced by the overwhelming need to comfort her. A smile began to grow inside him. Comfort had soon given way to desire, for both of them. He had read it in her eyes, felt it in the way she had returned his kisses. Later, in the bedroom, she had shown a passion equal to his own. It had been a revelation; he had never felt this way about any woman before, the need to cherish her, to protect her and put her happiness before his, in all things.

Beyond the dressing room door he could hear Dawkins moving about. There had been no sign of his estimable valet when he had carried Rosina into the room last night. Did the man know what had happened here? It was likely that he would guess, from the pile of hastily discarded clothes, but it made no difference. The fellow had always been the soul of discretion and when Conham informed him he would be wearing his new coat of blue superfine today, Dawkins would know at once that something out of the ordinary was about to take place.

Conham curbed his impatience and forced himself not to rush through his morning routine before going down to breakfast at the usual hour. Rosina would need time to change and break her own fast before she returned to the Manor. He would go to her office and casually invite her to join him in the morning room. There they would talk, uninterrupted. With her excellent grasp of such matters, she would understand that he had little to offer her, apart from his heart and a great deal of hard work, at least for a few years. He only hoped she would think it was enough.

By ten o'clock Conham could wait no longer. He made his way to the land steward's office and was surprised to find Davy Redmond there alone. The young man jumped up as he came in and Conham waved him back to his seat.

'Is Miss Brackwood not arrived yet?'

'She has been and gone, my lord.'

'Gone?' Conham's brows snapped together.

'Yes, my lord. She left this for you.'

Conham almost snatched the papers Davy held out to him and walked across to the window. There were two sheets, pinned in one corner. The second was folded up beneath Rosina's message, which was brief and to the point.

My lord...

So formal!

I have gone to Brackwood to search for my father's will. The attached arrived yesterday from Mr Palmer, the sec-

*ond witness. He has only recently returned to England
and learned of my enquiries from Professor MacDowell.*

*I should not be gone more than a few days and Davy
knows what needs to be done while I am away.*

I have taken your travelling chariot. Forgive me.

R

Stifling a curse, he read the letter she had pinned to her note.
Then he turned to Davy.

'When did she leave?'

'I—I am not sure, my lord.' The young man stuttered, startled by Conham's abrupt tone. 'I arrived here soon after eight
and she was already writing her note for you.'

Conham barely heard the last few words, he was already
heading out the door.

The travelling chariot was comfortably sprung and the seats
thickly padded, but Rosina was in no humour to appreciate its
luxuries, or the passing landscape. She was going over and over
Mr Palmer's letter in her head, and trying to reassure herself
that she was doing the right thing. His reply suggested that Papa
had hidden a copy of the will.

A very reasonable voice inside argued that Edgar would have
searched for it thoroughly, but that did not mean he would have
found it. Edgar had never done anything thoroughly in his life,
except drink to excess. No. Rosina was convinced the will was
still in the house, and she would not rest until she had visited
Brackwood and made her own search.

Her attention was caught by a familiar landmark and she sat
up. They were very close to the Crown, where she had ordered
the driver to stop. She needed to eat something before arriving at
Brackwood Court. Her reception there was unlikely to be cordial.

The chariot came to a halt before the entrance of the posting inn. Rosina collected her reticule from the seat beside her,
but when she looked up there was no liveried footman waiting to help her out. Conham was holding open the door, and
he looked furious.

Chapter Twenty-Two

'Lord Dallamire! What, what a surprise.'

After the slightest hesitation Rosina stepped down from the travelling chariot. Conham's riding dress and the two lathered horses being led away by his groom explained how he had caught up with her so quickly.

'It shouldn't be,' he said grimly.

He held out his arm and one look at his face told her not to ignore it. She placed her fingers on his sleeve and went with him into the inn, where a bowing landlord showed them immediately to a private parlour.

She preceded Conham into the room and spoke almost before the door had closed upon them.

'I am very sorry I took the travelling chariot without permission, my lord.'

'Damn the chariot!' he retorted, ripping off his gloves. 'What the devil do you mean by coming here without me?'

She made sure the large dining table was between them before she answered him.

'I did not wish to involve you in this.'

His eyes were the colour of granite this morning, and they glittered dangerously.

'By heaven, madam, I know you value your independence,

but this is the outside of enough! Do you think your brother is going to allow you to search his house? The man has already tried to kill you once.'

Rosina shuddered at his words, but she overcame it.

'That is why I needed your carriage. Edgar is unlikely to harm me if I have your driver and footman in attendance.'

'I would not be so sure of that.'

They glared at each other for a long moment, then Rosina sighed.

'Let us not fight, sir. Mr Palmer's letter was on my desk when I went into the office this morning. It was in the pile of correspondence Davy left for me yesterday.' She blushed, remembering the reason she had not dealt with it last night. 'You had only just arrived at the Manor and I did not want to drag you away again so soon. For what might turn out to be a mare's nest.'

'And did you think I would be happy to learn you had come here alone?' he demanded.

'No, I knew you would not, which is why I set off early. I beg your pardon, I thought you might try to dissuade me.'

Rosina looked at him across the table and saw the genuine concern in his eyes. She walked around to him, putting out her hands.

'I must do this, Conham. I need to know what my father's last wishes were.'

'I can understand that.' He clasped her fingers and looked down at them, his thumbs rubbing gently across the backs of her hands. 'I know this is important to you, but you must allow me to help you.'

'Do I have any choice?'

He met her eyes, the hard look fading. 'No.'

A tiny thread of relief rippled through Rosina.

'I should be glad of your company,' she admitted.

'Good. I shall order refreshments and then we will discuss what you intend to do.'

Within a very short time they were sitting down with a pot of coffee and slices of cake on the table between them.

'You read Mr Palmer's letter?' she asked him.

'Yes.' He drew it from his pocket and looked at it again. 'Palmer quotes your father as saying he would not keep the will in his desk but that he would be *keeping it close*.'

'Yes. Mr Palmer remembered that particularly because it was such an odd thing for my father to say.'

'Do you not think that means he would be keeping it on his person? If so, it was sure to have been found when he died.'

'I did consider that,' replied Rosina. 'However, if that had been the case then Mr Paxby would have known of it. After all, he was with Papa when he was taken ill. He helped undress him and get him to bed for the very last time.' She frowned. 'No, I think Papa secreted it somewhere in the house.'

'But surely, if there was a will, it would have been found by now.'

She raised her chin. 'Not necessarily.'

Conham knew that determined look. It would be useless to argue.

'Do you have a plan?' he asked her.

She nodded. 'Today is market day. When Edgar moved back to Brackwood he formed the habit of drinking at one of the taverns in the afternoon, to throw dice and play cards with anyone who had the money to join him. I doubt if his marriage has changed that. It is in part the reason I was in such haste to come here. I thought I would go to Brackwood Court while Edgar is out and talk with Lady Brackwood. I hoped I might persuade her to let me look over the house.'

'And if your brother is at home?'

'I shall have to think of something else.'

He raised one eyebrow. 'Housebreaking, perhaps?'

A faint flush bloomed on her cheek.

'Perhaps.'

Conham sighed. It was madness, even to contemplate such a thing, but he knew how much this meant to her.

'Very well, let us hope it will not come to that.' He took out his watch. 'Once we have finished here we will make our way to the Court. The market should be over by then and the taverns will be filling up.'

* * *

The sun was dropping towards the horizon when they reached their destination but the sky was clear, and Conham judged that there was a good hour of daylight left. As he jumped down from the carriage he took his first look at Rosina's old home.

Brackwood Court was a large, rambling building, built of local stone. Much of it appeared to be old. Tudor, he thought, looking at the stone-mullioned windows and high chimneys, but some later modifications had been carried out, including a square porch over the entrance. It was a handsome house and he could understand why she loved it.

Conham handed Rosina out and went with her to the door, where he enquired if Sir Edgar was at home. Upon learning that he was not, Rosina asked to see Lady Brackwood, and they were left to kick their heels in the hall while a stately butler carried a message to Her Ladyship.

'I do not recognise any of these people,' she muttered. 'Edgar has dismissed all Papa's loyal retainers.'

He knew she required a clear head for what needed to be done next and kept his response deliberately cool.

'Did you think he would not, after what he did to you?' His matter-of-fact tone worked. She squared her shoulders, hiding all signs of distress. Impulsively, he caught her hand and kissed it. 'Courage, Rosina.'

The gesture touched her heart. She was grateful for his support, but there was no time to tell him that. The butler returned and they were escorted up the ornately carved wooden staircase to the drawing room. It had changed little since Rosina had been here last. The furnishings looked more worn but the wood was highly polished and the flowers on the side table suggested that the house at least was well cared for.

The new Lady Brackwood was standing beside the fireplace, waiting to greet them.

'Sir Edgar is out,' she said quickly, twisting her hands together. 'I am not sure you should be here.'

'Thank you for agreeing to see me,' said Rosina, ignoring her remark. 'How is my little nephew?'

'He—he is doing very well,' replied their hostess, thrown off guard by this friendly enquiry.

'I am very pleased to hear that.' Rosina paused, then said, 'Lady Brackwood, how much do you know of my leaving this house?'

Harriet looked a little surprised. 'I know that you quarrelled with Edgar.'

'It was far worse than a quarrel, but never mind that now. When I left, I was unable to take all my personal belongings. Nothing valuable, but things that mean a great deal to me.'

'I am very sorry,' Lady Brackwood replied, looking genuinely dismayed. 'By the time I came here your room had been cleared. There can be nothing of yours left. Edgar said he wanted to remove every trace of you.'

Rosina shuddered. She felt Conham's hand on her back and was heartened by his presence. She tried again.

'Would you permit me to look in my father's study? He had some letters of mine, put away with the family papers.'

'No. That is not possible. The study is locked and Edgar keeps the key.'

'Ah, of course he does. But Lady Brackwood… Harriet. We are sisters, now. Surely you would not deny me one last look around the house, if I promise not to disturb anything?'

Rosina reached out to touch her arm and Harriet jumped away as if she had been burned.

'I c-cannot allow you to do that, Edgar would not like it.' She moved towards the bell pull. 'I am sorry. I think you should leave now.'

'Please, we wish you no harm,' said Rosina quickly. 'Surely you would not deny me the chance to say goodbye to my old home.' Harriet had stopped short of ringing the bell and Rosina added, 'I spent so many happy years here, you see. So many precious memories.'

She let the words hang, knowing she was playing on the other woman's sympathy.

Harriet stood, indecisive, wringing her hands. Then, just as she was about to speak, they heard the rumble of voices from the hall. Heavy footsteps sounded on the stairs and the door was thrown open so violently it crashed back against the side table.

'What the devil do you mean, letting that whore in here!'

Edgar came roaring into the room and Lady Brackwood fell back with a cry.

'Mind your manners, Brackwood!'

Conham stepped forward. Rosina knew his superior build and the sharp warning would be enough to make Edgar pause. From his flushed face and bloodshot eyes, it was clear that her brother was drunk. He glared at Conham then turned his head and addressed his wife.

'What are they doing here?' he demanded.

'Sh-she wanted to see her old rooms,' stammered Harriet, her face white. 'But I said no. Believe me, I was not going to let them. I was about to send them away.'

With a curse Edgar turned and glared at Rosina.

'You have no business here. Get out of my house.'

'Please, Edgar, I do not want to fight with you.'

'I said get out!'

'What have I done to deserve this?'

'You stole my birthright!'

Rosina stepped back as if he had slapped her.

'That's not true!'

'It is, damn you! Father made you mistress here, running the estate, organising everything. You turned him against me!'

'No, that's not true,' she cried. 'I helped Papa after Mama died, but that was only until you could come home and take over. I promise you, Edgar, he wanted to teach you, just as he had taught me.'

'Teach me? I never had a chance!' He raged at her, his lips flecked with spittle. 'You were always Father's favourite. So devilishly clever, so damned *c-capable*!'

Rosina stared, shocked at the malice in his voice.

'But you could have done as much, Edgar, if only you had applied yourself.'

'Why should I?' he threw at her. 'Why even bother when you do everything so much better?'

With a curse he swung away and began to pace the room.

'You were always in the way, criticising, meddling in the running of the estate,' he muttered, punching his fist into his palm. 'That was why you had to go. I couldn't let you stay here any longer. You were too good at everything. Always interfering, overriding my orders. You put me to shame with the tenants, the neighbours!'

She was aware of Conham moving to her side as her brother came to a halt before her, menacingly close.

'Oh, Edgar,' she said softly, 'I am so sorry. That was never my intention.'

Her words made no impression. There was nothing but angry loathing in his face as he glared at her.

'Get out, madam. Get out and take your *lover* with you!'

Conham's fists came up but Rosina quickly clutched his arm.

'No! He is drunk, my lord. You must not fight him.'

'Aye, how would that look?' Edgar sneered. 'Attacking a man in his own house.'

Rosina felt the muscles tense, hard as steel beneath his sleeve, and hung on tighter.

'Conham, please.'

The red mist was clearing from Conham's mind. Brackwood was swaying unsteadily on his feet. The fellow was no longer a threat. It was beneath him to knock down such a pitiful wretch. He heard Rosina's voice at his side, soft, pleading.

'Come away, my lord. Let us leave this place.'

'Very well, we will go. For now.'

He glanced back. Lady Brackwood was hunched in a chair, weeping softly. Heaven help her, with such a husband!

'Aye, go and devil take you both,' Brackwood jeered. He turned to his wife, hauling her to her feet. 'Come along, my dear, where are your manners? We must see our guests safely out of the house.'

Lady Brackwood was shrinking away from Edgar and Conham hesitated, loath to leave any woman at the mercy of such a bully. He felt Rosina tug gently on his arm.

'He is doing this for our benefit,' she murmured. 'He *wants* you to strike him. We should leave, now.'

Conham nodded. He escorted Rosina from the room, conscious that Brackwood and his wife were behind them. He opened the door and paused, allowing Rosina to go before him, but as he followed her out onto the landing he heard Lady Brackwood whisper something to her husband. It was met with a snarling curse, then a slap and a scream.

Conham swung around. Harriet was reeling, on the edge of collapse. Instinctively he stepped back to catch her as she fell, and at that moment Edgar barrelled past him.

'Rosina, look out!'

She had almost reached the staircase but turned back at Conham's shout, to see her brother hurtling towards her.

By the time Conham laid Harriet gently on the floor, Edgar had caught up with Rosina. She was backed against the landing railing and threw out her hands to hold him off. Frantically, she pushed him away and he swayed, stepping back and missing the top stair. Conham ran forward but he was too late. Brackwood swayed, arms flailing like a windmill as he lost his balance and toppled headlong down the stairs.

Rosina slumped against the handrail. After the commotion there was now only a terrible stillness. The silence seemed to go on forever, but it could only have been moments before Conham was running down the stairs. She glanced across the landing as Harriet came unsteadily out of the parlour and stared down at her husband, lying at the bottom of the stairs.

Collecting herself, Rosina hurried down to join Conham, who was kneeling beside Edgar. She stared at her brother's lifeless form. There was a small cut on his head, but apart from that and his dreadful pallor, there was no outward sign of injury.

'Is—is he…?'

'No, he breathes.' Conham tried to sound reassuring.

He assured himself that she was not about to faint before addressing the two footmen who had come running over. He barked out his instructions and when he turned back, Rosina was kneeling beside her brother, her fingers on the pulse in his neck.

'Don't move him,' he warned, 'I have sent for a doctor.'

'Can we not put him to bed?'

'Not yet. I saw a lot of broken bones when I was in the army. The surgeons told me many injuries are made far worse by moving the patient.'

He heard footsteps on the stairs and glanced up. Harriet had descended to the lowest stair.

'He is safe enough here, my lady,' he told her. 'But we need to keep him warm.'

At first, he thought she had not heard; she was staring down at the broken body on the floor, her face ashen. Then she nodded. 'I will fetch blankets.'

'I shall go and help her,' said Rosina, rising. 'I can do nothing here.'

She was very calm, but there was such anguish in her eyes that it tore at his heart.

'Yes, yes. Go and help.'

He watched her hurry after Harriet, knowing they would be better for being busy. For himself, there was nothing to do now but wait.

It was some time before the surgeon arrived. The ladies brought blankets to cover Edgar and then joined Conham in the vigil at the foot of the stairs. The patient slipped in and out of consciousness several times, and they gave him sips of water, doing their best to keep him still.

Conham said nothing, but what worried him most was that although Edgar threw his head from side to side and thrashed his arms, his legs beneath the covering blankets did not move.

He said as much to the doctor, once he arrived and examined Edgar. The man shrugged.

'Only time will tell.' He knelt by the patient, shaking his head. 'Drunk when he fell, was he? No need to deny it, I can smell it on him. I was expecting something like this. Well, well, let us put him to bed and we will see how he goes on. He will need careful nursing, night and day.'

Rosina stepped forward. 'I would like to help with that.'

Conham wanted to object but was silenced by her look, pleading with him to understand.

He gave her a slight nod and she turned back to address the doctor.

'I will stay, if Lady Brackwood will allow me?'

Rosina glanced at Harriet. The two of them had worked together, fetching blankets and bandages, finding a board in readiness for carrying the injured man upstairs to his bed, and she was relieved when the other woman agreed.

An hour later Edgar had been put to bed and Rosina went down to the hall to see Conham, who was preparing to leave.

'I cannot stay long,' she told him. 'Lady Brackwood is with my brother now, but she wants to go to the nursery soon, to attend to her baby.'

'Yes, of course,' he said, pulling on his gloves. 'It is too dark to return to the Manor tonight so I shall put up at the Crown, but as soon as I get back to Morton Gifford, I shall arrange for your bags to be packed.' He patted his pocket. 'I have your instructions for Mrs Goddard, your luggage should be with you by tomorrow night.'

'Thank you.' She hesitated, then, 'I am sorry. I never meant... I never knew Edgar felt so, so *belittled* by me! I feel all this is my fault.'

'No, Rosina, you must not blame yourself. Your brother is eaten up with jealousy.'

'But if I had acted differently...if I had not undermined him—'

He caught her hands. 'You did what you thought was best for Brackwood, what you thought your father would have wanted. Nothing can excuse what your brother did to you!'

'I know that, but... Oh, Conham, I cannot leave him while he is like this!'

'Stay then, if you must.' He touched her cheek, smiling a little. 'Do not worry about Morton Gifford. I will look after matters there with Davy until you are free to return. You will want to concentrate on looking after Sir Edgar. He is still your brother, even after everything he has done.'

'Yes. And although Harriet is very capable, she has the baby to consider and will need someone to help her nurse Edgar. It seems she has no one else, her family cast her off soon after she was married. I must stay. I hope you understand.'

He caught her hands.

'I do understand,' he said lightly, lifting first one then the other to his lips. 'It is my misfortune that I fell in love with an angel.'

'Oh, pray, do not say that,' she cried, blinking away tears. 'You know we can never be together.'

'We can and we will,' he said, kissing her.

The wail of a baby floated down from the upper floors and Rosina reluctantly pushed Conham away.

'I must go. Harriet needs to look after her son.'

He nodded. 'There is no time to explain it all now, but when this is over, we shall be married, I promise you!'

His smile almost broke her heart, but she bravely hid her tears until he had ridden off into the darkness.

Chapter Twenty-Three

For a full week Rosina worked with Harriet to nurse Edgar. At first he was too ill to know who was tending him, but as his mind recovered, he became increasingly angry to find her there, and she suggested they bring in one of the women from the village to help.

Rather than cause him distress, she took over the night watch, sitting with him while he slept during the long, dark hours between midnight and dawn. During the day, when she was not sleeping, she resumed the management of the estate. She dare not interfere too far, but her knowledge of Brackwood allowed her to fend off any immediate problems.

She also found herself growing closer to her sister-in-law. Harriet began asking her questions about Brackwood, and Rosina was only too pleased to talk about her old home and the village. She even drove Harriet around the land, something that Edgar had failed to do.

By the end of the third week, the doctor declared that Edgar was out of immediate danger and Rosina wrote to Davy, asking him to send the carriage. Despite the worry over her brother, she had taken some pleasure in seeing Brackwood again, but she knew she would be very glad to get back to Morton Gifford after one final night watch.

The doctor had said it was not strictly necessary now but Rosina wanted to do it. She felt she owed her brother that much. It was not too onerous a task, as long as Edgar was sleeping. A coal fire kept the room warm throughout the night and a lamp beside her chair gave sufficient light for her to occupy her time sewing or reading. She had been pleased to see that most of Papa's books remained in the small library, and she found one he had been particularly fond of, during his later years. She had read it before, several times, but still enjoyed it for its witty and sometimes cutting depiction of country society. She trimmed the lamp and settled down with her novel.

She had not read very far when one line jumped out at her:

> *If I could love a man who would love me enough to take me for a mere fifty pounds a year, I should be very well pleased.*

Rosina lowered the book, suddenly feeling slightly sick. Conham was such a man, she knew that, but there could be no happy ending to their story. Since taking her to his bed he was determined to marry her and count the world well lost. But that was impossible. A rich bride was not just desirable for Conham, it was a necessity. His mother had said as much. He had been born into a different world; he would be derided and despised by society if he neglected his duty. His friends would turn their backs on him.

Rosina might try to dismiss it as mere arrogance, but she knew Conham could not shrug off his obligations so easily. He might love her now, but it would not last. Not if it meant behaving in such a dishonourable way to his family, people that he loved.

Edgar stirred and Rosina went across to the bed. He murmured something, but did not wake. After straightening the bedcovers, she went back to her chair but she did not pick up the book again. There was not time to read the whole, so it was best to put it aside now, although she had no idea how else she would fill the remaining hours, save with her own thoughts.

They were not happy. Nursing Edgar had not taken all her time these past three weeks and she had visited Mr Paxby and his sister. There she learned even more about the discontent in the village and on the farms. It confirmed her own impression that matters at Brackwood were going from bad to worse.

Rosina leaned back in the chair and closed her eyes, remembering her original reason for coming here, to search for a new will. Since her brother's accident she had made no attempt to look for it, thinking it would be wrong, somehow, with Edgar being so ill. But now she began to think of the matter again. After all, it was not only Edgar who was suffering from Brackwood's ailing fortunes, there was his wife and son to consider.

She turned her mind to her father's last days. He had collapsed in this very room the night after he had dined with his friends. What if he had managed to hide the will somewhere in here?

She got up and wandered around the room, noting that the heavy dark wood furniture had been replaced by newer pieces with brass inlay and lions-claw feet. She saw Papa's mahogany dressing case sitting on Edgar's new dressing table and felt a sudden constriction in her throat. It brought back a host of memories, of happier times when Papa had been alive.

She gave herself a little shake. This was doing nothing to help her find the will and she forced herself to consider where it might be. If Papa had hidden it in any of the drawers or cupboards, or even between the mattress and the bed frame, it must have been found by Edgar or one of the servants when they turned out the room.

That only left the floorboards or the wainscot. She picked up the lamp and began to inspect the panelling. Beginning on one side of the door she made her way slowly around three of the walls, running her hands over the wood. It was worn smooth with age and polishing, but she could discern no gaps or loose panels. Edgar's bed was pushed against the last wall and she went back to it carefully, wary of allowing the light to disturb him. Nothing. Rosina moved around the bed. Hope was fading, but she thought that she might as well finish what she had started.

She had reached the final section of wainscot when her fingers felt a distinct ridge. The edge of one of the panels was definitely standing proud, but she had to move into the corner, where the wall adjoined the door frame, to see beneath it. She crouched down, holding the lamp towards the slight gap and her heart almost stopped.

Was that really something under the panelling or was she merely imagining it, because she wanted it so badly? She took a moment to steady herself and looked again. It was not easy to hold the lamp still, but yes, she was sure there was something in there.

Quickly, she went back to the dressing table and opened the dressing case. Inside were the usual silver-topped jars for holding powders or lotions and a selection of combs and brushes with ivory handles. She pulled out the small drawer beneath to reveal a row of smaller instruments, all necessary to a gentleman's toilet and each piece in its place on the green baize. She lifted out a pair of tweezers.

Her heart was pounding with anxiety that Edgar might wake as she went back to the gap in the panelling. Cautiously, she tried to extract the paper lodged beneath the wood. It was slow work, the folded sheet was tightly wedged into the narrow space, but finally she pulled out enough for her to be able to grip the document and ease it free from its hiding place.

Carefully she unfolded the paper.

I, Thomas George Brackwood of Brackwood Court in the County of Somersetshire, being of sound and disposing mind and memory...

Rosina was already in the hall when the Dallamire travelling chariot came to a halt on the drive of Brackwood Court. Taking her leave of Harriet, she stepped outside, only to stop in surprise when Conham jumped out of the carriage.

'I have come to take you home.'

His smile and the simple words set her heart soaring. It would be useless to deny her pleasure in seeing him, her countenance gave it away, but Rosina tried to contain her happiness. Despite everything she had to tell him, nothing had changed between them, except that her feelings for Conham had grown even stronger in the past three weeks. She knew it would be quite unbearable to remain at Morton Gifford knowing they could never marry.

He helped her into the carriage, gave orders to the driver and jumped in, sitting down beside her as the chariot moved off.

'Have you missed me?' he asked.

As if I had lost part of myself!

She could not say that of course. She held him off as he reached for her.

'Oh, Conham, I have so much to tell you. I have found the will.'

'The devil you have!'

Conham sat back and listened as she explained everything and showed him the paper she had extracted from behind the panelling.

'We should take this to Mr Shipton immediately,' he said, when he had read it. 'As executor and your father's attorney, he is by far the best person to deal with the matter. With your permission, we will go there now.'

Rosina nodded and he let down the window to give fresh instructions to the driver.

'There, it is done,' he said, resuming his seat. 'It is not so far out of our way.'

'Thank you. There will be enquiries to be made, and we do not know yet if the will is legally binding.'

'Have you told anyone else about it?' he asked her.

'No. Edgar is not well enough. He cannot leave his bed and it is not yet certain he will ever walk again.' She paused, saddened by the thought. 'I confess it did trouble me not to tell Harriet. We have become friends, you see. She did not confide in me, but I believe Edgar has been bullying her dreadfully. She has become a different person since the accident, far more assured.'

'I am very glad to hear that. But you know what this means?' He nodded towards the paper that she was still clutching in her hands. 'Your father has left all the unentailed land to you, for your lifetime.'

'Yes. If the will is proven then I shall have control of everything save Brackwood Court and the Home Farm. Having helped Harriet with the accounts for the past three weeks, I know my brother has already spent most of the dowry she brought with her, and without the rents and income from the farms and villages, he will not be able to pay his way.

'Edgar would have to listen to me, then. I am sure he must want Brackwood to thrive, if not for his own sake then for his son. Do you not think so?'

'No, I don't,' said Conham, bluntly. 'Are you not concerned he might make another attempt to harm you?'

'I thought of that.' She folded her hands in her lap. 'I am going to make a sworn statement, with all the facts of his previous attempt, and our other encounters since. I shall have it signed and sealed and give it to Mr Shipton for safekeeping, in case anything should happen to me. I think it will be as well to be prepared,' she told him. 'I should have done it before, rather than rely solely upon your protection.'

'But I *want* to protect you, Rosina. More than that I want to make you my wife!'

'Please, say no more!' Her anguished cry silenced him. 'I have too much to think of at present. Edgar may not even survive! If that is the case then his son will inherit, and Harriet will need my help whether the will is proven or not.' She gently pulled her hands free. 'I have a duty to my family, my lord, as you have to yours.'

'Duty!' He uttered the word like a curse. 'That damned word has always haunted me. But if we are to talk of duty, what of my obligation to you, now? I took you to my bed, madam. I *seduced* you!'

'I went willingly,' she replied. 'You owe me nothing because of what we did that night.'

'If you are with child—'

'I am not.' She was sitting very straight and still, only her hands, clasping and unclasping, betraying her agitation. 'My body has shown me,' she said, her cheeks flushed. 'You have no duty towards me, sir. I am not carrying your child.'

Conham shut his eyes. He had really thought she loved him, but it was not the case. She did not want to marry him, she would not even let him propose to her.

'By God, what a coil!'

She shrugged. 'Not at all. It is quite clear what we have to do.'

He said, after a moment, 'It is likely, then, that you will go back to Brackwood.'

'Yes, but not to the Court. Even if Edgar was not married, I would not live under his roof again. As it is, Harriet is mistress there now and she has the baby, too. She would not want me under her feet.' Rosina turned and looked out the window. 'But I could take a house close by. That would be essential if I am to run the estate. In either event I should have the one thing I have always wanted more than anything. To be independent.'

Conham listened to her cheerful voice and felt the leaden weight of her words on his spirits. She had always maintained she preferred her independence to marriage. He had thought he might change that, conceited fool that he was. She could have a comfortable life in Somerset, looking after the people and the land she loved. Had she not said more than once that Brackwood was her life?

When she looked back at him he dredged up a smile from somewhere deep inside.

'You would have your dream, then.'

'Yes.'

Rosina turned away again, pretending to study the familiar landscape. Now it was within reach, she realised that particular dream had been replaced months ago with another one. Something far more unattainable.

It was late by the time they reached Morton Gifford and Conham ordered the chariot to drive on to the lodge where, despite Rosina's protest, he insisted on walking with her to the door.

'Thank you for coming to fetch me, Conham.'

'Think nothing of it.'

She waited, wondering if he would kiss her, but he merely squeezed her hand before jumping back into the carriage.

'It is for the best,' she muttered to herself as she let herself into the lodge. 'If the new will is proven, Brackwood will need the income from the surrounding land. It has been neglected for the past year but I can change that. I must make it profitable, if not for Edgar's sake, then for Harriet and the child.'

And for herself, too, because independence was all she had left now. Even if her conscience would allow her to ignore the plight of her family and divert the funds to her own use, it would never make her the wealthy bride Conham needed.

With Rosina back at Morton Gifford, Conham knew there was no real need for him to remain, but he could not bring himself to leave. She would be heartbroken if the will should prove to be invalid, and he wanted to be there to support her.

He did his best to avoid Rosina, afraid she would see the hunger in his eyes. When it was necessary for them to meet and discuss estate matters Davy was usually present, and their encounters were always businesslike. On inclement days he found himself prowling the house like a prisoner, but when the weather was fine he was out of doors, visiting neighbours or spending the daylight hours riding through the Gloucester countryside.

However, he knew he could not stay forever. His man of business was urging him to come to London to deal with pressing financial matters. Also, his stepmother might have removed to the Dower House, but she was still writing to him, complaining of the slow progress in restoring Dallamire, and begging him to reconsider his decision not to marry an heiress.

After two weeks he decided it was time to leave the Manor. The latest correspondence from Berkshire concerned the next phase of improvements at Dallamire and he needed to decide how best to spend the limited funds at his disposal. Besides, Rosina was growing ever paler and more gaunt as she waited to hear news from Somerset: keeping his distance, not being able to comfort her, sliced like a knife into his soul.

Having made up his mind, Conham waited until Davy had left the Manor one morning before seeking out Rosina in her office. He knocked on the door and entered to find her sitting at her desk, staring at a letter in her hand.

'I beg your pardon, am I interrupting you?' She looked up and one glance at her face chased all other thoughts from his head. He said sharply, 'What is it?'

She said, in a colourless voice, 'Mr Shipton has written to me.'

'What does he say? Is the will invalid?'

Conham could not prevent a very selfish and ignoble burst of hope.

'Quite the opposite. Edgar has declared he will not contest the new will.'

'Oh.' He firmly squashed his disappointment. 'Is your brother fully recovered, then?'

'No. Harriet wrote to tell me that the doctors despair of his ever walking again, but he is sitting out of bed now and she says he is far more docile than before his accident.' She glanced down at the letter. 'I think this must be due to her influence. Mr Shipton says it will take time for everything to be finally settled, but my brother has agreed to my taking charge again and Harriet wants me to do so as soon as I can.'

'Well.' Conham strolled over to the window. 'That is good news for you.' He stared out at the winter landscape. It looked as dark and bleak as his mood, but he forced himself to say cheerfully, 'I am glad. You must be very pleased.'

Rosina had never felt more like weeping, but she said, in her brightest voice, 'Oh, good heavens, I am!'

He turned to face her. 'Well then. I will not stand in your way.'

'I beg your pardon?' She heard his words, but Conham was standing with his back to the wintry light coming in from the window and she could not see his face.

'Brackwood needs you. You should set to work, immediately.'

'But I am contracted as land steward here until Lady Day.'

'That can be changed. I worked with young Redmond while you were away and he proved himself very capable. I am sure he will make an excellent land steward.'

Rosina was well aware that Davy could easily take over as

her successor at Morton Gifford, but hearing Conham express the idea did not please her at all.

'You want to be rid of me!'

'There seems little point in you staying longer.'

He had stepped closer and she could see now that his face was inscrutable.

No, she thought, after a second look. He was *indifferent*.

Since her return from Brackwood he had been avoiding her. She knew it was partly her fault, she had given him to understand that she did not wish to marry him, but now it was clear why he had so readily accepted that. What she had thought was a grand passion, thwarted by his sense of duty, had been nothing more than infatuation. Now it was over and he wanted her gone with all speed. Odious, odious creature!

She was angry that he could think so little of her but there was something else, deep down. Panic. She was not ready to leave Morton Gifford. She did not really want to go.

It took every ounce of her control to maintain a business-like demeanour.

'I think not, my lord. My contract runs until the twenty-fifth of March and I shall honour that. There are matters to be dealt with here that I should like to see through to completion.' She gave him a cool, enquiring look. 'Unless you are dissatisfied with my work here?'

Rosina noted his scowl with satisfaction; her challenge had surprised him.

'Your work here has been exemplary, as well you know.'

'Thank you. Then Davy shall take over from me on Lady Day and not before. As you say, he is perfectly capable now and, should it be necessary for me to travel to Brackwood in the coming months, you will be able to rest easy, knowing that he will look after your interests here.'

'If that is what you wish, madam.'

'I do.' Having won that point, Rosina felt her resolution faltering. If he remained here much longer, she feared she would burst into tears. 'If that is all, my lord…'

'What? No. I came to tell you that I am leaving for Dallamire tomorrow. I intend to stop at Bellemonte on my way, to speak with Matt Talacre. Would you object if I told him now that you have heard from the attorney?'

She hesitated, but only for a moment. With Conham in Berkshire it would be useful to have someone nearby whom she trusted. Not that she could ever tell Matthew everything, of course.

'Yes, thank you, Matthew has proved himself a good friend to me. I have told him nothing of my visit to Brackwood and it would save me trying to put it all down in writing.'

'Very well. Goodbye, Rosina.'

'Goodbye, my lord.'

He held her gaze for a moment, as if waiting for her to say something more.

Go, Conham. Please go.

If he did not walk out soon she knew she would be lost. All pretence would be gone and she would throw herself at him, and beg him not to leave her at all.

Finally, just when she felt she could stand no more, he turned on his heel and strode out of the room.

Conham left Morton Gifford the following morning. He made no effort to see Rosina, merely leaving word with Davy that he could be reached at Dallamire, if she wished to contact him. He drove his curricle out through the gates and along the lanes at a smart pace, glad to concentrate upon keeping the spirited bays under control rather than allowing his thoughts to dwell on what he was leaving behind him.

There were no mishaps on the journey and he reached Bellemonte at midday. Leaving the curricle with his groom he set off in search of Matt, finally tracking him down to the little office he had set up for himself in the Pavilion.

'Conham, damme, this is a surprise! Come in, man, sit down and take a drink with me.'

'Thank you, no.' He threw his hat and gloves down on a chair. 'I cannot stop, I am on my way to Dallamire.'

Matt grinned. 'Off to tell your stepmama the good news, are you?'

'There is no good news.'

'Never tell me Rosina has refused you!'

'Yes—no. I did not ask her. That is why I have called, to stop you saying anything to her about the matter. It would only cause her distress.'

Conham swiftly told him about the new will.

'So, you see, Rosina will be leaving Morton Gifford in a few months.'

'I am astounded!' exclaimed Matt, when he had finished. 'The two of you have only had eyes for each other since we came into Gloucestershire. Rosina loves you, my friend, I would stake my life on it.'

'Then you would lose. Rosina's heart has always been at Brackwood. That is where she wants to be.'

But Matthew would not believe it.

'Have you told her that things have changed?' he demanded of Conham. 'That you are no longer in need of a rich wife?'

'What good would it do? Her brother is not contesting the will, which is almost an admission that it is valid. Rosina wants to return to Brackwood and continue with her father's plans to make the place profitable. It is what she has always wanted.'

'And if Sir Edgar dies?'

Conham felt his mouth twist into a bitter smile. 'Then she will devote herself to helping his widow, and providing a secure future for Edgar's son and heir.'

'The devil she will. Have you not told her how you *feel*? Surely you will not let her go without a fight!' Conham put up his hand, as if to ward off a blow, and Matt exploded. 'By God, man, don't be a fool. Go back now and talk to Rosina. Tell her you love her!'

'Confound it, how can I?' Conham raked a hand through his hair. 'Yes, I believe I can restore Dallamire without marrying a fortune, but it will take years. Possibly a lifetime of hard work and toil.'

'Much she'd care about that!'

'But *I* would care! And that is not the point. Rosina does not love me. Oh, she cares for me, a little. It would pain her to refuse me, and I do not want that. *If* she cannot go back to Brackwood, if it becomes a choice between working for someone else or marrying me, then perhaps, *perhaps* she might say yes. Until I know how things stand in the matter I will hold my peace. And so will you,' he finished, picking up his hat. 'You will say nothing about any of this to her. Promise me, Matthew, on your honour as an officer!'

Chapter Twenty-Four

It was Rosina's second spring at Morton Gifford, and bitter March winds were scouring the countryside. However, the days were growing longer, spring flowers dotted the hedgerows and Rosina clung to the hope that the weather would soon improve. That might lift her spirits, which had been uncharacteristically low throughout the winter. Her plans were all in place to quit Morton Gifford at the end of the month and move to Somerset. After that, all her ties to the Earl of Dallamire would be cut, with the exception of their mutual interest in Bellemonte.

She had heard nothing from Conham himself since his departure last winter. News of the earl was scarce, too. She scoured the London newspapers but there was no mention of him. The only news of any interest was that Miss Skelton had married Sir William Cherston. A baronet, not quite the noble rank Lady Skelton had wanted for her daughter, but Rosina hoped Amelia was happy with her choice.

From her office in the Manor, Rosina looked out at the leaden skies. Matthew was supposed to be calling today, to discuss his new plans for Bellemonte, but when she had walked across from the lodge this morning, a flurry of snow had caused her to think he might postpone his visit.

An hour later it was snowing heavily, and Rosina was just lighting the candles in her office when her visitor arrived.

'Matthew!' She went over to him, hands held out. 'I had quite given up on you.'

'It takes more than a little snow to stop me,' he said, kissing her cheek. 'To be truthful, I was more than halfway here when the snow began, and I decided it was easier to carry on than turn back. Although I may have to beg you to put me up tonight.'

'You know that will be no problem, Mrs Jameson is always pleased to see you here. She thinks almost as much of you as her master!'

Matt chuckled and put his case of papers on the desk. 'Talking of Conham, have you heard from him recently?'

'Why, of course.' Rosina went back to the fireplace. 'I correspond regularly with his secretary at Dallamire.'

'I am not talking of business letters, Rosina!'

'But what else should we discuss?'

She picked up the poker and stirred the coals. Matthew was a very good friend, but she could not bear to expose her wounded heart to him or anyone. When she looked up she saw that he was frowning at her and she fought hard to find a convincing smile.

'Pray sit down, Matthew. I will ring for some coffee and we can get to work!'

'So you see, Rosina,' said Matthew, smiling at her across the desk, 'Bellemonte is already showing a profit in its first full year under my control.'

'Oh, Matthew, I am so pleased for you.'

'And that's not all,' he went on. 'Your investment will return you a full fifty pounds this year. Almost as much as if you had invested it in government bonds.'

'Truly?' She pressed her hands to her cheeks. 'That is wonderful news!'

'Aye. Not a fortune, of course, but I expect the returns to improve next year, if you can afford to leave the money with me.'

'That is my intention.'

'You are sure you do not need it?' he asked her. 'For your new life in Somerset?'

'Ah, you have heard.'

'Yes. But I am grieved that you did not think fit to tell me of it yourself.'

'I beg your pardon. There never seemed to be the right time...'

He waved away her excuse.

'Too late for that now. Tell me instead what your plans are.'

'I move to Brackwood on the twenty-fifth, when my contract here ends. There is a small house in the village, which I shall make my home. I plan to allow myself a small salary from the estate funds and the rest will go back to Edgar. Or, more truthfully, to Harriet, who is slowly taking over the running of Brackwood Court. She is proving herself an excellent manager.'

'And Conham?'

'What about him?' She began to gather up the papers on her desk. 'This has nothing to do with the earl. We are agreed that Davy Redmond will take over here as manager. Now, I believe that is all our business concluded, Matthew, is it not?'

She smiled at him, holding his gaze and her breath, praying he would not say anything more about Conham. Finally, he nodded.

'Yes, that is all I need to discuss with you.' He glanced towards the window. 'However, since it has not stopped snowing all day, I shall not even attempt to drive to Bellemonte tonight.'

'I should think not,' she told him, relaxing a little. 'If I know Mrs Jameson, she will already have instructed Cook to prepare dinner for us.'

'Very well. I shall go and see if I can charm her into sending up some hot water for me, but I am afraid I shall have to dine with you in these clothes.'

Rosina chuckled. 'I am very glad. It means I shall not feel obliged to make my way back to the lodge and change!'

Matthew went off and Rosina set about putting away her ledgers. The news about Bellemonte was encouraging. The gardens had performed well, even through the winter, the Pleasure Baths were also showing a profit and Matt hoped to open the hotel in the coming months. She was pleased for him; he had worked so hard to make Bellemonte a success. And she was glad to see, when he had walked in earlier, that the ugly limp that had troubled him so much had disappeared. He looked like a man content with his lot.

'And so should you be content, Rosina Brackwood,' she told herself as she went around the office, snuffing the candles. 'Your future is more than secure now. You have sufficient income to live comfortably, should you need it.'

She extinguished the final light to leave only the glow from the fire.

'And you are returning to Somerset, your old home,' she went on. 'That should be enough for anyone.'

But the words had a hollow ring to them and they did not lift the leaden weight from her heart.

Dinner with Matt Talacre proved a welcome distraction for Rosina. They talked about Bellemonte and the weather, politics and art. She was genuinely glad to have Matt's company and when the covers were removed, she happily agreed to have a final glass of wine with him. Anything to delay returning to her lonely bed, where her thoughts would fly, as they always did, to Conham.

'I am very pleased you could come, Matthew,' she said, when he had refilled her glass from a fresh bottle. 'I have enjoyed talking with you this evening.'

'So, too, have I, although there is one subject we have not touched upon,' said Matt, his dark eyes suddenly serious. 'What the devil happened between you and Conham?'

'N-nothing,' she replied, startled.

'Did you know he wanted to marry you?'

She hesitated, staring down into her glass for a long moment.

'Yes. But he was just trying to be kind.'

'Kind be damned! He loves you, Rosina.'

'That's not true.' She shook her head. 'He likes me. Perhaps for a while he thought it was something more…but not now. And it could never have come to anything. He needs to marry a rich woman.'

'Not any more.' Matthew leaned forward. 'Do you know

what he has been doing these past months, Rosina? The steps he has been taking to improve his fortunes?'

'Of course I do. I know he has sold several properties, for example.'

'Did you also know he has persuaded the countess to decamp to the Dower House with the children? Or that he has sold timber from his estate to fund the latest repairs to Dallamire Hall?'

She raised her head. 'I do not need to know what is going on at Dallamire. My concern is Morton Gifford. Or it was,' she amended. 'From next month Davy Redmond will be land steward here and I shall be in Somerset.'

'And that is what you want?'

She pinned on her brightest smile. 'Of course it is. I shall be independent, which has always been my ambition.'

'But at what price, Rosina?'

She raised her hand. 'Stop this now, Matthew. This is none of your business.'

'But it is, when I see the two people I care about most in this world tearing themselves apart.'

'No, you are wrong. Conham cannot even bestir himself to see me before I leave Morton Gifford.'

'What?'

She bit her lip. 'I received a letter from his secretary. The earl is too busy to leave Dallamire. He is content for me to arrange matters as I wish in handing over to Davy Redmond.'

'I cannot believe he does not care. Rosina, I—'

'No more!' She pushed herself to her feet. 'I have had enough of this. Good night, M—'

'Believe me, madam, Conham is breaking his heart over you!'

She froze. Matthew went on.

'I have known Conham for ten years. We fought together, buried comrades together… Confound it, we are as close as family. Closer, in fact. He is not a man to wear his heart on his sleeve, but I *know* he loves you.'

Rosina sank back onto her chair. 'He has never said so.'

'Not at first, because he had nothing to offer you. Less than nothing.'

'How foolishly noble of him!'

'Aye, it was. But then he set about changing all that.'

'But why did he not write to me? Why did he not tell me about his plans?'

Matt laughed. 'Have you seen his letters? Conham is a man of action, Rosina. He does not express himself well with pen and ink. And besides, he was not sure he could do it and did not want to raise false hopes. Then in November, when he *did* think that he might be able to make it all work, he came back to propose to you.'

'But he didn't.'

'No, because you dashed off to Brackwood in search of that damned will.'

He refilled his glass and took a long drink. 'He has now convinced himself that you do not love *him*.'

Rosina crossed her arms, hugging herself. Conham had announced he was going to marry her, he had taken her to bed, but he had never said he loved her.

'He should have proposed, told me everything.'

Matt huffed. 'Did you really expect him to do so, when you were so intent on saving your old home?'

'I was trying to save *him*!'

She remembered how he had tried to kiss her, when he collected her from Brackwood. She had held him off. And she had refused to listen when he said he wanted to marry her, refused to let him explain.

I played my part too well. I pretended that Brackwood was all I really wanted, when really...

She looked up. 'Why have you not said anything of this to me before?'

'Conham swore me to silence. He believes that you want to return to Brackwood. That you do not love him.'

Tears started to her eyes. 'But I do. I do love him. Far too much to stop him from taking a rich wife. Someone with a large fortune.'

'And I am telling you he does not *need* to marry a fortune.' He pushed her wineglass towards her. 'If anyone should understand what is required to restore his neglected property, it should be you, Rosina! Thanks to your improvements, Morton Gifford is making more than enough to sustain itself and Conham is using some of the income to repair Dallamire Hall. Bellemonte, too, is showing a return. Not a great deal, to be sure, but enough to convince him there is a way forward that doesn't involve him marrying an heiress.

'He thought you could help him, Rosina. He thought you could work together to bring Dallamire back from the brink of ruin. But you have convinced him that you would prefer to live at Brackwood.'

'Yes, so he is free to find a more fitting wife.'

Matt threw out his hands and looked up at the ceiling.

'Damnation, woman, can't you see? He loves you, and if he can't have you, he won't marry anyone! He would rather tackle the restoration of Dallamire on his own than marry when his heart is elsewhere. Trust me, I know him better than I know myself.'

She shook her head, trying to make sense of everything she was hearing. Could it be possible? Could he truly love her? He had never said as much.

But he has shown you…time and again he has shown you how much he cares.

She frowned. 'But… Matthew, if you are such great friends, if Conham swore you to secrecy, why are you telling me this now?'

He grinned and held up his glass. 'Because I am drunk, madam, and not even a gentleman can be expected to keep his word when he is drunk!'

The snow was already melting when Rosina walked back to the Manor the next day. She was pleased to see it had not flattened the clusters of daffodils that glowed butter yellow in the early-morning sunshine. She always thought daffodils a very cheerful flower, a sign of hope for better things ahead, and today they exactly matched her mood.

She entered to find the butler in the hall and greeted him

with a smile. A far more genuine smile than she had managed for some time.

'Good morning, Jameson, has Mr Talacre broken his fast yet?'

'No, Miss Brackwood, he is still in his room. Breakfast is set for ten o'clock.' His eyes twinkled. 'Mrs Jameson insisted he should eat a good meal before setting out for Bellemonte.'

She nodded. 'An excellent idea. I shall take breakfast with him, if you will have another place set.'

'It shall be done. And Mr Redmond is already in the office, ma'am.'

'Thank you. Perhaps you could have coffee sent in for us. We have much to discuss!'

'I am sorry if I have delayed your departure, Matthew,' said Rosina, walking with him to the door of the Manor.

'Think nothing of it. The sun is shining, you see. There should be no difficulty in getting back to Bellemonte before dark.'

'Then I wish you a safe journey, my friend.'

She held out her hand and he kissed it.

'Thank you, Rosina. You will be quitting Morton Gifford yourself, soon. Is there anything I can do to help?'

'Nothing, thank you, it is all in hand. There is a great deal to be done here before Lady Day, but I shall manage, with Davy's help.'

'And when you leave? Perhaps you would like me to accompany you to—'

'That is very kind of you, Matthew, but no, I do not want you to come with me.'

He grinned. 'Because you wish to be independent?'

'Oh, no,' she said, twinkling up at him. 'Because I am going to find the earl, and I think you would be very much in the way!'

Chapter Twenty-Five

'There's some water here, sir, if Your Lordship is thirsty.'

Conham accepted the proffered flask with a word of thanks and drank deep. He was indeed thirsty. Hungry, too, having been on the roof of Dallamire Hall since daybreak. He had started by inspecting the gutters and the new lead flashing, and for the past half hour had been helping to haul up replacement coping for the stonemasons to repair the low parapet that ran around the edge of the roof. It was hot work, but he was discovering that he enjoyed hard, physical labour.

He had spent the past few months helping on the farms, laying hedges, mending fences and rebuilding barns. There had been no time for gentlemanly sports and pastimes but he found the work rewarding, even in the bad weather. It was honest toil and he was not ashamed of it, nor of helping the builders at work on the Hall. It gave him valuable experience and knowledge of how things were done and what was needed to keep Dallamire working. The exercise also tired him out and allowed him to sleep soundly.

Most nights, at least.

Conham wiped the sweat from his brow and glanced up at the sun. It was gone noon. He would go down soon and partake of his solitary nuncheon in the dining room while those working on the roof enjoyed the basket of cheese and bread and pickles that he had ordered to be sent up.

He gazed out over the countryside. There was undoubtedly a wonderful view from up here. The ornamental lake gleamed like a mirror, and he could see over the woods to the lush green hills beyond. How long was it since he had ridden out over his land, just for the sheer pleasure of it? In truth, he could not recall ever having done so since he became earl. As soon as he returned from France he had been beset by the obligations of running Dallamire.

He was about to turn away when a movement in the distance caught his eye. A carriage had emerged from the trees and was bowling along the drive towards the house.

'Oh, Lord, who is this now?' he muttered. His lawyer, perhaps, with more urgent papers to sign. Or another creditor, come to remind him of an overdue bill. 'I suppose I must go down and meet them.' He made his way across the roof to where a series of ladders was lashed to the scaffolding. 'Hell and damnation, 'tis All Fools' Day and I am clambering around on my own roof. Well, let them see me in all my dirt, perhaps that will convince them that I am not shirking my responsibilities!'

Rosina gazed eagerly out the window at the park that stretched to the horizon in every direction. They had left the main road some time ago and now, as the carriage emerged from the leafy shade of the woods and into the bright sunshine, she caught her first glimpse of Dallamire Hall.

The meandering drive was designed to give visitors an excellent view of the magnificent West Front. The main body of the Palladian mansion rose up, square and imposing, flanked by two low wings that stretched out like arms on either side. She felt a slight tremor of nerves. The house was even larger and more impressive than she had imagined. As the drive curled about again, she could see a lattice of scaffolding covering the south front, behind the Pavilion, and a number of figures moving about on the roof.

Rosina began to have doubts about the wisdom of her plan. What was she doing, arriving unannounced? With the amount of work being done on the house, it was unlikely that the earl would even be here. She clasped her hands together, prayer-like, and pressed them against her mouth as the carriage rattled around in a final sweeping curve and came to a halt in front of the house.

The coach rocked as one of the servants climbed down to open the door. Rosina took a deep breath and stepped out onto the drive. The magnificent central portico towered above her, while on either side, curling stone steps led up to the covered entrance.

No one appeared from the house to greet her, which heightened her apprehension that the earl might not be at home. Then she heard footsteps on the gravel and turned to see Conham striding quickly towards her.

Her heart missed a beat at the sight of him. He was dressed in serviceable boots and buckskins, but he wore neither coat nor waistcoat over the billowing white shirt that made his broad shoulders look impossibly wide. His auburn hair glinted in the sun, one unruly lock falling forward over his brow, and as he drew closer she could see his face was set and unsmiling.

'Miss Brackwood.'

His formality was not encouraging. All the rehearsed greetings she had prepared withered away as he crossed the final few yards and stopped before her.

Rosina's mouth dried. The top buttons of his shirt were undone and she could not keep her eyes from the smattering of dark hair exposed there. Heat surged through her body as she remembered the feel of it beneath her fingers when they were lying together in his bed, their naked bodies touching…

Oh, heavens, she was lost!

'Why are you here? Is something wrong?'

'N-no,' she stammered, dragging her gaze away from his chest but unable to look him in the eye. 'Nothing is wrong, exactly.'

Conham saw the rosy flush blooming on her cheek and cursed. He should have put on his coat before coming out. Rosina was the last person he had expected to see, and she was clearly upset to find him half-dressed. They were not lovers, after all.

Much to his regret.

A servant ran up, interrupting his thoughts. 'I beg your pardon, my lord, we was clearing the hall, and no one heard the carriage!'

'Thank you, Robert.' Conham forced his befuddled brain to think. 'Escort Miss Brackwood to the drawing room, if you please. And order refreshments to be taken in. Excuse me, ma'am. I will join you momentarily, once I am more…dressed.'

With that, he turned on his heel and strode off.

Rosina followed Robert up the steps, trying not to feel disheartened. She had gambled everything upon Conham being in love with her, but was he, really? He had not looked happy to see her. In fact, he had been distinctly ill at ease. Perhaps he had decided that his noble plans were unworkable. That he would prefer a rich bride after all.

Her heart sank. She thought he had never looked better, his skin tanned by the sun, those powerful long legs encased in buckskin and the white shirt rippling over his muscled shoulders. She felt quite weak with longing. He would have no difficulty finding a wife. How could any woman reject such a man? Perhaps he had already proposed to some beautiful heiress.

The drawing room was shady to the point of gloom. Opaque muslin sub-curtains covered the windows to prevent the light from fading the expensive furniture, and no fire burned in the hearth. Rosina took off her bonnet and gloves but she was not tempted to remove her pelisse. She did not feel at all welcome here.

When the refreshments eventually arrived, she ignored the cake but took a glass of wine. With nothing better to do, she carried it over to one of the windows, where she held aside one of the muslin curtains. The drawing room looked out over the gardens and lawn to a shimmering lake. It was a pretty view, but she thought the grounds sadly neglected. Not that it would take a great deal of work to restore the gardens, if someone was interested.

Since she did not expect to see Conham again for some time, she amused herself by planning the best way to set about it. She was busy mentally cutting back the shrubbery and restocking the flower beds when she heard the door open. She let the curtain fall and turned as Conham came in.

He was dressed now in a blue coat, grey satin waistcoat and a snowy white shirt and neckcloth. He had changed his buckskins and boots for tight-fitting pantaloons in dove grey and glossy black Hessians that would not look amiss in Piccadilly. It was a far more formal appearance, but it did not prevent her heart from skidding erratically at the sight of him. She said the first thing that came into her mind.

'Well, that is certainly a little more appropriate.'

His smile was perfunctory, a faint crease in his brows as his gaze swept over her. Then he looked towards the hearth.

'Ah. I beg your pardon, I quite forgot there is no fire. This room has not been used since the countess moved out. Also, we cannot light one because the men are repairing the chimney. I wondered why you were still wearing your pelisse. We could go to the morning room, if you would prefer?'

So polite, so formal!

'No, thank you, this is perfectly satisfactory.' Rosina felt her courage ebbing away. 'You are busy. I will not take up too much of your time.'

'Where is your maid?'

'I left her in Pangbourne. At the posting inn where we put up last night.'

His frown deepened. 'You should not be here alone, Rosina. You are no longer my employee.'

'No, but I thought I was your friend.'

He ignored that. 'You have come from Brackwood?'

'Yes.'

'And have you settled upon a house?'

'I am not going to rent a property there.'

'Oh? You have decided to live at Brackwood after all.'

'No, I would be very much in the way there.'

'I see. How is your brother?'

'The doctors do not think he will walk again.'

'I see. I am very sorry.'

Her hand fluttered. 'He is much altered, and Harriet is very firmly in charge. She is truly fond of Edgar and determined to keep to her marriage vows. She is also proving to be a very good housekeeper.' Rosina finished her wine and carefully placed the glass down on a table. 'We have advertised for a land steward.'

'May I ask why, when you are perfectly capable of doing the job?'

'Edgar would not welcome my…interference. Harriet and I have decided the best thing is to employ a capable steward to manage both Brackwood and the land Papa left to my care. Since most of the income I receive from it will go back to Brackwood, it is the most sensible solution.'

Conham frowned. She always put others before herself.

Except where you are concerned.

He thrust that thought aside.

'That need not prevent you from returning to the area, to be near your old home, your friends. You have sufficient money to live in comfort and independence. Why should you give up your dreams for your brother, after all he did to you?'

'Edgar will be far happier if I am not there.'

Her smile slipped a little and he exclaimed, 'Confound it, Rosina. Brackwood is all you have ever wanted!'

'It was, but I find now that it is not what I want at all.' She came a step closer. 'I wondered…that is, I came here to ask if, perhaps, you would like to marry me after all.'

Conham stared at her.

'Is this some sort of joke?' he demanded. 'Some fantastical jape for All Fools' Day?'

'No, no!'

Rosina had envisaged several answers to her question, but never that! She gave a ragged laugh.

'Oh, dear, I am making a mull of this. I am not quite a pauper and I thought, if you have not set your heart on a rich bride, that is…'

'No, Rosina, do not go on. It is too late for that!' She raised her brows at him and he said impatiently, 'Oh, Dallamire is safe, but it will take years to return the house and land to profit. There is little money for finery. I have reduced my staff, sold most of my horses and quite given up on visits of pleasure to the capital.'

'Do you think I care for that?'

'No, but I would care. You would be giving up your hard-won independence for…what? A life of damned hard work, full of debt and responsibilities.' He glanced down at his hands, rough and calloused from hard labour. No longer the hands of a gentleman. '*I* can bear the deprivation, but I will not inflict such hardship upon *you.*'

Her nerves already on edge, Rosina's temper snapped.

'Damn you, Conham, allow me to make my own decisions on that!'

Her unladylike language had shocked him. It had shocked her, too, but she could not stop now.

'How can you be so, so pompous, so nobly self-sacrificing?'

'Because I do not want you to suffer.'

'But I am already suffering!'

The words were out before she could stop them. He turned away, putting up a hand as if to silence her, but she had come this far and would say what she must. She thought bitterly that Edgar would approve. One last throw of the dice.

'I love you, Conham.'

She saw the slight shake of his head, sensed she was losing him and suddenly everything spilled out in a raging torrent.

'What would you have me do to prove it? Shall I…shall I build a willow cabin at your gate? Or, as I drove in, I noticed a pretty little gatehouse standing empty. You could rent that to me…'

'For God's sake, stop, Rosina!' he exclaimed. 'Do you think I haven't considered this, that you aren't constantly on my mind? I am not the husband you deserve. *I have nothing to offer you!*'

'Except love.'

The words fell into the abyss that yawned between them. She fixed her eyes on his broad back and went on quietly.

'If you can offer me that I would be satisfied.'

Rosina waited. She thought she heard a faint exhalation and saw the slightest lessening of tension in his figure. She stepped closer and put one hand gently on his shoulder.

'You see, I love *you*, Conham. Not your title. Not your wealth, or lack of it. I want to *be* with you. To live with you, work with you. If you will have me.'

Silence. Conham did not move. Her hand dropped. Matthew was wrong, he did not love her.

'I beg your pardon. My coming here has embarrassed you. I had best leave.'

'No, don't go.'

He turned, fixing her with a look from his grey, stormy eyes. She held her breath and waited for him to continue. Instead, he silently reached out and cupped the back of her head, pulling her close.

He kissed her, long, hard and very thoroughly, and the whole world exploded. He teased her lips apart and their tongues danced together. Rosina responded, feeling the heat of desire rushing through her body. She was almost swooning with it as he swept her up into his arms. He carried her over to the sofa, where he sat down with her on his lap and continued to plunder her mouth. Rosina sighed against his lips; every nerve end was on fire, she was trembling beneath his hands. When at last he broke off, she buried her face in his shoulder and clung to him.

'Oh, I thought you didn't want me,' she whispered.

'Want you! I have wanted you from the moment you cannoned into me in Queen Square.' She could feel his words, a rumble deep in his chest. 'I love you, Rosina, never doubt that, but I thought you wanted Brackwood and your independence more than you wanted me.'

She sighed. 'I thought so, too, at first. And then I had to persuade myself it was true. Because I knew I couldn't have you.'

'Even after I had taken you to bed? After I had said I would marry you?'

'I thought you were merely being noble.'

'There was nothing noble about it.' He settled her more securely on his lap and rested his cheek on her hair. 'I had come to Morton Gifford that day with the sole intention of throwing myself on your mercy and begging you to accept the hand of an impecunious earl. When I found you crying, I could not help myself. I wanted only to comfort you.' He sighed. 'I should have explained first!'

A chuckle escaped her. 'How could you? We were too busy kissing.'

She looked up then, but that was a mistake, because he immediately captured her mouth and for a long while she forgot everything, save the pure pleasure of his kiss. He unbuttoned her pelisse and she gave a little mewl of pleasure as he trailed a line of light butterfly kisses down her throat, gasping when his hand slid inside her bodice and cupped one breast.

He stopped. 'I beg your pardon, my hands are roughened with work.'

'Don't apologise,' she muttered, her voice ragged. 'And please, don't stop now!'

Conham lowered his head and kissed her again. Her body on fire, Rosina's fingers set to work on the buttons of his waistcoat. Clothes were abandoned amid a frenzy of passionate kisses, until they were lying naked together, oblivious of the cool air or the distant thud of hammers from the workmen on the roof.

When at last they were dressed again and Rosina was seated once more on the sofa with Conham's arm around her, she gave a long sigh.

'What a great deal of time we have wasted. If only I hadn't dashed off to Brackwood to search for that will!'

His arm tightened. 'When I read your note, I was afraid for you. I cursed your damned independence in going off alone.'

'My independence has caused a great deal of trouble,' she said in a small voice.

'But it also brought us together,' he reminded her.

'It did, but if I had not gone to Brackwood, Edgar would not have been injured.'

'And your father's estates would be in a fair way to being ruined,' he told her. 'We cannot live our lives on what might have been, my love. I regret, most deeply, that I didn't explain sooner that I had found a way out of our problems. That I could marry you and still fulfil my obligations. But it was never the right time, and after you found the will, I did not think there was any point in making you an offer. I thought I knew what your answer would be.'

'You see, I was right.' She raised her head and smiled up at him lovingly. 'You are nobly self-sacrificing.'

'But no more,' he declared. 'In future, I am going to take advantage of you, shamefully! I shall start by accepting your offer of marriage. You will keep your own income, of course. That must be included in the marriage settlement. But I warn you, there will be very little extra money to spare for fripperies or furbelows. No new carriages or grand tours of the Continent.'

'Unless my investment in Bellemonte comes good,' she murmured.

'Yes, but that will take years. I do not want to mislead you about our future, Rosina.'

'I know, and I am perfectly content,' she told him. 'All I want is to be allowed to help, to work with you to restore Dallamire. To be by your side day and night.'

'Especially at night!'

Rosina shivered deliciously at the wicked glint in his eyes.

'Well, madam,' he continued, 'will that do for you?'

'Oh, yes, Conham,' she said, melting back into his arms. 'That will do very well!'

* * * * *

HISTORICAL

Your romantic escape to the past.

Available Next Month

Tempted By Her Enemy Marquis Louise Allen
The Duke's Guide To Fake Courtship Jade Lee

....

Miss Anna And The Earl Catherine Tinley
The Lady's Bargain With The Rogue Melissa Oliver